Just LISTEN

Just LISTEN

a novel by

Sarah Dessen

Viking

Viking

Published by Penguin Group

Penguin Group (USA) Inc., 345 Hudson Street, New York, New York 10014, U.S.A.

Penguin Group (Canada), 90 Eglinton Avenue East, Suite 700, Toronto,
Ontario, Canada M4P 2Y3 (a division of Pearson Penguin Canada Inc.)

Penguin Books Ltd, Registered Offices: 80 Strand, London WC2R 0RL, England

First published in 2006 by Viking, a member of Penguin Group (USA) Inc.

10   12   14   15   13   11   9

LIBRARY OF CONGRESS CATALOGING-IN-PUBLICATION DATA

Dessen, Sarah.

Just listen : a novel / by Sarah Dessen.

p. cm.

Summary: Isolated from friends who believe the worst because she has not been
truthful with them, sixteen-year-old Annabel finds an ally in classmate Owen, whose
honesty and passion for music help her to face and share what really happened at
the end-of-the-year party that changed her life.

ISBN: 978-0-670-06105-1 (hardcover)

[1. Self-actualization—Fiction. 2. Interpersonal relations—Fiction. 3. Models
(Persons)—Fiction. 4. Family problems—Fiction. 5. High schools—Fiction.
6. Schools—Fiction.] I. Title.

PZ7.D455Jus 2006   [Fic]—dc22   2006000472

Printed in U.S.A.

Set in Century Book

Book design by Nancy Brennan

The best way out is always through.

—*Robert Frost*

Just LISTEN

Chapter
ONE

I taped the commercial back in April, before anything had happened, and promptly forgot about it. A few weeks ago, it had started running, and suddenly, I was everywhere.

On the rows of screens hanging over the ellipticals at the gym. On the monitor they have at the post office that's supposed to distract you from how long you've been waiting in line. And now here, on the TV in my room, as I sat at the edge of my bed, fingers clenched into my palms, trying to make myself get up and leave.

"It's that time of year again. . . ."

I stared at myself on the screen as I was five months earlier, looking for any difference, some visible proof of what had happened to me. First, though, I was struck by the sheer oddness of seeing myself without benefit of a mirror or photograph. I had never gotten used to it, even after all this time.

"Football games," I watched myself say. I was wearing a baby-blue cheerleader uniform, hair pulled back tight into a ponytail, and clutching a huge megaphone, the kind nobody ever used anymore, emblazoned with a K.

"Study hall." Cut to me in a serious plaid skirt and brown

cropped sweater, which I remembered feeling itchy and so wrong to be wearing just as it was getting warm, finally.

"And, of course, social life." I leaned in, staring at the me on-screen, now outfitted in jeans and a glittery tee and seated on a bench, turning to speak this line while a group of other girls chattered silently behind me.

The director, fresh-faced and just out of film school, had explained to me the concept of this, his creation. "The girl who has everything," he'd said, moving his hands in a tight, circular motion, as if that was all it took to encompass something so vast, not to mention vague. Clearly, it meant having a mega-phone, some smarts, and a big group of friends. Now, I might have dwelled on the explicit irony of this last one, but the on-screen me was already moving on.

"It's all happening this year," I said. Now I was in a pink gown, a sash reading HOMECOMING QUEEN stretched across my midsection as a boy in a tux stepped up beside me, extend-ing his arm. I took it, giving him a wide smile. He was a sopho-more at the local university and mostly kept to himself at the shooting, although later, as I was leaving, he'd asked for my number. How had I forgotten that?

"The best times," the me on-screen was saying now. "The best memories. And you'll find the right clothes for them all at Kopf's Department Store."

The camera moved in, closer, closer, until all you could see was my face, the rest dropping away. This had been before that night, before everything that had happened with Sophie, before this long, lonely summer of secrets and silence. I was a mess, but this girl—she was fine. You could tell in the way she stared out at me and the world so confidently as she opened her mouth to speak again.

"Make your new year the best one yet," she said, and I felt my breath catch, anticipating the next line, the last line, the one that only this time was finally true. "It's time to go back to school."

The shot froze, the Kopf's logo appearing beneath me. In moments, it would switch to a frozen waffle commercial or the latest weather, this fifteen seconds folding seamlessly into another, but I didn't wait for that. Instead, I picked up the remote, turned myself off, and headed out the door.

I'd had over three months to get ready to see Sophie. But when it happened, I still wasn't ready.

I was in the parking lot before first bell, trying to muster up what it would take to get out and officially let the year begin. As people streamed past, talking and laughing, en route to the courtyard, I kept working on all the maybes: Maybe she was over it now. Maybe something else had happened over the summer to replace our little drama. Maybe it was never as bad as I thought it was. All of these were long shots, but still possibilities.

I sat there until the very last moment before finally drawing the keys out of the ignition. When I reached for the door handle, turning to my window, she was right there.

For a second, we just stared at each other, and I instantly noticed the changes in her: Her dark curly hair was shorter, her earrings new. She was skinnier, if that was possible, and had done away with the thick eyeliner she'd taken to wearing the previous spring, replacing it with a more natural look, all bronzes and pinks. I wondered, in her first glance, what was different in me.

Just as I thought this, Sophie opened her perfect mouth, narrowed her eyes at me, and delivered the verdict I'd spent my summer waiting for.

"Bitch."

The glass between us didn't muffle the sound or the reaction of the people passing by. I saw a girl from my English class the year before narrow her eyes, while another girl, a stranger, laughed out loud.

Sophie, though, remained expressionless as she turned her back, hiking her bag over one shoulder and starting down to the courtyard. My face was flushed, and I could feel people staring. I wasn't ready for this, but then I probably never would be, and this year, like so much else, wouldn't wait. I had no choice but to get out of my car, with everyone watching, and begin it in earnest, alone. So I did.

I had first met Sophie four years earlier, at the beginning of the summer after sixth grade. I was at the neighborhood pool, standing in the snack-bar line with two damp dollar bills to buy a Coke, when I felt someone step up behind me. I turned my head, and there was this girl, a total stranger, standing there in a skimpy orange bikini and matching thick platform flip-flops. She had olive skin and thick, curly dark hair pulled up into a high ponytail, and was wearing black sunglasses and a bored, impatient expression. In our neighborhood, where everyone knew everyone, it was like she'd fallen out of the sky. I didn't mean to stare. But apparently, I was.

"What?" she said to me. I could see myself reflected in the lenses of her glasses, small and out of perspective. "What are *you* looking at?"

I felt my face flush, as it did anytime anybody raised their voice at me. I was entirely too sensitive to tone, so much so that even TV court shows could get me upset—I always had to change the channel when the judge ripped into anyone. "Nothing," I said, and turned back around.

A moment later, the high-school guy working the snack bar waved me up with a tired look. While he poured my drink I could feel the girl behind me, her presence like a weight, as I smoothed my two bills out flat on the glass beneath my fingers, concentrating on getting every single crease. After I paid, I walked away, studiously keeping my eyes on the pocked cement of the walkway as I made my way back around the deep end to where my best friend, Clarke Reynolds, was waiting.

"Whitney said to tell you she's going home," she said, blowing her nose as I carefully put the Coke on the pavement beside my chair. "I told her we could walk."

"Okay," I said. My sister Whitney had just gotten her license, which meant that she had to drive me places. Getting home, however, remained my own responsibility, whether from the pool, which was walking distance, or the mall one town over, which wasn't. Whitney was a loner, even then. Any space around her was her *personal* space; just by existing, you were encroaching.

It was only after I sat down that I finally allowed myself to look again at the girl with the orange bikini. She had left the snack bar and was standing across the pool from us, her towel over one arm, a drink in her other hand, surveying the layout of benches and beach chairs.

"Here," Clarke said, handing over the deck of cards she was holding. "It's your deal."

Clarke had been my best friend since we were six years old. There were tons of kids in our neighborhood, but for some reason most of them were in their teens, like my sisters, or four and below, a result of the baby boom a couple of years previously. When Clarke's family moved from Washington, D.C., our moms met at a community-watch meeting. As soon as they realized we were the same age, they put us together, and we'd stayed that way ever since.

Clarke had been born in China, and the Reynoldses had adopted her when she was six months old. We were the same height, but that was about all we had in common. I was blonde-haired and blue-eyed, a typical Greene, while she had the darkest, shiniest hair I'd ever seen and eyes so brown they were almost black. While I was timid and too eager to please, Clarke was more serious, her tone, personality, and appearance all measured and thoughtful. I'd been modeling since before I could even remember, following my sisters before me; Clarke was a total tomboy, the best soccer player on our block, not to mention a whiz at cards, especially gin rummy, at which she'd been beating me all summer.

"Can I have a sip of your drink?" Clarke asked me. Then she sneezed. "It's hot out here."

I nodded, reaching down to get it for her. Clarke had bad allergies year-round, but in summer they hit fever pitch. She was usually either stuffed up, dripping, or blowing from April to October, and no amount of shots or pills seemed to work. I'd long ago grown used to her adenoidal voice, as well as the omnipresent pack of Kleenex in her pocket or hand.

There was an organized hierarchy to the seating at our pool: The lifeguards got the picnic tables near the snack bar, while the moms and little kids stuck by the shallow end and the baby (i.e., pee) pool. Clarke and I preferred the half-shaded area behind the kiddie slides, while the more popular high-school guys—like Chris Pennington, three years older than me and hands-down the most gorgeous guy in our neighborhood and, I thought then, possibly the world—hung out by the high dive. The prime spot was the stretch of chairs between the snack bar and lap lane, which was usually taken by the most popular high-school girls. This was where my oldest sister, Kirsten, was stretched out in a chaise, wearing a hot-pink bikini and fanning herself with a *Glamour* magazine.

Once I dealt out our cards, I was surprised to see the girl in orange walk over to where Kirsten was sitting, taking the chair next to her. Molly Clayton, Kirsten's best friend, who was on her other side, nudged her, then nodded at the girl. Kirsten looked up and over, then shrugged and lay back down, throwing her arm over her face.

"Annabel?" Clarke had already picked up her cards and was impatient to start beating me. "It's your draw."

"Oh," I said, turning back to face her. "Right."

The next afternoon, the girl was back, this time in a silver bathing suit. When I got there, she was already set up in the same chair my sister had been in the day before, her towel spread out, bottled water beside her, magazine in her lap. Clarke was at a tennis lesson, so I was alone when Kirsten and her friends arrived about an hour later. They came in loud as always, their shoes thwacking down the pavement. When they reached their usual spot and saw the girl sitting there, they slowed, then looked at one another. Molly Clayton looked annoyed, but Kirsten just moved about four chairs down and set up camp as always.

For the next few days, I watched as the new girl kept up her stubborn efforts to infiltrate my sister's group. What began as just taking a chair escalated, by day three, to following them to the snack bar. The next afternoon, she got in the water seconds after they did, staying just about a foot down the wall as they bobbed and talked, splashing one another. By the weekend, she was trailing behind them constantly, a living shadow.

It had to be annoying. I'd seen Molly shoot her a couple of nasty looks, and even Kirsten had asked her to back up, please, when she'd gotten a little too close in the deep end. But the girl didn't seem to care. If anything, she just stepped up her efforts more, as if it didn't matter what they were saying as long as they were talking to her, period.

"So," my mother said one night at dinner, "I heard a new family's moved in to the Daughtrys' house, over on Sycamore."

"The Daughtrys moved?" my father asked.

My mother nodded. "Back in June. To Toledo. Remember?"

My father thought for a second. "Right," he said finally, nodding. "Toledo."

"I also heard," my mom continued, passing the bowl of pasta she was holding to Whitney, who immediately passed it on to me, "that they have a daughter your age, Annabel. I think I saw her the other day when I was over at Margie's."

"Really," I said.

She nodded. "She has dark hair, a bit taller than you. Maybe you've seen her around the neighborhood."

I thought for a second. "I don't know—"

"That's who that is!" Kirsten said suddenly. She put down her fork with a clank. "The stalker from the pool. Oh my God, I *knew* she had to be way younger than us."

"Hold on." Now my father was paying attention. "There's a stalker at the pool?"

"I *hope* not," my mother said, in her worried voice.

"She's not a stalker, really," Kirsten said. "She's just this girl who's been hanging around us. It's so creepy. She, like, sits beside us, and follows us around, and doesn't talk, and she's always listening to what we're saying. I've told her to get lost, but she just ignores me. God! I can't believe she's only *twelve*. That makes it even sicker."

"So dramatic," Whitney muttered, spearing a piece of lettuce with her fork.

She was right, of course. Kirsten was our resident drama queen. Her emotions were always at full throttle, as was her mouth; she never stopped talking, even if she was well aware you weren't listening to her. In contrast, Whitney was the silent type, which meant the few words she uttered always carried that much more meaning.

"Kirsten," my mother said now, "be nice."

"Mom, I've tried that. But if you saw her, you'd understand. It's strange."

My mother took a sip of her wine. "Moving to a new place is difficult, you know. Maybe she doesn't know how to make friends—"

"She obviously doesn't," Kirsten told her.

"—which means that it might be your job to meet her halfway," my mother finished.

"She's *twelve*," Kirsten said, as if this was on par with being diseased, or on fire.

"So is your sister," my father pointed out.

Kirsten picked up her fork and pointed it at him. "Exactly," she said.

Beside me, Whitney snorted. But my mom, of course, was already turning her attention on me. "Well, Annabel," she said, "maybe you could make an effort, if you do see her. To say hello or something."

I didn't tell my mother I'd already met this new girl, mostly because she would have been horrified she'd been so rude to me. Not that this would have changed her expectations for my behavior. My mother was famously polite, and expected the same of us, regardless of the circumstances. Our whole lives were supposed to be the high road. "Okay," I said. "Maybe I will."

"Good girl," she said. And that, I hoped, was that.

The next afternoon, though, when Clarke and I got to the pool, Kirsten was already there, lying out with Molly on one side and the new girl on the other. I tried to ignore this as we got settled in our spot, but eventually I glanced over to see Kirsten watching me. When she got up a moment later, shooting me a look, then headed toward the snack bar, the new girl immediately following her, I knew what I had to do.

"I'll back in a second," I told Clarke, who was reading a Stephen King novel and blowing her nose.

"Okay," she said.

I got up, then started around by the high dive, crossing my arms over my chest as I passed Chris Pennington. He was lying on a beach chair, a towel over his eyes, while a couple of his buddies wrestled on the pool deck. Now, instead of sneaking glances at him—which, other than swimming and getting beaten at cards, was my main activity at the pool that summer—I'd get bitched out again, all because my mother was insistent we be raised as the best of Good Samaritans. Great.

I could have told Kirsten about my previous run-in with this girl, but I knew better. Unlike me, she did not shy away from confrontation—if anything, she sped toward it, before overtaking it completely. She was the family powder keg, and I had lost track of the number of times I'd stood off to the side, cringing and blushing, while she made her various displeasures clear to salespeople, other drivers, or various ex-boyfriends. I loved her, but the truth was, she made me nervous.

Whitney, in contrast, was a silent fumer. She'd never tell you when she was mad. You just knew, by the expression on her face, the steely narrowing of her eyes, the heavy, enunciated sighs that could be so belittling that words, any words, seemed preferable to them. When she and Kirsten fought—

which, with two years between them, was fairly often—it always seemed at first like a one-sided argument, since all you could hear was Kirsten endlessly listing accusations and slights. Pay more attention, though, and you'd notice Whitney's stony, heavy silences, as well as the rebuttals she offered, few as they were, that always cut to the point much more harshly than Kirsten's swirling, whirly commentaries.

One open, one closed. It was no wonder that the first image that came to mind when I thought of either of my sisters was a door. With Kirsten, it was the front one to our house, through which she was always coming in or out, usually in mid-sentence, a gaggle of friends trailing behind her. Whitney's was the one to her bedroom, which she preferred to keep shut between her and the rest of us, always.

As for me, I fell somewhere between my sisters and their strong personalities, the very personification of the vast gray area that separated them. I was not bold and outspoken, or silent and calculating. I had no idea how anyone would describe me, or what would come to mind at the sound of my name. I was just Annabel.

My mother, conflict-adverse herself, hated it when my sisters fought. "Why can't you just be *nice*?" she'd plead with them. They might have rolled their eyes, but a message sank in with me: that being nice was the ideal, the one place where people didn't get loud or so quiet they could scare you. If you could just be nice, then you wouldn't have to worry about arguments at all. But being nice wasn't as easy as it seemed, especially when the rest of the world could be so mean.

By the time I got to the snack bar, Kirsten had disappeared (of course), but the girl was still there, waiting for the guy behind the counter to ring up her candy bar. *Oh well*, I thought, as I walked up to her. *Here goes nothing.*

"Hi," I said. She just looked at me, her expression unreadable. "Um, I'm Annabel. You just moved here, right?"

She didn't say anything for what seemed like a really long while, during which time Kirsten walked out of the ladies' room behind her. She stopped when she saw us talking.

"I," I continued, now even more uncomfortable, "I, um, think we're in the same grade."

The girl reached up, pushing her sunglasses farther up her nose. "So?" she said, in that same sharp, snide voice as the first time she'd addressed me.

"I just thought," I said, "that since, you know, we're the same age, you might want to hang out. Or something."

Another pause. Then the girl said, as if clarifying, "You want me to hang out. With you."

She made it sound so ridiculous I immediately began backtracking. "I mean, you don't have to," I told her. "It was just—"

"No," she cut me off flatly. Then she tilted her head back and laughed. "No *way*."

The thing is, if it had just been me there, that would have been it. I would have turned around, face flushed, and gone back to Clarke, game over. But it wasn't just me.

"Hold on," Kirsten said, her voice loud. "What did you just say?"

The girl turned around. When she saw my sister, her eyes

widened. "What?" she said, and I couldn't help but notice how different this, the first word she'd ever said to me, sounded as she said it now.

"I said," Kirsten repeated, her own voice sharp, "*what* did you just say to her?"

Uh-oh, I thought.

"Nothing," the girl replied. "I just—"

"That's my sister," Kirsten said, pointing at me, "and you were just a total bitch to her."

By this point, I was already both cringing and blushing. Kirsten, however, put her hand on her hip, which meant she was just getting started.

"I wasn't a bitch," the girl said, taking off her sunglasses. "I only—"

"You were, and you know it," Kirsten said, cutting her off. "So you can stop denying it. And stop following me around, too, okay? You're creeping me out. Come on, Annabel."

I was frozen to the spot, just looking at the girl's face. Without her sunglasses, her expression stricken, she suddenly *looked* twelve, just staring at us as Kirsten grabbed my wrist, tugging me back to where she and her friends were sitting.

"Unbelievable," she kept saying, and as I looked across the pool I could see Clarke watching me, confused, as Kirsten pulled me down onto her chair. Molly sat up, blinking, reaching up to catch the untied straps of her bikini.

"What happened?" she asked, and as Kirsten began to tell her, I glanced back toward the snack bar, but the girl was gone. Then I saw her, through the fence behind me, walking across the parking lot, barefoot, her head ducked down. She'd left all her stuff on the chair beside me—a towel, her shoes, a bag with a magazine and billfold, a pink hairbrush. I kept waiting for her to realize this and turn back for it. She didn't.

Her things stayed there all afternoon: After I'd gone back to sit with Clarke, and told her everything. After we played several hands of rummy, and swam until our fingers were pruny. After Kirsten and Molly left, and other people took their chairs. All the way up until the lifeguard finally blew the whistle, announcing closing time, and Clarke and I packed up and walked around the edge of the pool, sunburned and hungry and ready to go home.

I knew this girl was not my problem. She'd been mean to me, twice, and therefore was not deserving of my pity or help. But as we passed the chair, Clarke stopped. "We can't just leave it," she said, bending over to gather up the shoes and stuff them into the bag. "And it's on our way home."

I could have argued the point, but then I thought again of her walking across the parking lot, barefoot, alone. So I pulled the towel off the chair, folding it over my own. "Yeah," I said. "Okay."

Still, when we got to the Daughtrys' old house, I was relieved to see all the windows were dark and there was no car in the driveway, so we could just leave the girl's stuff and be done with it. But as Clarke bent down to stick the bag against the front door, it opened, and there she was.

She had on cutoff shorts and a red T-shirt, her hair pulled back in a ponytail. No sunglasses. No high-heeled sandals. When she saw us, her face flushed.

"Hi," Clarke said, after a just-long-enough-to-be-noticed

awkward silence. Then she sneezed before adding, "We brought your stuff."

The girl just looked at her for a second, as if she didn't understand what she was saying. Which, with Clarke's congestion, she probably didn't. I leaned over and picked up the bag, holding it out to her. "You left this," I said.

She looked at the bag, then up at me, her expression guarded. "Oh," she said, reaching for it. "Thanks."

Behind us, a bunch of kids coasted past on their bikes, their voices loud as they called out to one another. Then it was quiet again.

"Honey?" I heard a voice call out from the end of the dark hallway behind her. "Is someone there?"

"It's okay," she said over her shoulder. Then she stepped forward, shutting the door behind her, and came out onto the porch. She quickly moved past us, but not before I saw that her eyes were red and swollen—she'd been crying. And suddenly, like so many other times, I heard my mother's voice in my head: *Moving to a new place is tough. Maybe she doesn't know how to make friends.*

"Look," I said, "about what happened. My sister—"

"It's fine," she said, cutting me off. "I'm fine." But as she said it, her voice cracked, just slightly, and she turned her back to us, putting a hand to her mouth. I just stood there, totally unsure what to do, but as I looked at Clarke, I saw she was already digging into the pocket of her shorts to pull out her ever-present pack of Kleenex. She drew one out, then reached around the girl, offering it to her. A second later, the girl took it, silently, and pressed it to her face.

"I'm Clarke," Clarke said. "And this is Annabel."

In the years to come, it would be this moment that I always came back to. Me and Clarke, in the summer after our sixth-grade year, standing there behind that girl's turned back. So much might have been different for me, for all of us, if something else had happened right then. At the time, though, it was like so many other moments, fleeting and unimportant, as she turned around, now not crying—surprisingly composed, actually—to face us.

"Hi," she said. "I'm Sophie."

Chapter
TWO

"Sophie!"

Finally it was lunchtime, which meant that this, the first day of school, was now at least half over. All around me, the hallway was packed and noisy, but even with locker doors clanging and the droning of various announcements from the intercom, I could still hear Emily Shuster's voice, clear as day.

I looked down the hall to the main staircase and sure enough, she was coming toward me, her red head bobbing through the crowd. When she finally emerged about two feet from where I was standing, our eyes met, but only fleetingly. Then she was quickly moving on, down the hall to where Sophie was waiting for her.

Since Emily had been my friend first, I'd thought maybe, just maybe, she might still be. Apparently not. The lines had been drawn, and now I knew for sure I was standing outside of them.

I had other friends, of course. People I knew from my classes, and from the Lakeview Models, which I'd been doing for years now. It was becoming clear, though, that my self-imposed isolation during the summer had been more effective than I'd realized. Right after everything happened, I'd cut myself off entirely, figuring this was safer than risking people judging me. I blew off phone calls and avoided people when I saw them out at the mall or the movies. I didn't want to talk about what had happened, so it seemed safest not to talk at all. The result, however, was that now all morning, when I'd stopped to say hello to girls I knew, or walked up to groups of people chatting, I'd felt an instant coolness and distance, one that lingered until I made my excuses and walked away. Back in May, all I'd I wanted was to be alone. Now I'd gotten my wish.

My association with Sophie didn't help, of course. Hanging out with her made me a party to all her various social crimes and misdemeanors—and there were many—so there was a wide portion of the student body that was not exactly rushing to embrace me. To the girls Sophie had insulted and isolated while I stood by doing nothing, my own taste of this medicine was nothing short of deserved. If Sophie couldn't be ostracized, I was the next best thing.

Now I headed down to the main lobby, stopping in front of the long row of glass doors that looked out over the courtyard. Outside, the various cliques—jocks, art girls, pols, burnouts—were scattered across the grassy spaces and walkways. Everyone had a place, and once I'd known mine: the long wooden bench to the right of the main walkway, where Sophie and Emily were sitting. Now I was wondering if I should even go out at all.

"It's that time of year again," someone called out in a falsetto voice from behind me. There was a burst of laughter, and as I turned around, I saw a group of football players hanging out by the front office. A tall guy with dreadlocks was imitating the way I'd held out my arm to that guy in the commercial, while the rest of them snickered. I knew they were just goofing around, and maybe another time it wouldn't have bothered me. But now, I felt my face flush as I pushed the doors open in front of me and stepped outside.

There was a long wall to my right, so I headed toward it, looking for a spot, any spot, to sit down. There were only two people sitting on it, the distance between them just big enough to make it clear they weren't together. One was Clarke Reynolds. The other was Owen Armstrong. It wasn't like I had a lot of choices of seating or company, so I sat down between them.

The bricks were warm on my bare legs as I busied myself pulling out the lunch my mother had packed for me that morning: open-faced turkey sandwich, bottled water, and a nectarine. I uncapped the water, taking a big sip, before I finally allowed myself to take a look around. As soon as I glanced over at the bench, I saw Sophie was watching me. When our eyes met, she smiled a thin-lipped smile, shaking her head before looking away.

Pathetic, I heard her say in my head, then pushed this thought away. It wasn't like I wanted to sit with her, either. Then again, I never would have expected to find myself in my current company, either, with Clarke on one side and the Angriest Boy in School on the other.

At least Clarke I knew, or had once known. All the information I possessed about Owen Armstrong I'd gotten from a distance. Like that he was tall and muscular, with broad shoulders and thick biceps. And he always wore boots with thick rubber soles that made him seem even bigger, his steps heavier. His hair was dark and cut short, spiking up a bit at the top, and I'd never once seen him without his iPod and earphones, which he wore inside, outside, in class, out of class. And while I knew he had to have friends, I'd never seen him talk to anyone.

Then there was the fight. It had happened the previous January, in the parking lot before first bell. I'd just gotten out of my car when I saw Owen, backpack over his shoulder, earphones on as always, heading down to the main building. On the way, he passed Ronnie Waterman, who was leaning up against his car, talking with a bunch of his buddies. Every school has someone like Ronnie—a total jerk, famous for tripping people in the hallways, the kind of guy who yells "Nice ass!" when you walk past him. His older brother, Luke, had been his total opposite, captain of the football team and student-body president, totally nice and well liked, and because of this, people put up with his annoying little brother. But Luke had graduated the year before, and now Ronnie was on his own.

Owen was just walking along, minding his own business, and Ronnie shouted out something to him. When he didn't respond, Ronnie pushed off his car and crossed over to block Owen's path. Even from where I was standing, I could tell this was a bad idea; Ronnie wasn't small, but he was tiny compared to Owen Armstrong, who was a full head taller at least, not to mention much wider. Ronnie, however, didn't seem to notice this. He said something else to Owen, and Owen just looked at him for a second, then stepped around him. As he started walking again, Ronnie hit him in the chin.

Owen stumbled, but only slightly. Then he dropped his bag, pulling back his other arm and letting go in a solid arc, where it connected square in the center of Ronnie's face. I could hear it, that smack of fist against bone, from where I was standing.

Ronnie went down within seconds—his body first, knees buckling, then shoulders, followed by his head, which bounced slightly when it hit the ground. Owen, for his part, dropped his hand, stepped over him calm as you please, then picked up his bag and kept walking, the crowd that had gathered parting quickly, then scattering outright to let him through. Ronnie's friends were already gathering around him, someone was calling for the parking-lot guard, but all I could remember was Owen just walking away—same pace, same stride as before, as if he hadn't even stopped.

At the time, Owen was still relatively new; he had been at our school for a only month. As a result of this incident, he got suspended for another. When he came back, everyone was talking about him. I heard that he'd done time in juvenile hall, been kicked out of his previous school, and was in a gang. There were so many rumors that a few months later, when I heard he'd been arrested for fighting at a club over the weekend, I just assumed it wasn't true. But then he'd just disappeared, never coming back to school. Until now.

Up close, though, Owen didn't really look like a monster. He was just sitting there, in sunglasses and a red T-shirt, drumming his fingers on his knee and listening to his music. Even so, I figured it was best not to get caught staring at him, so after unwrapping my sandwich and taking a bite, I took a breath and turned my attention to my right side, and Clarke.

She was at the far end of the wall, a notebook open in her lap, eating an apple with one hand while scribbling something with the other. Her hair was pulled back at her neck in a simple elastic, and she was wearing a plain white T-shirt, army pants, and flip-flops, the glasses she'd started to wear the year earlier, small and tortoiseshell, perched on her nose. After a moment, she glanced up and over at me.

She had to have heard about what happened the previous May. Everyone had. As the seconds passed and she didn't turn away, I wondered if maybe she might have finally forgiven me. That perhaps, just as a new rift had started, I could mend an old one. It would be only fitting, now that we'd both been shunned by Sophie. It gave us something in common again.

And she was still looking at me. I put down my sandwich, then took in a breath. All I had to do, right now, was say something to her, something great, something that might—

But then, suddenly, she turned away. Pushed her notebook into her bag, zipping it shut, her body language stiff, her elbow extended in a sharp angle in my direction. Then she hopped down off the wall, slid her bag over her shoulders, and walked away.

I looked down at my sandwich, half-eaten, and felt a lump rise in my throat. Which was just so stupid, because Clarke had hated me forever. This, at least, was not new.

For the rest of lunch, I just sat there, making a point of not looking at anyone. When I checked my watch and saw I had only five minutes to go, I figured the worst part was over. I was wrong.

I was stuffing my water bottle into my bag when I heard a car pull into the turnaround at the end of the wall. I glanced over to see a red Jeep pulling up to the curb. The passenger door opened and a dark-haired guy climbed out, sticking a cigarette behind his ear as he ducked down, saying something to the person behind the wheel. As he shut the door and started to walk away, I got a look at the driver. It was Will Cash.

I felt my stomach physically drop, as if from a great height, straight down. Everything narrowed, the sounds around me falling away as my palms sprang into sweat, my heartbeat loud in my ears, *thump thump thump.*

I could not stop staring at him. He was just sitting there, one hand on the wheel, waiting for the car in front of him—a station wagon out of which some girl was unloading a cello or some other big instrument—to move along. After a second, he shook his head, irritated.

Shhh, Annabel. It's just me.

A million red Jeeps must have passed before my eyes in the last few months, and despite myself I'd checked each one for his face, this face. But only now, here, was it actually him. And while I had told myself that in broad daylight I could be strong and fearless, I felt as helpless as that night, as if even in the wide open, the bright light of day, I still wasn't safe.

The girl finally got her case out of the station wagon, then waved to the driver as she shut the door. As the car pulled forward, Will glanced over at the courtyard, and I watched his eyes move across the people there, barely seeming to register anyone in particular. Then he looked at me.

I just stared at him, my heart pounding in my chest. It lasted only a second, and I saw no recognition, nothing on his face but a blank stare, as if I were a stranger, just anyone. Then he was moving forward, the car a red blur, and it was over.

Suddenly, I was aware again of the noise and commotion around me: people bustling past to their next class, calling out to one another, tossing trash into the nearby can. Still, I kept my eyes on the Jeep, watching as it climbed the hill that led toward the main road, creeping away from me, bit by bit. And then, in the midst of all the noise and voices, movement and change, I turned my head, cupped a hand to cover my mouth, and threw up in the grass behind me.

When I turned back around a few moments later, the courtyard was mostly empty. The jocks had vacated the other wall, the grass beneath the trees was bare, Emily and Sophie had left their bench. It wasn't until I had wiped my mouth and glanced to my other side that I saw Owen Armstrong was still there, watching me. His eyes were dark and intense, and I was so startled that I quickly looked away. When I glanced back a minute later, he was gone.

Sophie hated me. Clarke hated me. Everybody hated me. Or, maybe not everybody.

"The Mooshka people *loved* your pictures," my mother was saying, her happy voice a complete contrast to how I felt as I sat in a long line of traffic, trying to get out of the parking lot after seventh period. "Lindy said they called her and were just raving."

"Really," I said, switching my phone to my other ear. "That's great."

I tried to sound enthusiastic, but the truth was I'd totally forgotten that a few days earlier my mother had told me that Lindy, my agent, was sending my pictures over to a local swimwear company called Mooshka Surfwear that was hiring for their new ad campaign. Suffice to say modeling was not my top concern these days.

"However," she continued, "Lindy says they'd like to see you in person."

"Oh," I said as the line crept another inch or so forward. "Okay. When?"

"Well," she replied, "actually . . . today."

"Today?" I said, as Amanda Cheeker, driving what looked like a brand-new BMW, totally cut me off, not even looking as she pulled out in front of me.

"Yes. Apparently one of their advertising heads is in town, but only until tonight."

"Mom." I inched forward incrementally, then craned my neck, trying to see who was causing the holdup. "I can't. It's been a really crappy day, and—"

"Honey, I know," she said, as if she actually did, which was totally not the case. Having raised three daughters, my mom was well versed in the politics of girls, which had made it easy for me to explain Sophie's sudden and utter disappearance from my life with the standard "She's just acting so weird," and

"I have no idea what happened." As far as she knew, Sophie and I had just drifted apart; I couldn't imagine what she would have thought if I told her the real story. Actually, I *could* imagine, which was why I hadn't and had no intention of doing so. "But Lindy says they're *really* interested in you."

I glanced in my side mirror, taking in my flushed face, flat hair, and the flecks of mascara around my eyes, the result of finally breaking down in tears in a bathroom stall after sixth period. I really did look as bad as I felt. "You don't understand," I said as I moved up barely one car length. "I didn't sleep well last night, I look really tired, I'm all sweaty—"

"Oh, Annabel," she said, and I felt a lump rising in my throat, reacting immediately to her soft, understanding tone, so welcome after this long terrible day. "I know, sweetie. But it's just one thing, and then you'll be done."

"Mom." The sun was in my eyes, and all I could smell was exhaust. "I'm just—"

"Listen," she said. "How about this. Come home, you can take a quick shower, I'll make you a sandwich and do your makeup. Then I'll drive you over, we'll get it done, and you won't have to think about it again. Okay?"

That was the thing with my mother. There was always a How About This, some deal she was able to manufacture and sell to you that, while being not very different from the original proposition, at least sounded better. Before, saying no had been my prerogative. Now, doing so would make me unreasonable.

"All right," I said as traffic finally started moving at a

decent pace. Up ahead, I could see the security guard waving people around a blue Toyota with a crushed back bumper. "When's the appointment?"

"Four o'clock."

I glanced at my watch. "Mom, it's three thirty right now, and I'm not even out of the parking lot. Where's the office?"

"It's at . . ." she said. I heard paper rustling. "Mayor's Village."

Which was a good twenty minutes away. I'd be lucky to get there on time if I headed straight there, and even then I'd need serious stoplight mercy. "Great," I said. "There's no way."

I knew I was being difficult, not to mention petulant. I also knew I'd go to the meeting and put on my best face, because being difficult and petulant was about as bad as I got when it came to my mother. After all, I was the nice one.

"Well," she said now, in her small voice. "I could call Lindy and tell her you just can't do it, if you like. I'm happy to do that."

"No," I said as I finally reached the top of the parking lot, putting on my blinker. "It's okay. I'll go."

I'd been modeling for as long as I could remember. Actually, it was even before that. I'd done my first shoot when I was nine months old, wearing onesies for a SmartMart Sunday circular, a job I'd gotten when my mother, her sitter having fallen through, had to bring me along to one of my sister Whitney's go-sees. The woman hiring asked her if I was available, my mother said yes, and that was that.

The whole modeling thing had started, though, with Kirsten. She was eight when a talent agent caught up with my mom and dad in the parking lot after her ballet recital, offering them a card and saying they should give him a call. My father had laughed, assuming it was a scam, but my mom was intrigued enough to take Kirsten in for an appointment. The agent had immediately set her up for an audition for a local car-dealership commercial, which she didn't get, followed by a print ad for Easter festivities at the Lakeview Mall, which she did. My modeling career began with onesies, but Kirsten could claim bunnies, or at least one very big one, leaning over to put a shiny egg in her basket as she, in a puffy white dress, smiled into the camera.

Once Kirsten started getting regular work, Whitney wanted to try it as well, and soon they were both making the rounds, often even going up for the same jobs, which only added to the natural friction between them. Their looks, though, were as distinct and different as their temperaments. Whitney was the beauty, with the perfect bone structure and haunting eyes, while Kirsten was somehow able to convey her bubbly personality with just one look. Whitney did better in print, but Kirsten popped on screen. And so on.

Because of this, by the time I started modeling, my family was well known on the local circuit, which consisted mostly of print ads for department and discount stores and regionally cast and shot commercials. While my dad chose to take a hands-off approach to us working—as he did to everything even vaguely girly, from Tampax to broken hearts—my mother thrived on it. She loved ferrying us to jobs, talking business with Lindy on the phone and gathering pictures to update our books. But when she was asked about it, she always pointed out first that it was our choice, not hers. "I would have been happy to have them making mud pies in the backyard," I'd heard her tell people a million times. "But this is what they wanted to do."

In truth, though, my mother loved the modeling, too, even if she didn't want to admit it. But I believed it was even more than that. In some way, I thought that it had saved her.

Not at first, of course. Initially, for her, our modeling was just a fun hobby, something for her to do when she wasn't having to work at my dad's office, which we joked was the most fertile place on the planet, as the secretaries were always getting pregnant, leaving it to my mom to answer the phones until he found a replacement. But then, the year I turned nine, my grandmother died, and something changed.

My own memories of my grandmother are distant, muted, based more on photographs I'd seen than on any real events. My mom was an only child and very close to her own mother, even though they lived on opposite coasts and saw each other only a few times a year. They talked on the phone almost every morning, usually while my mom had her midmorning cup of coffee. Like clockwork, if you came into the kitchen around ten thirty, you'd find her in the chair facing the window, stirring cream into a mug, the phone cocked between her ear and shoulder. To me, it always sounded like the most boring of conversations, solely about people I'd never met, or whatever my mom had cooked the night before, or even my own life, which sounded deadly dull, as well, relayed this way. For my mom, though, it was different. Crucial. How much so, we didn't realize until after my grandmother was gone.

It wasn't like my mom had ever been some pillar of strength. She was a quiet woman, soft-spoken, with a kind face—the sort of person you'd look for if you were out in public somewhere and something bad happened, an instant comfort. I'd always relied on my mom to be just that, exactly as she always had been, which was why the change in her in the weeks following my grandmother's funeral was so strange. She just got . . . quieter. Still. There was suddenly something haunted and tired about her face, so obvious that even I, at nine, could see it. At first, my dad just assured us that it was the normal grief process, that my mother was tired, and she'd be fine. But as time went on, she didn't get better. Instead she started sleeping later, and then later, until she sometimes didn't get out of bed at all. When she was up, I'd sometimes come into the kitchen midmorning to find her sitting in that same chair, empty mug in her hands, looking out the window.

"Mom," I'd say, and she wouldn't respond, so I'd say it again. Sometimes it took three times before she'd slowly begin to turn her head, but when she did I would suddenly feel scared, like I didn't want to see her face after all. Like in those few moments, she might have changed again, shifting deeper into someone I didn't recognize.

My sisters remembered this time better than I did, as they were older and therefore privy to more information. And in typical fashion, they each had their own way of dealing with it. It fell to Kirsten to take care of things around the house, like cleaning and making our lunches, when my mom wasn't up to it, which she did with her usual bravado, as if nothing was wrong at all. Whitney, on the other hand, I often found outside my mother's half-closed bedroom door, listening or peering in, but she'd always move on when I saw her, not meeting my eyes. As the youngest, I wasn't sure how to react, other than to just try not to make trouble or ask too many questions.

My mother's condition quickly grew to dictate our lives. It was the barometer by which we judged everything. In my mind, it all came down to the first glimpse I had of her each morning. If she was up and dressed at a decent hour and making breakfast, things would be okay. But if she wasn't and I found my dad in the kitchen instead, doing his best with cold cereal and toast, or even worse, if neither of them was in sight, I knew it was not going to be a good day. Maybe it was a rudimentary system, but it worked, more or less. And it wasn't like I had a lot else to go on.

"Your mother isn't feeling well," was all my dad would say when we asked after her as we sat around the dining-room table, my mother's place glaringly empty, or when she didn't emerge from her room all day, the only view of her a lump under the covers, barely visible in a sliver of light from the drawn shades. "We all just need to do the best we can to make things easy for her until she feels better. Okay?"

I remember nodding, and seeing my sisters doing the same. But *how* to do this was another thing entirely. I had no idea how to make things easier, or even if I'd done something to make them difficult in the first place. What I did get was that it was paramount that we protect my mom from anything that might upset her, even if I wasn't sure what those things were. So I learned another system: When in doubt, keep it out—out of earshot, out of the house—even if this meant, really, just keeping it in.

My mother's depression, or episode, or whatever it was—I never got a concrete term, which made it all the more hard to define—had been going on for about three months when my dad convinced her to go see a therapist. At first she went reluctantly, quitting after a couple of sessions, but then she started up again, and this time she stuck with it, continuing for the next year. Still, there wasn't some sudden change—one particular day that I came into the kitchen at ten thirty and there she was, bright and cheerful, like she'd been waiting for me to appear. Instead, it was a slow process, little increments, like moving a half a millimeter a day so that you only really notice progress from a distance. First she stopped sleeping all day, then she began to get up midmorning, then finally she started to cook breakfast every once in a while. Her silences, so noticeable at the dinner table and everywhere else, slowly became less extended, a little conversation here, a comment there.

In the end it was the modeling, though, that convinced me we were over the worst of it. Since my mom had been the one who got us to jobs and dealt with Lindy as far as scheduling and auditions, we'd all been working a lot less while she was sick. My dad had taken Whitney to a couple of jobs, and I'd had one shoot that was booked way in advance, but things had definitely slowed down—enough so that when Lindy called one day during dinner about a go-see, even she was assuming we'd take a pass.

"That's probably best," my dad said, glancing back at all of us at the table before taking the phone farther into the kitchen. "I just don't think the time's right."

Kirsten, who was chewing on a piece of bread, said, "Right for what?"

"A job," Whitney told her, her voice flat. "Why else would Lindy call during dinner?"

My dad was rummaging in the drawer by the phone now, finally digging out a pencil. "Well, okay," he said, grabbing a nearby notepad. "I'll just take down the info, but most likely . . . right. What was that address, again?"

My sisters were both watching him as he scribbled it down, probably wondering what the job was for, and for whom. But I was looking at my mom, who had her eyes on my dad as well, even as she drew her napkin out of her lap, dabbing the corners of her mouth. When he came back in, settling into his chair and picking up his fork, I waited for my sisters to ask for details. But instead, my mom spoke first.

"So what was that about?"

My dad looked at her. "Oh," he said, "just an audition tomorrow. Lindy thought we might be interested."

"We?" Kirsten said.

"You," my dad told her, scooping some beans onto his fork. "I told her it probably isn't a good time. It's in the morning, and I've got to be at the office. . . ."

He trailed off, not bothering to finish—not that he had to. My dad was an architect and busy enough with his own work, plus taking care of my mom and keeping up the house, without having to deal with running us all over town. Kirsten knew this, even though it was obvious she was disappointed. But then, in the quiet as we all went back to eating, I heard my mom take in a breath.

"I could take her," she said. We all looked at her. "I mean, if she wanted to go."

"Really?" Kirsten asked. "Because that would be—"

"Grace," my dad said, his voice concerned. Kirsten sat back in her chair, now quiet. "You don't have to."

"I know." My mom smiled, a wan smile, but a smile just the same. "It's just one day, though. One thing. I'd like to."

So the next day, my mom was up for breakfast—I remember that, clearly—and when Whitney and I left for school, she and Kirsten headed off to an audition for a local bowling alley commercial. Kirsten got the job. It was by no means her first ad, and not a very big one, as things went. But every time it ran afterwards, and I saw her bowl that perfect strike (edited in, as my sister was a terrible bowler, the queen of the gutter ball), I thought about that night at the table and how, finally, it seemed like things might be getting back to normal.

And they did, more or less. My mom started taking us around to auditions again, and while she wasn't always cheerful and perky, maybe she actually never had been in the first place. Maybe that, like so much else, I'd only imagined, or assumed. Still, as that year went on, I had trouble trusting that things were really getting better. As hopeful as I wanted to be, I always felt like I was holding my breath, sure that it wouldn't last. And even when it did, the fact that what had happened to my mom had come on so suddenly, with no beginning or true end, made it seem that much more likely to reappear in the same fashion. Back then, I always felt like it would take only one bad event, one disappointment, for her to leave us again. Maybe I felt that way still.

This was one reason why I hadn't yet told my mom I wanted to quit modeling. The truth was that all summer, when I went to go-sees, I felt strange, nervous in a way I never had before. I didn't like the scrutiny, having to walk in front of people, strangers staring at me. At one fitting for a swimsuit shoot in June, I'd kept cringing when the stylist tried to adjust my bathing suit, a lump rising in my throat even as I apologized and said I was fine.

Each time I got close to telling my mom about this, though, something would happen to stop me. I was the only one left modeling now. And while it is hard enough to take away something that makes a person happy, it's even more difficult when it seems like it's the *only* thing.

Which was why, when I got to Mayor's Village fifteen minutes later, I was not surprised to find my mother waiting for me. As I turned in, I was struck, as always, by how *small* she was. Then again, my perspective was a bit skewed, as I was five-eight, and even at that the shortest of my sisters: Kirsten had a half inch on me and Whitney was five-ten. My father loomed above all of us at six-two, leaving my mother to always look sort of odd when we were all together, like one of those which-one-of-these-is-not-like-the-other puzzles we used to do in elementary school.

As I pulled in beside her car, I saw Whitney was in the passenger seat, her arms crossed over her chest. She looked irritated, which was neither surprising nor new, so I didn't dwell on it as I grabbed my makeup bag from my purse and went around to meet my mother, who was standing by her bumper, the hatch open.

"You didn't have to come," I said.

"I know," she replied, not looking up as she handed me a Tupperware container with a plastic fork balanced on top of it. "Fruit salad. I didn't have time to make a sandwich. Sit down."

I sat, then opened the container, digging in the fork to take a bite. I realized I was starving, which made sense, considering I'd thrown up the small amount of lunch I'd managed to get down. God, what a crappy day.

My mother took my makeup bag from me and began to rummage through it, taking out an eye-shadow compact and my powder. "Whitney," she called out, "hand those clothes back here, would you?"

Whitney sighed loudly, then turned around, reaching for the shirts that were hanging from the hook on the door behind her. "Here," she said flatly, barely extending them over the backseat. My mother reached for them, her fingertips falling short, so I turned around to get them for her. As my hand closed over the hangers and I tried to pull them toward me, Whitney held on for a second longer, her grip surprisingly strong as our eyes met. Then she let go, suddenly, and turned back around.

I was trying to be patient with my sister. To remember, at times like this, that it wasn't *her* I was upset with, but her eating disorder. But at times like this, it looked a lot like Whitney, and vice versa, so it was hard to tell the difference.

"Have some water," my mother said now, handing me an open bottle as she took the shirts from me. "And look here."

I took a sip, staying still as she dusted powder across my

face. Then I closed my eyes, listening to cars go by on the highway behind us, as she applied shadow and liner before beginning to rifle through the shirts, the hangers clanking. I opened my eyes to see her holding a pink suede top out at me.

Shhh, Annabel. It's just me.

"No," I said. It came out harsher than I meant, my voice sharp. I took in a breath, forcing myself to sound more normal as I added, "Not that one."

She looked surprised, glancing at it, then back at me again. "Are you sure? It looks wonderful on you. I thought you loved this shirt."

I shook my head, then looked away quickly, focusing on a minivan that was passing by, one of those MY CHILD IS AN HONOR STUDENT stickers on the back window. "No," I told her again. She was still watching me, so I added, "It cuts me weird, or something."

"Oh," I heard her say. She offered me a blue scoop-neck instead. "Here," she said as I looked at it more closely, seeing a price tag hanging from it. "Hop in and change. It's three fifty."

I nodded, then got down off the bumper, walking around to the backseat door and pulling it open. I climbed in, bending down to pull off my tank top, and froze. "Mom," I said.

"Yes?"

"I don't have a bra."

I heard her heels on the pavement as she came around the car. "You don't?"

I shook my head, trying to stay low in the seat. "I had a tank top on; it's got one built in."

My mother thought for a second. "Whitney," she said. "Give—"

Whitney shook her head. "No way."

Now it was my mother's turn to sigh. "Honey, please," she said. "Just help us out, okay?"

And so, as we had for the last nine months or so, we had to wait, and worry, about Whitney. After what felt like a long silence, she finally pulled her arms up under her shirt, fumbled around, then drew a beige bra out of the collar, dropping it back behind her. I grabbed it off the floor, putting it on—we weren't exactly the same size, but it was better than nothing— then pulled the shirt over it. "Thanks," I said, but, of course, she ignored me.

"Three fifty-two," my mother said. "Let's go, honey."

I got out of the car, then walked back around to where she was waiting, holding my purse. She handed it to me, then looked at my face one last time, examining her handiwork. "Close your eyes," she said, reaching forward carefully to draw a clump of mascara off one of my eyelashes. When I opened them, she smiled at me. "You look beautiful."

"Yeah, right," I said, but then she gave me a look, so I added, "Thank you."

She tapped her watch. "Go ahead. We'll wait for you."

"You don't have to. I'll be fine."

The car's engine started suddenly as Whitney turned the key, and then she was rolling down the window, extending her arm outside. She was wearing long sleeves, as always, but you could see a bit of her wrist, pale and so thin, as she tapped her fingers on the side of the car. My mother looked at her, then back at me.

"Well, I'll at least wait for you to get inside," she said. "Okay?"

I nodded, then leaned forward to kiss her just above her cheek, so as not to smudge my lipstick. "Okay."

When I got to the building, I turned around. She lifted her hand, waving, and as I did the same I glanced beyond her at Whitney, whose face I could see framed in the side mirror. She was watching me, too, her face expressionless, and, like so often lately, I felt a twinge, something twisting in my stomach.

"Good luck," my mother called out, and I nodded, then looked back at Whitney. But she'd slid down in her seat and disappeared from view, leaving the mirror empty.

Chapter
THREE

Whitney had always been skinny. While Kirsten was voluptuous and curvy, and I was more wiry and athletic, my middle sister had been born with the true model's body, tall and rail-thin. Kirsten and I were always being told by photographers that while we had pretty faces, we were too plump or too short, respectively, to get serious print work. Early on, though, it was clear Whitney had real potential.

So it only made sense that the summer after her senior year, Whitney would move to New York to try her luck modeling there. This was the same thing Kirsten had done two years earlier. After she'd begged my parents to let her move in with two older girls she knew from our agency, they'd agreed on the condition that she also enroll in some college courses. Though at first Kirsten had kept up the balance, once she'd gotten some print work and a couple of commercials, school had fallen by the wayside. Even with the work, though, she still earned the bulk of her money with waitress and hostessing gigs.

Not that this bothered her all that much. Since high school, when she discovered boys and beer—not necessarily in that order—Kirsten's focus on modeling had dwindled considerably. While Whitney always made sure to get plenty of sleep before a job and arrived on time without fail, Kirsten was much more likely to roll in late, with bedhead and a hangover. One time she'd showed up for a Kopf's prom dress shoot with a hickey so large they couldn't even totally cover it with make-up. When the ads ran, weeks later, she'd laughed as she pointed it out to me—a brown circle, barely visible under the strap of her princesslike gown.

My mother had had higher hopes for Whitney. Two weeks after graduation, they packed her stuff and drove up to move her into the apartment where Kirsten was now living alone. To me, this cohabitation seemed like a bad idea from the start. My mom and dad, though, were firm: Whitney was only eighteen, and she needed some family looking out after her, and since my parents were already helping with Kirsten's rent, she couldn't really complain. (Although she did, of course.) Besides, my mom said, my sisters were older now, their various conflicts all in the past.

Once Whitney was moved in, my mom stayed on for a little while getting her settled, signing her up for a couple of courses and accompanying her to her first few appointments with agencies. Each night, she called after dinner to fill my dad and me in on what was going on, sounding happier than I'd ever heard her as she reported on celebrity sightings, meetings with agents, and the hectic, amazing pace of New York. Within a week, Whitney had her first go-see, landing her first job soon afterwards. By the time my mom left a month later, she was working much more than Kirsten ever had. Everything was going exactly as planned . . . until it wasn't.

My sisters had been living together for about four months when Kirsten started calling my mom and saying Whitney was acting strange. That she'd lost weight, hardly seemed to be eating at all, and was really snippy every time Kirsten tried to broach either topic. At first there didn't seem to be much cause for concern. Whitney had always been moody, and even my parents hadn't expected their living situation to go completely smoothly. Most likely, my mom reasoned, Kirsten was being overly dramatic, and if Whitney had lost a little weight, well, she *was* working in a very competitive market, which meant more pressure about her appearance. As she gained confidence, things would even out.

The next time we saw Whitney, though, the change in her was obvious. Before she'd looked lithe, elegant; now, she was gaunt, and her head seemed too big for her body, weighing down her neck. She and Kirsten flew down together for Thanksgiving, and when we picked them up from the airport, the contrast was startling. There was Kirsten, with her round cheeks and clear blue eyes, wearing a bright pink sweater, her skin warm against mine as she threw her arms around me, shrieking how much she'd missed us all. And beside her, Whitney, in sweatpants, a long-sleeved black turtleneck, no makeup, her skin pale. It was a shock, but at first no one said anything, instead just exchanging hellos and hugs and the basic how-was-the-trip banter. As we walked into baggage claim, though, my mother finally broke.

"Whitney, honey," my mother said. "You look *exhausted*. Is that cold you had still hanging on?"

"I'm fine," Whitney said.

"No, she isn't," Kirsten informed us flatly, pulling her suitcase off the carousel. "She doesn't eat. Ever. She's killing herself."

My parents exchanged a look. "Oh, no, she's just been sick," my mother said. She looked at Whitney, who was glaring at Kirsten. "Right, honey?"

"Wrong," Kirsten told her. To Whitney, she said, "Like we talked about on the plane: Either you tell them, or I will."

"Shut up," Whitney said, her voice clenched.

"Now, now," my father said. "Let's just get the bags."

This was typical. My father, the lone male in our estrogen-heavy household, had always dealt with any kind of emotional situation or conflict by doing something concrete and specific. Discussion of cramps and heavy flow at the breakfast table? He was up and out the door to change the oil on one of our cars. Coming home in tears for reasons you just didn't want to discuss? He'd go make you a grilled cheese, which he'd probably end up eating. Family crisis brewing in public place? Bags. Get the bags.

My mother was still studying Whitney, her face concerned. "Honey?" she said, her voice soft, as my dad yanked another suitcase off the belt. "Is this true? Is something wrong?"

"I'm fine," Whitney said again. "She's just jealous that I'm working so much."

"Oh, please!" Kirsten said. "I could give a *shit* about that, and you know it."

My mother's eyes widened, and again I thought of her amongst us, so small, fragile. "Watch your language," my dad said to Kirsten.

"Dad, you don't understand," she told him. "This is serious. Whitney has an eating disorder. If she doesn't get help, she'll—"

"Shut up!" Whitney shrieked, her voice suddenly shrill. "Just shut up!"

This eruption was so startling—we were only used to Kirsten freaking out, ever—that we all just stood there for a second, as if gauging whether it had really happened. But then I saw people in the crowd glancing over at us, making it clear. I saw my mother's face flush, embarrassed.

"Andrew," she said, moving closer to my father. "I don't—"

"Let's go to the car," my dad told us, picking up Whitney's suitcase. "Now."

We went. In silence, my mother and father walking ahead, his arm clamped over her shoulder, Whitney behind them, head bent down against the breeze, Kirsten and I bringing up the rear. As we walked, she slid her hand down to enclose mine, her palm warm in the cold. "They have to know," she said, but when I turned my head, she was looking away, and I wondered if she was actually talking to me at all. "It's the right thing to do. I have to do it."

When we got in the car, no one spoke. Not as we pulled out of the deck, not when we got on the highway. In the backseat, stuck between my sisters, I kept feeling Kirsten taking in a breath, like she might say something, but no words came. On my other side, Whitney was pressed up against the window, looking out, her hands in her lap. I kept staring at her wrists, which looked thin and knobby and pale against the black of her sweatpants. My parents, up front, both stared straight ahead, and occasionally I'd see my father's shoulder move, and I knew he was patting my mom's hand, consoling her.

As soon as we pulled into the garage, Whitney was pushing her door open. Within seconds, she covered the few feet to the door that led to the kitchen, disappearing inside and slamming it behind her. Beside me, Kirsten sighed.

"Okay," she said quietly as my dad cut the engine. "We need to talk."

They did, but I wasn't allowed to hear what they said. It was made clear to me ("Annabel, why don't you go do some homework?") that I was not to be part of this conversation. Instead, I stayed in my room, math book open in my lap, straining to make out some of what was happening downstairs. I could hear my father's low tones, my mom's higher ones, and the occasional indignant shift in tone from Kirsten. On the other side of my wall, Whitney, in her room, was silent.

Finally, my mom came upstairs, passing my room to knock on Whitney's door. When there was no reply, she said, "Whitney, honey. Let me in." Nothing. She stood there for what felt like a full minute or two before suddenly I heard the lock turn, and then the door open and shut again.

I went back downstairs, where I found Kirsten sitting at the kitchen table with my father, an untouched grilled cheese on a plate in front of her. "Look," she was saying as I opened the cabinet to pull out a glass, "she explains it all away really well. She'll have Mom brainwashed in three seconds."

"I'm sure that's not true," my dad told her. "Give your mother some credit."

Kirsten shook her head. "She's sick, Daddy. She hardly ever

eats, and when she does she's really weird about it. She'll eat one quarter of an apple for breakfast or, like, three saltines for lunch. And she works out all the time. The gym around the corner is open twenty-four hours, and sometimes I wake up and she's gone, and I know she's there."

"She might not be," my dad said.

"I followed her. A few times. She runs on the treadmill for hours. Look, I had a friend when I first moved to the city, her roommate was like this. She got down to eighty pounds or something; they had to put her in the hospital. It's serious."

My dad was quiet for a second. "Let's just get her side of things," he said finally. "And then we'll see where we are. And Annabel?"

I jumped. "Yes?"

"Maybe go finish that homework?"

"Okay," I said. I finished my water, then put my glass in the dishwasher and headed back upstairs. As I forced myself back to parallelograms, I could hear my mother talking to Whitney next door, her voice low and soothing. I was almost done with my work when her door opened.

"I know," my mom was saying. "How about this: Take a shower, and a nap, and I'll wake you up when it's time for dinner. Okay? Everything will look better then."

I heard a sniffle, which I assumed was Whitney agreeing to this, and then my mother was walking past my door again. This time, she looked in at me.

"Everything's all right," she said. "Don't worry."

Looking back, I don't doubt my mom believed this at the time. I learned later how Whitney had completely reassured her, saying she was just overworked and overtired, and while she had been working out more and eating less because she had found she was a little bigger than the girls she was going up against for jobs, it was by no means to extreme levels. If Kirsten thought she wasn't eating, she maintained, it was because they kept totally different hours, as Kirsten worked nights and Whitney worked days. Personally, she'd said, she felt that there was more to this than just concern. Since arriving in New York, Whitney had clearly been working more than Kirsten ever had, and perhaps that wasn't sitting well. Maybe she was just jealous.

"I am not jealous!" I heard Kirsten say, her voice angry, a few minutes after my mother went downstairs. "Don't you see, she's tricked you. Open your *eyes!*"

There was more, of course, but I couldn't hear it. And by the time I was called for dinner an hour later, whatever had happened was over, and we were back in default Greene family mode, pretending everything was just fine. And from the outside, I was sure it at least looked that way.

My father designed our house, and at the time it was the most modern one in the neighborhood. Everyone called it "The Glass House," although it really wasn't all glass, only the front. From the outside, you could see our entire downstairs: the living room, split by the huge stone fireplace, the kitchen beyond, and past that the pool in the backyard. You could also see the stairs and part of the second floor—the doorways to my room and to Whitney's, and the landing between them, split by the chimney. The rest was tucked away behind, out of sight. So while it seemed like you were seeing everything, you really weren't. Just bits and pieces that looked like a whole.

The dining room was right at the front of the house, though, so when we ate dinner, we were always in full view. From my seat at the table, I could always see when cars passing slowed down slightly, the drivers glancing in at us for this snapshot, a happy family seated around a hearty meal. But everyone knows looks can be deceiving.

That night, Whitney ate her dinner; it was the first time, but by no means the last, that I noticed this. Kirsten drank too many glasses of wine, and my mother kept saying how wonderful it was we were all together, finally. And repeat, for the next three days.

The morning they left, she sat them both down at the kitchen table and asked them each to make her a promise. She wanted Whitney to take better care of herself, get more sleep, and keep to a healthy diet. Kirsten she asked to keep an eye on Whitney and try to be sympathetic to the pressure she was under living in a new city and working so hard. "Okay?" she said, looking from one of them to the other, then back again.

"Okay," Whitney said. "I promise."

Kirsten, though, just shook her head. "It's not me," she said to my mother, pushing back her chair and standing up. "I warned you. That's all I'm going to say. I told you, and you are choosing not to listen to me. I just want us all to be clear on that."

"Kirsten," my mother said, but she was already gone, walking out to the garage, where my father was putting the suitcases into the car.

"Don't worry," Whitney said, getting up and kissing my mom on the cheek. "Everything's fine."

For a while, it seemed like it was. Whitney kept getting jobs, including a shoot for *New York* magazine, her biggest yet. Kirsten got a new hostessing gig at a very famous restaurant, and a cable TV commercial. If they weren't getting along, we didn't hear about it—instead of one weekly phone call where they passed the receiver between them, now they each called separately, Kirsten usually in the late morning, Whitney in the evenings. Then, about a week before they were due home for Christmas, we got a call during dinner.

"I'm sorry, what?" my mother said, the phone to her ear as she stood in the doorway that led from the kitchen to the dining room. My dad glanced over at her as she lifted her other hand, putting it over her free ear to hear better. "What did you say?"

"Gracie?" My dad pushed his chair back, getting to his feet. "What is it?"

My mom shook her head. "I don't know," she said, handing over the phone. "I can't . . ."

"Hello?" my dad said. "Who is this? . . . Oh . . . I see . . . Right . . . Well, that's a mistake, I'm sure. . . . Hold on, I'll find the right information."

As he put the phone down, my mother said, "I couldn't understand her, what was she saying?"

"There's a problem with Whitney's insurance card," he told her. "Apparently she was at the hospital today."

"The hospital?" My mother's voice crept up to that scary, shaky octave that always made my own heart instantly start beating faster. "Is she all right? What happened?"

"I don't know," my dad said. "She's already been discharged, there's just a problem with the billing. I have to find her new card. . . ."

As my dad went up to his office to look for it, my mom got back on the phone and tried to get information from the woman who'd called. Citing privacy reasons, though, she wouldn't tell much, only that Whitney had been brought in by ambulance that morning and left a few hours earlier. The minute my dad cleared up the billing issue, he called Kirsten and Whitney's apartment. Kirsten answered.

"I tried to tell you," was all she said. I could hear her voice from where I was sitting. "I tried."

"Put your sister on the phone," my father told her. "Now."

Whitney got on, and I could hear her talking quickly, her voice high and cheery, as my parents both leaned into the receiver, listening. Later, I'd get the story she told them: that it was no big deal, she'd just been really dehydrated—a result of an ongoing sinus infection—and fainted at a shoot. It sounded worse than it was, and the ambulance was just the result of someone panicking. She hadn't told us because she didn't want my mother to worry, and it really was nothing, nothing at all.

"Maybe I should come up there," my mother said. "Just to make sure."

No, Whitney said, there was no point, they'd be home for Christmas in two weeks, and that was all she needed, a real break, to get some sleep, and she'd be totally well again. "Are you sure?" my mother asked.

Yes. She was positive.

Before they hung up, my father asked to talk to Kirsten again. "Is your sister all right?" he asked her.

"No," Kirsten told him. "She's not."

But still, my mother didn't go. This was the biggest mystery, the one thing that, looking back, I could never quite figure out. For whatever reason, she chose to believe Whitney. It was a mistake.

When Whitney flew home for Christmas, she came alone, as Kirsten had to stay an additional few days for work. My dad went to the airport to pick her up, and my mom and I were in the kitchen, fixing dinner, when they returned. When I took my first glance at my sister, I couldn't believe my eyes.

She was so thin. Emaciated. It was obvious, even though she was wearing even baggier clothes than the last time I'd seen her, and more layers as well. Her eyes looked sunken in her face, and you could see all the tendons in her neck, moving like puppet strings whenever she turned her head. I just stared at her.

"Annabel," she said, annoyed. "Come give me a hug."

I put down the vegetable peeler I was holding, then moved tentatively across the room. As I wrapped my arms around her, I felt like I might break her, she felt so brittle. My father was standing behind her with her suitcase, and as I looked at his face I knew that he, too, was shocked by the change in her in only a month's time.

My mother did not acknowledge any of this, at least not out loud. Instead, as I let go of Whitney, she stepped forward, smiling, and pulled her close. "Oh, honey," she said. "You've had such a hard time."

As she leaned down over my mother's shoulder, Whitney

slowly closed her eyes. The lids seemed almost translucent, and I felt a shudder run through me.

"We're going to get you well," my mother said, "starting right now. Go freshen up, and we'll sit down for dinner."

"Oh, I'm not hungry," Whitney said. "I ate while I was waiting for my plane."

"You did?" My mother looked hurt. She'd been cooking all day. "Well, surely you can at least manage some vegetable soup. I made it specially for you, and it's just what you need to get your immune system up."

"Really, I just want to sleep," Whitney said. "I'm so tired."

My mom glanced at my dad, who was still looking at Whitney, his face serious. "Well, okay, then maybe you should lie down for a while. You can eat when you wake up. Okay?"

But Whitney didn't eat. Not that night, which she slept straight through, not stirring each time my mother came in with a tray. Not the next morning; she was up at the crack of dawn, claiming to have already eaten breakfast when my father, the earliest riser in our house, came downstairs to make his coffee. At lunch, she was asleep again. Finally, at dinner, my mother made her sit down with us.

It started the minute my dad began to serve. Whitney was sitting beside me, and as he started to carve the roast beef, putting pieces on plates, I was distinctly aware of how she was unable to sit still, twitching nervously, pulling at the cuff of her baggy sweatshirt. She crossed and uncrossed her legs, took a sip of her water, then tugged at her cuff again. I could feel the stress coming off of her, palpable, and as my father put a full plate in front of her heaped with meat, potatoes, green beans, and a big hunk of my mother's famous garlic bread, she lost it.

"I'm really not hungry," she said quickly, pushing it away. "I'm not."

"Whitney," my father said. "Eat your food."

"I don't *want* it," she said angrily, as across the table, my mother looked so hurt I could hardly stand it. "This is about Kirsten, isn't it? She told you to do this."

"No," my mother said, "this is about you, honey. You need to get well."

"I'm not sick," Whitney said. "I'm fine. I'm just tired, and I'm not going to eat if I'm not hungry. I won't. You can't make me."

We all just sat there, watching her as she tugged at her cuffs again, her eyes on the table. "Whitney," my father said, "you're too thin. You need—"

"Don't tell me what I need," she said, pushing back her chair and getting up. "You have no *idea* what I need. If you did, we wouldn't even be having this conversation."

"Honey, we want to help you," my mother said, her voice soft. "We want—"

"Then leave me alone!" She slammed the chair against the table, making all our plates jump, and then stomped out. A second later, I heard the front door open and shut, and then she was gone.

This is what happened next: After doing his best to calm my mother down, my dad got in the car and went out to look for Whitney. My mother took up a position in a chair in the foyer, in case he somehow didn't find her, and I quickly finished my dinner, then I covered all their plates with plastic wrap, put them in the fridge, and did the dishes. I was just finishing up when I saw my dad's car coasting back into the driveway.

When he and Whitney came back in, she wouldn't look at anyone. Instead, she kept her head low, eyes on the floor, as my father explained that she was going to eat some food and then go back to sleep, in the hopes that things would look better tomorrow. There wasn't a discussion of this deal, or how they had come about it. It was already decided.

My mother asked me to go upstairs then, so I didn't get to see Whitney eat her dinner, or hear if there were any more arguments about it. Later, though, when the house was so quiet I knew everyone else was asleep, I went downstairs. There was only one plate left of the three I'd wrapped up, and while it looked like it had been poked at since, it was nowhere near clean.

I got a snack, then went into the TV room, where I watched a rerun of a reality makeover show and some of the local news. When I finally headed back upstairs, it was that weird time of night when the moon was shining really brightly through the glass, lighting everything up. There was always something strange about seeing so much moonlight inside, and as I passed through it, I covered my eyes.

The hallway that led to my room and Whitney's was lit up as well, the only shaded part in the middle, from the chimney. As I stepped into that sudden dark, I smelled the steam.

Or felt it. All I knew was that suddenly, it was like the very air changed, becoming heavier and more moist, and for a second I just stood there, breathing it in. The bathroom was all the way at the other end of the hall, and there was no light beneath the door, but as I moved toward it, the steam got thicker and more pungent, and I could hear the sound of water splashing. It seemed so bizarre. I could understand leaving a faucet running, but the shower? Then again, Whitney had been acting weird ever since she got home, so anything was possible. I finally reached the half-open door, pushing it open.

Immediately it hit against something, then swung back at me. I eased it open again, the steam now thick in my face, already condensing on my skin. I couldn't see anything, and all I could hear was water, so I reached blindly to my right, my hand moving over the wall until I found the switch.

Whitney was lying on the floor, at my feet. It was her shoulder the door had hit when I first tried to open it. She was curled up, slightly, a towel knotted around her, her cheek pressed against the linoleum. The shower, as I'd suspected, was on full blast, and water was pooling in the bottom, too much for the drain to handle.

"Whitney?" I said, crouching down beside her. I couldn't imagine what she'd been doing here in the dark, alone, so late at night. "Are you—"

Then I saw the toilet. The lid was up, and inside was this yellowy mix, tinged with red that I knew, somehow, with one look, was blood.

"Whitney." I put my hand on her face. Her skin was hot, wet, and her eyelids fluttered. I reached down, shaking her shoulder. "Whitney, wake up."

She didn't. But she did move, just enough that the towel

came loose. And then, finally, I saw what my sister had done to herself.

She was all bones. That was the first thing I thought. Bones and knobs, every bump of her spine protruding and visible. Her hips poked out at angles, her knees were skinny and pale. It seemed impossible that she could be so thin and still be alive, and even more so that she'd been able to somehow hide this. As she shifted again, though, I saw it, the one thing that would stick with me forever: the sharpness of her shoulder blades as they rose out of her skin, looking like the wings of a dead baby bird I'd once found in our backyard, hairless and barely born, already broken.

"Daddy!" I screamed, my voice so loud in the tiny room. *"Daddy!"*

The rest of the night I remember only in bits and pieces. My father, fumbling to put on his glasses as he ran down the hallway in his pajamas. My mother behind him, standing in that one shaft of light at the other end of the hall, illuminated, her hands to her face as he pushed me aside, then crouched down beside Whitney, putting his ear to her chest. The ambulance, the swirling lights of which made the entire house seem like a kaleidoscope. And then the silence once it was gone, with Whitney and my mother inside, my father following in his car behind. I was told to stay where I was, and wait for word.

I didn't know what to do. So I went back to the bathroom and cleaned it up. I flushed the toilet, looking away as I did so, then mopped up the water that had spilled out on the floor, and took the towels I used down to the washing machine, putting them in. Then I went and sat in the living room, in all that moonlight, and waited.

It was my father who finally called two hours later. The sound of the phone ringing jerked me awake, and as I picked up the receiver, the sun was rising in the front of the house, the sky streaked with pinks and reds. "Your sister is going to be okay," he said. "When we get home, we'll explain what's happening."

After we hung up, I went back to my room and crawled into bed, sleeping two more hours until I heard the garage door open and knew they were home. When I came down to the kitchen, my mother was making a pot of coffee, her back to me. She had on the same clothes as the night before, her hair uncombed.

"Mom?" I said.

She turned around, and when I saw her face, my stomach dropped. It was just like all those years ago: her face so tired, eyes swollen from crying, her very features haunted. A sudden panic made me want to wrap myself around her, putting myself between her and the world and everything it could do to her, to me, to any of us.

And then it happened. My mother started crying. Her eyes welled up, and she looked down at her hands, which were trembling, and then she was sobbing, the sound seeming so loud in the quiet of the kitchen. I stepped forward, not knowing how to handle this. Luckily, I didn't have to.

"Grace." My father was standing in the doorway to the hall that led to his office. "Honey. It's all right."

My mother's shoulders were shaking as she drew in a breath. "Oh, God, Andrew. What did we—"

And then my father was moving across the room toward her, taking her in his arms, his big frame encompassing hers. She buried her face in his chest, the sobs muffled in his shirt, and I stepped back, over the threshold, out of sight, and sat down in the dining room. I could still hear her crying, and the sound was awful. But seeing it was worse.

Eventually, my dad got my mother calmed down and sent her upstairs to shower and try to get some rest. Then he came back down and sat across from me.

"Your sister is very sick," he said. "She's lost an extreme amount of weight and apparently hasn't been eating normally for months now. Her system just shut down last night."

"Is she going to be okay?" I asked.

He ran a hand over his face, taking a moment before answering. "The doctors feel," he said, "that she needs to go immediately to a treatment facility. Your mother and I . . ." He trailed off, looking past me, out at the pool. "We just want what's best for Whitney."

"So she's not coming back?"

"Not right away," he told me. "It's a process. We just have to see how it goes."

I looked down at my hands, which I had spread out in front of me on the table, the wood cool on my palms. "Last night," I said, "when I first saw her, I just . . ."

"I know." He pushed his chair out, standing up. "But she's going to get help now. Okay?"

I nodded. Clearly, my dad was not up for discussing the emotional impact of what had happened. He'd given me the facts, what prognosis there was, and that was all I'd get.

After a couple of days in the hospital, Whitney was trans-
ferred to a treatment center, which she hated so much she initially refused to speak to my parents when they visited. Still, it
was helping her, as she began gaining weight, bit by bit, day by
day. As for Kirsten, she arrived on Christmas Eve to find my
parents exhausted and stressed out, me just trying to stay out
of the way, and any hope of holiday cheer completely out of the
question. Which did not prevent her from dropping a bomb of
her own.

"I've made a decision," she announced as we sat at dinner
that night. "I'm giving up modeling."

My mother, at the end of the table, put down her fork.
"What?"

"I'm just not into it anymore," Kirsten said, taking a sip of
her wine. "Truth be told, I haven't been for a while. And it's not
like I've been working that much anyway. But I just decided to
make it official."

I glanced at my mom. She was already so tired and sad, and
this clearly was not helping. My dad was watching her, too. He
said, "Don't do anything rash, Kirsten."

"I'm not. I've thought about it a lot." Of all of us, she was
the only one still eating, scooping up a forkful of potatoes as
she said this. "I mean, let's face it, I'm never going to be a hundred and five pounds. Or five-ten, for that matter."

"You've gotten plenty of work just as you are," my mom
said.

"Some work," Kirsten corrected her. "It's by no means a living. I've been doing this since I was eight. I'm twenty-two now.
I want to do something else."

"Such as?" my dad said.

Kirsten shrugged. "I don't know yet. I've got the hostess thing at the restaurant, and I have a friend who owns a salon who offered me a receptionist job. So the bills will be covered, for the most part. I'm thinking I might sign up for some classes or something."

My dad raised his eyebrows. "School," he said.

"Don't sound so surprised," Kirsten replied, although I had to admit, this was shocking to me, as well. Even before she'd stopped taking classes in New York, she'd never been much for academics. In high school the classes she hadn't missed because of modeling she skipped, usually preferring to spend her time with whatever scruffy, free-spirited boyfriend she had at the time. "Most girls my age have already graduated and have real careers. I feel like I've missed out on a lot, you know? I want to get my degree."

"You could take classes and still model," my mother said. "It doesn't have to be an either/or situation."

"Yes, it does," Kirsten replied. "For me, it does."

Under different circumstances, maybe my parents would have pushed to discuss this further. But they were tired, and while Kirsten might have been known best for her directness, her stubbornness ran a close second. It shouldn't have been all that surprising anyway, as she'd hardly been committed to modeling for years now. Coming so close to Whitney's collapse, however, it meant more. Especially to me, although I didn't realize it at the time.

Whitney stayed at the treatment center for thirty days, during which time she gained ten pounds. She wanted to return to

New York once she was released, but my parents insisted she move back home instead, as the doctors felt strongly a return to modeling would risk any progress she'd made, or would make. That was in January, and since then she'd been going to an outpatient program, seeing an additional therapist twice a week, and sulking around the house. Meanwhile, Kirsten had kept to her word, enrolling in some classes at a New York college while juggling her other two jobs. Surprisingly, given her high-school experience, she loved school, calling each weekend happy and bubbling over with details about her classes and what she was studying. Again, my sisters were at extremes and yet similar at the same time: Each was starting over, but only one by choice.

There were some weeks when it seemed like Whitney was really getting better, gaining weight, clearly on her way. And then there were others when she'd refuse to eat breakfast, or get caught doing forbidden crunches in her room late at night, and only the threat of having to go back into the hospital and be force-fed was enough to make her get back in line. Through it all, one thing remained constant: She would not talk to Kirsten.

Not when she called. Not even when she came home for a weekend in the spring. At first Kirsten was hurt, then angry, before finally retaliating with her own silence. The rest of us were stuck in the middle, filling the awkward pauses with chatter that always fell short. Since then, while my mom and dad had both traveled up to see her at various times, she'd made a point of not coming back home.

It was weird. As a kid, I'd always hated it when my sisters

fought, but them not talking at all was worse. Their complete and total lack of communication, now going on nine months, was scary in how permanent it felt.

The changes in my sisters over the last year were both evident and sensory. One you could spot on sight, while the other you heard about the moment you were in earshot, whether you wanted to or not. As for me, I found myself where I'd always been, stuck somewhere in the middle.

But I had changed, too, even if only I could tell. I was different. As different as my family was that night it all began from what we appeared to be—the five of us, a happy family, sharing a meal in our glass house—to anyone in a car passing by on the road outside, looking in.

Chapter
FOUR

For the first week of school, Sophie ignored me completely. Which was hard. But when she did begin to speak to me, I quickly realized I much preferred the silence.

"Whore."

It was always just one word. One word, said clearly and with enough spite to sting. Sometimes it came from behind me, floating over my shoulder when I wasn't expecting it. Other times, I could see her coming, and took it right in the face. The one thing that was always the same was that her timing was impeccable. The moment I started to feel a little better or have a half-decent moment in an okay day, she was right there to make sure it didn't last.

This time, she was walking by as I sat on the wall during lunch. Emily was with her—Emily was always with her, these days—and I didn't look at them, instead just focusing on the notebook in my lap and the history paper I was working on. I'd just written the word *occupation*, and I kept my pen to the page, making both *o*'s darker and darker, until Emily and Sophie passed.

There was a karmic aspect to this, although I didn't like to think about it. The truth was, it hadn't been that long ago that I'd been the one who walked alongside Sophie while she did her dirty work, when I was the person who, while not taking part in the slur, didn't stop it, either. Like with Clarke.

Thinking this, I looked up, glancing around the courtyard until I found her sitting at one of the picnic tables with a few of her friends. She was at the end of the bench, a textbook open in front of her, half listening to the conversation between the girls next to her as she flipped through the pages. Clearly, sitting alone on that first day for her had been optional. She hadn't come anywhere near the wall, or me, since.

But Owen Armstrong remained. Other people came and went from our wall, some in groups, some by themselves, but only he and I were there every single day. We always kept an understood distance between us—about six feet, give or take a few inches—that whoever arrived second was always sure to honor when they sat down. There were other constants, too. He never ate, that I saw; I always had a full lunch, courtesy of my mother. He seemed completely unaware, and uncaring, of what anyone else was doing, while I spent the hour convinced everyone was staring at and discussing me. I did homework; he listened to music. And we never, ever spoke.

Maybe it was because I was spending so much time alone. Or the fact that there were only so many minutes of my lunch hour I could spend doing homework. Whatever the reason, I'd become somewhat fascinated with Owen Armstrong. Every day, I made it a point to take a few sideways glances at him, cataloging something else about his appearance or habits. So far, I'd garnered quite a bit of information.

For instance, the earphones. He *never* seemed to take them off. Clearly, he loved music, and his iPod was always either in his pocket, his hand, or lying on the wall beside him. I'd also noticed that his reactions when he was listening varied. Usually he sat totally still except for his head bobbing, slowly and almost imperceptibly. Occasionally he drummed his fingers on his knee, and in very rare instances, he hummed along, barely loud enough for me to hear, and then only when no one was passing or talking nearby. Those were the times I wondered most what he was listening to, although I imagined it to be just like him, dark and angry and loud.

Then there was his appearance. His size, of course, you saw first: the height, the big wrists, the enormity of his mere presence. But there were little things, too, like his dark eyes, which were either green or brown, and the two identical rings—each flat, wide, and silver—he wore on the middle finger of each hand.

Now, as I glanced over at him, he was sitting with his legs stretched out in front of him, leaning back on his palms. A swath of sunlight was falling across his face, and his earphones were on, his head bobbing slightly, eyes closed. A girl carrying a piece of poster board walked past me, then slowed as she approached him, and I watched her as she carefully stepped over his feet, like Jack from "Jack in the Beanstalk" creeping past the sleeping giant. Owen didn't stir, and she scurried on.

I'd once felt this same way about Owen as well, of course. Everyone did. But there was something about our daily proximity that had made me relax, or at least not jump every time he looked my way. These days I was more worried about Sophie, who was a credible threat, or even Clarke, who had made it clear that yes, she still hated me.

It seemed odd that Owen Armstrong could seem somehow safer than the only two best friends I'd ever had. I was beginning to see, though, that the unknown wasn't always the greatest thing to fear. The people who know you best can be riskier, because the words they say and the things they think have the potential to be not only scary but true, as well.

I had no history with Owen. But Sophie and Clarke were different. There was a pattern here, some sense of connection, even if I didn't want to see it. It didn't seem fair or right, but I couldn't help but wonder if maybe all of this, and where I found myself, wasn't so accidental. Maybe it was just what I deserved.

After that night when Clarke and I returned her stuff to her at her house, Sophie started to hang out with us. It wasn't a specific invitation as much as she was just eased in. Suddenly there was a third beach chair, another hand dealt into the card game, one more Coke to carry when it was your turn to go get drinks. Clarke and I had been best friends for so long it was kind of nice to have a fresh take on things, and Sophie definitely provided that. In her bikinis and makeup, full of stories of the boys she'd dated in Dallas, she was totally different from us.

She was also loud and bold, completely unafraid to talk to guys. Or wear whatever she felt like wearing. Or say what was on her mind. She wasn't unlike Kirsten in this fashion, but while my sister's forthrightness always made me uneasy,

Sophie's was different. I liked it, almost envied it. I couldn't say what I wanted, but I could always count on her to speak up, and the events she set into motion—always a little risky, at least for me, but fun at the same time—were ones I never would have gotten to experience left to my own devices.

Still, there were moments when I felt uneasy around Sophie, although it was hard to put my finger on why, exactly. As much as we hung out and she became part of my day-to-day life, I couldn't forget how mean she'd been to me that first day at the snack bar. Sometimes I'd just look at her while she was telling a story, or painting her nails as she lay on the end of my bed, and wonder why she had done that. And in the next beat, if she'd do it again.

For all her bravado, though, I knew Sophie had her own problems. Her parents had just recently divorced, and while she'd mentioned repeatedly all the stuff her dad bought her when she lived in Texas—clothes, jewelry, anything she wanted—one day I'd overheard my mom and one of her friends discussing the divorce, which was apparently very ugly. Sophie's dad had left for a much younger woman, and there'd been a bitter battle over their house in Dallas. Mr. Rawlins supposedly wasn't in contact with Sophie or her mom at all. But Sophie never mentioned this, and I didn't ask about it. I figured if she wanted to talk about it, she would.

In the meantime, she hardly held back on anything else. For instance, she was always telling me and Clarke we were immature. Everything, apparently, was wrong: our clothes (so childish), our activities (boring), and our experiences (nonexistent). While she was interested in my modeling and seemed fascinated with my sisters—who both pretty much ignored her, as they did me—she was always giving Clarke a hard time.

"You look like a boy," she said one day when we all went to the mall. "You could look really cute, if you tried. Why don't you wear some makeup or something?"

"I'm not allowed," Clarke told her, blowing her nose.

"Please," Sophie said. "It's not like your parents have to know. Just put it on when you leave, take it off before you go home."

But Clarke wasn't like that, and I knew it. She got along well with her mom and dad, and wouldn't lie to them. Sophie, however, wouldn't let up. If it wasn't Clarke's lack of makeup, it was her clothes, or her constant sneezing, or the fact that she had to be home a full hour before either of us, meaning that whatever we did as a group always had to be cut short in order to make sure she got in on time. If I'd been paying more attention, maybe I would have seen what was happening. As it was, though, I just attributed it to us all getting used to one another, and figured everything would work out eventually—at least until that night in early July.

It was a Saturday, and we were all spending the night at Clarke's. Her parents were out at some symphony concert, so we had the house to ourselves to make a frozen pizza and watch movies. Typical Saturday. We'd preheated the oven, and Clarke was seeing what was on pay-per-view when Sophie arrived, dressed in a denim miniskirt, a white tank top that showed off her tan, and white sandals with thick heels.

"Wow," I said as she came in, her heels clacking against the floor. "You look nice."

"Thanks," she replied, as I followed her into the kitchen.

"You're pretty dressed up for pizza," Clarke told her, then sneezed.

Sophie smiled. "This isn't for pizza," she said.

Clarke and I looked at each other. I said, "Then what is it for?"

"Boys," she said.

"Boys?" Clarke repeated.

"Yeah." Sophie hopped up on the counter, crossing her legs. "I met a couple of guys today, walking home from the pool. They said they'd be hanging out there tonight and we should come meet them."

"The pool is closed at night," Clarke told her, sliding the pizza onto a cookie sheet.

"So?" Sophie said. "Everyone goes up there. It's not a big deal."

I knew instantly Clarke was not going to go for this. First, because her parents would kill her if they found out. Second, because she always followed the rules, even the ones everyone else ignored, like taking a shower before getting in the pool and always getting out of the water the second the lifeguard announced adult swim. "I don't know," I said as I thought this. "We probably shouldn't."

"Oh, come *on*, Annabel," Sophie said. "Don't be a wuss. Besides, one of these guys was asking about you specifically. He'd seen us together and asked if you would be there."

"Me?" I said.

She nodded. "Yeah. And he's *cute*. His name's Chris Pen-something. Penner? Penning—"

"Pennington," I said. I could feel Clarke looking at me; she was the only one who knew how I felt about him, the crush I'd had forever. "Chris Pennington?"

"That's it," Sophie said, nodding. "You know him?"

I glanced at Clarke, who was now making a point of focusing on putting the pizza in the oven, adjusting it on the rack. "We know who he is," I said. "Right, Clarke?"

"He's *so* hot," Sophie said. "They said they'd be there around eight, and they'd have some beers."

"Beers?" I said.

"God, calm down," she said, laughing. "You don't have to drink if you don't want to."

Clarke shut the oven with a bang. "I can't go out," she said.

"Oh, you can too," Sophie said. "Your parents won't even know."

"I don't *want* to," Clarke finished. "I'm staying here."

I just looked at her, knowing I should say the same thing, but for some reason, the words just didn't come. Probably because all I could think about was Chris Pennington, who I'd watched at the pool a million afternoons, asking about me. "Well," I said, forcing myself to speak, "maybe—"

"Then me and Annabel will go," Sophie said, hopping off the counter. "No big deal. Right, Annabel?"

Now Clarke did look at me. She turned her head, and I felt those dark eyes watching me carefully. Suddenly I felt that imbalance, that unevenness of three, with me left to choose which way to go. On the one side was Clarke, my best friend, and our entire routine, everything we'd always done and known. On the other was not only Sophie and Chris Pennington but this whole other world, unchartered and open, at least for a little while, this one night. I wanted to go.

"Clarke," I said, taking a step toward her. "Let's just go for a little while, like, a half hour. Then we'll come back and eat the pizza and do the movie and all that. Okay?"

Clarke wasn't an emotional person. She was instead a born stoic, extremely logical, her entire approach to life one of figuring out problems, stating solutions, and moving on. But in that moment, as I said this, I saw something rare on her face: surprise, followed by hurt. It was so unexpected, though, and gone so quickly, that it was hard to know if I'd really seen it at all.

"No," she said. "I'm not going." And with that, she walked across the room to the couch, sitting down and picking up the remote. A second later, she was scrolling through channels, images and color flickering across the screen.

"All right then," Sophie said with a shrug. Then she turned to me. "Come on," she said.

She started toward the front door, and for a second, I just stood there. Everything about the Reynoldses' kitchen and this night was so familiar: the smell of pizza in the oven, the two-liter Coke on the countertop, Clarke in her spot on the couch, my spot open and waiting for me beside her. But then I looked down the hallway to Sophie, who was now standing in the open door. Behind her, it was just barely dark, the streetlights flickering on, and before I could change my mind, I walked toward her and stepped outside.

Even years later, I remembered that night so well. Like how it felt, after climbing through the hole in the pool fence, to walk across the dark parking lot, right up to Chris Pennington, who smiled at me and said my name aloud. And the way the beer he'd brought tasted as I took my first sip, fizzy and light in my mouth. Then later, after he walked me around the back of the pool, how it felt to kiss him, his lips warm against mine, my back pressed up against the cool of the wall behind me. Or hearing Sophie laughing in the distance, her voice carrying over the still water from wherever she was with his best friend, a guy named Bill who moved away at the end of that summer. All of these things register, but there is one image, one moment, that rises above them all. That was later, when I glanced over the pool fence to see someone standing across the street, under a streetlight. A small girl with dark hair, in shorts and no makeup, who could hear our voices but not see us.

"Annabel," she called out. "Come on, it's late."

We all stopped talking. I could see Chris squint as he looked into the dark. "What was that?"

"Shhh," Bill said. "Someone's out there."

"It's not someone," Sophie said, rolling her eyes. "It's Ca-*larke.*"

"Ca-w*hat*?" Bill said, laughing.

Sophie reached up, pinching her nose shut with two fingers. "Ca-*larke,*" she repeated, her voice sounding so like Clarke's, stuffed up and adenoidal, that it was startling. I felt a pang in my chest as everyone laughed, and I looked back over at her again, knowing she could hear it. She was still there, across the street under the light, but I knew she would come no farther, and that it was my job to leave now and go to her.

"I better—" I said, stepping forward.

"Annabel." Sophie leveled her gaze at me. At the time this was new, but later I'd come to recognize her expression, a mix of annoyance and impatience. It was the look she'd give me a million times over the years, whenever I wasn't doing what she wanted. "What are you doing?"

Chris and Bill were both watching us. "It's just," I began, then stopped. "I should just go."

"No," Sophie said. "You shouldn't."

I should have just walked away, from Sophie, from all of it, and done the right thing. But I didn't. I told myself later it was because Chris Pennington had his hand on the small of my back and it was summer, and earlier, his lips on mine, hands in my hair, he had whispered to me that I was gorgeous. Really, though, it was this moment with Sophie, my fear of what would happen if I stood up to her, that stopped me. And shamed me for years to come.

So I stayed where I was, and Clarke went home, and later, when I tried to go back to her house, the lights were off, the door locked. I went up anyway, but unlike that night we'd gone to Sophie's, the door didn't open. Instead, Clarke left me waiting, as I had done to her, and eventually I went home.

I knew she was really mad at me. I assumed, though, that we'd work it out. It was just one night—I'd made a mistake; she'd come around. But the next day, when I walked up to her at the pool, she wouldn't even look at me and ignored my repeated hellos, turning away when I sat down on the chair beside her.

"Come on," I said. No response. "It was stupid of me to go. I'm sorry, okay?"

But it wasn't okay, clearly, as she still wouldn't look at me, giving me only her sharp profile. She was so mad, and I felt so helpless, I couldn't stand to sit there, so I got up and left.

"So what?" Sophie said when I went to her house and told her what had happened. "Why do you even care she's pissed?"

"She's my best friend," I told her. "And now she hates me."

"She's just a kid," she replied. I was sitting on her bed, watching her as she stood in front of her bureau mirror. She picked up her brush, giving her hair a few strokes. "And to be honest, she's kind of a nerd, Annabel. I mean, is that how you really want to spend your summer? Playing cards and listening to her sniffle? Please. You hooked up with Chris Pennington last night. You should be happy."

"I am," I said, although I wasn't sure this was true, even as I said it.

"Good." She put down her brush, then turned around, looking at me. "Now come on. Let's go to the mall or something."

And that was that. Years of friendship, all those card games and pizza nights and sleepovers, finished in less than twenty-four hours. Looking back, maybe if I had approached Clarke again, we could have worked things out. But I didn't. It was like the passing time and my guilt and shame opened up a chasm, wider and wider. Once, I might have been able to leap it, but eventually it was too distant to even look across, much less find a way to the other side.

Clarke and I would run into each other again, of course. We lived in the same neighborhood, rode the same bus, went to the same school. But we never spoke. Sophie became my best friend, although nothing ever happened with Chris Pennington, who, despite all the things he'd said in the dark that night, never talked to me again. As for Clarke, she found a new group of friends on the soccer team, which she joined in the fall, going on to be a starting forward. Eventually we were so different, and moving in such different crowds, that it was hard to believe we'd ever been close at all. In my photo albums, though, there was page after page of proof—the two of us at backyard cookouts, riding bikes, posing on her front steps, that ever-present pack of Kleenex between us.

Before Sophie, people knew who I was because of my sisters and my modeling, but it was only once we were friends that I was popular. And there was a difference. Sophie's particular brand of fearlessness was perfect for navigating the cliques and various dramatics of middle school and high school. The bossy girls and whispered comments that had always unnerved me didn't bother her at all, and I found it was much easier to cross the various social barriers once she'd already busted through them for me. Suddenly, everything I'd always watched and envied from a distance—the people, the parties, and especially the boys—was not only closer but altogether possible, and all because of Sophie. It made the other things I had to put up with, like her moodiness, and everything that had happened with Clarke, seem almost worth it. Almost.

At any rate, everything with me and Clarke and Sophie had happened ages ago. But this past summer, I'd found myself thinking about Clarke a lot, especially when I was alone at the pool. So much would have been different if I'd just stayed in that night, taken my spot beside her, and let Sophie go on without me. I'd made my choice, though, and I couldn't take it back.

Although sometimes, in the late afternoon, when I'd close my eyes and start to drift off, listening to kids splashing in the water and the lifeguard's whistle, it almost seemed like nothing had changed. At least until later, when I'd jerk awake to find myself in the shade, the air suddenly cooler, long past time to go home.

When I got home from school, the house was empty and the light on the answering machine was blinking. I pulled an apple out of the fridge, polishing it on my shirt as I walked across the room to play the messages. The first one was from Lindy, my agent.

"Hi, Grace, it's me, returning your call. Sorry it took so long, my assistant quit and I've had this useless temp manning the phones, it's been a total disaster. But anyway. No news yet, but I have a call in to the Mooshka office, so we'll hopefully hear something soon. I'll keep you posted, hope all is well, love to Annabel. Bye!"

Beep. I'd hadn't thought about the Mooshka go-see for days, but clearly it was on my mother's mind. I didn't want to think about it now either, so I moved on to the next message, which was from Kirsten. She was famous for leaving long, rambling missives, often having to call back for a part two when the machine cut off on her, so as soon as I heard her voice, I pulled out a chair.

"It's me," she began, "just calling to say hello, see what's going on. I am right this minute walking to class; it's a gorgeous day here. . . . Don't know if I told you guys, but I signed up for a communications class this semester, heavily recommended by a friend, and I am just loving it. It's taught with a psychology angle, and I'm just learning so much. . . . And the TA who runs my recitation is *brilliant.* I mean, a lot of times in lectures I just find myself zoning out, even if I feel the material is interesting, but Brian, he's just riveting. Seriously. He's even got me considering a minor in communications, just because I'm getting so much out of the class. . . . But there's also my film-making class, which really interests me, so I just don't know. Anyway, I'm almost to class now, hope all of you are well, miss you love you bye!"

Kirsten was so used to being cut off she always sped up at the end of her messages, so she blurted out this last part, barely beating the beep. I reached over, hitting the SAVE button, and the house was quiet again.

I stood, picking up my apple, and crossed through the dining room. When I got to the foyer I stopped, as I often did, to look at the big black-and-white photo that hung opposite the front door. It was a horizontal shot of my mom and the three of us girls, standing on the jetty near my uncle's summer house. Each of us was all in white: Kirsten in white jeans and a plain V-neck T-shirt, my mother wearing a sundress, Whitney in a bathing suit top and drawstring pants, me in a tank top and long skirt. We were all tan, the water spread out wide to the corners of the frame behind us.

It had been taken three years earlier during one of our extended family beach trips; the photographer was a friend of a friend of my father's. At the time it had seemed spontaneous, him casually suggesting we pose, but in fact my dad been planning it for weeks as a gift for my mother for Christmas. I remembered how we'd followed the photographer, a tall, lithe man whose name I forgot, out across the sand to the jetty. Kirsten had stepped up first, then extended her hand to help my mother, while Whitney and I brought up the rear. The rocks were hard to navigate, and I remembered Kirsten guiding my mom along the jagged edges until we got to a flat spot and gathered together.

In the picture, we are all intertwined: Kirsten's fingers are wrapped in my mother's, Whitney has her arm over her shoulder, and I'm in front, curved slightly toward my mom as well, my arm around her waist. My mother is smiling, as is Kirsten, while Whitney is just staring into the camera, her beauty, as usual, breathtaking. Even though I remembered smiling each time the flash popped, my expression in the final product is not one I recognize, my face caught somewhere between Kirsten's broad grin and Whitney's gorgeous hauntedness.

The picture was beautiful, however, the composition perfect. People always commented on it, as it was the first thing you saw when you walked in the door. In the last few months, though, it had started to look kind of eerie to me. Like I couldn't just see the fine white-on-black contrast, or the way our features repeated themselves, in different measure but always similar, across our faces. Instead, when I studied it, I saw other things. Like how Whitney and Kirsten stood so close to each other, no space between them. The way my own face looked different, more relaxed. And how small my mother seemed with all of us bent around her, pulling her closer, shielding her with our bodies, as if without us to hold her down, she might just fly away.

I picked up my apple, taking another bite just as my mother's car pulled into the garage. A second later I heard doors shutting and voices as she and Whitney came inside.

"Hello there," my mother said when she saw me, putting down the bag of groceries she was carrying on the counter with a thump. "How was school?"

"Fine," I said, stepping back as Whitney brushed past, not acknowledging me and taking the corner quickly, disappearing upstairs. It was Wednesday, which meant she'd just come from her shrink's, which always put her in a mood. I'd thought seeing a therapist was supposed to make you feel better, not worse, but apparently, it was more complicated than that. But then everything was more complicated for Whitney.

"There was a message from Lindy," I told my mom.

"What'd she say?"

"The Mooshka people haven't called yet."

My mom looked disappointed, but only for a moment. "Oh, well. I'm sure they will." She walked to the sink, turned on the faucet, and lathered up her hands with liquid soap, looking out the window at the pool. In the afternoon light she looked kind of tired—Wednesdays took a toll on her, too.

"And Kirsten called. She left a long message," I said.

She smiled. "You don't say."

"The upshot," I said, "is she likes her classes."

"Well, that's nice to hear," she said, drying her hands on a dishtowel. She folded it, putting it back by the sink, then came to sit down beside me. "So. Tell me something that happened to *you* today. Something good."

Good. I thought for a second about what was going on with

Sophie, my daily observations of Owen Armstrong, the fact that Clarke still hated me. None of these things fell under this heading, or anywhere near it. As the seconds ticked by, I could feel myself starting to panic, desperate for something to offer up to her to make up for the Mooshka people, for Whitney's mood, for everything. She was still waiting.

"There's this guy in my gym class," I said finally. "He's kind of cute, and he talked to me today."

"Really," she said, smiling. Score. "What's his name?"

"Peter Matchinsky," I told her. "He's a senior."

This was not a lie. Peter Matchinsky *was* in my gym class and he was kind of cute and a senior. And he had talked to me that day, although it was only to ask me what Coach Erlenbach had just said about our upcoming swim test. Normally, I didn't stretch the truth to my mom, but in the last few months I'd learned to forgive myself these little trespasses, because they made her happy. Unlike the real truth, which would be the last thing she wanted to hear.

"A cute senior," she said, sitting back in her chair. "Well. Tell me more."

And I would. Even though there wasn't much else. If I had to, I'd pad the edges of the story, filling it in, trying to make it substantial enough to nourish this need, her hunger for my life, at least, to somehow be normal. The worst part was that I had things I wanted to tell my mother, too many to count, but none of them would go down so easy. She'd been through too much, between my sisters—I could not add to the weight. So instead, I did my best to balance it out, bit by bit, word by word, story by story, even if none of them were true.

• • •

Most mornings before school, it was just me and my mom at breakfast, my dad only joining us if he got a late start to the office. Whitney never got out of bed before eleven if she could help it. So when I came down a couple of weeks later to find her showered, dressed, and sitting at the table with my car keys in front of her, I had a feeling something was up. I was right.

"Your sister's going to drive you to school today," my mother said. "Then she's going to take your car and do a little shopping, see a movie, and pick you up this afternoon. Okay?"

I looked at Whitney, who was watching me, her mouth a thin line. "Sure," I said.

My mother smiled, then looked from my sister to me, then back to my sister again. "Great," she said. "Everything works out."

She did her best to sound casual as she said this, but it was clear from her tone she was anything but. Since Whitney had come home from the hospital, my mother preferred to keep her both busy and within sight, which was why my sister was always dragged on errands and to my mother's appointments. Whitney was constantly arguing for more freedom, but my mom worried that given it, she'd binge or purge, or exercise, or do something else forbidden. Clearly, something had shifted, although what it was or why, I had no idea.

When we walked out to the car, I automatically headed for the driver's side, then stopped when I saw Whitney doing the same thing. For a second, we both just stood there. Then she said, "I'll drive."

"Okay," I told her. "That's fine."

The ride was awkward. I didn't realize until we were on the road how long it had actually been since I'd been alone with Whitney. I had no idea what to say to her. I could ask about shopping, but it might bring up body-image issues, so I tried to think of other topics. Seeing a movie? Traffic? I had no idea. So I just sat there, silent.

Whitney wasn't talking, either. I could tell it had been a while since she'd driven. She was being very cautious, pausing a beat longer at stop signs than necessary, letting people in front of us. At a red light, I looked across to see two business-men in an SUV staring at her. They were both in suits—one in his twenties, one my father's age—and instantly I felt defen-sive, protective of her, even though I knew she would have hated this if she knew it. Then, though, I realized they weren't looking at her because she was skinny, but because she was so striking. I'd forgotten that once, my sister had been the most beautiful girl I'd ever seen. The world, or at least some of it, still seemed to feel the same way.

We were about a mile from school when I finally decided to try and say something. "So," I said, "are you excited about today?"

She glanced at me, then looked back at the road. "Excited," she repeated. "Why would I be excited?"

"I don't know," I said as we turned into the school entrance. "Maybe because, you know, you have a whole day to yourself."

For a second, she didn't answer, focusing instead on pulling over to the curb. "It's a day," she said finally. "I used to have a whole life."

I wasn't sure what to say to that. "Okay, well, see you later!" seemed glib, if not totally inappropriate. So instead I just pushed open the door and reached into the back for my bag.

"I'll see you at three thirty," she said.

"Right," I said.

She put on her blinker, looking over her shoulder. I shut the door, and she eased into traffic and drove away.

I pretty much forgot about Whitney for the rest of the day, as I had a literature test that afternoon that I was totally nervous about. For good reason, as it turned out. Even though I had studied most of the night before *and* gone to the review session Mrs. Gingher offered at lunch, there had still been some questions that completely stumped me. There was nothing I could do but just sit there, staring at them and feeling like a total moron, until she announced time and I had to turn it in.

As I headed down the steps to the main building entrance to meet Whitney, I dug out my notes and started to go through them, trying to figure out what I'd missed. There was a big crowd making its way across the turnaround, and I was so engrossed that I didn't even see the parked red Jeep until I was walking right in front of it.

One minute I was scanning the notes I'd taken on Southern literature, trying to find a quote that had completely escaped me; the next, I was glancing up at Will Cash. This time, he'd seen me first. He was staring right at me.

I looked away, fast, quickening my pace as I walked in front of his bumper. I was almost to the curb when he called out to me. "Annabel," he said.

I knew I should just ignore him. But even as I thought this, my head was already turning, as if by instinct. He was sitting there, wearing a plaid shirt, unshaven, a pair of sunglasses perched on his forehead, as if they might slip down at any moment.

"Hey," he said. I was close enough to the car now to feel the A/C just barely wafting out the open window.

"Hi." Just one word, but it came out twisted, mangling itself as it squeezed up my throat.

He didn't seem to notice any of my nervousness as he slid an elbow out the window, then glanced over at the courtyard beyond me. "Haven't seen you around at the parties lately," he said. "You still hanging out?"

A breeze blew across me then, catching the edge of my notes, making them flutter, the sound like little wings. I tightened my fingers on the paper. "No," I managed. "Not really."

I felt a chill go up my neck, and I wondered if I was going to faint. I couldn't look at him, so I kept my eyes down, but in my side vision, I could see his hand, resting on the open window, and I found myself staring at it, the long tapered fingers drumming idly on the Jeep's door.

Shhh, Annabel. It's just me.

"Well," he said, "see you around, I guess."

I nodded, and then, finally, I was turning back around and walking away. I took in a breath, trying to remind myself that I was surrounded by people, safe here. But then I felt it, the ultimate proof otherwise: my stomach gurgling, rising up, the one response I could never control. *Oh my God*, I thought, quickly stuffing my papers into the top of my bag. I pulled it over my shoulder, not taking the time to zip it, then started walking toward the nearest building, praying that I could hold it together until I was to the bathroom. Or at least out of sight. But I didn't get that far.

"What was *that*?"

It was Sophie. She was right behind me. I stopped walking, but the bile kept rising. After so many times of her just saying one word, to hear these three was overwhelming. And then she was speaking again.

"What the hell do you think you're doing, Annabel?" she said.

Two younger girls scurried past me, their eyes wide. I tightened my hand around the strap of my bag, swallowing again.

"Didn't you get enough that night? You need more or something?"

Somehow, I started to move forward again. *Don't get sick, don't look back, don't do anything*, I kept telling myself, but my throat felt raw, my head light.

"Don't you ignore me," Sophie was saying now. "Turn around, bitch!"

All I wanted—all I'd ever wanted—was just to get away. To be somewhere small where I could crowd in and feel safe, all four walls pressed around me, no one staring or pointing or yelling. But here I was in the wide open, in full view. I might have just given in, letting her do whatever she wanted, like I had for weeks now, but then something happened. She reached out and grabbed my shoulder.

And something snapped in me. Snapped hard, like a bone, or a branch, a clean break. Before I even knew what I was doing, I'd whirled around and was facing her, reaching up with hands that I wasn't even sure were mine to push her away, my palms hitting her chest, hard, and knocking her backwards, stumbling. It was primal and immediate and surprised both of us, but most of all, me.

She lost her footing, her eyes wide, but then caught herself quickly and started toward me again. She had on a black skirt and a bright yellow tank top, her arms tan and wiry beneath it, her hair spilling loose over her shoulders. "Oh my God," she said, her voice low, and I somehow moved backwards, my feet thick underneath me. "You better—"

The crowd around us was closing in now, bodies jostling. Above the movement, I could hear the whirring of the security guard approaching on his golf cart. "Break it up," he called out. "Move on to the parking lot or bus area."

Sophie stepped closer to me. "You're a whore," she said, her voice low, and I heard a hiss from somewhere, that low *oooooh*, followed by the guard's voice, second warning.

"Stay away from my boyfriend," she said, her voice low. "Do you hear me?"

I just stood there. I could still feel the pressure of her chest against my hands, how it felt to push her, something solid giving way. "Sophie . . ." I said.

She shook her head, then stepped forward, brushing past me. Her shoulder hit mine, hard, and I stumbled, bumping someone behind me before righting myself. Everyone was staring, a blur of faces fluctuating, shifting, as she moved through them, and then their eyes all turned to me.

I pushed through the bodies beside me, one hand over my mouth. I could hear people talking, laughing, as the crowd gave way, bit by bit, and I finally reached the outer edge. The main building was right in front of me, a row of tall bushes in front of it that led around its back side. I ran toward them, their prickly leaves scraping my hands as I pushed through. I didn't make it far, and could only hope I was out of sight as I bent over, one hand clutching my stomach, and got sick in the grass, coughing and spitting, the sound rough in my ears.

When I was finished, my skin felt clammy, and there were tears in my eyes. It was horrible and embarrassing, and one of those moments when you just want more than anything to be alone. Especially when you suddenly realize you're not.

I didn't hear the footsteps. Or see the shadow. Instead, from where I was crouched on the ground, the green of the grass filling my vision, the first thing I made out were hands, a flat silver ring on the middle finger of each. One was clutching my notes. The other was reaching out for me.

Chapter
FIVE

Owen Armstrong looked like a giant, his hand enormous as it stretched toward me. Somehow I found myself extending my own back to him, and then he was folding his fingers over mine, pulling me to my feet. I stood steady for about a second before my head went light and woozy and I stumbled.

"Whoa," he said, reaching out to steady me. "Hold on. You better sit down."

He eased me back two steps, and I felt the building behind me, the bricks cool against my back. I slid down the wall slowly, until I was on the grass. From this new vantage point, he seemed even bigger.

Suddenly, he dropped his bag off his shoulder. It hit the ground with a clank, and then he was crouching down beside it, reaching in and digging around. I heard objects bumping against each other as they were moved and redistributed, and it occurred to me that maybe I should be concerned about this. Finally, his hand stopped digging, and he sat back, slightly. I braced myself as he worked his hand out of the bag, bit by bit, and came up with . . . a pack of Kleenex. A small one, bent and wrinkled, and he pressed them against his chest—which was enormous, oh my God—smoothing them out, before pulling one free and handing it to me. I took it the same way I'd taken his hand—in disbelief, and very carefully.

"You can have the whole pack," he said. "If you want."

"That's okay." My voice sounded hoarse. "One is fine." I pressed it to my mouth, taking a breath through it. He put the pack by my foot anyway. "Thank you," I said.

"No problem."

He sat down on the grass beside his bag. Because I'd gone to that review session at lunch, I hadn't seen him all day, but he looked pretty much the same as always: jeans, T-shirt fraying at the hem, thick-soled black wingtips, earphones. Up close—or closer—I could also see he had a few freckles, and that his eyes were green, not brown. I could hear voices rising up from the courtyard; they sounded like they were floating over our heads.

"So, um," he said, "are you okay?"

I nodded, the response instant. "Yeah," I said. "I just felt sick all of a sudden, I don't know . . ."

"I saw what happened," he said.

"Oh," I said. I felt my face flush. So much for trying to save face. "Yeah. That was . . . pretty bad."

He shrugged. "Could have been worse."

"You think?"

"Sure." His voice was not rumbly like I would have guessed, but instead low and even. Almost soft. "You could have punched her."

I nodded. "Yeah," I said. "I guess you're right."

"It's good you didn't, though. Wouldn't have been worth it."

"No?" I said, even though, truthfully, I hadn't even considered this.

"No. Not even if it felt good at the time," he said. "Trust me."

The weirdest thing of all was that I did. Trust him, that is. I looked down at the pack of tissues he'd given me, picking them up and taking out another one. Just as I did, I heard a buzzing from my bag. My phone.

I pulled it out, glancing at the caller ID. It was my mother, and I debated for a second whether I should pick up. I mean, it was weird enough to be sitting there with Owen without getting my mom involved. Then again, it wasn't like I had that much to lose at this point, considering he'd already seen me vomit—twice, actually—and freak out in front of half the student body. We were kind of past formalities. So I answered.

"Hello?"

"Hi, honey!" Her voice was loud, so much so that I wondered if Owen could hear it. I pressed the phone closer to my ear. "How was your day?"

By now, I'd detected the nervous shrillness that crept into her cadence when she was worried but pretending not to be. "It was fine," I said. "I'm fine. What's up?"

"Well," she said, "Whitney's still at the mall. She found some great sales, but then she missed the early movie. And she *really* wanted to see it, so she called to say she was staying later."

I switched the phone to my other ear as there was a burst of voices around the side of the building. Owen glanced over at them, but a second later they moved on. "So she's not coming to pick me up?"

"Well, no, as it turns out," she replied. Of course Whitney would push the limits the very first day she got her freedom. And of course my mother would say oh, yes, stay later, that's fine, but then completely freak out. "But I can come get you," she said now, "or maybe you could get a ride with one of your friends?"

One of my friends. Yeah, right. I shook my head, then ran a hand through my hair. "Mom," I said, trying to keep my voice even, "it's just that it's kind of late, and—"

"Oh, it's fine! I'll come get you right now!" she said. "I'll be there in fifteen minutes."

She didn't want to come, and we both knew it. Whitney might call, or show up. Or, even worse, not show up. Not for the first time, I wished both of us could just say what we meant. But that, like so much else, was impossible.

"It's fine," I told her. "I'll get a ride."

"Are you sure?" she asked, but already, I could hear her relaxing, thinking that this problem, at least, was resolved.

"Yes. I'll call if I can't."

"Do that," she said. And then, just as I might have been getting angry, "Thank you, Annabel."

When I hung up, I just sat there, holding my phone in my hand. Once again, everything was revolving around Whitney. It might have been just a day to her, but this one had really sucked for me. And now, I was walking home.

I glanced back up at Owen. In the time I'd been contemplating this newest problem, he'd pulled out his iPod and was messing with it. "So you need a ride," he said, not looking at me.

"Oh, no," I said quickly, shaking my head. "It's just my sister . . . she's being a pain."

"Story of my life," he said. He hit one last button, then slid it back in his pocket and stood up, brushing off his jeans. Then he reached down, grabbing his bag, and hoisted it over his shoulder. "Come on."

I'd endured a lot of scrutiny since the beginning of the school year. It was *nothing*, however, compared to the looks Owen and I got as we walked up to the parking lot. Every person we passed stared, most of them openly, with a few bursting into whispers—"Oh my God, did you see that?"—before we were even out of earshot. Owen, however, didn't seem to notice as he led me to an old-style blue Land Cruiser with about twenty CDs in the passenger seat. He got behind the wheel, then cleared them out and reached across to open the door for me.

I got in, then reached down for the seat belt. I was just about to pull it across me when he said, "Hold on. That's sort of busted," and gestured for me to hand it to him. When I did, he pulled it over me—his hand at what struck me as a very formal and polite distance from my stomach—then yanked up the buckle from the seat, holding it at an angle and sliding the belt in. Then, from the pocket on his own door, he pulled out a small hammer.

I must have looked alarmed—GIRL 17, FOUND DEAD IN SCHOOL PARKING LOT—because he glanced at me and said, "It's the only way it works." He tapped the buckle with the hammer three times in the center, before pulling at the belt to make sure it was locked in. When it was, he stuck the hammer back in the pocket and cranked the engine.

"Wow," I said, reaching down and giving it a little tug. It didn't budge. "How do you get it off?"

"Just push the button," he said. "That part's easy."

As we started through the parking lot, Owen rolled down his window, resting his arm there, and I took a look around the interior of the car. The dashboard was battered, the leather of the seats cracked in places. Plus, it smelled like smoke, faintly, although I could see the ashtray, which was partly open, was clean and filled with coins, not butts. There were some headphones on the backseat, along with a pair of Doc Martens oxblood boots and several magazines.

Most of all, though, I saw CDs. *Tons* of CDs. Not just the ones he'd cleared out for me and dumped on the backseat floor, but stacks and stacks of others, some store-bought, many more clearly home-burned, piled haphazardly on the seats and the floor. I glanced back at the dashboard in front of me. While the car was dated, the stereo looked practically new, not to mention advanced, rows of lights blinking.

Just as I thought this, we reached the stop sign at the top of the parking lot and Owen put on his blinker, looking both ways. Then he reached out for the stereo, nudging up the volume button with the side of his thumb before taking a right.

Even with all the lunches during which I'd studied him, and all the details I'd thereby managed to ascertain, there was still one unknown, and this was it: Owen's music. I had my hunches, though, so I braced myself for punk rock, thrash metal, something fast and loud.

Instead, after a bit of staticky silence, I heard . . . chirping. Lots of chirping, like a chorus of crickets. This was followed, a moment later, by a voice chanting in a language I didn't understand. The chirping grew louder, then louder, and the voice did as well, so it was like they were calling to each other, back and forth. Beside me, Owen was just driving, nodding his head slightly.

After about a minute and a half, my curiosity got the better of me. "So," I said, "what is this?"

He glanced over at me. "Mayan spiritual chants," he said.

"What?" I said, speaking loudly to be heard over the chirping, which was really going now.

"Mayan spiritual chants," he repeated. "They're passed down, like oral traditions."

"Oh," I said. The chanting was so loud now it was verging on shrieking. "Where did you get this?"

He reached forward, turning the volume down a little bit. "The library at the university," he said. "I checked it out of their sound-and-culture collection."

"Ah," I said. So Owen Armstrong was spiritual. Who knew? Then again, who would have thought I would be sitting in his car, listening to chants with him? Not me. Not anybody. And yet, here we were.

"So you must *really* like music," I said, looking back at the stacks of CDs.

"Don't you?" he replied, switching lanes.

"Sure," I said. "I mean, everybody does, right?"

"No," he said flatly.

"No?"

He shook his head. "Some people *think* they like music, but they have no idea what it's really all about. They're kidding themselves. Then there are people who feel strongly about music, but just aren't listening to the right stuff. They're misguided. And then there are people like me."

I just sat there for a second, studying him. He still had his elbow out the window and was sitting back in his seat, his head just brushing the ceiling above him. Up close, I was realizing he was still kind of intimidating, but for different reasons. His size, yes, but other things, too—like those dark eyes and wiry forearms, plus his intense gaze, which he now turned on me for a moment before directing his attention back to the road. "People like you," I said. "What kind of people are those?"

He hit his blinker again and began to slow down. Up ahead, I could see my old middle school, a yellow school bus pulling out of the parking lot. "The kind who live for music and are constantly seeking it out, anywhere they can. Who can't imagine a life without it. They're enlightened."

"Ah," I said, like this actually made sense to me.

"I mean, when you really think about it," he continued, "music is the great uniter. An incredible force. Something that people who differ on everything and anything else can have in common."

I nodded, not sure what to say to this.

"Plus there's the fact," he went on, making it clear he didn't need me to reply anyway, "that music is a total constant. That's why we have such a strong visceral connection to it, you know? Because a song can take you back instantly to a moment, or a place, or even a person. No matter what else has changed in you or the world, that one song stays the same, just like that moment. Which is pretty amazing, when you actually think about it."

It *was* pretty amazing. As was this conversation, so wholly unlike anything I could or would have ever imagined. "Yeah," I said slowly. "It is."

We drove on for a second, in silence. Except for the chanting.

"What I mean to say," he said, "is yes. I like music."

"Got it," I said.

"And now," he said as we turned into the school's lot, "I'll apologize in advance."

"Apologize? For what?"

He slowed, finally stopping at the curb. "My sister."

There were several girls standing around the main entrance to Lakeview Middle, and I quickly scanned their faces, trying to guess which one was related to Owen. The girl with the instrument case and the braid, leaning against the building, an open book in her hands? The tall blonde with the big Nike duffel bag and the field-hockey stick, drinking a Diet Coke? Or the easiest bet, the dark-haired girl with the pixie cut, wearing all black, who was lying on a nearby bench, her arms crossed tightly over her chest, staring up at the sky with a pained expression?

Just then, though, I heard a clank right outside my window. When I turned my head, I saw a small, thin, dark-haired girl dressed head to toe in pink: ponytail tied with a pink ribbon, shiny pink lip gloss, hot-pink T-shirt, jeans, and pink platform flip-flops. When she saw me, she shrieked.

"Oh my God!" she gasped, her voice muffled by the window between us. "It's *you!*"

I opened my mouth to say something, but before I could, she disappeared from the window, a pink blur. A second later, the back door creaked open, and she scrambled inside. "Owen, oh my God!" she said, still at full, excitable volume. "You didn't tell me you were friends with Annabel Greene!"

Owen glanced at her through the rearview. "Mallory," he said, "take it down a notch."

I started to turn around to say hello, but she was already leaning forward, poking her head between my seat and Owen's, so close to me I could smell bubblegum breath. "This is unbelievable," she said. "I mean, it's you!"

"Hi," I said.

"Hi!" she shrieked, then jumped up and down a little bit in the seat. "Oh my God, I love your work. I really do."

"Work?" Owen said.

"Owen, come on." Mallory sighed. "She's a Lakeview Model, hello? And she's done tons of local ads. And that commercial, you know the one I love, with the girl in the cheerleading uniform?"

"No," Owen said.

"That's her! I can't believe this. I can't wait to tell Shelley and Courtney, oh my God!" Mallory grabbed her bag and unzipped it, pulling out a cell phone. "Oh! Maybe you can say hello to them, that would be so cool, and—"

Owen turned around in his seat. "Mallory."

"Just a sec," she said, pushing buttons. "I just want to—"

"Mallory." His voice was lower now, more stern.

"Hold on, Owen, okay?"

Owen reached out, taking the phone from her. She watched it leave her hands, eyes wide, then looked up at him. "Come on! I just wanted her to say hello to Courtney."

"No," he said, putting the phone on the console between us.

"Owen!"

"Put on your seat belt," Owen told her as he pulled away from the curb. "And take a breath."

After a short pause, Mallory proceeded to do both of these things, audibly. When I glanced back again, she was sitting there, in full pout mode, her arms crossed over her chest. When I looked at her, she brightened up immediately. "Is that a Lanoler sweater?"

"A what?"

She leaned forward, smoothing her fingers over the yellow cardigan I'd thrown on that morning. "This. It's gorgeous. Is it a Lanoler?"

"You know," I said, "I'm not—"

Her hand moved to my collar, pulling it down to check the tag. "It is! I knew it. Oh my God, I want a Lanoler sweater so *bad*, I have forever—"

"Mallory," Owen said, "don't be a label whore."

Mallory dropped her hand. "Owen!" she said. "R and R."

Owen gave her a look in the rearview. Then he sighed, loudly. "What I meant to say, Mallory," he said, sounding pained, "is that your focus on labels and material goods troubles me."

"Thank you," she replied. "And I understand and appreciate your concern. But, as you know, fashion is my life."

I looked at Owen. "R and R?"

"Rephrase and Redirect," Mallory told me. "It's part of his Anger Management. If he says something inflammatory, you can tell him it hurts your feelings, and he has to say it another way."

Owen was looking at her through the rearview, a flat expression on his face. "Thank you, Mallory," he said.

"You're welcome," she replied. Then she smiled at me, big, and bounced in the seat again.

For a second, we drove in silence, which gave me a moment to catch up, or try to, with all this newfound knowledge about Owen Armstrong's personal life. So far, only the fact that he'd been in Anger Management wasn't a surprise. Mallory, the music, and, of course, the fact that I was privy to either of these things were shockers in the biggest sense of the word. On the other hand, I wasn't sure what I'd been expecting. I mean, he had to have a family and a life. I'd just never really taken the time to picture it. It was like when you're a little kid and you run into your teacher or librarian at the grocery store or Wal-Mart and it's just so startling, because it never occurred to you they existed outside of school.

"So I really appreciate the ride," I said to Owen. "I don't know how I would have gotten home otherwise."

"It's no problem," he said. "I just have to make a couple of—"

This thought was interrupted, however, by the sound of Mallory sucking in a breath. "Oh my God," she said. "I'm going to get to see your *house*?"

"No," Owen said curtly.

"But we're taking her home! I'm here!"

"We're dropping you off first," he told her.

"Why?" she said.

"Because," Owen told her as we moved through an intersection, turning off the main road, "I have to go by the station, so Mom said to bring you by the store."

Mallory sighed, sounding pained. "But Owen—"

"No buts," he said. "It's already decided."

Another thump as Mallory slumped, dramatically and dejectedly, against the seat behind her. "It's so not fair," she said a second later.

"Life isn't fair," Owen told her. "Get used to it."

"R and R!" she said.

"No," Owen said. Then he reached forward, nudging up the volume on the radio, and the chirping started up again.

We drove along with just the Mayan chants for a few minutes, long enough for me to actually start to get used to them. Then, suddenly, I felt breath in my ear. "When you did that commercial," Mallory asked, "did you get to keep the clothes from that?"

"Mallory!" Owen said.

"What?"

"Can you just relax and listen to the music?"

"This isn't music! This is crickets and screaming." To me she said, "Owen is a total music Nazi. He won't let anyone listen to anything other than the weird stuff he plays on his radio show."

"You have a radio show?" I asked Owen.

"It's just a local thing," he told me.

"It's his *life*," Mallory said dramatically. "He spends all week getting ready for it, worrying about it, even though it's on when normal people aren't even up yet."

"I'm not playing music for normal people," Owen said. "I'm playing music for people who are—"

"Enlightened, we know," Mallory said, rolling her eyes. "Me personally? I listen to 104Z. They play all the top-forty stuff, lots of good songs you can dance to. I like Bitsy Bonds. She's my favorite singer. I went to her concert last summer, with all my friends? It was *so* fun. Do you know her song 'Pyramid'?"

"Um," I said. "I don't know."

Mallory sat up straighter, tossing back her hair. "'Stack it up, higher and higher, the sun's above, it's full of fire, kiss me here so I'll know you did, baby I'm falling, pyramid!'"

Owen winced. "Bitsy Bonds isn't a *singer*, Mallory. She's a product. She's fake. She has no soul; she doesn't stand for anything."

"So?"

"So," he said, "she's more famous for her belly button than her music."

"Well," Mallory said, "she does have a *great* belly button."

Owen just shook his head, clearly bothered, as he turned off the main road into a small parking lot. There was a row of stores to the left, and he turned into a space in front of one that had a mannequin in the front window wearing a poncho and some flowing earth-toned pants. The sign on the door said DREAMWEAVERS. "Okay," he said. "We're here."

Mallory made a face. "Great," she said sarcastically. "Another afternoon at the store."

"Your parents own this place?" I asked.

"Yes," Mallory grumbled as Owen picked up her phone from the center console, giving it back to her. "It's *so* unfair. Here I am, obsessed with clothes, and my mom has a clothing store. But it's all stuff I wouldn't ever wear in a million years. Not even if I was *dead*."

"If you were dead," Owen told her, "you'd have bigger problems than what you were wearing."

Mallory looked at me then, her expression grave. "Annabel, seriously. It's all, you know, natural fabrics and fibers, Tibetan batiks, vegan shoes."

"Vegan shoes?" I said.

"They're awful," she whispered. "Awful. They're not even *pointy*."

"Mallory," Owen said. "Please get out of the car."

"I'm going, I'm going." Still, she took her time gathering up her bag, undoing her seat belt, and unlocking the door. "It was really nice to meet you," she said to me.

"You, too," I said.

She slid out, shutting the door behind her, and started into the store. As she pushed the door open, she looked back, then waved at me excitedly, her hand blurring. I waved back, and then Owen was pulling away, back to the main road. Without Mallory, the car seemed smaller, not to mention quieter.

"Again," he said, as we slowed for a red light, "I'm sorry."

"Don't be," I told him. "She's cute."

"You don't live with her. Or have to listen to her music."

"104Z," I said. "All the hits, with less of the lip."

"You listen to that station?"

"I have before," I said. "Especially when I was in middle school."

He shook his head. "It would be different if she had no access to good music. If she was deprived of culture. But I've made her tons of CDs. She just won't listen to them. Instead, she chooses to fill her head with that pop crap, listening to a station where they pretty much just play the occasional songs between commercials."

"So on your show," I said, "it's different."

"Well, yeah." He glanced over at me, shifting gears as we headed back onto the main road. "I mean, it's community radio, so there aren't commercials. But I think you should be responsible about what you're putting out there for people to hear. If it can be pollution or art, why wouldn't you choose art?"

I just looked at him. Clearly, I had really misjudged Owen Armstrong. I wasn't sure who I'd thought he was, but it wasn't this person sitting beside me.

"So where do you live?" he asked me, switching lanes as we approached a stoplight.

"The Arbors," I said. "It's a few miles past the mall; you can just—"

"I know it," he said. "The station is just a couple of blocks from there. I have to stop in there for a second, if that's okay."

"Sure," I said. "That's fine."

The community radio station was in a squat, square building that had once been a bank. There was a metal tower beside it, as well as a somewhat droopy banner hanging across the front entrance. WRUS it said in big black letters. COMMUNITY RADIO: RADIO FOR US. There was a big window in front, on the other side of which I could see a man sitting in a broadcast booth wearing headphones and speaking into a microphone. There was a lit-up sign in the corner of the window that said O AIR: apparently, the N was burned out.

Owen pulled into a space right up front, then cut the engine before turning around in his seat to pick through some CDs on the floor. After gathering up a few, he pushed open the door. "Back in a sec," he said.

I nodded. "Okay."

Once he disappeared inside, I started checking out some of the handwritten names on the CD cases, none of which I recognized: THE HANDYWACKS (ASSORTED), JEREMIAH REEVES (EARLY STUFF), TRUTH SQUAD (OPUS). Suddenly, I heard a beep, then turned my head to see a Honda Civic pulling into the spot next to me. Which wouldn't have been noteworthy, really, except the driver had on a bright red helmet.

It wasn't the kind football players wear, exactly, but something a little bigger, with more padding. The guy wearing it looked to be about my age and was dressed in a black sweatshirt and jeans. He waved at me, and I waved back, tentatively, and then he was rolling down his window.

"Hi," he said. "Is Owen inside?"

"Yeah," I said slowly. His eyes were big, blue, and long-lashed in the small cutout of the faceplate, and his hair was past his shoulders, pulled back in a ponytail that was poking out from under the helmet. "He said he'd be back in a second."

He nodded. "Cool," he said, sitting back in his seat. I was trying not to stare at him, even though it was kind of hard. "I'm Rolly, by the way," he said.

"Oh. Hi. I'm Annabel."

"Nice to meet you." He reached down to his cup holder, picking up a paper cup with a straw poking out of it and taking a sip. He was just putting it back when Owen came out of the building.

"Hey," Rolly called out to him. "I was just driving by and saw your car. I thought you had to work today."

"At six," Owen told him.

"Oh. Well, that's cool," Rolly said, sitting back in his seat with a shrug. "Maybe I'll come by or something."

"Do that," Owen said. "And Rolly?"

"Yeah?"

"You know you still have your helmet on, right?"

Rolly's eyes widened, and he lifted up his hands to his head, carefully. Then his face flushed, almost as red as the helmet. "Oh," he said, pushing it off. Underneath, his hair was matted down, and there were creases across his forehead. "Yeah. Thanks."

"No problem. I'll see you in a bit."

"Okay." Rolly put the helmet on the seat beside him, smoothing a hand over his head as Owen climbed back behind the wheel. As we backed away, I waved at him again, and he nodded, smiling, his face still slightly pink.

Once back on the main road, we drove for a moment before Owen said, "It's for his job. Just so you know."

"The helmet," I said, clarifying.

"Yeah. He works at this self-defense place. He's an attacker."

"An attacker?"

"The one people practice on," he told me. "You know, once they learn the techniques. That's why he has to wear padding."

"Oh," I said. "So . . . you guys work together?"

"No. I deliver pizzas. This is it, right?" he asked as we came up on the entrance to my neighborhood. I nodded and he put his blinker on, then turned in. "He does the radio show with me."

"Does he go to Jackson?"

"Nope. The Fountain School."

The Fountain School was an "alternative learning space," also known as the Hippie School. It had a very small student body and an emphasis on personal expression, and offered electives like batik and Ultimate Frisbee. Kirsten had dated several somewhat crunchy guys from there, back in the day.

"Left or right?" Owen asked as we came up to a stop sign.

"Straight. For a while," I told him.

As we headed farther into my neighborhood, not talking, I got the same feeling I'd had that morning with Whitney, like I should at least attempt to make conversation. "So," I said finally, "how'd you end up with a radio show?"

"It's something I've always been sort of interested in," Owen said. "And right after I moved here, I heard about this course they have at the station where they teach the basics. After you take it, you can write up a show proposal. If they approve it, they give you an audition and, if they like what you do, a time slot. Me and Rolly got ours last winter. But then I got arrested. So that put us back a bit."

He said this so nonchalantly, as if he was talking about a vacation to the Grand Canyon, or attending a wedding. "You got arrested?" I asked.

"Yeah." He slowed for another stop sign. "I got in a fight at a club. With some guy in the parking lot."

"Oh," I said. "Right."

"You heard about it?"

"Maybe something," I said.

"So why'd you ask?"

I felt my face get hot. Ask a bold question, you'd better be prepared to answer one. "I don't know," I said. "Do you believe everything you hear?"

"No," he said. Then he looked at me for a moment, before turning back to the road. "I don't."

Right, I thought. Okay. So I wasn't the only one who had heard some rumors. It was only fair, though. Here I'd had all these assumptions about Owen based on what had been said about him, but it hadn't occurred to me that there were stories about me out there as well. Or at least one.

We drove on in silence through two more stop signs. Then, finally, I took a breath and said, "It's not true, if that's what you were wondering."

He was downshifting, the engine grinding as we slowed to take a corner. "What isn't?" he said.

"What you heard about me."

"I haven't heard anything about you."

"Yeah, right," I said.

"I haven't," Owen said. "I'd tell you if I had."

"Really."

"Yeah," he said. I must have looked doubtful at this, because he added, "I don't lie."

"You don't lie," I repeated.

"That's what I said."

"Ever."

"Nope."

Sure you don't, I thought. "Well," I said. "That's a good policy. If you can stick to it."

"I don't have a choice," he replied. "Holding stuff in doesn't really work for me. Learned that the hard way."

I had a flash of Ronnie Waterman going down in the parking lot, his head bouncing off the gravel. "So you're always honest," I said.

"Aren't you?"

"No," I told him. This came so easily, so quickly, it should have surprised me. But for some reason, it didn't. "I'm not."

"Well," he said as we approached another stop sign, "that's good to know, I guess."

"I'm not saying I'm a liar," I told him. He raised his eyebrows. "That's not how I *meant* it, anyway."

"How'd you mean it, then?"

I was digging myself a hole here, and I knew it. But still, I tried to explain myself. "It's just . . . I don't always say what I feel."

"Why not?"

"Because the truth sometimes hurts," I said.

"Yeah," he said. "So do lies, though."

"I don't . . ." I said, then trailed off, not sure exactly how to put this. "I just don't like to hurt people. Or upset them. So sometimes, you know, I won't say exactly what I think, to spare them that." The ironic thing was that saying this out loud was actually the most honest I'd been in ages. If not ever.

"But that's still a lie," he said. "Even if you mean well."

"You know," I replied, "I find it really hard to believe you're always honest."

"Believe it. It's true."

I turned to face him. "So if I were to ask you if I looked fat in this outfit," I said, "and you thought I did, you'd say so."

"Yes," he said.

"You would not."

"I would. I might not say it that way, exactly, but if I thought you didn't look good—"

"No way," I said flatly.

"—and you'd *asked*," he continued, "I'd tell you. I wouldn't just offer it up, though. I'm not a hateful person. But if you asked for my opinion, I'd give it."

I shook my head, still not believing him.

"Look," he said, "like I said, for me, not saying how I feel when I feel it is a bad move. So I don't do it. Look at it this way: I might be saying you're fat, but at least I'm not punching you in the face."

"Are those are the only options?" I asked.

"Not always," he replied. "Just sometimes. And it's good to know your options, right?"

I could feel myself about to smile, which was just so strange that I turned my head as we came up to another stop sign. There was a car parked on the street ahead, halfway down, facing us. A second later, I realized it was mine.

"Still straight?" Owen asked.

"Um, no," I told him, leaning closer to the glass. Sure enough, it was Whitney behind the wheel. She had a hand to her face, her fingers spread to cover her eyes.

"Then . . . what? Right? Left?" Owen asked. He dropped his hand from the wheel. "What's wrong?"

I looked at Whitney again, wondering what she was doing so close to home, parked. "That's my sister," I said, nodding at the car.

Owen leaned forward, looking at her. "Is . . . is she okay?"

"No," I said. Maybe not lying was contagious; this reply came out automatically, before I could pick other words to explain. "She's not."

"Oh," he said. He was quiet for a second. "Well, do you want to—"

I shook my head. "No," I told him. "Take a right."

He did, and I slid down slightly in my seat. As we passed Whitney, it was clear she was crying, her thin shoulders shaking, her hand still pressed to her face. I felt something catch in my own throat and then we were moving on, leaving her behind.

I could feel Owen watching me as we reached the next

stop sign. "She's sick," I said. "She has been for a while now."

"I'm sorry," he said.

This was what you were supposed to say. What anyone would say. The weird thing was, after everything he'd just told me, I knew Owen meant it. Honest, indeed.

"Which is yours?" he asked me now, as we turned onto my street.

"The glass one," I told him.

"The glass—" he began, but then stopped, as it came into view. "Oh. Right."

It was the time of day when the sun hit the glass just so, the golf course reflected almost perfectly in the second story. Downstairs, I could see my mother standing at the kitchen counter. She'd started walking to the door when we pulled up, then stopped when she realized it was just me and not Whitney. I thought about my sister, sitting two streets over, and my mom, worrying here at home, and felt that familiar pull in my stomach, a mix of sadness and obligation.

"Man," Owen said, looking up at it. "That's really something."

"People in glass houses," I said. I looked back in at my mother, who was still at the counter, watching us. I wondered if she was curious about Owen or too distracted to even notice I was in a car she didn't recognize, much less with a boy. Maybe she thought it was Peter Matchinsky, that nice senior from my gym class.

"Well," I said, reaching down for my bag. "Thanks for the ride. For everything."

"No problem," he said.

I heard a car coming up behind us, and a second later, Whitney was pulling into the driveway. It wasn't until she parked and got out that she looked up and saw me and Owen. I lifted my hand, waving at her, but she ignored me.

I knew already what would happen when I went inside. Whitney would be stomping around, ignoring my mother's cheerful, leading questions. Eventually she'd get fed up and go upstairs, slamming her door, and then my mom would be upset, but pretend not to be. Even so, I'd worry over her until my dad got home, at which time we'd all sit down for dinner and pretend everything was fine.

Thinking this, I looked back at Owen. "So when is it?" I asked. "Your radio show."

"Sundays," he replied. "At seven."

"I'll listen," I told him.

"In the morning," he added.

"Seven in the *morning*?" I asked. "Really?"

"Yeah," he replied, picking at the steering wheel. "It's not the ideal time slot, but you take what you can get. Insomniacs are listening, at least."

"*Enlightened* insomniacs," I said.

He looked at me for a second, as if I'd somehow surprised him, saying this. "Yeah," he said, and smiled. "Exactly."

Imagine that, I thought. *Owen Armstrong smiling*. In a bizarre day, this was the most surprising thing yet. "Well," I said, "I guess I should go."

"Okay. I'll see you around."

I nodded, then reached down, undoing the seat belt. Sure enough, one click and I was free. Harder to get in than out, like so little else.

As I shut the door behind me, Owen put the car into gear, beeping the horn once as he drove off. Sure enough, as I turned to look up at my house, Whitney was climbing the stairs, taking the steps two at a time. My mother was still at the kitchen island, staring out the back window.

I don't lie, Owen had said, with the same flat certainty someone else might tell you they didn't eat meat or know how to drive. I wasn't sure I could even fathom it, but I still envied Owen his easy bluntness, the ability to open himself out into the world instead of folding deeper within. Especially now, as I headed inside, where my mother was waiting for me.

Chapter
SIX

"Okay, girls, quiet down. Attention here, please! We're getting ready to start, so listen for your name. . . ."

I'd been doing Lakeview Models since I was fifteen. Every summer, tryouts were held to pick sixteen girls for mall promotions like posing with cub scouts at a Pinewood Derby event or handing out balloons at the Harvest Festival Petting Zoo. The models also appeared in print ads, did fashion shows, and were part of the annual Lakeview Mall calendar, which was distributed along with the new phone book every year. That was what we were shooting today. We were supposed to have been done the day before, but the photographer was slow, so we'd all been called back now, on a Sunday afternoon, to finish.

I yawned, then sat back against the potted plant behind me, taking a look around the room. The newer girls were all together in a corner, talking too loudly, while a couple of people I knew from previous years were gossiping about some party. The only two seniors sat apart from everyone else, one with her head back, eyes closed, the other flipping through an SAT prep book. Finally, across the room from me, also sitting alone, was Emily Shuster.

I'd met Emily at the last calendar shoot. She was a year younger than me and had just moved to town. She didn't know anyone, and while everyone was waiting around, she'd come and sat down next to me. We started talking, and just like that, we were friends.

Emily was, in a word, sweet. She had short red hair and a heart-shaped face, and when I'd invited her out with me and Sophie that night after the shoot, she'd been thrilled. When I pulled up to her house, she was already outside waiting, her cheeks pink from the cool air, as if she'd been there awhile.

Sophie was less enthusiastic. Plainly put, she had issues when it came to other girls, especially pretty ones, even though she herself was gorgeous. Whenever I had Lakeview Model stuff, or landed a big job, she always got a little moody. There was stuff about her that bothered me, too. Like how she sometimes snapped at me and acted like I was stupid, and often wasn't nice to other people unless she had a reason to be—and sometimes, not even then. The truth was, my friendship with Sophie was complicated, and at times I wondered why she was my best friend, when more often than not I was either tiptoeing around her or having to ignore one barbed comment or another. But then I'd remember how much things had changed for me since we'd started hanging out—from that night with Chris Pennington on, so much had happened that I never would have experienced otherwise. And really, when you came down to it, I didn't have anyone else. Sophie made sure of that, too.

The night I met Emily, we were going to a party at the A-

Frame, a house just outside of town that was rented by a few guys who'd gone to Perkins Day, the local private school, a couple of years earlier. They had a band called Day After, and after graduation they'd stuck around, playing club dates and trying to get a record deal. In the meantime, they had parties almost every weekend that attracted a mix of high-school students and various locals.

From the moment the three of us walked into the party that night, I could feel people looking at Emily. She *was* a beautiful girl, but being with us—especially Sophie, who was well known not only at our school but at Perkins Day, as well—made her suddenly that much more noteworthy. We weren't even halfway to the keg when Greg Nichols, an obnoxious junior, made a beeline for us.

"Hey, guys," he said, "what's up?"

"Go away, Greg," Sophie told him over her shoulder. "We're not interested."

"Speak for yourself," he said, completely undeterred. "Who's your friend?"

Sophie sighed, shaking her head.

I said, "Um, this is Emily."

"Hi," Emily said, flushing.

"Hel-lo," Greg replied. "Let me get you a beer."

"Okay," she said. As he walked off, glancing back at her, she turned to me, her eyes wide. "Oh my God," she said. "He's really cute!"

"No," Sophie told her. "He's not. And he's only talking to you because he's already hit on everyone else here."

Emily's face fell. "Oh," she said.

"Sophie," I said. "Honestly."

"What?" she said as she picked some lint off her sweater, scanning the crowd. "It's true."

It probably was. But that didn't mean she had to *say* it. This was typical Sophie, though. She believed everyone had a place, and it was her job to make sure you knew yours. She'd done it with Clarke. She did it with me. And now, it was Emily's turn. But while I'd just stood by all those years earlier, this time I felt I had to do something, if only because I was the reason Emily was even there in the first place. "Come on," I said to her. "Let's go get a beer. Sophie, you want one?"

"No," she said curtly, and turned away from me.

By the time I got a drink and went to look for her, she'd disappeared. *So she's pissed,* I thought. *That's nothing new, I'll smooth it over in a second.* But then Greg Nichols had reappeared, and I didn't want to leave Emily alone with him. It took us twenty minutes to extricate ourselves, at which point I left Emily with some girls she knew and finally went looking for Sophie. I found her on the back porch, smoking, alone.

"Hi," I said, but she ignored me. I took a sip of my beer, looking out over the swimming pool below the deck. It was empty and covered in leaves, a lawn chair parked at the bottom.

"Where's your friend?" she asked me.

"Sophie," I said. "Come on."

"What? It's just a question."

"She's inside," I said. "And she's your friend, too."

"No," she said, snorting. "She's not."

"Why don't you like her?"

"She's a freshman, Annabel. And she's—" She stopped,

taking another drag of her cigarette. "Look, if you want to hang out with her, go ahead. I don't."

"Why not?"

"I just don't." She turned, looking at me. "What? We don't have to be joined at the hip, you know. You don't have to do everything I do."

"I know that," I said.

"Do you?" She exhaled, a stream of smoke billowing out between us. "Because, really, you've never done *anything* without me. From the day we met, I'm the one who's gotten all the guys, found out about all the parties. Before you met me, you were just sitting around passing tissues to Ca-larke Rebbolds."

I took another sip from my cup. I hated when Sophie was like this—nasty, all sharp edges. I hated it even more when I thought it was my fault, which clearly this was. "Look," I told her, "I just invited Emily along because she doesn't know any-one."

"She knows you," she said. "And now Greg Nichols."

"Funny."

"I'm not being funny," she told me. "I'm just telling it like it is. I don't like her. If you want to hang out with her, go ahead. I'm not interested." Then she dropped her cigarette on the deck, grinding it out with her boot, turned around, and went inside.

I felt uneasy watching her go, nervous. Like maybe she was right, that without her I really would be nothing. A part of me knew this wasn't true, but there was this small sliver of doubt, nagging like a splinter. With Sophie, it was always all or nothing. You were either with her—or, more specifically, following her—or against her. There was no in between. So while being her friend was often hard, being on her bad side would be much, much worse.

I glanced at my watch, realizing Emily had to be home soon, and went to look for her, working my way through the party until I found her talking to a girl from the models. I hung out with them for a while, letting Sophie cool down. By the time we had to leave, I figured her little mood had passed.

When I went to look for her, though, she'd disappeared again. She wasn't outside. Or in the kitchen. Finally I turned down a hallway and spotted her at the other end, opening a door. She saw me, then turned away, slipping inside. I took a deep breath, then headed toward it, knocking twice.

"Sophie," I said. "It's time to go."

No answer. I sighed, crossing my arms over my chest, and stepped closer to the door. "Okay," I said, "I know you're mad at me, but let's just go, and we can talk about it later. All right?"

Still nothing. I looked at my watch again—if we didn't leave soon, Emily would be late for curfew. "Sophie," I said, reaching down for the knob. It wasn't locked, so I turned it, slowly, pushing it open and starting to step inside. "Just—"

I stopped speaking. And walking. Instead, I just stood there, in the half-open door, staring at Sophie, who was leaning against the wall opposite, a boy pressed against her. He had one hand under her shirt, the other moving down her thigh, and his head was ducked down, his lips on her neck. As I jerked back over the threshold, startled, he turned and looked at me. It was Will Cash.

"We're busy," he said, his voice low. His eyes were red, his lips inches from her shoulder.

"I—" I said "—I'm sorry . . ."

"Go home, Annabel," Sophie told me, moving her hand up into his hair, her fingers moving through where it curled, just barely, over his collar. "Just go home."

I stepped back, shutting the door, and just stood there in the hallway. Will Cash was one of the Perkins Day guys. He played guitar in the band and was a senior that year. While he was cute—very cute, the kind of guy you couldn't help but notice—he also had a reputation for being sort of a jerk, as well as a serial dater, at least in the short term. He was always with one girl or another, but never for long. Sophie, for her part, preferred jocks and clean-cut types and hated anyone even slightly alternative. Clearly, though, she was making an exception. At least for the time being.

That night, I tried to call her several times, but she never answered. The next day, around noon, when she finally called me, she didn't even mention Emily or what had happened between us. All she wanted to talk about was Will Cash.

"He's amazing," she told me. She'd given me the barest of details before announcing she was coming over, as if this subject was too big for a simple phone discussion. Now, she was sitting on my bed, flipping through an old *Vogue*. "He knows everybody, he's this amazing guitar player, and he's so freaking smart. Not to mention sexy. I could have kissed him all night long."

"You looked happy," I said.

"I was. I *am*," she said, turning a page and leaning in to

examine a shoe ad. "He is just what I need right now."

"So," I said, keeping Will's hit-and-run reputation in mind, "you're gonna see him again?"

"Of course," she said, like this was a stupid question. "Tonight. The band's playing at Bendo."

"Bendo?"

She sighed, reaching up to pull her hair back behind her neck with one hand. "It's a club, over on Finley?" she said. "Come on, Annabel, you have to have heard of *Bendo*."

"Oh," I said, although I hadn't. "Yeah."

"They go on at ten," she said, flipping another page. "You can come, if you want."

She wasn't looking at me as she asked this, and her voice was flat, no intonation. "No," I said. "I can't. I have to be up early tomorrow."

"Suit yourself," she said.

So that night, I sat at home, and Sophie went to Bendo to see the band, after which, I heard later, she went back to the A-Frame and slept with Will. Despite all her bragging and talk, he was her first, and from then on, he was all she cared about.

For me, though, it was difficult to see the appeal. While Sophie claimed that Will was sweet and funny and hot and smart (as well as a million other adjectives) none of these things really came to mind whenever I found myself face-to-face with him. Will *was* good-looking and incredibly popular. But he was also hard to read, the kind of guy who is just attractive enough that a warm personality is almost required to make him approachable. Will didn't have that. Instead, he came off as standoffish, as well as eerily intense, and whenever I found myself having to make conversation with him—in the car, when Sophie ran in to pay for gas, or at parties, when we both were looking for her—I felt nervous, entirely too aware of how he stared at me or let long silences fall between us.

Even worse, it was like he knew he unsettled me, almost as if he *liked* it. Usually I attempted to make up for my uneasiness by talking too much or too loudly, or both. And when I did, Will would just keep his eyes level, no expression on his face, as I floundered on endlessly before finally sputtering to a stop. I was sure he thought I was stupid. I *sounded* stupid, like a little girl trying too hard to impress. At any rate, I did my best to avoid him, although it wasn't always possible.

Other girls, though, didn't seem to have this problem, and because of it, dating Will turned out to be a full-time job, even for a girl as hardworking as Sophie. From the very start, there were rumors, and it seemed like everywhere they went Will knew someone, usually female. Add in the fact that they went to different schools, which made the stories we heard second- or thirdhand of his wandering eye and—if the constant rumors were to be believed—hands that much harder to con-firm. Plus there was the being-in-a-band factor. Plainly put, Sophie had her work cut out for her, and their relationship quickly became defined by a recognizable cycle: Will interacts in any way with some girl, rumors abound, Sophie goes after said girl, then after Will, they argue, break up, get back together. And on and on.

"I just don't understand why you put up with this," I said to her late one night as we drove too fast through a strange neighborhood, yet again looking for the house of some girl she'd heard had been flirting with Will at a party.

"Of course you don't," she snapped, running a stop sign as we took a sharp right. "You've never been in love, Annabel."

I said nothing to this, because it was true. I'd dated a few guys but had never had anyone serious. Although, if this was love, I thought, as we screeched around another curve, Sophie leaning across me to scan house numbers, her face flushed, I had to wonder if that was really such a bad thing.

"Will could have any girl he wanted," she said, slowing down a bit as we approached a row of houses on the left. "But he chose me. He's *with* me. And I will be damned if I let some bitch decide she's going to change that."

"They were just talking, though," I said. "Right? I mean, that doesn't mean anything, necessarily."

"Just talking, alone, at a party, in a room with no one else, is *not* just talking," she snapped. "If you know a guy has a girlfriend—especially if that girlfriend is me—there's absolutely no reason you should be doing anything with him that could be taken the wrong way. It's a choice, Annabel. And if you make the wrong one, you have only yourself to blame when there are consequences."

I sat back in my seat, keeping quiet as she pulled up in front of a small white house. The front porch light was on, and there was a red Jetta in the driveway, a Perkins Day field hockey sticker on the back bumper. If I'd been bolder—or just very stupid—I might have pointed out that it couldn't just be that all the girls in town had it in for Sophie's relationship, that Will had to have *some* culpability in all the rumors. But then I looked at her face, and something in her expression reminded me of that day at the pool all those years ago, when she'd shown up and immediately zeroed in on Kirsten being her friend. It didn't matter that my sister ignored her or was outright rude to her. When Sophie decided she wanted something, she wanted it. And for all the drama, being with Will had made her more envied than ever. She didn't have to follow the most popular girl around anymore. She *was* the most popular girl. Because of this, I wondered if the way she saw Will wasn't, really, all that different from how I saw her; while staying could be difficult, doing without entirely would be much, much harder.

So I'd sat there in the car as she got out, dodging the thrown brightness of the porch light as she walked up the driveway to the Jetta. I wanted to look away as she took the key clutched in her hand and dragged it across its pretty red flank, spelling out what this girl now was to her. But I didn't. I watched, the way I always did, only turning away as she came back toward me, when I was already a partner to the crime.

The irony was that even though I'd seen Will and Sophie go through their drama enough times to know it by heart, I was still completely surprised when I suddenly found myself a part of it. One bad move on one night, and the next thing I knew it was *me* she was after—me who was the slut, the whore—and me cut out, not only of her life, but the one I'd come to know as my own, as well.

• • •

"Annabel," Mrs. McMurty, the director of the Models, said now as she passed behind me, "you're up next, okay?"

I nodded, then stood up, brushing myself off. Across the room, I could see one of the new girls, a tall brunette, posing awkwardly with a large blue serving platter from the kitchen store. The calendar shoot was always kind of weird. Each girl got a month, and you had pose with products from a particular store in the mall. The year before, I'd been unlucky enough to draw Rochelle Tire and got stuck with whitewalls and radials.

"Hold it out, like you're offering something," the photographer said, and the girl reached forward, extending her neck. "Too much," he said, and she flushed, then pulled back.

I started up toward where the photographer was, working my way around a few girls who were leaning against the wall. I was almost there when Hillary Prescott stepped in front of me, blocking my path.

"Hey, Annabel."

Hillary and I had started in the Models together. While initially we'd been kind of friends, I'd quickly learned to keep my distance, as she was a huge gossip. She was also an instigator, more than happy to not only report the dish but stir it up as well.

"Hi, Hillary," I said. She was unwrapping a stick of gum, which she now popped in her mouth, then offered the pack to me. I shook my head. "What's going on?"

"Not much." She reached up, twisting a strand of hair around her finger, looking at me. "How was your summer?"

If it had been anyone else, I would have offered up my standard answer—"Fine"—without even thinking. But since it was Hillary, I was on my guard. "Good," I said, keeping my voice curt. "How was yours?"

"Totally boring," she replied, sighing. She chewed her gum for a moment: I could see it, pink and shiny, on her tongue. "So what's up with you and Emily?"

"Nothing," I said. "Why?"

She shrugged. "It's just, you guys always used to hang out. Now you're not even talking to each other. Just seems kind of weird."

I glanced over at Emily, who was examining her fingernails. "I don't know," I said. "Things change, I guess."

I could feel her looking at me, and I knew, despite her questions, that she knew exactly what had happened, or most of it. Still, I'd be damned if I filled in the rest of the details. "I better go," I told her. "I'm up next."

"Right," she said, narrowing her eyes at me as I stepped around her. "See you later."

I took my place against the wall, then settled to wait again, yawning. It was two in the afternoon, but I was exhausted. And it was all Owen Armstrong's fault.

That morning I'd happened to wake up briefly and glance at the clock right at 6:57 A.M. Just as I was about to roll back over, I remembered Owen's show. He'd been on my mind a lot that weekend, if only because I was suddenly aware of every little white lie I told, from the "Fine" I replied when my dad asked me how school was on Friday to how I'd nodded when my mom asked me the night before if I was excited about getting back to the Models. Cumulatively, it seemed like a lot of dishonesty, enough so that I found myself wanting to keep my word whenever possible. I'd told Owen I would listen to his show. So I did.

When I first turned it on at seven sharp, I could hear only static. I leaned closer to the radio, pressing my ear to it, just as there was an explosion of noise: a sudden burst of guitar, a clanging of cymbals, followed by someone screaming. I jerked, startled, whacking the radio with my elbow and knocking it off the bed. It hit the floor with a bang but kept playing, now at full blast.

Whitney started banging on the other side of the wall as I grabbed it, turning it down as quickly as I could. When I finally pulled it back to my ear—carefully this time—the song was still going, the words the singer was saying (or screeching, really) indecipherable. I had never heard music like this, if it was even music at all.

Finally, with a burst of cymbals, it was over. The next song, though, was no better. Instead of thrashing guitars, it was some sort of electronic piece, consisting of various beeps and blips with a man talking over them, reciting what sounded, to me anyway, like a shopping list. Plus, it went on for five and a half minutes, which I knew because I was watching the clock the entire time, praying for it to finish. When it finally did, Owen came on.

"That was Misanthrope with 'Descartes Dream,'" he said. "Before that, we had Lipo with 'Jennifer.' You're listening to Anger Management, here on WRUS, your community radio station. Here's Nuptial."

Which was another long techno piece, followed by something that sounded like old men reciting poems about whaling ships, their voices gruff and uneven, after which came a solid two minutes of very drippy-sounding harp music. It was such a mishmash, I couldn't even begin to adjust to it. Instead, for a full hour, I sat there, listening to song after song, waiting for one I could actually either a) understand or b) enjoy. It didn't happen. Clearly, I was not going to be enlightened. Just exhausted.

"Annabel," Mrs. McMurty called out, jerking me back to the present. "We're ready for you."

I nodded, then stepped over to stand in front of the backdrop, which was now decorated with several plants: a spider plant, some ferns, and a big palm tree in a pot with wheels. Clearly, this year I'd drawn Laurel's Florals. At least it was better than tires.

The photographer was one I hadn't met before, and he didn't say hello as I stepped in front of him, too busy messing with his camera as a prop guy pushed the rolling pot closer to me. A frond brushed my cheek.

The photographer glanced up at me. "We need more plants," he said to Mrs. McMurty, who was standing off to the side. "Or else I'm just going to have to shoot really close."

"Do we *have* more plants?" Mrs. McMurty asked the prop guy.

He glanced into the adjoining room. "A couple of cacti," he said. "And one ficus. But it's looking kind of sick."

There was a pop as the light meter went off. I reached up,

trying to push the frond out of my face. "Good," the photographer said, coming closer and moving it back. "I like that. Kind of a reveal thing. Do it again."

I did, holding back a sneeze as a branch tickled my face. Behind the photographer, I could see the other girls watching me—the new models, the seniors, Emily. But while I'd had so much trouble lately with being stared at, in this setting it was familiar, what was supposed to happen. If only for a few minutes, I could stop thinking of everything inside to focus only on the surface: one glimpse, one glance, one look. This one.

"Good," the photographer said. A cactus was moving closer in my side vision, but I kept my eyes on him as he moved around me, the flash popping as he directed me to come out, emerge, again and again.

That night, after my mom had gone to bed, and Whitney was locked away in her room, I went downstairs for a glass of water. My dad was sitting in the den just beyond the kitchen, the TV on in front of him, his feet up on the ottoman. When I flicked on the light, he turned around.

"You," he said, "are just in time for a great documentary on Christopher Columbus."

"Really," I said, pulling a glass out of the cabinet.

"It's fascinating," he said. "You want to watch with me? You might just learn something."

My dad loved the History Channel. "It's the story of the world!" he always said, when the rest of us complained about having to watch yet another show about the Third Reich, the fall of the Berlin Wall, or the Great Pyramids. Usually he capitulated, allowing himself to be outvoted, and was subsequently subjected to the Style Network, HGTV, or an endless series of reality shows. When he was alone later at night, though, the TV was all his. Still, he always seemed eager for company, as though history was even better when you had someone to share it with.

Usually, that someone was me. While my mom went to bed early, Whitney claimed boredom, and Kirsten always talked too much no matter what you were watching, my dad and I were a good match in the evenings, sitting together as history unfolded before us. Even if it was a show I knew he'd seen before, he still acted interested, nodding and saying, "Hmm," and "You don't say," as if the narrator could not only hear him, but required this feedback to continue.

In the last few months, though, I'd stopped watching with him. I wasn't sure why, but each time he asked, I suddenly felt tired, too tired to keep up with world events, even if they had already happened. There was something so heavy about the burden of history, of the past. I wasn't sure I had it in me to keep looking back.

"No thanks," I said now. "It's been a long day. I'm pretty tired."

"All right," he said, sitting back and picking up the remote. "Next time."

"Yeah. Definitely."

I picked up my water and walked over to his chair, and he leaned sideways, offering his cheek for me to kiss good night. After I did, he smiled, then hit the volume button, the sound of the narrator rising as I walked out of the room.

"In the fifteenth century, explorers yearned for . . . "

Halfway to the stairs I stopped, taking a sip of my water, then turned back and looked at him. The remote was now on his stomach, the light of the TV flickering across his face. I tried to picture myself retracing my steps, moving back to take my place on the couch, but I just couldn't. So I left him there alone to watch history repeat, the same events retold again and again, on his own.

Chapter
SEVEN

The entire weekend, I'd wondered what to expect when I next saw Owen at school. If anything would be different after what had happened on Friday, or we'd go back to our shared silence and distance, as if nothing had happened. A few minutes after he sat down, he made the choice for us.

"So. Did you listen?"

I put my sandwich down, turning to face him. He was in his normal spot, wearing jeans and a black crewneck. His iPod was out as well, earphones hanging around his neck.

"To your show?" I said.

"Yeah."

I nodded. "I did, actually."

"And?"

Despite the fact that I'd spent most of the weekend realizing how often I fibbed or outright lied to keep the peace, my first instinct at this moment was to do just that. Honesty in principle was one thing. In someone's face, another.

"Well," I began. "It was . . . interesting."

"Interesting," he repeated.

"Yeah," I said. "I'd, um, never heard those songs before."

He just looked at me, studying my face for what felt like a very long time. Then he startled me by standing up and taking three strides, quickly closing the distance between us before sitting down beside me. "Okay," he said. "Did you really listen?"

"Yeah," I said, trying not to stammer. "I did."

"I don't know if you remember," he said, "but you *did* tell me that you lie."

"I didn't say that." He raised an eyebrow. "I said I often hold back the truth. I'm not doing that this time, though. I listened to the whole show."

He still didn't believe me, it was obvious. And not exactly surprising.

I took a breath. "'Jennifer' by Lipo. 'Descartes Dream' by Misanthrope. Some song with a lot of beeping—"

"You *did* listen." He sat back, nodding his head. "Okay, then. Now tell me what you really thought."

"I told you. It was interesting."

"Interesting," he said, "is not a word."

"Since when?"

"It's a placeholder. Something you use when you don't want to say something else." He leaned a little closer to me. "Look, if you're worried about my feelings, don't be. You can say whatever you want. I won't be offended."

"I did. I liked it."

"Tell the truth. Say something. Anything. Just spit it out."

"I—" I began, then stopped myself. Maybe it was the fact that he was so clearly on to me. Or my sudden awareness of how rarely I was honest. Either way, I broke. "I . . . I didn't like it," I said.

He slapped his leg. "I *knew* it! You know, for someone who lies a lot, you're not very good at it."

This was a good thing. Or not? I wasn't sure. "I'm not a liar," I said.

"Right. You're *nice*," he said.

"What's wrong with nice?"

"Nothing. Except it usually involves not telling the truth," he replied. "Now. Tell me what you really thought."

What I really thought was that I felt very unsettled, as if somehow, Owen Armstrong had figured me out, and I hadn't even realized it. "I liked the show format," I said, "but the songs were kind of . . ."

"Kind of what?" He waggled his fingers at me. "Give me some adjectives. Other than interesting."

"Noisy," I said. "Bizarre."

"Okay." He nodded. "What else?"

I looked at his face carefully, gauging it for signs that he was offended, or bothered. There were none, so I continued. "Well, the first song was . . . painful to listen to. And the second, the Misanthrope one . . ."

"'Descartes Dream.'"

"It put me to sleep. Literally."

"That happens," he said. "Go on."

He said this so easily, like he wasn't bothered in the least. So I did. "The harp music sounded like something you'd hear at a funeral."

"Ah," he said. "Okay. Good."

"And I hated the techno."

"All of it?"

"Yes."

He nodded. "Well. Okay, then. That's good feedback. Thank you."

And that was that. He pulled out his iPod and started pushing buttons. No tantrums, no hurt feelings, no offense. "So . . . you're okay with that?" I asked.

"That you didn't like the show?" he replied, not looking up. "Yeah."

He shrugged. "Sure. I mean, it would have been cool if you had. But most people don't, so it's not exactly surprising."

"And that doesn't bother you," I said.

"Not really. I mean, at first, it was kind of disappointing. But people recover from disappointment. Otherwise we'd all be hanging from nooses. Right?"

"What?"

"Hey, what about the sea shanty?" he asked. I just looked at him. "The men chanting about sailing the open sea. What was your take on that one?"

"Weird," I said. "Very weird."

"Weird," he repeated slowly. "Huh. Okay."

Just then I heard voices, and footsteps, and turned my head just in time to see Sophie crossing the courtyard with Emily. I'd been so distracted by what had happened with Owen on Friday that initially, I'd forgotten about the confrontation that preceded it. That morning, though, on the way to school, the dread set in as I began wondering what would happen. But so far, I'd only crossed paths with Sophie once, at which point she'd glared at me, mumbling a "slut" as she went by. Same old, same old.

Now, though, she glanced over at me, her eyes widening slightly before she nudged Emily with her elbow. Then they were both staring at me, and I felt my face flush as I looked down at my backpack at my feet.

Owen, for his part, did not notice this as he put his player down, running a hand through his hair. "So you didn't like any of the techno?" he asked. "Like, not even one aspect?"

I shook my head. "No," I said. "Sorry."

"Don't be sorry, it's your opinion. There's no right and wrong in music, you know? Just everything in between."

Just then, the bell rang, surprising me. I was so used to lunch being interminable, but this one had flown by. I reached down, balling up what was left of my sandwich as Owen hopped off the wall, slipping his player in his pocket and grabbing his earphones.

"Well," I said, "I guess I'll see you around."

"Yeah." He started to put on his earphones as I grabbed my bag, sliding off the wall. "See you later."

As he walked away, I took another look at the bench. Sure enough, Sophie and Emily were still staring. I watched as Sophie said something, and Emily smiled, shaking her head. I could only imagine what they would say about us, what stories they would come up with. None of them could be weirder than the truth: that Owen Armstrong and I just might be friends.

Thinking this, I glanced over, finding him in the crowd. He'd put on his earphones and was headed up to the arts building, his bag over his shoulder. They'd been watching him, too, but he hadn't even noticed. If he did, I was pretty sure he wouldn't care anyway. And for that, more than the honesty, the directness, and everything else, I envied him most of all.

I didn't get the Mooshka job. This was neither upsetting nor surprising, at least to me, although my mother did seem disappointed. Personally, I was just relieved the whole thing was over, and ready to move on. But the next day, as I took out my lunch, a note fell out with it.

> *Annabel,*
>
> *I just wanted to tell you that I'm so proud of you for all you've accomplished, and not to be discouraged about the Mooshka campaign. It was very competitive, Lindy said, and they did think highly of you. She and I have arranged to talk today about some other things she's lining up, which sound very exciting. I'll fill you in tonight. Have a great day.*

"Bad news?"

I jumped, startled, then glanced up to see Owen was standing in front of me. "What?"

"You looked stressed," he said, nodding at the note in my hand. "Something wrong?"

"No," I said, folding the note and putting it down beside me. "Everything's fine."

He walked over to the wall, sitting down not right next to me, as he had the day before, but not as far away as he once had, either. I watched him as he slid his iPod out of his pocket, then leaned his palms back on the grass beside us, surveying the courtyard.

I was aware, during all of this, that with my last response, I hadn't exactly been honest with him. Of course, he never would have known this. Or cared, probably. Still, for some reason, I felt the need to Rephrase and Redirect. As it were.

"It's just this thing with my mom," I said.

He turned his head, and I wondered if maybe he thought I was crazy, or had no idea what I was talking about. "Thing," he repeated. "Just so you know; that's a *serious* placeholder."

Of course it is, I thought. Still, I clarified. "It has to do with my modeling."

"Modeling?" He looked confused. "Oh, right. Like Mallory was talking about. You were in a commercial or something?"

"I've been doing it since I was a kid. Both my sisters did it, too. But lately, I've been wanting to quit."

And there it was. The one thing I'd only said in my head, now finally out there, and to Owen Armstrong, of all people. This was so big a step for me that I probably could have stopped right there. But for whatever reason, I continued.

"And anyway," I said, "it's complicated, because my mom's really into it, and if I quit, then she'll be upset."

"But you don't want to do it anymore," he said. "Right?"

"Yeah."

"So you should tell her that."

"You say that like it's easy," I said.

"Isn't it?"

"No."

There was a burst of laughter from the doors to our left as a group of freshmen came out, talking too loudly. Owen looked over at them, then back at me. "Why not?" he asked.

"Because I don't do confrontations."

He glanced over at Sophie, who was sitting on her bench with Emily, then slowly slid his eyes back to me.

"Well," I added, "I don't do confrontations *well*."

"What happened between you two, anyway?"

"Me and Sophie?" I asked, although I knew what he meant. He nodded. "It was just . . . we had a falling-out over the summer."

He didn't say anything; I knew he was waiting for more details. "She thinks I slept with her boyfriend," I added.

"Did you?"

Of course he would ask, point-blank. But still, I felt my face flush. "No," I said. "I didn't."

"Maybe you should tell her that," he said.

"It's not that simple."

"Huh," he said. "Call me crazy, but I'm sensing a theme here."

I looked down at my hands, thinking again that I had to be awfully simple for him to deduce so much about me in less than a week. "So if you were me," I said, "you would—"

"—just be honest," he finished. "On both counts."

"You say that like it's easy, too," I told him.

"It's not. But you can do it. It just takes practice."

"Practice?"

"In Anger Management," he said, "we had to do all this role-playing stuff. You know, to get used to handling things in a less volatile way."

"You role-played," I said, trying to picture this.

"I had to. It was court-ordered." He sighed. "But I have to say, it was kind of helpful. You know, so that when and if something similar did happen, you had some kind of road map for dealing with it."

"Oh," I said. "Well, I guess that makes sense."

"All right, then." He slid a little closer to me. "So say I'm your mom."

"What?" I said.

"I'm your mom," he repeated. "Now tell me you want to quit modeling."

I could feel myself blushing. "I can't do that," I said.

"Why not?" he asked. "Is it so hard to believe? You think I'm not a good role-player?"

"No," I said. "It's just—"

"Because I am. *Everyone* wanted me to be their mother in group."

I just looked at him. "I just . . . It's weird."

"No, it's hard. But not impossible. Just try it."

A week earlier, I hadn't even known what color his eyes were. Now, we were family. At least temporarily. I took in a breath.

"Okay," I said. "So—"

"Mom," he said.

"What?"

"The more accurate the exercise, the more effective it is," he explained. "Go all out, or don't go at all."

"Okay," I said again. "Mom."

"Yes?"

This is so weird, I thought. Out loud, I said, "The thing is, I know that the modeling thing is really important to—"

He held up a hand in the STOP position. "R and R. Rephrase and Redirect that."

"Why?"

"*Thing*. Like I said, major placeholder, super vague. In confrontations, you have to be as specific as possible, to avoid misunderstandings." He leaned a little closer to me. "Look, I know it's weird," he said. "But it works. I promise."

This was little comfort, though, as I proceeded to cross over from simply uncomfortable to borderline humiliated. "I know my modeling is very important to you," I said, "and that you really enjoy it."

Owen nodded, gesturing for me to go on.

"But to be honest . . . " I reached up, tucking a piece of hair behind my ear. "It's just that lately, I've been thinking about it a lot, and I feel like . . ."

The thing was, I knew this was just a game. Practice, not real. But even so, I felt something seizing up in me, like an engine sputtering to a stop. I had too much at stake here—failing would not only reveal my weakness about confrontation, but embarrass me in front of him, as well.

He was still waiting.

"I can't do it," I said, and looked away.

"You so had it, though!" he said, slapping the wall with the palm of his hand. "You were right there."

"I'm sorry," I said, picking up my sandwich again. My voice sounded tight as I said, "I just . . . I can't."

He looked at me for a moment. Then he shrugged. "All right," he said. "No big deal."

We sat there, both of us silent for a second. I had no idea what had just happened, but it did feel like a big deal, suddenly. Then I heard Owen take in a breath.

"Look," he said, "I'm just going to say this: It's got to suck, you know? Keeping something like that in. Walking around every day having so much you want to say, but not doing it. It's gotta make you really mad. Right?"

I knew he was talking about modeling. But hearing this, I thought of something else, the thing I could never admit, the biggest secret of all. The one I could never tell, because if the tiniest bit of light was shed upon it, I'd never be able to shut it away again.

"I should go," I said, stuffing my sandwich back into the bag. "I . . . I have to talk to my English teacher about this project I'm supposed to be doing."

"Oh," he said. I could feel him watching me, and made a conscious effort not to look back. "Sure."

I stood up, grabbing my bag. "I'll, um, see you later."

"Right." He picked up his iPod. "See you around."

I nodded, and then, somehow, I was walking away, leaving him behind. I waited until I was at the main doors to look back.

He was just sitting there, head ducked down, listening to his music like nothing had happened at all. I had a flash of my first impression of him—that he was dangerous, a threat. I knew now he wasn't, at least not in the ways I'd thought then. But there *was* something frightening about Owen Armstrong:

he was honest and expected the same from everyone else. And that scared me to death.

When I first walked away from Owen, I felt relieved. But it didn't last.

The real truth, I realized as the day wore on, was that even though I hardly knew Owen, I'd actually been *more* honest with him than anyone else in a long time. He knew about what had happened between me and Sophie, about Whitney's illness, and that I hated modeling. This seemed like an awful lot to reveal to someone who, in the end, I couldn't even risk being friends with. But I didn't know it for sure until I saw Clarke.

It was after seventh period, in the hallway, and she was opening her locker. Her hair was in two spriggy pigtails, and she had on jeans, a black shirt, and shiny Mary Janes. As I watched, a girl I didn't know passed behind her, saying her name, and Clarke turned, smiling, and said hello back to her. It was all totally normal, just another moment in another day, but something in it struck me, and I found myself going back, back, all the way to that night down by the pool. Another time I'd been afraid of conflict, afraid to be honest, afraid even to speak. I'd lost a friend then, too. The best friend, really, I'd ever had.

It was too late to try and alter what had happened between me and Clarke, but there might still be time to change something else. Maybe even me. So I went to look for Owen.

In a school of over two thousand students, it was easy to lose yourself, not to mention someone else. But Owen definitely stood out in a crowd, so when I couldn't find him or the

Land Cruiser, I figured I'd missed him. When I got into my car and pulled out onto the main road, though, I spotted him. He was on foot, walking down the center of the median, his back-pack over one shoulder, earphones on.

It wasn't until I was right up to him that it occurred to me this might be a mistake. But you get only so many do-overs in this life, so many chances to, if not change your past, alter your future. So I slowed down and lowered my window.

"Hey," I called out, but he didn't hear me. "Owen!" Still no response. I moved my hand to the center of my steering wheel and pushed down, hard, on the horn. Finally, he turned his head.

"Hey," he said as someone behind me beeped angrily before whizzing past. "What's up?"

"What happened to your car?" I asked him.

He stopped walking, then reached up, pulling the earphone out of his left ear. "Transportation issues," he said.

This is it, I told myself. *Say something. Anything. Just spit it out.*

"Story of my life," I told him, then reached over, pushing open my passenger door. "Get in."

Chapter
EIGHT

The first thing that Owen did when he got in my car was bump his head on what I hadn't realized—until that particular moment anyway—was a pretty low ceiling. "Oof," he said, reaching up to rub his forehead just as one of his knees whacked the dashboard. "Man. This is a small car."

"Is it?" I said. "I've never really noticed, and I'm five-eight."

"Is that tall?"

"I used to think so," I said, glancing at him.

"Well, I'm six-four," he replied, trying to push his seat, which was already back as far as it would go, even farther away from the dashboard. Then he moved his arm, trying to balance it on the window, but it was too big, so he changed position, crossing it over his chest, before finally letting it drop to hang beside him. "So I guess it's all relative."

"You okay?" I asked.

"Fine," he said, altogether unbothered, as if this sort of thing happened all the time. "Thanks for the ride, by the way."

"No problem," I said. "Just tell me where you're going."

"Home." He moved his arm again, still trying to fit into the seat. "Just keep straight. You don't have to turn for a while."

We rode without talking for a few minutes. I knew this was the time to say what was on my mind, to explain myself. I took in a breath, bracing myself.

"How do you *stand* it?" he said.

I blinked. "I'm sorry?"

"I mean," he said, "it's just so silent. Empty."

"What is?"

"This," he said, gesturing around the car. "Driving in silence. With no music."

"Well," I said slowly, "to be honest, I didn't realize we were, actually."

He sat back, his head bumping the headrest. "See for me, it's immediate. Silence is so freaking loud."

This seemed either deep or deeply oxymoronic. I wasn't sure which. "Well," I said, "my CDs are in the console in the center if you—"

But he was already pulling it open and taking out a stack of CDs. As he began to work his way through them, I glanced over, suddenly nervous.

"Those aren't really my favorites," I said. "They're just the ones I have in here right now."

"Huh," he said, not looking up. I turned back to the road, hearing the cases clacking as he flipped through them. "Drake Peyton, Drake Peyton . . . so you're into that frat-boy hippie rock stuff?"

"I guess," I said. This was bad, I thought. "I saw him live summer before last."

"Huh," he said again. "More Drake Peyton . . . and Alamance. That's alt-country, right?"

"Yeah."

"Interesting," he said. "Because I wouldn't have pegged you for . . . Tiny? This is his most current album, right?"

"I got it over the summer," I said, slowing for a red light.

"Then it is." He shook his head. "You know, I have to admit, I'm surprised. I never would have pegged you for a Tiny fan. Or any rap, for that matter."

"Why not?"

He shrugged. "I don't know. Bad assumption, I guess. Who made you this one?"

I glanced at the disc he was holding, immediately recognizing the slanting print. "My sister Kirsten."

"She's into classic rock," he said.

"Since high school," I said. "She had a Jimmy Page poster on her wall for years."

"Ah." He scanned the track list. "She has good taste, though. I mean, there's Led Zeppelin here, but at least it's not 'Stairway to Heaven.' In fact," he said, sounding impressed, "'Thank You' is my favorite Led Zeppelin song."

"Really?"

"Really. It's got that kind of cheesy, power-ballad feel. Kind of ironic, yet truthful. Can I put it on?"

"Sure," I said. "Thanks for asking."

"You gotta ask," he said, reaching forward and sliding the CD into my stereo. "Only a real asshole takes liberties with someone else's car stereo. That's serious."

The player clicked a couple of times, and then I heard music, faintly. Owen reached forward for the volume button, then glanced at me. When I nodded, he turned it up. Hearing the opening chords, I had a pang of missing Kirsten, who, during her rebellion-filled senior year, had developed a passion for seventies-era guitar rock, which, at its height, had her listening to Pink Floyd's *Dark Side of the Moon* on repeat for what seemed like weeks at a time.

Thinking this, I looked back over at Owen, who was drumming his fingers on his knee. Kirsten, of course, would never hesitate to say what was on *her* mind. So with her song playing in my ears, I decided to follow suit. Or try to. "So about today," I said. He looked over at me. "I'm sorry about what happened."

"What happened?"

I fixed my eyes on the road ahead, feeling my face flush. "When we were doing the role-playing, and I freaked out and walked away."

I was expecting an "It's okay" or maybe a "Don't worry about it." Instead, he said, "That was freaking out?"

"Well," I said. "I guess. Yeah."

"Huh," he said. "Okay."

"I didn't mean to get so upset," I explained. "Like I said, I just don't do confrontations very well. Which I guess was obvious. So . . . I'm sorry."

"It's all right." He tried to sit back again, his elbow knocking the door. "In fact . . ."

I waited for him to finish this thought. When he didn't, I said, "What?"

"It's just, to me, that wasn't really freaking out," he said. "No?"

He shook his head. "To me, freaking out is raising your voice. Screaming. Veins bulging. Hitting people in parking lots. That kind of thing."

"I don't do that," I said.

"I'm not saying you should." He reached up, running a hand through his hair; as he did so, the ring on his middle finger caught the light, glinting for a second. "It's just a semantic issue, I guess. Take this next right."

I did, turning onto a tree-lined street. All the houses were big, with wide front porches. We passed a group of kids in a cul-de-sac playing roller hockey, then some moms on a corner, grouped around a pack of strollers.

"This is it, up here," he told me. "The gray one."

I slowed down, then pulled over to the curb. The house was beautiful, with a wide front porch with a swing, and bright pink flowers in pots lining the steps. A yellow cat was lying on the front walk, stretched out in the sunshine. "Wow," I said. "Great house."

"Well, it's not glass," he said. "But it's okay."

We sat there for a second, our situation now reversed from last time, me waiting for him to go inside. "You know," I said finally, "I just wanted to say you were right about what you said earlier. It is kind of hard to hold a lot in. But for me . . . it's sometimes even harder to let it out."

I wasn't sure why I felt compelled to bring this up again. Maybe to finally explain myself. To him, or to me.

"Yeah," he said. "But you gotta get stuff out. Otherwise it just festers, and eventually, you just blow."

"See, that's the part I can't deal with," I said. "I can't take it when people are angry."

"Anger's not bad," he said. "It's human. And anyway, just because someone's upset doesn't mean they'll stay that way."

I looked down at my steering wheel, picking at the edge. "I don't know," I said. "In my experience, when people I'm close with have gotten upset with me, that's it. It *is* forever. Everything changes."

Owen didn't say anything for a second. I could hear a dog barking from some house down the street. "Well," he said, "maybe you weren't as close with them as you thought."

"Meaning what?"

"Meaning that if someone is really close with you, your getting upset or them getting upset is okay, and they don't change because of it. It's just part of the relationship. It *happens*. You deal with it."

"You deal with it," I said. "I wouldn't even know how to do that."

"Well, that makes sense," he said. "Considering you never let it happen in the first place."

The CD was still going, now playing a song by Rush as a minivan drove past us, kicking up some leaves. I had no idea how many minutes had passed while we'd been sitting there. It seemed like a long time.

"You sure have a lot of answers," I said.

"I don't," he replied, reaching down to twist one of his rings around his finger. "I'm just doing the best I can, under the circumstances."

"How's that going?" I asked.

He glanced up at me. "Well, you know," he said. "It's day to day."

I smiled. "I like your rings," I said, nodding at his hands. "Are they the exact same?"

"Sort of. And not really." He reached down, sliding the one off his left hand and handing it to me. "They're kind of a before-and-after thing. Rolly made them for me. His dad's a jeweler."

The ring was heavy in my palm, the silver thick. "He made this?"

"Not the ring," he said. "The engraving. On the inside."

"Oh." I tilted the ring slightly, peering along the interior curve. There, in all capital letters, in formal, very elegant type, it said GO FUCK YOURSELF. "Nice," I said.

"Classy, huh?" he said. He made a face. "That was me pre-arrest. I was a little . . ."

"Angry?"

"You could say. He made this one when I finished the Anger Management course." He slid the ring off his other middle finger, then held it up to my face. In the same type, same size, it said OR NOT.

I laughed. "Well," I said, handing it back to him. "It's always good to know your options."

"Exactly." Then he smiled at me, and I felt another flush come over my face, but not the embarrassed or anxious kind—a different sort entirely. One I never would have thought I'd feel around Owen Armstrong. Ever. The moment was broken, however, by a voice.

"Annabel!"

I looked to my right—it was Mallory. Sometime during this exchange, she'd appeared at Owen's window, where she was now smiling widely and waving. "Hi!"

"Hi," I said.

She gestured for Owen to put his window down, which he did, slowly, and clearly somewhat reluctantly. As soon as there was a space big enough, she stuck her head in. "Oh my God, I love your shirt! Is that from Tosca?"

I glanced down. "Maybe," I said. "My mom got it for me."

"You're so lucky! I love Tosca. It's, like, my favorite store in the whole world. Are you coming in?"

"Coming in?" I asked.

"To the house. Are you staying for dinner? Oh, you *totally* have to stay for dinner!"

"Mallory," Owen said, rubbing a hand over his face. "Please stop shrieking."

She ignored him, sticking her head in even farther. "You could see my room," she said, her eyes wide, excited. "And my closet, and I could show you—"

"Mallory," Owen said again. "Back away from the car."

"Do you like my outfit?" she asked me. She stepped back so I could see it: plain white tee, short jacket over it, rolled-up jeans, and shiny boots with thick soles. After doing a little spin, she stuck her head back in the window. "It's inspired by Nicholls Lake; she's my favorite singer right now? She's, like, punk."

Owen sat back, his head bonking against the headrest. "Nicholls Lake," he said in a low voice, "is *not* punk."

"Yes, she is," Mallory told him. "And see? Today, so am I!"

"Mallory, we've talked about this. Remember? Did we not discuss the true definition of punk?" Owen said. "Have you even *listened* to that Black Flag CD I gave you?"

"That was so loud," she said. "And plus you can't even sing along. Nicholls Lake is better."

Owen took in another shuddering breath. "Mallory," he said. "If you could just—"

Just then, a tall dark-haired woman—Owen's mom, I assumed—appeared in the doorway of the house, calling her. Mallory shot her an annoyed look. "I have to go in," she announced, then leaned in even farther, so her face was inches from Owen's. "But you'll come over another time, right?"

"Sure," I told her.

"Bye, Annabel."

"Good-bye," I said.

She smiled, then stood up, and waved at me. I waved back, and Owen and I watched her climb the front stairs and head down the walk, turning to look back at us every few steps or so.

"Wow," I said. "So she's punk, huh?"

Owen didn't answer me. Instead, all I could hear was him inhaling, loudly, several times in a row.

"Is this you freaking out?" I asked.

He exhaled. "No. This is me annoyed. I don't know what it is about her. There's just something about sisters. They can make you freaking crazy."

"Story of my life," I said.

Another silence. In every one that fell, I told myself this

time, he was going to get out and leave, and this would be over. And each time, I wanted it to happen even less.

He said, "You say that a lot, you know."

"What?"

"'Story of my life.'"

"You said it first."

"Did I?"

I nodded. "That day, behind the school."

"Oh." He was quiet for a moment. "You know, when you think about it, that's kind of a weird thing. I mean, it's meant to be sympathetic, right? But it's kind of not. Like you're telling the other person there's nothing unique about what they're saying."

I considered this as a couple of kids on Rollerblades whizzed past, hockey sticks over their shoulders. "Yeah," I said, finally, "but you could also look at it the other way. Like you're saying no matter how bad things are for you, I can still relate."

"Ah," he said. "So you're saying you relate to me."

"No. Not at all."

"Nice." He laughed, turning his head to look out the window. I caught the quickest flash of his profile, and remembered all those days I'd spent studying him from a distance.

"Okay," I said. "Maybe a little."

He turned back, facing me, and I felt it again. Another pause, just long enough for me to wonder what, exactly, was happening. Then he pushed the door open. "So," he said, "um, thanks again for the ride."

"No problem. I owed you."

"No," he said, "you didn't." He untangled himself from the seat. "I'll see you tomorrow, or something."

"Yeah. See you then."

He got out, shutting the door behind him, then grabbed his bag and started up the steps. I watched him until he went inside.

As I pulled away from the curb, the whole afternoon seemed so strange, surreal. There was so much filling my head, too much to even begin to understand, but as I drove, I suddenly realized something else was bothering me: The CD had stopped and there was no music. Before, I probably wouldn't have even noticed, but now that I had, the silence, if not deafening, was distracting. I wasn't sure what this meant. But I reached forward and turned on the radio anyway.

Chapter
NINE

Beauty and the Beast. The Odd Couple. Shrek and Fiona. I had
to hand it to the rumor mill: Over the next couple of weeks,
they came up with lots of names for me and Owen and whatever it was we were doing every day on the wall at lunch. For
me, it was harder to define. We weren't together by any means,
but we weren't strangers. Like so much else, we fell somewhere in the middle.

Whatever the case, some things now were just understood.
First, that we'd sit together. Second, that I'd always give him a
hard time about not eating anything—he'd confessed to me he
spent his lunch money on music, always—before sharing whatever I'd brought. And third, that we would argue. Or not argue,
exactly. *Discuss.*

Initially, it was only about music, Owen's favorite subject
and the one about which he felt the most strongly. When I
agreed with him, I was brilliant and enlightened. When I didn't,
I had the Worst Taste in Music in the World. Usually the most
spirited exchanges came at the beginning of the week, as we
discussed his radio show, which I now listened to faithfully
every Sunday morning. It was hard to believe that once I'd

been so nervous to tell him what I thought. Now, it came naturally.

"You've got to be kidding!" he said one Monday, shaking his head. "You didn't like that Baby Bejesuses song?"

"Was it the one that was all touch-tones?"

"It wasn't all touch-tones," he said indignantly. "There was other stuff, too."

"Like what?"

He just looked at me for a second, half of my turkey sandwich poised in his hand. "Like," he said, then took a bite, which meant he was stalling. After taking his time chewing and swallowing, he said, "The Baby Bejesuses are innovators of the genre."

"Then they should be able to put together a song using more than a phone keypad."

"That," he said, pointing at me with the sandwich, "is I-Lang. Watch it."

I-Lang meant Inflammatory Language. And like R and R and placeholders, it had become part of my daily vocabulary. Hang out with Owen long enough, and you got an Anger Management tutorial, free of charge.

"Look," I said, "you know I don't like techno music. So maybe, you know, you should stop asking me my opinion of techno songs."

"That is such a generalization!" he replied. "How can you just rule out an entire genre? You're jumping to conclusions."

"No, I'm not," I said.

"What do you call it, then?"

"Being honest."

He just looked at me for a second. Then, with a sigh, he took another bite of the sandwich. "Fine," he said, chewing. "Let's move on. What about that thrash metal song by the Lipswitches?"

"Too noisy."

"It's supposed to be noisy! It's thrash metal!"

"I wouldn't mind the noise, if there were other redeeming qualities," I told him. "It's just someone wailing at the top of their lungs."

He popped the last bit of crust into his mouth. "So no techno and no thrash metal," he said. "What's left?"

"Everything else?" I said.

"Everything else," he repeated slowly, still not convinced. "Okay, fine. How about the last song I played, the one with glockenspiel."

"The glockenspiel?"

"Yeah. By Aimee Decker. There was a stand-up bass, and some yodeling at the beginning, and then . . ."

"Yodeling?" I said. "Is that what that was?"

"What, now you don't like *yodeling*, either?"

And on and on. Sometimes, it got heated, but never to the point where I couldn't handle it. The truth was, I looked forward to my lunches with Owen, more than I ever would have admitted.

Between our discourses on early punk, big band and swing, and the questionable redeeming qualities of techno music, I was learning more and more about him. I now knew that although he'd always had a passion for music, it wasn't until his parents divorced a year and a half earlier that he'd become, to use his word, obsessed. Apparently the split had been pretty ugly, with accusations going back and forth. Music, he told me, was an escape. Everything else was ending and changing, but music was this vast resource, bottomless.

"Basically," he said one day, "when they wouldn't talk to each other, I got stuck in the middle, doing all the go-between work. And of course, it was always the *other* one who was terrible and inconsiderate. If I agreed, I was screwed, because someone got offended. But if I disagreed, that was taking sides, too. There was no way to win."

"That must have been hard," I said.

"It sucked. That's when I started really getting into the music thing, all the obscure stuff. If nobody had heard it, nobody could tell me what I was supposed to think about it. There was no right and wrong there." He sat back, waving away a bee that was circling around us. "Plus, around that same time, there was this college radio station out in Phoenix that I started listening to—KXPC. There was this one guy who had a late-night shift on the weekends . . . he played some seriously obscure shit. Like tribal music, or seriously underground punk, or five full minutes of a faucet dripping. Stuff like that."

"A faucet dripping," I said. He nodded. "That's music?"

"Obviously not to everyone," he replied, shooting me a look. I smiled. "But that was kind of the point. It was, like, this whole uncharted territory. I started writing down the stuff he was playing, and looking for it at record stores and online. It gave me something to focus on other than all the stuff going down at home. Plus, it came in handy when I needed to drown out the screaming downstairs."

"Really? Screaming?"

He shrugged. "It wasn't that bad. But there were definitely some freak-outs on both sides. Though, to be honest, the silence was worse."

"Worse than screaming?" I said.

"Much," he said, nodding. "I mean, at least with an argument, you know what's happening. Or have some idea. Silence is . . . it could be anything. It's just—"

"So freaking loud," I finished for him.

He pointed at me. "Exactly."

So Owen hated silence. Also on his list of dislikes: peanut butter (too dry), liars (self-explanatory), and people who didn't tip (delivering pizza didn't pay that well, apparently). And those were only the ones I knew about so far. Maybe it was because of his stint in Anger Management, but Owen was very open about the things that pissed him off.

"Aren't you?" he asked one day, when I pointed this out to him.

"No," I said. "I mean, I guess I am about some things."

"What makes you mad?"

Instinctively, I looked over at Sophie, who was on her bench, talking on her cell phone. Out loud I said, "Techno music."

"Ha-ha," he said. "Seriously."

"I don't know." I picked the crust of my sandwich. "My sisters, I guess. Sometimes."

"What else?"

"I can't think of anything," I said.

"Please! You're seriously saying the only thing that bugs

you is siblings and a genre of music? Come on. Are you not human?"

"Maybe," I said, "I'm just not as angry as you are."

"Nobody's as angry as I am," he replied, hardly bothered. "That's a fact. But even *you* have to have something that really pisses you off."

"I probably do. I just . . . can't think of one right this second." He rolled his eyes. "And besides, what do you mean no one's as angry as you are? What about Anger Management?"

"What about it?"

"Well," I said, "wasn't the point that you not be angry anymore?"

"The purpose of Anger Management isn't to make you not angry."

"No?"

He shook his head. "No. Anger is inevitable. Anger Management is just what it sounds like: It's supposed to help you deal with it. Express it in a more productive way than, say, hitting people in parking lots."

If at first I'd doubted it, I didn't now: Owen was always this honest. Ask a question, you got an answer. For a while, though, I'd tested him, soliciting his opinion on various things, like my clothes ("Not your best shade," he told me about a new peach-colored shirt), his initial impression of me ("Too perfect and completely unapproachable"), and the state of his love life ("Nonexistent, currently").

"Is there anything you won't tell someone?" I finally asked him one day, just after he'd told me that, while my new haircut looked fine, he preferred it longer. "Like, at all?"

"You just asked me what I thought," he pointed out, helping himself to a pretzel from the bag between us. "Why ask me, if you don't want me to be honest?"

"I'm not talking about my hair. I'm talking in general." He gave me a doubtful look, popping the pretzel into his mouth. "Seriously. Do you ever think to yourself, maybe I shouldn't say this? Maybe it's not the right thing to do?"

He considered this for a second. "No," he said finally. "I told you. I don't like liars."

"It's not lying, though. It's just not telling."

"You're saying there's a difference?"

"There is," I said. "One is actively deceiving. The other is just not saying something out loud."

"Yes, but," he replied, pulling out another pretzel, "you're still participating in a deception. Except it's just to yourself. Right?"

I just looked at him, turning this thought over in my mind. "I don't know," I said slowly.

"In fact," he continued, "that's worse than lying, when you really think about it. I mean, at the very least you should tell yourself the truth. If you can't trust yourself, who can you trust? You know?"

I would never have been able to tell him so, but Owen inspired me. The little white lies I told on a daily basis, the things I kept in, each time I was not totally honest—I was aware of every one now. I was also cognizant of how good it felt to actually be able to say what I thought to someone. Even if it was just about music. Or not.

One day at lunch, Owen put his backpack on the wall

between us, unzipped it, and pulled out a stack of CDs. "Here," he said, pushing them toward me. "For you."

"Me?" I said. "What is this?"

"An overview," he explained. "I planned to do more, but my burner was acting up. So I could only do a few."

To Owen, "a few" CDs meant ten, by my count. Looking at the top few, I saw that each had a title—TRUE HIP HOP, CHANTS AND SHANTIES (VARIOUS), TOLERABLE JAZZ, ACTU-AL SINGERS ACTUALLY SINGING—with the tracks listed beneath in a neat block print. It occurred to me that they were probably the result of a pointed discussion about stoner rock we'd had the day before, when Owen decided that maybe my knowledge of music was so "stunted and wanting" (his words) due to a lack of exposure. So here was his remedy: a personal primer, divided into chapters.

"If you really like any of these," he continued, "then I can give you more. When, you know, you're ready to go in depth."

I picked up the stack, flipping through the rest of the titles. There was one for country music, the British Invasion, folk songs. When I reached the one at the very bottom, though, I saw that the cover was blank, except for two words: JUST LISTEN.

Instantly, I was suspicious. "Is this techno?" I asked him.

"I can't believe you'd just assume that," he said, offended. "God."

"Owen," I said.

"It's not techno."

I just looked at him.

"The point is," he said as I shook my head, "that all the oth-ers are set lists, set concepts. An education, if you will. You should listen to them first. And then, when you've done that, and you think you're ready, really ready, put that one on. It's a bit more . . . out there."

"All right," I said. "I'm *officially* wary now."

"You might totally hate it," he admitted. "Or not. It might be the answer to all life's questions. That's the beauty of it. You know?"

I looked down at it again, studying the cover. "'Just Listen,'" I said.

"Yeah. Don't think, or judge. Just listen."

"And then what?"

"And then," he said, "you can make up your mind. Fair enough, right?"

This did seem fair to me, in fact. Whether it was a song, a person, or a story, there was a lot you couldn't know from just an excerpt, a glance, or part of a chorus. "Yeah," I said, sliding it back to the bottom the stack. "Okay."

"Grace," my father said, glancing at his watch again. "It's time to go."

"Andrew, I know. I'm almost ready." My mother bustled across the kitchen, picking up her purse and putting it over her shoulder. "Now, Annabel, I'm leaving money for pizza tonight, and tomorrow you girls can make whatever you want. I just went shopping, so there's plenty of food. Okay?"

I nodded, as my dad shifted in the doorway.

"Now," my mom said, "what did I do with my keys?"

"You don't need your keys," my father told her. "I'm driving."

"And I'm going to be in Charleston all day tomorrow and

half of Monday while you're in meetings," she replied, putting her purse down again and starting to dig through it. "I might need to get out of the hotel for a while."

My father, who by my count had already been standing in the open door to the garage for a full twenty minutes, leaned against the doorjamb, exhaling loudly. It was Saturday morning, and my parents were supposed to have left for South Carolina for the long weekend, and some big architecture conference, ages ago. "Then you can use mine," he told her, but she ignored him and began taking stuff out of her purse, laying her wallet, a pack of Kleenex, and her cell phone on the counter. "Grace. Come on." She didn't budge.

When my dad had first proposed this trip, he'd pitched it as a great getaway to one of their very favorite cities. When he was in meetings, she could shop and see the sights, and in the evenings, they'd eat at the best restaurants and enjoy some quality time together. It had sounded great to me, but my mother had hesitated, not sure she wanted to leave me and Whitney alone. Especially since Whitney had been in a worse mood than usual since the week before, when she'd started a new therapy group. Against her wishes. With, in her words, a "freak."

"Whitney, please," my mother had said one night at dinner, when the subject first came up. "Dr. Hammond thinks this group could really help you."

"Dr. Hammond is an idiot," Whitney replied. My father shot her a look, but if she saw this, she ignored it. "I know people who have worked with this woman, Mom. She's a nutcase."

"I find that hard to believe," my dad said.

"Believe it. She's not even a real psychiatrist. A lot of the doctors in my program think she's way out there. Her methods are really unorthodox."

"Unorthodox how?" he asked.

"Dr. Hammond," my mom said, and this time, Whitney rolled her eyes at his name, "says that this woman, Moira Bell, has had great success with many of his patients *because* she takes a different approach."

"I'm still not getting what's so different about this woman," my dad said.

"She does a lot of hands-on exercises," my mother told him. "It's not just sitting and talking."

"You want an example?" Whitney put down her fork. "Janet, this girl I know from the hospital? When she was in Moira Bell's group, she had to learn how to make fire."

My mother looked confused. "Make fire?"

"Yeah. Moira gave her two sticks, and her assignment was to rub them together until she made fire. Until she could make fire consistently, every time she did it."

"And what, exactly," my dad said, "was the purpose of this exercise?"

Whitney shrugged, picking up her fork again. "Janet said it was supposed to have something to do with being self-sufficient. She also said Moira Bell was crazy."

"That does sound different," my mother said. She looked worried, like she was picturing Whitney burning the entire house down.

"I'm just saying," Whitney said, "that it's going to be a waste of time."

"Give it a try," my dad told her. "Then make up your mind."

Her mind, though, had clearly already been made up, at least judging by how the rest of the night went—all her typical slamming, sighing, and sulking tacked up a notch. The next day, after attending the group as scheduled, she'd come back in one of the worst moods yet. Now, she'd been back twice, and while she hadn't yet burned down the house, my mother was still nervous. I kind of was as well, since I was the one stuck behind with her.

My dad, though, felt it was time to trust Whitney with more responsibility. She'd never be independent if my mother kept hovering, he said, and they'd only be gone for two days. He'd even called Dr. Hammond, who signed off on the arrangement. Still, my mother wasn't convinced, which was why she was stalling now, going through her purse contents yet again as my father glanced at his watch.

"I just don't understand," she said, opening the purse wider. "I had them last night, and I can't imagine where they've gotten to. . . ."

Just then, I heard the front door shut. A moment later, Whitney came around the corner, wearing yoga pants, a T-shirt, and sneakers, her hair pulled back in a ponytail. In one hand, she was carrying a bag from Home & Garden. In the other, my mother's keys.

"Ah," my father said, walking over to my mom. "Mystery solved." He picked up the purse, pushing everything on the counter back into it. "Let's go. Before we lose anything else."

They went, finally, and I watched from the kitchen table as

they backed up the driveway. The last glimpse I got of my mom, she was turning her head to look back at the house as they drove away.

Once they were gone, I pushed out my chair, standing up, then looked over Whitney, who was messing with whatever she'd bought at Home & Garden, her brow furrowed as she studied the bag's contents. "Well," I said. "I guess it's just the two of us."

"What?" she said, not looking up at me.

All around me, the house felt empty. Quiet. It was going to be a long weekend. "Nothing," I told her. "Never mind."

Luckily, I had other things to do besides be ignored by my sister. Well, one thing.

The Lakeview Mall Fall Fashion Show was the next weekend, and that afternoon, I had to go to a meeting about the rehearsal schedule. When I got to Kopf's, it was in the midst of a typically hectic Saturday, complete with an in-store appearance by a pop singer named Jenny Reef, who was doing a promotion with, of all things, Mooshka Surfwear. The juniors department was packed with girls, a long line snaking all the way back to lingerie while a bouncy pop song played on a constant loop from a nearby boom box.

"Annabel!"

I turned around, and there was Mallory Armstrong. She was smiling big and coming toward me at a fast clip, her progress impeded somewhat by the poster, CD, and camera she was carrying. Following behind her at a more leisurely pace was her mom, whom I recognized from the day I'd dropped Owen at his house. "Hi!" Mallory said. "I can't believe it—are you a Jenny Reef fan, too?"

"Um," I said as another throng of girls rushed past us to get in line, "not really. I had to come in for a meeting. . . ."

"For the Models?"

"Yeah," I said, "actually. We have this fashion show next weekend."

"The Fall Fashion Show. I know! I'm so excited, I'm totally coming," she said. "Can you believe Jenny Reef is, like, here? She signed my poster!"

She unrolled it so I could see. Sure enough, there was Jenny Reef, looking very surferesque and Californian, posing on a beach. There was a guitar stuck in the sand on one side of her, a surfboard on the other. Written beneath it, in black sharpie, it said: TO MALLERY. HANG TEN WITH ME AND MOOSHKA SURFWEAR. LOVE, JENNY.

"Wow," I said as her mom walked up to us. "That's cool."

"And I got a free CD and a picture!" Mallory said, bouncing slightly on the balls of her feet. "I wanted to get a Mooshka T-shirt, too, but . . ."

"But you already have a thousand T-shirts," her mom finished for her. Looking at her, I could see where Owen got his height: She was taller than me, with dark hair pulled back at the neck, and was wearing jeans and a knitted pullover. I took a quick glance at her shoes, noting that they were not pointy, and wondered if they were vegan. "Hi," she said to me. "I'm Teresa Armstrong. And you are?"

"Mom!" Mallory shook her head. "This is Annabel Greene, I can't believe you don't recognize her."

"I'm sorry," Mrs. Armstrong said. "Should I?"

"No," I said.

"Yes," Mallory said, turning to her mom. "Annabel's from the Kopf's commercial, the one I'm, like, obsessed with?"

"Ah," her mom said, smiling politely. "Right."

"And she's friends with Owen. *Good* friends."

"Really," Mrs. Armstrong said, sounding surprised. She smiled at me. "Well. That's nice."

"Annabel's in the fashion show I was telling you about next weekend," Mallory explained. To me she said, "Mom isn't very into fashion. But I'm trying to educate her."

"And I," Mrs. Armstrong said with a sigh, "am trying to get Mallory more interested in issues, and less in pop stars and clothes."

"Hard to do," I said.

"Almost impossible." She pushed her purse farther up onto her shoulder. "But I'm doing my best."

"Hello Kopf's shoppers!" a voice suddenly boomed from a speaker overhead. "Thank you for coming out today for our exclusive in-store appearance by Jenny Reef, sponsored by Mooshka Surfwear! Please join us in a few minutes, at one o'clock, when Jenny will perform her newest single, 'Becalmed,' in the Kopf's Café, located adjacent to the men's department. We'll see you there!"

"Did you hear that? She's performing!" Mallory grabbed her mom's hand. "We *have* to stay."

"We can't," Mrs. Armstrong told her. "We have to be at the women's center at one thirty for group."

"Mom," Mallory groaned. "Please not today. Please?"

"We have a mother-daughter discussion group," Mrs. Armstrong explained to me. "Once a week, we get together, six moms and six girls, and discuss issues that are pertinent to our personal growth. The group is led by this wonderful women's studies professor from the university, Boo Connell? It's really—"

"So totally boring," Mallory finished for her. "Last week I fell asleep."

"Which was very unfortunate, because the topic was menstruation," Mrs. Armstrong said. "It's a manifestation of many changes and beginnings for women. . . . The discussion was really fascinating."

Mallory gasped. "Mom! You are not talking about getting your period with Annabel Greene!"

"Menstruation is nothing to be embarrassed about, sweetie," her mom said as Mallory flushed a deeper shade of pink. "I'm sure even models get their periods."

Mallory put a hand to her face. "Oh," she said, "my God." Then she closed her eyes, as if she wanted to disappear, or maybe was pretending she already had.

"I should go," I said, the voice coming over the loudspeaker again. "It was, um, nice to meet you."

"You, too," Mrs. Armstrong said.

I smiled at Mallory, who was still standing there looking mortified. "See you later," I said.

She nodded. "Okay. Bye, Annabel."

I started back toward the conference room. I'd only taken a couple of steps, though, when I heard Mallory hiss, "Mom, I can't believe you did that to me."

"Did what?"

"*Humiliated* me like that," Mallory said. "You owe me an apology."

"Honey," Mrs. Armstrong said, sighing, "I'm really not clear on what the problem is. Maybe if you . . ."

I didn't get to hear the rest, as I was passing through the cosmetics department, where a mob of women were getting makeovers, and their voices drowned everything out. When I reached the conference room, though, I turned back to see Mallory and her mom were still where I'd left them. Mrs. Armstrong had squatted down in front of her daughter and was listening, nodding occasionally, as Mallory spoke.

Inside the conference room, I could hear Mrs. McMurty telling everyone to quiet down, that it was time to get started. Still, I stayed where I was a moment longer, watching as Mrs. Armstrong finally stood and she and Mallory started toward the exit. Mallory didn't look particularly happy, but when, after a few steps, her mom reached down for her fingers, she didn't pull away. Instead, she wrapped her hand around her mom's, quickening her pace, and they walked out the doors together.

When I got home later that afternoon, Whitney was out on the front steps. There was a row of four small flowerpots lined up in front of her, a bag of potting soil beside them, and she was sitting there, a small shovel in one hand, with an annoyed expression on her face.

"Hi," I said as I headed up the walk toward her. "What are you doing?"

She didn't answer me at first, instead just ripping open the potting-soil bag and plunging the shovel in. But then, as I stepped around her, toward the door, she said, "I have to plant herbs."

I stopped walking. "Herbs?"

"Yeah." She scooped some thick soil out of the bag, dropping it into one of the tiny pots with a thunk, some spilling over the sides. "For my stupid therapy group."

"Why herbs?"

"Who knows?" She filled another pot, just as messily, then reached up, wiping her face. "This is what Mom and Dad are paying Moira Bell one fifty an hour for, to tell me to grow some freaking rosemary." She picked up a stack of seed packets from beside her foot, flipping through them. "And basil. And oregano. And thyme. Money well spent, right?"

"It does seem kind of weird," I said.

"Because it *is*," she replied, scooping out more dirt for the third pot. "It's also stupid and a waste of time and not going to work. It's almost winter. You can't grow stuff in winter."

"Did you tell her that?"

"I tried to. But she doesn't care. She doesn't care about anything except making sure she makes you look like an ass." She dumped dirt into the last pot, making it wobble, but it didn't fall over. "'You can grow them inside,' she said, all chirpy. 'Just find a sunny window.' Yeah, right. I'll kill these things in days. And even if I don't, what the hell am I supposed to do with a bunch of herbs?"

I watched as she picked up the basil packet, ripping it open, and dumped out some seeds into her hand. "Well," I said, "you can use them to cook, or something."

She'd been about to plant the seeds, but now she looked up at me, her expression flat, unreadable. "Cook," she repeated. "Right."

I felt my face flush. Again, I'd managed to say something wrong, even when I hadn't really thought I'd said anything at all. Thankfully, the phone began to ring inside, and I headed to get it, grateful for a reason to shut a door between us.

By the time I reached the kitchen, the machine had already picked up. There was a beep, and then Kirsten came on.

"Hello?" she said, her voice loud, as always. "Anybody there? It's me, pick up if you are. . . . God, where is everyone? And I had good news, too. . . ."

I picked up the receiver. "What good news?"

"Annabel! Hi!" Her voice jumped a couple of octaves, a marked contrast to Whitney's flat monotone. I sat down, getting comfortable—if Kirsten's messages were long, actually being on the phone with her could kill an entire afternoon. "I'm so glad you're home, how are you?"

"Okay," I said, sliding my chair a bit to the right. Looking across the dining room, I could see Whitney shaking seeds into a flowerpots, her brow wrinkled as she concentrated. "How are you?"

"Fabulous." Of course she was. "You know that filmmaking class I was telling you about? The one I'm taking this semester?"

"Yeah," I said.

"Well," she continued, "we had to do a five-minute short for our midterm grade, right? They only pick two to be shown for this, like, showcase night that everyone goes to. And mine got picked!"

"That's great," I said. "Congratulations."

"Thank you." She laughed. "I have to tell you, I know it's just this school thing but I am so psyched. This class, and the communications one I'm taking . . . I mean, they've just really changed the way I look at things. Like Brian says, I'm learning to tell, but also to show. And I—"

"Wait," I said. "Who's Brian?"

"The TA in my communications course. He helps the professor run the class, and handles the smaller discussion group I'm in on Fridays. He's amazing, just so smart. God! Anyway, I'm really proud of this piece I did, but now I have to get up and introduce it next weekend in front of everyone. I am so nervous I can't even tell you."

"Nervous?" Of all the adjectives I would have used to describe my sister, this would never have been one of them. "You?"

"Well, yeah," she said. "Annabel, I have to get up and talk about my film in front of total strangers."

"You used to get up and walk in front of strangers," I pointed out. "In bathing suits, even."

"Oh, that's different," she said.

"How?"

"Because that's just . . ." She trailed off, sighing. "This is personal. Real. You know?"

"Yeah," I said, although I wasn't sure I did, really. "I guess."

"Anyway, it's a week from today. So you'll have to think good thoughts for me. Okay?"

"Sure," I said. "So . . . what's it about?"

"My short?"

"Yeah."

"Oh. Well, it's kind of hard to explain. . . ." she said before, of course, commencing to do just that. "Basically, though, it's about me. And Whitney."

I looked outside again at Whitney, who was ripping open another seed packet, wondering how she'd react to this. "Really," I said.

"I mean, it's a fictional thing, of course," she said. "But it's based on that time when we were kids, out on our bikes, and she broke her arm. Remember? I had to ride her home on my handlebars?"

I thought for a second. "Yeah," I said. "Wasn't that . . . "

"Your birthday," she said. "Your ninth birthday. Dad missed the party to take her to the hospital. She got back with her cast just in time for cake."

"Right." It was coming back to me. "I do remember that, actually."

"Well, it's basically about that. But different. It's hard to explain. I can e-mail it to you, if you want. I mean, I'm still tinkering with it, but you could get the general idea."

"I'd love to see it," I said.

"You'll have to tell me if it's terrible, though."

"I'm sure it isn't."

"I guess I'll find out on Saturday." She sighed. "Anyway,

look, I better go. I just wanted to tell you guys about it. Everything okay there?"

I looked out at Whitney again. She'd put another layer of soil into the pots and had now picked up a hose to water them, her eyes narrowed as the drops sputtered out. "Yeah," I said. "Everything's fine."

As I hung up the phone, I heard the front door open. A moment later, when I crossed through the foyer, Whitney was lining her flowerpots up in the dining-room window. I stood in the archway, watching her arrange them on the sill in a neat row, brushing off their rims with her fingers. When she was done, she stood up, planting her hands on her hips. "Oh, well," she said. "Here goes nothing."

"Or not," I said.

She glanced over at me, and I wondered if she was going to snap at me or make a typically sarcastic remark. "We'll see," she said, then dropped her hands and started toward the kitchen.

As she turned on the faucet and began washing her hands, I walked over to the window to look at the flowerpots. The dirt in them was black and fragrant, spotted with fertilizer, and I could see beads of water here and there, glinting in the sunlight. Maybe it was a stupid exercise, and you couldn't grow things in winter. But there was something I liked about the idea of those seeds, buried so deep, having at least a chance to emerge. Even if you couldn't see it beneath the surface, molecules were bonding, energy pushing up slowly, as something worked so hard, all alone, to grow.

Chapter
TEП

By that afternoon, my mother had already left two messages: one letting us know they'd arrived at their hotel, and the other reminding me where she'd left the pizza money, a subtle hint to make sure that we (i.e., Whitney) ate dinner. *Message received,* I thought as I walked down to the kitchen. The money was on the counter with a list of several places that delivered. My mother was nothing if not prepared.

"Whitney?" I called up the stairs. No answer. Which didn't mean she wasn't there, just that she probably didn't feel like responding. "I'm ordering the pizza. Is cheese okay?"

Another silence. *Fine,* I thought. *Cheese it is.* I picked a number at random and dialed.

After ordering, I headed up to my room and settled in to listen to the discs Owen had made me, beginning with one entitled PROTEST SONGS (ACOUSTIC AND WORLD). I made it through three tracks about unions before nodding off, only to wake up with a start when I heard the doorbell ring.

I sat up just as Whitney passed my room and padded down the stairs to answer it. After brushing my teeth, I followed her.

When I got to the foyer, she was standing at the door, which was open, blocking my view of both her and whoever was on the other side. Still, I could hear their voices.

". . . not so much their newer stuff, but the earlier albums," she was saying. "I have a couple of imports I got from a friend that are awesome."

"Really," another, deeper voice—a guy—replied. "UK imports, or somewhere else?"

"UK, I think. I'd have to check."

Maybe it was because I'd just woken up, but there was something familiar about some part of this scene, although I couldn't put my finger on exactly what it was.

"What do I owe you again?" Whitney asked.

"Eleven eighty-seven," the guy replied.

"Here's a twenty. Just give me five back."

"Thanks." I took another step. Now, I was sure I knew that voice. "The thing about Ebb Tide," it continued, "is that they're really an acquired taste."

"Totally," Whitney said.

"I mean, most people don't even . . ."

I stepped around the door, and sure enough, it was Owen. Standing there on the mat in front of my door, earphones dangling around his neck, counting out dollar bills into my sister's hand She was nodding as he spoke and looking at him with a much warmer expression than she'd given me in, oh, a year. When he saw me, he smiled.

"See," he said to Whitney, "case in point. Annabel is *not* an Ebb Tide fan. She hates techno, in fact."

Whitney looked at me, then back at Owen again, clearly confused. "She does?"

"Yup. Despite my best efforts to convince her otherwise," he said. "She's very stubborn, once she's made up her mind. Totally honest, totally opinionated. But I guess you already know that."

Whitney just looked at me as he said this, and I knew what she was thinking: that this was not me at all, not by a long shot. It didn't sound exactly right to me either, but for some reason, her incredulousness bothered me.

"Anyway," he said now, bending down to the plastic carrier at his feet and unzipping it to pull out a pizza box. "Here you go. Enjoy it."

Whitney nodded, still looking at me, and took it from him. "Thanks," she said. "Have a good night."

"You, too," Owen replied as Whitney turned, walking into the dining room toward the kitchen.

I stepped into the center of the open doorway, watching Owen as he shoved the wad of money in his hand into his pocket, then picked up the carrier. He had on jeans and a red T-shirt that said SLICE O'CHEESE! Of all the numbers for pizza places my mom left me, I'd called this one. Who knew? But I had to admit, I was happy to see him.

"Your sister," he said to me now, "is an Ebb Tide fan. She has *imports*."

"And that's good?"

"*Very* good," he replied. "It's almost enlightened. Imports take effort."

"Do you talk about music with every single person you meet?"

"No," he said. I just looked at him. Behind me, I heard Whitney cut on the TV.

"Well, not always. In this case, I had on my earphones, and she asked me what I was listening to."

"And it just so happened to be a band she knows and loves."

"That's the universality of music," he said cheerfully, switching the carrier to his other arm. "It's a bonding thing. It brings people together. Friend and foe. Old and young. Me and your sister. And—"

"Me and your sister," I finished for him. "And your mom."

"My mom?" he asked.

"I met her today, at the mall. At the Jenny Reef thing."

His face fell. "You went to see *Jenny Reef*?"

"I *love* Jenny Reef," I said, and he winced. "She's much better than Ebb Tide."

"That," he said, his voice serious, "is not *even* funny."

"What's wrong with Jenny Reef?" I said.

"Everything is wrong with Jenny Reef!" he shot back. *Here we go*, I thought. "Did you even *see* the poster she signed for Mallory? With the product plug in her autograph? I mean, it's so abhorrent that anyone could consider themselves an artist and then sell out so completely to the corporate machine, in the name of—"

"Okay, okay, calm down," I said, figuring I should fess up before he popped a vein. "I didn't go to see Jenny Reef. I had a meeting for the Models at Kopf's."

He sighed, shaking his head. "Thank God. You had me worried there for a second."

"What happened to there being no right and wrong in music?" I asked him. "Or does that not apply to teenage pop stars?"

"It applies," he said flatly. "You're entitled to an opinion about Jenny Reef. It would just dismay me if you were really a fan."

"But have you really given her a chance? Remember," I said, holding up my hand, "don't think or judge. Just listen."

He made a face at me. "I *have* listened to Jenny Reef. Not necessarily by choice, but I have. And my opinion is that she's a publicity whore who has allowed her music, if that's even what you want to call it, to be hijacked and compromised in the name of materialism and big business."

"Well," I said. "As long you don't feel too strongly about it."

Suddenly I heard a low buzz, and he reached around to his back pocket, pulling out a cell phone, glancing at the screen. "Pie up, gotta go," he said, stuffing the carrier under his arm. "You know, as much as you might want me to, I can't just stand here and argue with you about music all night."

"No?" I said.

"No." He stepped back from the door. "However, if you want to continue this discussion some other time, I'd be more than happy to do so."

"Like Tuesday?"

"Sounds good." He started down the steps. "I'll see you then, okay?"

I nodded. "Bye, Owen."

"And don't forget the show tomorrow!" he called out over his shoulder as he headed for his truck. "We're doing all techno. A full hour of dripping faucets."

"Are you joking?"

"Maybe. You'll have to listen to find out, though."

I smiled, then stood there, watching him as he climbed inside the Land Cruiser. He turned the stereo on first, then put the car in gear. Of course.

When I got to the living room, Whitney was settled on the couch, drinking a bottled water. The pizza was on the counter. She didn't say anything, her eyes on the TV—which was showing something about a sitcom actress who'd had a cocaine problem—as I helped myself to a plate and a slice and sat down at the table in the kitchen.

"Are you . . ." I began, then stopped myself. "Aren't you hungry?"

She kept her eyes on the TV as she said, "I'll eat in a minute."

Fine, I thought. My mother wouldn't be happy, but then again she wasn't here. And I was starving. As I began to take a bite, though, Whitney muted the TV and said, "So how do you know that guy?"

"He goes to my school," I said, then swallowed. She was watching me, so I added, "We're friends."

"Friends," she repeated.

I thought of Mrs. Armstrong's surprised smile as she reacted to this same word, hours earlier. "Yeah," I said. "We sometimes hang out at lunch."

She nodded. "Is he friends with Sophie, too?"

"No," I said. I didn't know why, but instantly, my guard was up, and I wondered why she was asking this. Or, actually, why we were even talking at all, when she'd been the one who'd been so resistant to my attempts at conversation all day long. But then I remembered her face when Owen had described me as honest, how clear it was this surprised her, so I added, "I'm not really friends with Sophie these days."

"You're not?"

"No."

"What happened?"

Why do you care? I wanted to ask. Instead, I said, "We had a fight last spring. It got kind of ugly. . . . We don't really talk."

"Oh," she said.

I looked back down at my plate, wondering why I had suddenly decided to share this with Whitney, of all people. It seemed like a mistake, and I sat there, waiting for her to say something snarky or mean, but she didn't. Instead, she just turned back to the TV, and a moment later, I heard the volume come on.

On the screen, the actress was now telling her story, dabbing her eyes with a Kleenex as she did so. I looked from her to Whitney, who was sitting in my father's chair. Who knew she was an Ebb Tide fan, that she had imports, that she was possibly, in Owen's view anyway, enlightened? On the other hand, though, it wasn't like she knew that much about me, either. Maybe we could have remedied this over a long weekend, but we weren't. Instead, we just sat there, together but really apart, watching a show about a stranger and all her secrets, while keeping our own to ourselves, as always.

The next morning, Owen kicked off his show with a techno song that went on, no joke, for a full eight and a half minutes. All of which I spent telling myself that I was fully entitled to go back to sleep, and yet somehow not able to do so.

"That was Prickle with 'Velveteen,'" he said, when it was finally over. "Off of their second disc, *The Burning*, which is probably one of the best techno records ever released. Hard to believe some people don't even like that kind of music, isn't it? You're listening to Anger Management. Got a request? Call us at 555–WRUS. Here's Snakeplant."

I rolled my eyes, but didn't roll over. Instead, I listened to the entire show, as was my habit now, while Owen played some rockabilly, some Gregorian chants, and a song in Spanish he described as "like Astrid Gilberto, and yet not." Whatever that meant. Finally, in the last few moments before eight o'clock, I heard the beginning of notes of a song that sounded familiar. Although why I wasn't sure until he came on again.

"This has been Anger Management, here on your community radio station, WRUS, 89.9. We'll wrap up today with a long-distance dedication to a regular listener, to whom we say: Look, don't be ashamed of the music you love. Even if, in our humble opinion, it's not really music at all. We know why you really went to the mall yesterday. See you next week!"

Only then did it hit me: It was the Jenny Reef song, the one they'd been playing nonstop at the mall the day before. As it began, I sat up, grabbing for my phone.

"WRUS, Community Radio."

"I did not go to the mall to see Jenny Reef," I said. "I told you that yesterday."

"Are you not enjoying the song?"

"Actually," I said, "I am. It's better than just about everything else you played."

"Funny."

"I'm not joking."

"I'm sure you aren't," he said. "Which, frankly, is just plain sad."

"Almost as sad as you playing Jenny Reef on your show. What is this, all the hits with none of the lip?"

"It was meant to be ironic!"

I smiled, reaching up to tuck a piece of hair behind my ear. "Just keep telling yourself that."

He sighed loudly, the noise filling the receiver. "Enough about Jenny Reef. Answer me this. How do you feel about bacon?"

"Bacon?" I repeated. "Which song was that?"

"It's not a song. It's a food. You know, bacon? Pork product? Sizzles in a frying pan?"

I actually pulled the phone away from my ear, looked at it, then put it back.

"What do you say? You up for it?" he was saying.

"Up for what?" I asked.

"Breakfast."

"Now?" I said, glancing at the clock.

"What, you have plans already?"

"Well, no, but—"

"Cool. Pick you up in twenty minutes."

And then he just hung up. I put the phone back on its base, then turned, looking at myself in the mirror over my bureau. *Twenty minutes*, I thought. *Okay.*

In nineteen and a half, I'd managed to shower, throw on some clothes, and get out to my front stoop, where I was waiting when Owen pulled into the driveway. Whitney was still asleep, allowing me to forgo an explanation, which was handy since I didn't exactly have one. As I walked over to the car, Rolly, who was in the front passenger seat, pushed open his door and got out, leaving it open for me.

"You remember Rolly, right?" Owen said.

"Yeah," I said, as he nodded at me. "But you don't have to move. I can sit in back."

"It's no problem," he told me, climbing into the backseat. "Besides, I have to make sure I have all my gear for later."

"Gear?" I said as I got in, shutting the door behind me. Owen gestured for me to put on my seat belt, which I did, letting him work the hammer to get it buckled.

"For work. I've got to do a class today," Rolly explained. As I turned around, I saw he was holding the same red helmet he'd been wearing the first time I saw him. Also on the seat were several pads of all sizes: a large one that looked like something an umpire would wear, several that were tube-shaped, and some thick gloves. "It's an intermediate level. Gotta make sure I'm well covered."

"Right," I said as Owen shifted into reverse, backing out of my driveway. "So, how do you end up with a job like that?"

"Same way as most," he replied, putting the pad down. "I

answered an ad. Initially, I was just helping out answering phones and enrolling people for classes. But then one guy got a groin injury and quit, so I got promoted to attacker."

"Or demoted," Owen said. "Depending on how you look at it."

"Oh, no," Rolly told him, shaking his head. He had a really sweet face, I was noticing. Where Owen was big and broad, more the attacker style, Rolly was smaller and wiry, with bright blue eyes. "Attacking is *much* better than clerical work."

"It is?" I asked.

"Sure. I mean, for one, it's exciting," he said. "And another, you really get to meet people on such a personal level. There's a real bonding in someone beating the crap out of you."

I glanced over at Owen, who was switching gears with one hand and adjusting the stereo with the other. "You can look at me all you want," he said, keeping his eyes on the road. "I am not commenting on that."

"Fighting brings people together," Rolly said. "In fact, a lot of the women who take my classes come up and hug me afterwards. People connect with me. It's happened tons of times."

"But only once," Owen added, "that really mattered."

Rolly sighed. "True," he said. "Very true."

"Meaning what?" I asked.

"Rolly's in love with a girl who punched him in the face," Owen explained.

"Not the face," Rolly corrected him. "The neck."

"Apparently," Owen told me, "she has a mad right hook."

"It was impressive," Rolly agreed. "It was at this expo I worked, at the mall? We had a table, you know, and people could enter a drawing for a free class, and take a hit at me, for fun."

Owen put on his turn signal, shaking his head.

"Anyway," Rolly continued, "she comes up with some friends, and Delores—that's my boss—starts her spiel about the classes and invites them to hit me. Her friends won't do it, but she steps right up. Looks me in the eye. And wham! Right in the collarbone."

"You had your pads on, though, right?" I said.

"Of course!" he said. "I'm a professional. But still, even through the pads, you can tell when someone packs a wallop. And this girl did. Plus, she was gorgeous. Lethal combination. But before I can even say anything, she just smiles at me, says thanks, and walks away. Gone. Just like that. I never even got her name."

We were merging onto the highway now, picking up speed. "Wow," I said. "That is quite a story."

"Yeah," he said, nodding, his expression solemn. He put his hands on top of the helmet in his lap, folding them carefully. "I know."

Owen rolled down his window, letting some air in. Then he took in a deep breath. "Oh, yeah," he said. "We're almost there."

I turned around; all I could see was highway. "Where?"

"Two words," Owen said. "Double bacon."

Five minutes later, we were pulling into the parking lot of the World of Waffles, a twenty-four-hour breakfast place right off the interstate. *So they like breakfast*, I thought. Then the breeze shifted, and suddenly I smelled it: bacon. The scent was pungent, heavy, and inescapable.

"Oh my God," I said as we headed inside. Owen and Rolly were taking deep, full breaths on either side of me. "That is—"

"Great, I know," Owen said. "It didn't used to be like this. I mean, they had bacon, but not at this level. But then this new place opened up on the other side of the highway—"

"The Morning Café," Rolly said, wrinkling his nose. "So subpar. Famously soggy pancakes."

"—and they had to get competitive. So now, every day is Double Bacon Day." He stepped up, pulling the door open for me. "Great, right?"

I nodded, then stepped inside. The first thing I noticed was that the smell was stronger, if that was even possible. The second was that the room, which was small and crammed with tables and booths, was freezing.

"Oh," Owen said once he glanced over and saw I had my arms wrapped around myself. "Forgot to warn you about the cold thing. Here." He shrugged off the jacket he was wearing, handing it to me. I started to protest, but he said, "They keep it cold so people don't stay too long. Believe me, if you're chilly now, you'll be frozen in ten minutes. Take it."

I did, then slipped it on. Of course it was huge on me, the cuffs completely covering my hands. I pulled it tighter around me as we followed a tall, slim waitress whose name tag said DEANN to a booth by the window. Behind us, a woman was quietly nursing a baby, her head ducked down. On our other side, there was a couple about our age eating waffles, both in running clothes: The girl had blonde hair and an elastic around her wrist, while the guy was taller and darker, the bottom part of a tattoo just visible under his shirtsleeve.

"I recommend the chocolate-chip pancakes," Rolly told me after Deann had brought coffee and left us to examine the menu. "With lots of butter and syrup. And bacon."

"Ugh," Owen said. "I keep it basic: eggs, bacon, biscuit. Done."

Pork seemed to be required, so when Deann returned I ordered a waffle and, yes, bacon. Although I wasn't sure I needed it; I felt like I'd already eaten an entire side just by breathing.

"So you guys do this every week," I said, taking a sip of my water.

"Yeah." Owen nodded. "Since the first show. It's a tradition. And Rolly always pays."

"That's not tradition," Rolly said. "It's because I lost a bet."

"How long do you have to pay?"

"Forever," Rolly told me. "I had my chance, and I blew it. And now I pay. Literally."

"It's not really forever," Owen said now, tapping his spoon against his water glass. "Just until you talk to her."

"And when is that going to happen?" Rolly asked.

"The next time you see her."

"Yeah," he said glumly. "The next time."

I looked at Owen. "The girl with the hook," he explained. "In July, we saw her out at a club. First time we ever saw her anywhere. And Rolly'd been talking about her nonstop since she clocked him—"

Rolly flushed. "Not *nonstop*."

"—and here's his chance," Owen finished. "But he can't act."

"The thing is," Rolly said, "I'm a big believer in the perfect moment. They don't come around that often."

This deep thought was punctuated—or interrupted, depending on how you looked at it—by Deann arriving with our food. I had never seen so much bacon in my life; it was crammed around the edge of the waffle, literally falling off my plate.

"So there I am," Rolly said, beginning to butter his pancakes, "trying to figure out an in, and her sweater falls off the back of her chair. It's like it's meant to be, you know? But I freeze up. I can't do it."

Beside me, Owen had already popped a piece of bacon in his mouth and was chewing it while peppering his eggs.

"The thing is," Rolly said, "it's a big deal when you finally get the chance to do the one thing you want to do—need to do—more than anything. It can kind of scare the crap out of you."

He pushed the syrup over to me, and I picked it up, putting some on my waffle. "I bet," I said.

"Which is why," Owen said, "I said that if he picked up the sweater and talked to her, I'd pay for breakfast forever. And if he *didn't* do it, he had to foot the bill."

Rolly took another bite of his pancakes. "I actually got up and started over there. But then she turned around, and I—"

"Choked," Owen said.

"Panicked. She saw me, and I got all flustered, and I kept walking. Now I have to pay for breakfast for eternity. Or, until I actually make good on the bet, which is unlikely because I haven't seen her since."

"Wow," I said. "That's quite a story."

He nodded somberly, just as he had earlier in the car. "Yeah," he said. "I know."

By the time we left an hour later, all the bacon was gone and I was so full I thought I would bust. Back in the car I reached for my seat belt, pulling it across me, then stopped just short of the buckle as Owen slid it in for me, then grabbed the hammer again. His hands were right at my waist as he tapped its center, his head ducked down by my shoulder. I looked at his dark hair, the sprinkle of freckles by his ear, those long lashes, but then he was already done, pulling away.

All the way into town, I watched Rolly in the side mirror as he put on his padding for work: first the big chest piece, then the tubes on his arms and legs, gradually growing more substantial and less recognizable in front of my eyes. He put on the helmet just as we pulled up to the strip mall where EmPOWerment! was located.

"Thanks for the ride," he said, opening the door and easing himself down to the ground. The padding on his legs was so thick he had to take short, halting steps, his arms held out to his sides. "I'll call you later."

"Sounds good," Owen told him.

As we drove home, the scenery blurring past, I thought back to that first day, and how strange it had been to find myself with him. Now it was almost normal. Outside, the neighborhood was quiet, a few sprinklers going, a man in his robe padding out down the driveway to pick up his paper, and I found myself remembering what Rolly had said earlier about the perfect moment. This seemed like one, suddenly, the right time to say something to Owen. To thank him, maybe, or just to let him know how much his friendship had meant to me in the last couple of weeks. But just as I was getting up the nerve to say something, he beat me to it.

"So. Have you listened to any of the CDs I burned for you?"

"Yeah," I said as we turned onto my street. "I actually started the protest song one yesterday."

"And?"

"Fell asleep," I told him. He winced. "But I was really tired. I'll try it again and let you know."

"No rush," he said, pulling up in front of my house. "These things take time."

"No kidding. You gave me a lot to listen to."

"Ten CDs," he replied, "is not a lot. It's barely a smattering."

"Owen. It's, like, a hundred and forty songs. Minimum."

"If you want a real education," he continued, ignoring this, "you can't just sit and wait for the music to come to you. You have to go to the music."

"Are you suggesting some sort of pilgrimage?"

I was joking. Judging by the serious look on his face, however, he was not. "You could call it that," he said.

"Uh-oh," I said, sitting back in my seat. "What would *you* call it?"

"Going to a club to see a band," he replied. "A good band. Live. Next weekend."

The first thing that popped into my mind was a question: *Are you asking me out?* The second, following rapidly behind, was that if I actually asked it, he'd answer in full truth, and I was not sure I wanted that. If he said yes, it would be . . . what? Great. And terrifying. If he said no, I'd feel like an idiot.

"A good band," I repeated instead. "Good according to who?"

"To me, of course."

"Oh."

He raised an eyebrow. "And to *others*, too," he said. "It's Rolly's cousin's band."

"Are they—"

"No. Not techno," he answered flatly. "They're more kind of a loose rock, original songs, somewhat jokey but solidly alternative."

"Wow," I said. "That's quite a description."

"The description means nothing. It's the music that counts," he said. "And the music, you will like. Trust me."

"We'll see," I said, and he smiled. "So when is this loose-rock-original-songs-somewhat-jokey-but-solidly-alternative band playing?"

"Saturday night," he replied. "It's an all-ages show, at Bendo. There's an opener, so they'll go on around nine."

"Okay."

"Okay, as in you'll go?"

"Yeah."

"Cool."

I smiled as, behind him in my house, I saw Whitney appear at the top of the stairs. She had on her pajamas and was yawning, one hand to her mouth, as she started down to the foyer, her shadow stretching across the wall beside her. Once at the bottom of the stairs, she crossed into the dining room, then bent down over her flowerpots in the front window. After a moment, she reached out, pressing down the soil in one of them, then turned another so the opposite side faced the light. Then she sat back on her heels, her hands in her lap, and studied them.

I glanced at Owen, who was watching her as well, and wondered what this looked like to him. From the outside, it had to seem so different from what it really was. Move on to the next house and you'd see something else, another glimpse, another story. This one wasn't even mine to tell, but for whatever reason, I found myself wanting to do it anyway.

"They're herbs," I said to Owen. "She just planted them yesterday. They're, um, part of her therapy."

He nodded. "You said she was sick. What's wrong? If you don't mind my asking."

"She has an eating disorder," I told him.

"Oh."

"She's a lot better than she was," I added. And this was true. In fact, I'd watched her eat two pieces of pizza the night before. Much later than I ate, and only after blotting off any semblance of grease, and then cutting them into many small pieces. But she did eat them, so that had to count for something. "I mean, when we first found out, it was really bad. She was in the hospital for a while last year."

We both watched as Whitney stood up, brushing a piece of hair out of her face. I wondered if she suddenly looked different to Owen, as if knowing this information had changed her to him. I studied his expression, but there was no way to tell.

"That must have been hard," he said, as she turned, starting around the dining-room table. "Watching her go through that."

As Whitney stepped through the archway to the kitchen, she disappeared. A second later, I spotted her again, crossing in front of the island. That was the thing I always forgot about being outside our house, how it seemed like you could see everything, but certain things were blocked out, hidden. "Yeah," I said. "It was. It was awful. It really scared me."

This time, I didn't think about the fact that I was telling the truth. I didn't have that moment when I felt myself take the leap, daring to be honest. Instead, it just happened. Owen turned and looked at me, and I swallowed, hard. Then, as I so often found myself doing when I had his attention, I continued.

"The thing about Whitney," I said, "is that she was always really private. So you never knew if anything was wrong with her. My sister Kirsten, she's the total opposite, the kind of person who always volunteers *too* much information. So, like, when Kirsten was unhappy, you knew it even if you didn't want to. Whereas with Whitney, you had to draw it out of her. Or figure it out some other way."

Owen looked back at the house, but Whitney had disappeared again. "What about you?" he said.

"What about me?"

"How can they tell when something's wrong with you?"

They can't, I thought, but I didn't say this. Couldn't say this. "I don't know," I said. "I guess you'd have to ask them."

A big SUV blew past us then, kicking up a bunch of leaves that had been raked to the curb. As they fluttered across the windshield, I glanced back over at my house to see Whitney climbing the stairs again, a bottled water in her hand. This time, she glanced outside. When she saw us, she slowed her steps, briefly, before continuing on to the landing.

"I should go in," I said, reaching down to undo my seat belt. "Thanks again for breakfast."

"No problem," Owen said. "Don't forget about the pilgrimage, okay? Saturday. Nine o'clock."

"Got it." I opened my door, sliding out, then shut it behind me. As I walked around the front bumper, he cranked the engine, then waved at me. It wasn't until I got halfway down the driveway that I realized I was still wearing his jacket. I whirled around, only to see him taking the corner, a blue blur, disappearing. Too late.

I unlocked the front door, stepping inside, then slid the jacket off, folding it over my arm. There was something clunky in the outside pocket, and I reached in, my fingers groping until they brushed a solid object. Even before I pulled it out, I knew what it was: Owen's iPod. It was nicked and scratched beyond all belief, a faint crack across the screen, his earphones wrapped around it. And despite the cold of the World of Waffles, it was warm in my hand.

"Annabel?"

I jumped, then looked up; Whitney was at the top of the stairs, staring down at me. "Hi," I said.

"You're up early."

"Yeah," I said. "I, um, went out for breakfast."

She narrowed her eyes at me. "When did you leave?"

"A while back," I said, starting up the stairs. As I got to the landing, she stepped aside, just barely, so I had to squeeze past her. I heard her sniff once. Then twice. *Bacon*, I thought.

"I better go start on my homework," I said, heading toward my room.

"Okay," she said slowly. But she stayed where she was, still watching, as I shut my door behind me.

Because I had never once seen Owen without his iPod, I assumed he would notice its absence pretty quickly. So when the phone rang later that afternoon, I picked it up expecting to hear him already in deep music withdrawal. But it wasn't Owen; it was my mother.

"Annabel! Hi!"

When my mother was nervous, her cheerfulness quotient skyrocketed. The line was almost crackling from her forced perkiness. "Hi," I said. "How's your trip going?"

"Just fine," she said. "Right now your father's playing golf, and I just got my nails done. We've been so busy, but I figured I should check in. How are things going?"

This was actually her third call in thirty-six hours. But I played along anyway.

"Good," I said. "Not much is happening."

"How's Whitney?"

"Fine."

"Is she there now?"

"I don't know," I said. I sat up, then got off the bed, walking to my door and opening it. "I can check—"

"Did she go out?" she asked.

"I'm not sure," I said. *God*, I thought. "Hold on." I stepped out into the hallway, then put the phone to my chest, listening for a second. I didn't hear the TV, or any noise from downstairs, so instead I walked a few paces to Whitney's door, which was closed, but not entirely. I knocked, lightly.

"Yeah?"

When I pushed it open, she was sitting on her bed, cross-legged, writing in a notebook in her lap. "Mom's on the phone," I said.

She sighed, then reached out her hand, palm up, and I stepped over, giving her the receiver. "Hello? . . . Hi. . . . Yes, I'm here. . . . I'm fine. . . . Everything's fine. You don't have to keep calling, you know."

Then my mother said something, and Whitney sat back against her headboard. As she listened, offering up a series of mmm-mhms and uh-huhs, I glanced out her window. Even though our rooms were adjacent, her view of the golf course, where a man in checked pants was now taking a practice swing, looked totally different to me, like it might have been another place altogether.

"Yeah, okay," she was saying now, reaching up to smooth a hand over her hair. Looking at her, I thought again how beautiful she was—even in jeans and a T-shirt, no makeup, she was breathtaking. So much so that it was hard to believe she could ever have looked at herself and seen anything else. "I'll tell her. . . . Okay. . . . Bye."

She dropped the phone from her ear, hitting the OFF button. "Mom says she'll see you tomorrow," she said. "They'll be back by dinnertime."

"Oh," I said as she handed the receiver back to me. "Right."

"And we can either eat spaghetti for dinner tonight or go

out." She sat back, pulling her legs up to her chest, then looked at me. "What do you want to do?"

I hesitated, wondering if this was a trick question. "I don't care," I said. "Spaghetti is fine."

"All right. I'll fix it in a little while."

"Okay. I can help, if you want."

"Whatever," she said. "We'll figure it out later." She leaned forward, picking up a pen from beside her foot and uncapping it. I could see now that the top page of the notebook in her lap was filled with her print, and I wondered what she was writing. After a moment, she looked up at me. "What?"

"Nothing," I said, realizing I was still standing there, staring at her. "I'll, um, see you in a bit."

I went back to my room and sat down on my bed, picking up Owen's iPod. It seemed strange, and maybe kind of wrong, to have it here in my room, not to mention in my hands. Still, I found myself unwrapping the earphones, then hitting the power button. After a second, the screen blinked to life. When the menu appeared, I clicked on SONGS.

There were 9,987 to choose from. *Good God*, I thought, as I scrolled down through the list for a minute, titles blurring past. I remembered what he'd said about drowning things out. It was what he'd done during the divorce, but also every day, I realized, when he walked around with his earphones on. Ten thousand songs could fill a lot of silence.

I clicked back to the menu, then scrolled to PLAYLISTS. Another long list popped up: A.M. SHOW 8/12, A.M. SHOW 8/19, CHANTS (IMPORTED). And then: ANNABEL.

I lifted my finger off the button. It was probably just one of the CDs he'd made for me, I thought. But still, I found myself hesitating, the same way I had earlier in the truck. Wanting to know, but not. This time, though, I broke.

When I clicked on the button, the screen changed, pulling up a list of songs. The first one was "Jennifer" by a band called Lipo. Which sounded slightly familiar. As was "Descartes Dream," by Misanthrope, the second song, which I went ahead and clicked on. It only took a moment to recognize it as one of the songs from the first show of Owen's I'd listened to. Not liked, but listened to. And discussed with him afterwards.

They were all there. Every song we'd ever talked or argued about, listed in careful order. The Mayan chants, from the first day he'd given me the ride. "Thank You," by Led Zeppelin, from when I'd picked him up. Entirely too much techno, every thrash metal song. Even Jenny Reef. As I listened to a bit of each, I thought of all the times I'd seen Owen with his earphones on and wondered what he was listening to, much less thinking about. Who would have ever guessed that it might have been me?

I glanced over at the clock—it was 4:55. Owen had to be missing this by now. No big deal. I'd just drive over to his house and drop it off. Easy.

Halfway down the stairs, though, I heard a crash, followed by a muttered "shit." When I poked my head into the kitchen, Whitney was shoving a saucepan back into the cupboard.

"Everything okay?" I asked.

"Fine." She stood up, brushing her hair out of her face. On the island in front of her, there was a jar of pasta sauce, a box of spaghetti, a cutting board with a red pepper and a cucumber on it, and a bag of lettuce. "Are you going out or something?"

"Um," I said. "I was . . . just for a little while. Unless you want me to—"

"No, I'm fine." She picked up a box of spaghetti, her eyes narrowing as she read the back of it.

"Oh. Okay," I said. "Well, I'll be back by—"

"It's just . . ." She put the box down. "I'm not sure which pot I'm supposed to use for pasta."

I put Owen's coat down on the table, then crossed the room to the cabinet next to the stove. "This one," I told her, pulling out the large stock pan and the strainer pot that fit inside of it. "It's easier to drain that way."

"Oh," she said. "Right. Sure."

I carried it to the sink, filling it up with water, and put it on the stove. I could feel her watching me as I turned on the burner. "It'll take a while," I told her. "If you cover it, it cuts down the time some."

She nodded. "Okay."

I walked back over to the chair where I'd left Owen's coat, then stood there, watching, as she took a smaller pot out of the cabinet and put it on the stove. Then she picked up the pasta sauce, popping off the top and dumping it in. All of this she did very slowly and deliberately, as if she were splitting atoms. Which wasn't really all that surprising, as Whitney hardly ever cooked for herself. My mother monitored all her meals, fixed her snacks and sandwiches, even the cereal she ate for breakfast. I realized that if this was weird for me to watch, it had to be really strange for her to do. Especially alone.

"Do you want me to help?" I asked her as she pulled a spoon out of the drawer by the stove and stuck it into the pasta sauce, stirring it tentatively. "I don't mind."

For a minute, she didn't say anything, and I wondered if I'd offended her. But then, not turning around, she said, "Sure. I mean, if you want to."

So that night, for the first time I could remember, I fixed dinner with my sister. We didn't talk much, other than her asking me the occasional question (what temperature to put the oven on for garlic bread, or how much spaghetti to make) and me answering (350, all of it). I set the table while she tackled the salad in her typically slow and methodical way, cutting up the vegetables so carefully and grouping them by color on the cutting board. Once everything was done, Whitney and I sat down together in the dining room, just the two of us. As I slid into my seat, I glanced over at her flowerpots in the windowsill.

"They look good there," I said as she sat down.

"I guess," she replied, picking up her napkin. Her plate was mostly salad, with only a tiny bit of pasta, but I didn't say anything, if only because I knew my mom would have. "Now they just have to actually grow."

I twirled some spaghetti around my fork, then took a bite. "This is good," I told her. "Perfect."

"It's pasta," she said with a shrug. "It's easy."

"Not always," I told her. "If you don't cook it enough, it's crunchy in the middle. And if you cook it too much, it's mushy. It's a fine line."

"Really," she said.

I nodded. For a moment, we were both quiet, just eating. I looked over at the pots again, the golf course beyond, so green it was almost unreal.

"Thank you," Whitney said.

I wasn't sure if this was for the cooking compliment, or the salad, or just sticking around. I didn't care, either. I was just happy to take it, for whatever it was.

"You're welcome," I said, and she nodded, as outside, a car drove past, then slowed, the driver glancing in at us before moving on.

Chapter
ELEVEN

"It's Annabel!"

I had not even taken my finger off Owen's doorbell, but somehow Mallory was already on the other side. Then the knob rattled and the door swung open.

At first, I almost didn't recognize her, as she was wearing an incredible amount of makeup: base, eyeliner and shadow, way too much rouge, and fake eyelashes, one of which was unpasted and sticking to her eyebrow. She also had on a tight, strapless black dress and very high-heeled sandals, on which she was teetering as she gripped the doorknob.

Grouped around her, all staring at me, were four other girls, also dressed and made up: a short, dark-haired girl with glasses, wearing a black dress and wedge heels; two identical redheads with green eyes and freckles, each in jeans and high-cut crop-tops; and a chubby blonde in what looked like a prom dress. In the small space of the doorframe, the smell of hair-spray was overpowering.

"Annabel!" Mallory shrieked, jumping up and down. Her hair, done up high above her head in some sort of faux-Mohawk, did not move. "Hi!"

"Hi," I said. "What are you—"

Before I could finish, she reached out, grabbing my hand and yanking me over the threshold. "You guys," she said as the other girls stepped back, still staring, "oh my God, this is Annabel Greene, can you even believe it?"

The blonde in the prom dress, studying me with her very pink lips pursed, said, "You were in that commercial."

"Duh!" Mallory told her. She reached up, finally adjusting her eyelash. "She's the Kopf's girl. And a Lakeview Model."

"What are you doing here?" one of the redheads asked.

"Well," I said, "I was in the neighborhood, and—"

"She's friends with my brother. *And* with me." Mallory squeezed my hand again, her palm hot against mine. To me she said, "You're just in time for our photo shoot. You can help us with our poses!"

"Actually, I can't stay," I said. "I just stopped in for a second."

This was what I'd told Whitney, too, after dinner. That I had something to bring by a friend's, and I'd be back within the hour. She'd just nodded, although she was looking at me sort of strangely, like she was wondering if I might come home smelling of bacon.

"Do you like my outfit?" Mallory asked now, striking a pose, one hand behind her neck, eyes turned up to the ceiling. She held it for a moment, then resumed her normal standing position. "We're doing all these different looks. I'm Evening Elegant."

"We're Daytime Casual," one of the redheads told me, planting a hand on her hip. Her sister, who had more freckles, nodded, her face solemn.

I looked at the dark-haired girl with the glasses. "Classy Workplace," she mumbled, tugging at her black dress.

"And I," the blonde announced, twirling so her dress swished, "am Fantasy Engagement."

"You are not," Mallory said. "You're Nighttime Formal."

"Fantasy Engagement," the blonde insisted, taking another spin. To me she added, "This dress cost—"

"Four hundred dollars, we know, we know," Mallory said, annoyed. "She thinks she's a big deal just because her sister was a debutante."

"When are we taking pictures?" one of the redheads asked. "I'm tired of being Daytime Casual; I want to wear a dress."

"In a second!" Mallory snapped, irritated. "First Annabel has to see my room. Then she can advise us on our looks."

She started to pull me toward the stairs, the other girls clomping along behind us. "Is Owen here?" I asked.

"Somewhere," she said as we started up the steps. The dark-haired girl was beside me now, studying me with a serious expression, while the other three whispered behind me. "You should see the pictures we took last time at Michelle's, they were so good! I had this one where I was European Flair? It was fabulous."

"European Flair?" I asked.

She nodded. "I wore a beret and a plaid skirt, and posed with a loaf of French bread. It was awesome."

"I want to be European Flair," the girl in black said. "This dress is boring. And how come you always get to be Evening Elegant?"

"Just wait a second!" Mallory hissed as we came up on a

closed door. She stepped in front of it, clasping her hands to her chest. "Okay," she said. Her eyelash had come loose again. "Prepare yourself for the ultimate model experience."

This did not sound very promising. I glanced behind me; the other girls were all staring at me, still. I turned back to Mallory. "All right," I said slowly.

She reached down, twisting the knob, then pushed the door open. "Here it is," she said. "Can you believe it?"

I couldn't. The wall in front of me, like the ones on either side, was covered from top to bottom with pictures from magazines. Model after model, ad after ad, celebrity after celebrity. There were blondes, brunettes, redheads. High fashion, prom fashion, casual fashion, showbiz fashion. One beautiful, high-cheekboned face after another, striking a pose this way, that way, every possible way. There were so many pictures, cut out and edges overlapping, that you couldn't even see the wall behind them.

"Well?" Mallory said. "What do you think?"

Truth be told, it was all completely overwhelming, even before she pulled me forward, pointing at one specific face. It was only after I moved closer that I realized it was mine.

"See," she said, "this is from the Lakeview Models calendar last year, when you were April, and posed with the tires? Remember?"

I nodded, and then she was pulling me a few feet to the right, pointing again. Meanwhile, the other girls had scattered, the redheads flopping onto the nearby bed, where they were flipping through a stack of magazines, while the blonde and the dark-haired girl jockeyed for position on the chair that faced a nearby vanity.

"And this," Mallory said, her finger inches from the wall, "is the Boca Tan ad that was in the program for a basketball game I went to last year at the university. See, your hair is blonder there, right?"

"Right," I said. I looked slightly orange, as well. So strange. I'd forgotten all about that. "It sure is."

Another tug, and the photos blurred as we moved again, this time in the opposite direction, coming to a stop on the far left. "But this one," she said, "is my all-time favorite. That's why I have it right next to my bed."

I leaned in closer. It was a collage of shots from the Kopf's back-to-school commercial: me in the cheerleader uniform, on the bench with the girls behind me, at a desk, on the arm of the cute boy in the tux. "Where did you get photos?" I asked her.

"It's a screen capture," she said proudly. "I burned the commercial to a DVD, then uploaded it and saved the images on my computer. Cool, huh?"

I leaned in, looking even more closely, remembering, as I did each time I saw the commercial, that day in April when I'd shot it. I was so different then; everything was different then.

Mallory dropped my hand, leaning in beside me. "I just love that commercial," she said now. "At first, it was because of the cheerleading outfit, because I was really into that this summer? But then it was all about the clothes, and the story. . . . I mean, it's great."

"The story," I said.

"Yeah." She turned to look at me. "You know, that you're this girl, and you're going back to high school after a great summer."

"Oh," I said. "Right."

"At first, it's, like, all the stuff that happens right at the beginning of school. Like cheering at the big game. And studying for tests, and hanging out with all your friends on the quad."

Hanging out with all my friends on the quad, I thought. *Right.*

"And then," she said, "it ends with the first dance, where you get the hot guy, which means the *rest* of the year will be even better." She sighed. "It's like you have this great life, and get to do all this cool stuff. All the stuff high school should be. You're like—"

I looked at her again. Her face was inches from the pictures, still staring. "The girl who has everything," I said, remembering the director's words.

She turned to face me, nodding. "*Exactly,*" she said.

I wanted to tell her, right then, that this wasn't true. That I was far from the girl who had everything; that I wasn't even that girl in the pictures, if I ever had been. No one's life was really like that, one glorious moment after another, especially mine. A real set of snapshots from my back-to-school experience would be something else entirely: Sophie's pretty mouth forming an ugly word, Will Cash smiling at me, me alone behind the building retching in the grass. This was the real truth about me going to back to school. The story of my life.

I heard heavy footsteps in the hallway, then a heavy sigh. "Mallory, I told you, if you want me to take pictures, let's go ahead and do it. I've got a show to work on and I don't—"

I stood up; Owen was standing in the open doorway. When he saw me, his eyes widened. "—have all night," he finished. "Hey. What are you doing here?"

"She came for my party," Mallory told him.

Owen narrowed his eyes. "You came for this?"

"You're helping with the photo shoot?" I replied.

"No," he said. "I just—"

"We needed a photographer," Mallory explained to me, "for the group shots. And now we have a stylist, too! This is perfect." She clapped her hands. "Okay, everyone, downstairs and into position. We'll do our group pictures first, then move on to individual. Who has our shoot list?"

The dark-haired girl got up off the chair by the mirror, reaching into her pocket to pull out folded piece of paper. "Here," she said.

"Okay," Owen said as Mallory took it from her, "tell me why you're really here."

"Fashion is my life," I told him. "You know that."

Mallory cleared her throat. "Daytime Casual first," she said, pointing to the redheads, "followed by Workplace Classy, Evening Elegant, and Nighttime Formal."

"Fantasy Engagement," the blonde corrected her.

"Downstairs!" Mallory said. "Let's go!"

The redheads got off the bed, heading for the door, the dark-haired girl in the black following along. The blonde, in comparison, took her time, shooting me a look as she passed.

"Hi, Owen," she said as she walked by him, the hem of her dress dragging on the carpet.

Owen nodded at her, a flat expression on his face. "Hello, Elinor," he said. At the sound of her name, her face flushed pink and she picked up speed, darting out the door and down the hallway, where she was greeted with a burst of giggling.

Mallory followed her friends, then stopped in the doorway, turning back to look at us. "Owen," she said, "I'll need you downstairs in five, ready to shoot. Annabel, you can style and supervise."

"Watch the tone, Mallory," Owen told her. "Or you'll be taking self-portraits."

"Five minutes!" she said. Then she clomped down the hallway, her voice rising up as she continued to order her friends around.

"Wow," I said to Owen as their voices faded. "This is quite a production."

"Tell me about it," he said, sitting down on the edge of the bed. "And mark my words: it will end in tears. It always does. These girls have no concept of thinking toward the middle."

"Thinking toward what?"

"The middle," he repeated as I sat down next to him. "It's an Anger Management term. It means not only thinking in extremes. You know, either I get what I want or I don't. Either I'm right or I'm wrong."

"Either I'm Fantasy Engagement or I'm Nighttime Formal," I added.

"Right. It's dangerous to think like that, because nothing is totally cut-and-dry," he said. "Unless, apparently, you're thirteen."

"Miss Fantasy Engagement does seem like a bit of a diva."

"Elinor?" He let out a breath. "She's a piece of work."

"She seems to like you quite a bit."

"Stop it," he said, shooting me a dark look. "That's I-Lang. Big-time."

"You know that whole model-photographer-hookup thing," I said, bumping him with my knee. "It's practically required."

"Why are you here, again?"

"I just came by to drop this off." I held up his jacket. "I forgot to give it back to you this morning."

"Oh," he said. "Thanks. But you could have waited until Tuesday, if you wanted."

"I would have," I told him, reaching into the pocket and pulling out the iPod, "except for this."

His eyes widened. "Oh, man," he said, taking it from me. "That I would have missed."

"I figured you probably were already."

"Not yet," he said. "But I was about to start planning next week's show, so pretty soon, I would have. Thanks."

"You're welcome."

There was a burst of noise from downstairs, what sounded like someone either cheering or wailing. "See?" Owen said, pointing at the open door. "Tears. Guaranteed. No middle."

"Maybe we should just hide out here," I said. "Might be safer."

"I don't know," he said, glancing around at the walls. "Looking at all these pictures gives me the creeps."

"At least you're not in them," I told him.

"You? There are ones of you here?"

I pointed at the pictures from the commercial, and he got up, walking over to look closer. "It's nothing special," I said. "Really."

He studied the pictures long enough that I began to regret pointing them out. "It's strange," he said finally.

"Gee," I said. "Thanks a lot."

"No, I mean, you don't look like you, or something." He paused, leaning in a little closer. "Yeah. I mean, you look familiar, but not like the same person at all."

I sat there for a second, a little weirded out, because actually this was how I felt, too, when I looked at the older ads I'd done, especially the Kopf's commercial. That girl *was* different from who I was now, more whole and unbroken and okay than the one I saw in the mirror these days. I'd just thought I was the only one who noticed.

"No offense," Owen said.

I shook my head. "It's fine."

"I mean, it's a nice picture." He peered at it again. "I just think you look better now."

At first, I thought maybe I'd heard him wrong. "Now?" I said.

"Yeah." He glanced up at me. "What did you think I meant?"

"I don't . . ." I began, then stopped. "Never mind."

"You think I'd tell you that you looked better here?"

"Well," I said, "you *are* honest."

"I'm not a jerk, though," he replied. "You look good. You just don't look like you. You look . . . different."

"Different bad," I said.

"Different different."

"Super vague," I pointed out. "Placeholder. *Double* place-holder."

"You're right," he said. "What I mean is, looking at this, I think, *Huh, that's not Annabel. That doesn't look like her at all.*"

"What do I look like?"

"Like this," he said, nodding at me. "My point is, I don't know you as someone who gets their picture taken in a cheer-leading outfit. Or even as a model, period. That's not you to me."

I wanted to ask him to explain further, to say what I was to him, exactly. But then I realized maybe he just had. I already knew he thought of me as honest, direct, even funny—all things I had never thought about myself. Who knew what else I could be, what kind of potential there was in the differences between that girl and the one he saw now. So many possibilities.

"Owen!" Mallory yelled up the stairs. "We're ready for you now!"

Owen rolled his eyes. Then he walked over, holding out his hand to help me to my feet. "Okay," he said. "Come on."

Looking up at him, I realized that this, too, was part of my real back-to-school days: Along with Sophie and Will and every-thing horrible, there was Owen, reaching out a hand to me. And now, as I reached up, closing my fingers over his, I was grate-ful more than ever for something, finally, to hold on to.

Owen was right about the tears. Within an hour, we had a melt-down.

"It's not fair!" said the dark-haired girl, whose name I now knew was Angela, her voice wavering.

"You look good," Mallory told her, adjusting her boa. "What's the problem?"

I knew. In fact, it was pretty obvious. While Mallory and the others were alternating between Evening Elegant and Nighttime Formal (or, depending on how you looked at it, Fantasy Engagement), Angela had been continually assigned Workplace Classy, which was clearly the least favorite of the chosen looks. Now, she looked down at her plain black skirt, black blouse, and flats. "I want to do Evening Elegant," she protested. "When is it my turn?"

"Owen!" Elinor, the blonde, called out, tugging a tube top down over her stomach. "Are you ready for me?"

"No," Owen muttered as she moved in toward him, tossing her hair and putting a hand on her hip. "Not even close."

The shoot was quite a production. Not only had the girls pushed back the furniture in the living room and draped a white sheet over the mantel for a backdrop, there was also a dressing and makeup area (the powder room) and background music (mostly Jenny Reef, Bitsy Bonds, and Z104; Owen's offer to put together a mix was roundly rejected).

"It will be your turn," Mallory, who was now in a gold bathing-suit top and sarong, the boa over her shoulders, told Angela. "But Workplace Classy is very important. Someone has to do it."

"Then why don't you?"

Mallory sighed, blowing her bangs out of her face. "Because my look is better suited to evening," she explained as the redheads, who'd moved on to swimwear, practiced for the beach action shots by tossing a soccer ball back and forth.

"With your glasses, you look better doing serious corporate looks."

I glanced at Angela, whose upper lip was now trembling slightly. "You know," I said, "maybe she could take off her glasses."

"I'm ready!" Elinor said to Owen. "Go ahead! Get the shot!"

Owen, who was standing in front of the couch, winced as he lifted the camera to his eye. In my experience, models did not ever boss the photographer, but that was clearly not the case here. Instead, Owen just kept his finger on the shutter pretty much nonstop, taking shot after shot as the girls arranged themselves every which way. Now, as Elinor blew a kiss to the camera, and to him, he looked appalled.

As a stylist, I'd been told it was my job to stay in the powder room/dressing area and supervise wardrobe, which consisted of the piles of clothing and shoes that were scattered on the countertops, floor, and nearby stairs. After my few early suggestions—less cleavage and makeup, for starters—had been completely ignored, I'd been mostly watching Owen and trying not to laugh.

"You know," he said now, as Elinor dropped to the floor and began to writhe toward him, her elbows clunking across the hardwood, "I'm thinking we're about done here."

"But we haven't even gotten the group shots!" Mallory said.

"Then you better get those together," he told her. "Your stylist and photographer get paid by the hour, and you can't afford us for much longer."

"Okay, fine," Mallory grumbled, tossing her boa over one shoulder. "Everyone together in front of the backdrop, now!"

The redheads grabbed their ball and headed over, while Elinor got to her feet, pulling up her tube top again. I looked at Angela, who was standing in the archway to the living room, arms crossed over her chest, her upper lip seriously shaking now. Three could be a crowd, I thought. But so could five.

"Hey," I said, and she turned around, looking at me. "Come on. Let's get you into something else."

I could hear Mallory telling everyone how to stand as Angela followed me back to the powder room, where I surveyed the options. "This is cute," I said, picking up a red skirt. "What do you think?"

Angela sniffled, then reached up, adjusting her glasses. "It's all right," she said.

"And maybe we can pair it with . . ." I glanced around, then grabbed a black top with spaghetti straps. "This. And some really high heels."

She nodded, taking the skirt from me. "Okay," she said, starting down the hallway to the side bedroom there. "I'll go change."

"You do that," I told her. "I'll find the shoes."

"Angela!" Mallory yelled. "We need you in here!"

"Just a sec," I called out, bending down and rummaging through the pile of shoes by my feet. I'd picked out one strappy sandal and was looking for its mate when I felt someone watching me. When I glanced up, Owen was standing there, holding the camera.

"One sec," I said. "We're changing our look."

"I heard." He stepped into the powder room, leaning against the door and watching me as I finally found the shoe, wedged under a puffy parka. "That was nice of you. Helping her out."

"Well," I said, "modeling can be an ugly business."

"Yeah?"

I nodded as I stood up, glancing down the hallway for Angela, then leaned against the opposite side of the doorframe, facing him, the shoes dangling from my hand. After a moment, he lifted up the camera to his eye. "Don't," I said, putting my hand over my face.

"Why not?"

"I hate having my picture taken."

"You're a *model*."

"That's why," I told him. "It's gotten old."

"Come on," he said. "Just one."

I dropped my hand but didn't smile as his finger moved to the shutter. Instead, I just looked at him, through the lens, as the flash popped. "Nice," he said.

"Yeah?"

He nodded, turning the camera over to look at the display on the back. I stepped closer, looking down at it as well. Sure enough, there I was, the doorframe behind me. My hair was unbrushed, a few strands loose around my face, I had on no makeup, and it wasn't my best angle. It also wasn't a bad picture. I moved in closer, studying my face, the faint light behind it.

"See?" Owen said. I could feel his shoulder against mine, his face only inches away, as we both peered down at the image. "*That's* what you look like."

I turned my head to say something to this—what, I had no

idea—and his cheek was so close, right there. I looked up at him, and then, before I knew what was happening, he was turning his head slightly, bending down to me. I closed my eyes, and then his lips were right there, soft on mine, and I stepped closer, pressing myself against—

"I'm ready for my shoes."

We both jumped, startled; Owen bonked his head on the doorframe. "Shit," he said.

Heart pounding, I looked down at Angela, who was staring up at us, her expression serious. "Shoes," I said, handing them over. "Right."

Owen was rubbing his head, his eyes closed. "Man," he said. "That smarts."

"Are you okay?" I asked. He nodded, and I reached out, touching his temple, then kept my fingers there for a moment, his skin warm, smooth to the touch, before taking my hand away.

"Owen!" Mallory yelled from the living room. "We're ready! Let's go!"

Owen pushed off the doorframe and started into the living room while Angela, now strapped into her shoes, slowly made her way along behind him. I stayed where I was for a moment, then glanced at myself in the powder-room mirror, amazed at what had just happened. I studied my reflection for a second, then stepped away from it, out of my own sight.

When I got to the living room, all drama had been forgotten, and the group shot was in full swing, all five girls posing wildly as Owen moved dutifully around them. I leaned in the archway, watching as each girl vamped in her own way: a hip shimmy, an arched neck, fluttering lashes.

The song playing in the background was the kind Owen hated: all poppy, bouncy beats, a girl's perfectly engineered voice sliding effortlessly over the instruments. Mallory reached over to the CD player on the floor beside her, cranking the volume, and the girls all shrieked, beginning to dance, their hands waving over their heads. Owen stepped aside as they bounced and twirled, then turned the camera on me, holding it there as the girls blurred past between us. I wasn't sure exactly what he was seeing, but now I had an idea. So this time, I smiled.

When I pulled into my driveway later that night, all the lights in the house were off except in Whitney's room. I could see her in the chair by her window, sitting with her feet tucked up under her. She had that same notebook open in her lap and was writing, her hand moving slowly across the page. For a moment I just sat there, watching her, the one thing I could make out in the dark.

I'd left Owen's just in time. Elinor, Angela, and the twins had tired of both the photo shoot and Mallory's bossiness and were on the verge of some sort of fashion mutiny, the house was a wreck, and Owen's mom—apparently a bit of a neat freak—was due home at any moment. I'd offered to stay and help clean up, or play peacemaker, but he declined.

"I can handle it," he said, as we stood on the front steps. "If I were you, I'd get out while I could. It's only going to go downhill from here."

"So optimistic," I said.

"No," he replied as, inside, I heard an indignant shriek, followed by a door slamming. He turned his head, glancing toward the door, then back at me. "Just realistic."

I smiled, then moved down one step, pulling my keys out of my pocket. "So I'll see you at school, I guess."

"Yup," he said. "See you then."

Neither of us moved and I wondered if he would kiss me again. "Okay," I said, feeling my stomach flip-flop. "I'm, um, going."

"Right." He stepped a little closer to the edge of the step where he was standing, and I moved forward on mine, meeting him halfway. As he leaned down to me and I closed my eyes, I could hear something, a *thunk-thunk-thunk* noise, growing both louder and closer. The doorknob rattled, and we both jumped back as Mallory, wearing thick wedge heels, a black catsuit, and the green boa, burst out onto the porch.

"Wait!" she said, clomping across to me, her hand outstretched. "Here. These are for you."

She handed me a stack of pictures, so fresh from the printer I could smell ink. The one on the top was of her in her gold bathing-suit top, the shot taken close with the feathers from the boa framing her face, drifting upwards toward the edges. I flipped through the next few, which featured a couple of group poses, Elinor writhing on the floor and, finally, Angela in the outfit I'd picked out for her. "Wow," I said. "These are great."

"They're for your wall," she said. "So you can look at me sometimes."

"Thank you," I told her.

"You're welcome." She turned to Owen. "Mom just called from the car. She'll be home in ten minutes."

"Right." Owen sighed. To me he said, "I'll see you later."

I nodded, and then they were walking inside, where I could hear the other girls arguing, Mallory waving at me one last time before shutting the door. A moment later, he said something, and the girls quieted down, quick. By the time I started down the steps, I couldn't hear a thing.

Now, I got out of my car and started up the walk, Mallory's pictures in my hand. The entire ride home all I'd been able to think about was Owen's face, coming closer to mine, how it felt when he'd kissed me, barely long enough to count and yet still unforgettable. I felt my face flush as I pushed open the door, then started up the stairs.

"Annabel?" Whitney called out when I got to the top. "Is that you?"

"Yeah," I said. "I'm back."

As I reached for my door, hers opened and she stepped out into view. "Mom called again," she said. "I told her you'd gone to a friend's house. She asked who, but I said I didn't know."

For a moment we just looked at each other, and I wondered if I was supposed to explain myself further. "Thanks," I said finally as I pushed my door open and turned on the light. I put the pictures on the bureau, then shrugged off my coat, tossing it over my desk chair. When I turned back around, she was standing in my doorway.

"I told her maybe you'd call her when you got in," she said. "But you probably don't have to."

"Okay," I said.

She shifted slightly, leaning against the doorjamb. As she did so, she saw the pictures. "What are these?" she asked.

"Oh, nothing," I said. "They're just . . . they're silly."

She picked them up, cradling them in her open hand as she worked through them, her expression moving from impassive to curious to, at one shot of Elinor sprawled on the floor, somewhat horrified.

"My friend's little sister was having a modeling slumber party," I said, walking over to stand beside her as she kept moving through the stack. There were the redheads, side by side, doing a mirror-image pose, and Angela in her black dress, the dreaded Workplace Classy. There were a few more of Mallory as well, doing a full range of looks: pensive, dreamy, and, perhaps due to something Owen had just said, annoyed. "They get all dressed up and take shots of themselves."

Whitney paused to study a shot of Elinor in her white dress, looking pensive. "Wow," she said. "That's quite a look."

"It's called Fantasy Engagement."

"Huh," she said, flipping to the next picture, which was Elinor again, this time sprawled on the floor, mouth half open. "What's that called?"

"I don't think that has a name," I said.

She withheld further comment, flipping to the next shot, which was of Mallory in a red top, facing the camera. Her lips were pursed, her eyelashes enormous. "She's kind of cute," she said, tilting the picture slightly. "Good eyes."

"Oh, God," I said, shaking my head. "She'd *die* if she heard you say that."

"Really."

I nodded. "She's model-obsessed. You should see her room. It's all pictures from magazines, everywhere you look."

"She must have been thrilled you were there, then," she said. "A real-live model."

"I guess," I said, watching as she kept flipping, past a series of group shots: all the girls' faces pressed together, then each of them looking a different direction, as if waiting for five separate buses. "It was kind of weird for me, actually."

Whitney was quiet for a second. Then she said, "Yeah. I know what you mean."

Like so much else that had happened that weekend, I found myself in this unexpected moment with my sister almost holding my breath. Finally I said, "I mean, we never did that, you know? When we were kids."

"We didn't have to," she said as Angela's picture came up, her dark eyes so serious, skin pale in the camera's flash. "We had the real thing."

"Yeah," I said. "But this might have been more fun. Less pressure, anyway."

I felt her cut her eyes at me as I said this, and too late I realized she thought I was talking about her. I waited for her to snap or say something nasty, but she didn't, instead just handing me back the pictures. "Well," she said. "I guess we'll never know."

As she stepped out into the hallway I looked down at the pictures; Mallory's boa shot was back on top. "Sleep well," I said.

"Yeah." She glanced over at me, the light behind her, and I was struck by the simple perfection of her cheekbones and lips, so striking and accidental all at once. "Good night, Annabel."

Later, when I got into bed, I picked up the pictures again, then sat back in bed, flipping through them. After going through the stack twice, I got out of bed and went to my desk, digging around in the top drawer until I found some pushpins. Then I tacked the pictures up, in rows of three, on the wall above my radio. *So you can look at me sometimes*, Mallory had said, and as I turned off my light I did just that. The moon, coming in, was slanted across them, making them bright, and I kept my eyes on them as long as I could. At some point, though, I could feel myself falling asleep, and I had to turn away, back to the dark.

Chapter
TWELVE

My mother returned from her first vacation in over a year rested, manicured, and rejuvenated. Which would have been great, if her newfound energy hadn't been directed at the one thing I least wanted to think about, but now could not avoid: the Lakeview Models Fall Fashion Show.

"So you've got to be at Kopf's today for a fitting, tomorrow for a rehearsal," she said to me as I poked at my breakfast before school. "And the final run-through is on Friday. Your hair appointment is on Thursday, and I booked your nail stuff for Saturday morning, early. Okay?"

After an entire weekend to myself, not to mention the last few months with very few work commitments, this did not sound okay. It sounded painful. But I didn't say anything. As much as I was dreading the week and the show, at least I had something to look forward to afterwards, which was going to Bendo with Owen.

"You know, something occurred to me this weekend," my mom continued. "The Kopf's people are probably just about to start casting for the spring campaign. So this show is a great opportunity for them to see you in person, don't you think?"

Hearing this, I felt a twinge of dread, knowing I should tell her I wanted to quit modeling. But then I had a flash of me and Owen on the wall, role-playing this very scenario, and how even when it was just a game I hadn't been able to get the words out. Across from me, my mother was sipping her coffee, and I knew that this, right now, was the perfect moment. She'd dropped a sweater, and I could just pick it up. But like Rolly, I froze up. And stayed silent. I'd do it later, I told myself. After the show. I would.

At the same time that I was walking down a runway at the mall, modeling winter clothes, my sister Kirsten would also be in front of a crowd, albeit for a different reason. The day before, she'd finally e-mailed her short piece to me as promised. Because I was used to Kirsten explaining—if not overexplaining—everything that was any part of her life whatsoever, the message she'd sent with it took me by surprise.

Hi, Annabel, here it is. Let me know what you think. Love, K.

At first, I'd actually scrolled down through the body of the e-mail, looking for the rest of the message—if my sister was long-winded on the phone, her e-mails were equally verbose. But there was nothing else.

I hit the DOWNLOAD NOW button, then watched as blue squares filled up the screen. When it was done, I clicked on PLAY.

The first shot was of grass. Green, beautiful grass, just like the kind on the golf course across the street, i.e., totally chemically induced, filling the screen from one side to the other. Then the camera pulled back, back, to show it was the yard in front of a white house with pretty blue trim, and two figures on bikes blurred past.

The camera cut, and we were suddenly facing two girls as they rode toward us. One, a blonde, looked to be about thirteen; the other, a brunette, was thinner and more slight, lagging a little bit behind.

Suddenly the girl in front looked back at the other, then began pedaling faster, pulling away from her. As she did so, the camera cut back and forth between her pedaling, wind blowing back her hair, and pretty images of the neighborhood: a dog asleep on the sidewalk, a man picking up his paper, the blue, blue sky, a sprinkler sending water in an arc over a flower bed. As she kept on, picking up speed, the images came faster and faster, repeating, until the camera cut to a shot of the road ahead, coming to a *T*. She skidded to a stop, then turned around. Behind her, in the distance, you could just see a bike lying in the middle of the road, one wheel spinning, the smaller girl sitting beside it, holding her arm.

The next shot was of the blonde skidding to a stop beside her. "What happened?" she asked.

The younger girl shook her head. "I don't know," she said.

The blonde pushed herself over, closer. "Here," she said. "Get on."

In the next shot, the smaller girl was balanced on the handlebars, holding her arm, as the blonde pedaled up the street. Again the camera cut between them and images of the neighborhood, although both were different now: the dog lunging and barking as they passed, the man stumbling as he reached for his paper, the sky gray, the sprinkler hissing as water splatted a nearby car, then ran in streaks down the side. It was the same, and yet so different, and when the house rose up in the distance, it looked different, too. The blonde pedaled up the driveway, the camera pulling back as she did so, then stopped as the younger girl slid off the handlebars, holding her arm tight against her. They dropped the bike onto the grass and started toward the house. They climbed the steps. The door opened for them, but you couldn't see who was on the other side. As they disappeared inside, the camera panned down until the grass filled the screen again, side to side, scarily green and bright and fake. And then it was over.

I just sat there for a moment, staring at the screen. Then I hit PLAY and watched it again. And a third time. I still wasn't sure what to make of it, even as I reached for the phone and dialed Kirsten's number. But when she answered, and I told her I liked it but didn't get it, she wasn't upset. Instead, she said that was the whole point.

"What, that I be confused?" I asked.

"No," she said, "that the meaning not be spelled out. It's supposed to be left up to your interpretation."

"Yes, but *you* know what it means," I said. "Right?"

"Sure."

"And that is?"

She sighed. "I know what it means to *me*," she said. "For you, it's going to be different. Look, film is personal. There's no right or wrong message. It's all what you take from it."

I looked at the screen again, which I'd paused on the last shot of that green grass. "Oh," I said. "Okay."

It was just so bizarre. Here was my sister, queen of the

overshare, holding out on me. Holding *back*. I was used to having to guess with some people, but never Kirsten, and I wasn't sure I liked it. She, however, sounded happier than I'd heard her in months.

"I'm just so glad you liked it. And had such a strong reaction!" She laughed. "Now all I need is for everyone there on Saturday to feel the same way, and everything will be great."

Great for you, I thought, when we hung up a few minutes later. As for me, I was still confused. And, I had to admit, intrigued. Enough to watch the film two more times, studying it frame by frame.

Now, as my father came into the kitchen, running late, and my mom jumped up to bustle around him, I brought my plate to the sink, running some water over it. Through the window in front of me, I could see Whitney sitting on a chaise by the pool, a cup of coffee beside her. Normally she was sleeping at this hour, but lately she'd started getting up early. It was just one recent change among many.

At first the shifts were small, but still noticeable. She'd recently become somewhat social—a couple of days earlier she'd gone out for coffee with people from Moira Bell's group—and had also begun working a few mornings a week at my dad's office answering phones, filling in for yet another pregnant secretary. When she was home, she'd started to spend at least some of her time outside her room. It happened in stages: First her door went from always being shut to slightly ajar, to finally being open occasionally. Then I noticed she was hanging out in the living room instead of shut away upstairs. And just the previous day I'd come home from school to find her sitting at the dining-room table, books stacked all around her, writing on a legal pad.

I'd been ignored for so long that it was still my tendency to hesitate before addressing Whitney. This time, though, she spoke first.

"Hey," she said, not looking up. "Mom's out running errands. She said not to forget about rehearsal at four thirty."

"Right," I said. Her arm was crooked across the pad, her pen making a scratching noise as it moved across the paper. In the window, her herb pots were in full sunlight, although they hadn't shown any sign of sprouting yet. "What are you doing?"

"I have to write a history."

"A history?" I repeated. "Of what?"

"Well, actually, it's two histories." She put down her pen, stretching her fingers. "One of my life. And one of my eating disorder."

It was weird to hear her say this, and after a moment, I realized why. Even though it had pretty much dominated our family dynamic for almost a year, I'd never heard Whitney acknowledge her problem out loud. Like so much else, it was known but not discussed, present but not officially accounted for. From the way she said it, though, so matter-of-factly, it sounded like she, at least, was used to it.

"So they're two separate things?" I asked.

"Apparently. At least according to Moira." She sighed, although this time, when her therapist's name came up, she sounded more tired than annoyed. "The idea is that there is some separation, even if it doesn't always seem like it. That we had a life before we had a disorder."

I moved closer to the table, glancing at the books stacked beside her. *Starving for Attention: Eating Disorders and Adolescents* was the title of one; there was a slimmer volume called *Hunger Pains* beneath it. "So you have to read all those books?"

"I don't *have* to." She picked up her pen again. "They're just to fill in the factual stuff, if I need it. But the personal history is all my memories. We're supposed to do it one year at a time." She nodded at the pad in front of her. On the top line, I could see she'd written ELEVEN (11). There was nothing else on the page.

"Must be kind of weird," I said. "Thinking back, year by year."

"It's hard. Harder than I thought it would be." She opened a book by her elbow, flipping through the pages, then shut it. "I don't remember that much, for some reason."

I glanced over at her pots again, the sun spilling across them. On the other side of the window and across the street, the golf course was green and bright.

"You broke your arm," I said.

"What?"

"When you were eleven," I said. "You broke your arm. You fell off your bike. Remember?"

For a moment she just sat there. "That's right," she said finally, nodding. "God. Wasn't that, like, right after your birthday?"

"*On* my birthday," I told her. "You got back in your cast just in time for cake."

"I can't believe I forgot that," she said. She shook her head again, looking down at the paper before picking up her pen and clicking it open. Then she began to write, her script filling the top line. I started to mention Kirsten's movie, and how it had reminded me of this, but then I stopped myself. She'd already filled three lines and was still going; I didn't want to interrupt. So I backed out of the room and left her to it. When I passed by again an hour later, she was still going, and this time she didn't look up. She just kept writing.

Now as I turned away from the sink, I looked over at my mother, wondering if I asked her about what had happened on that day, my ninth birthday, just a month or two before her own mother died, what she would remember. The green, green grass, like Kirsten. That it happened just before my party, like me. Or, like Whitney, nothing at all, at least at first. So many versions of just one memory, and yet none of them were right or wrong. Instead, they were all pieces. Only when fitted together, edge to edge, could they even begin to tell the whole story.

"Get in."

I looked at Owen, raising one eyebrow. A minute earlier, I'd been walking across the Kopf's parking lot to my car, leaving yet another fashion-show rehearsal, when someone screeched into the space beside me. I'd looked over, startled, expecting to see a white kidnapper van. Instead, it was Owen in the Land Cruiser, already reaching over to push the passenger door open.

"Is this an abduction?" I asked.

He shook his head, gesturing impatiently with one hand for

me to get in the car, while adjusting the stereo with the other. "Seriously," he said, as I slowly climbed into the seat. "You have *got* to hear this."

"Owen," I said, watching him continue to push buttons on the console, "how did you know I was here?"

"I didn't," he replied. "I was just up at that light, heading home, when I looked over and saw you. Check this out."

He reached for the volume knob, turning it up. A second later, a whooshing sound filled my ears, followed by what sounded like a violin, but at rapid speed, and electrified. The result was a noise that would have been unsettling at a normal volume. Cranked as it was, though, I felt the hairs on my neck stand on end.

"Great, right?" Owen said, grinning widely. He was bobbing his head as the chords bounced over us. In my mind, I pictured one of those cardiac monitor machines, each sound causing my own heart to spike, the needle jumping off the screen.

I could feel myself wincing even as I said—or yelled— "What is this?"

"They're called Melisma," he yelled back as there was a boom of bass, loud enough to shake my seat. Over at the next car, a woman loading her squirming toddler into a car seat glanced over at us. "It's a music project. These awesome string players, synthesized and blended with various world beats, influenced by—"

Then he said something else, which was drowned out by a sudden burst of rapid drumbeats. I watched his lips move until it subsided, picking back up as he said, "—really a collaborative thing, this whole new music initiative. Incredible, right?"

Before I could answer, there was a bang of cymbals, followed by a fizzing noise. Call it reflex, or self-preservation, or just common sense, but I just couldn't help myself: I pressed my palms over my ears.

Owen's eyes widened, and I realized what I'd done. As I dropped my hands, though, the song suddenly ended, so the sound of them hitting the seat on either side of me was incredibly loud. Especially compared to the awkward silence that followed.

"You did not," Owen said finally, his voice low, "just cover your ears. Did you?"

"It was an accident," I said. "I just—"

"That's *serious*." He reached forward, shaking his head, and turned down the CD. "I mean, it's one thing to listen and respectfully disagree. But to shut it out entirely, and not even give it a chance—"

"I gave it a chance!" I said.

"You call that a chance?" he asked. "That was five seconds."

"It was long enough to form an opinion," I said.

"Which was?"

"I covered my ears," I told him. "What do *you* think?"

He started to say something, then stopped, shaking his head. Beside us, the woman in the minivan was now backing out. I watched her slide past his window. "Melisma," Owen said after a moment, "is innovative and textured."

"If by textured you mean unlistenable," I said quietly, "then I agree."

"I-Lang!" he said, pointing at me. I shrugged. "I can't believe you're saying that! This is the perfect marriage of instrument and technology! It's unlike anything anyone's ever done before! It sounds incredible!"

"Maybe in the car wash," I muttered.

He'd drawn in another breath, to continue this rant, but now he let it out, one big whoosh, then turned his head to look at me. "What did you just say?"

Like covering my ears, this had happened without my really realizing it. There had been a time when I was painfully aware of everything I said or did around Owen. The fact that this was no longer the case was either good or very bad. Judging by the look on his face—a mix of horrified and offended—I had a feeling it was probably the latter. At least right at this moment.

"I said . . ." I cleared my throat. "I said, maybe it sounds incredible in the car wash."

I could feel him staring at me, so I busied myself picking at the edge of my seat. Then he said, "Which means what?"

"You know what it means," I said.

"I truly do not. Enlighten me."

Of course he'd make me explain it. "Well," I said slowly, "you know, everything sounds better when you're driving through the car wash. It's just, like, a fact. Right?"

He didn't say anything, just stared at me.

"My point is," I said, clarifying, "it's not my thing. I'm sorry. I shouldn't have covered my ears; that was rude. But I just—"

"Which car wash?"

"What?"

"Which is this magical listening station, whereupon all musical worth is decided?"

I just looked at him. "Owen."

"Seriously, I want to know."

"It's not any one car wash," I said. "It's the car-wash phenomenon. You really don't know about it?"

"I don't," he repeated. Then he reached down, shifting into reverse. "But I will. Starting now."

Five minutes later, we were pulling up to 123SUDS, the automated drive-through car wash that had been down the street from my neighborhood for as long as I could remember. I'd grown up going there fairly often, mostly because my mom loved it. My dad would always tell her that the only way to get a car truly clean was to do it by hand—as he often did, on warm sunny days, in the driveway—and that 123SUDS was a waste of time and money. But my mom didn't care. "It's not about the wash, anyway," she'd tell him. "It's the *experience*."

Going there was never really planned. Instead, we'd just be passing by and she'd suddenly turn in, sending my sisters and me scrambling to collect change from the floorboards and center console to feed into the machine. We always chose the basic wash, skipping the hot wax, sometimes adding on the optional Armor All on the tires. Then we'd roll up all the windows, sit back in our seats, and go in.

There was just something about it. Driving into that dark bay, the water suddenly whooshing down like the biggest and most sudden thunderstorm ever. It would beat across the hood and trunk, pouring down the other side of your window, washing all the pollen and dust away, and if you closed your eyes you could almost imagine you were floating along with it. It was eerie and incredible, and when you spoke you always whispered, even if you didn't know why. More than anything, though, I remembered the music.

My mother loved classical stuff—it was all she played in her car, which drove my sisters and me nuts. We'd beg for regular radio, anything from this century, but she was stubborn. "When you drive, you can listen to whatever you like," she'd say, then crank up Brahms or Beethoven to drown out our irritated sighs.

But in the car wash, my mother's music sounded different. Beautiful. It was only then that I could close my eyes and enjoy it, understanding what it was that she heard every time.

When I finally got my own license, I could play whatever I wanted, which was great. But still, the first time I went through 123SUDS alone, I flipped around my radio dial to find something classical, for old times' sake. Just as I was rolling in, though, the station faded and my tuner jumped to the next one, which was playing a loud, twangy country song, also not something I would have chosen on my own. But it was strange. Sitting there, the brushes moving overhead, water spilling down my window, even the song that was playing—something about driving an old Ford under a full moon—sounded perfect. As if it didn't matter what was on, but instead how hard I was listening, there in the dark.

I told Owen all this on the ride over, explaining how since then, I'd been convinced that anything sounded good at the car wash. He looked dubious, however, as he pushed quarters into the cashier station, and I had to wonder if my theory was about to debunked.

"So what now?" he asked as the machine spit out his

receipt and the red light beside the bay dropped to green. "We just drive in?"

"You've never done this?" I asked him.

"I'm not much for car upkeep simply for aesthetics' sake," he said. "Plus, I think there's a hole in my roof."

I motioned for him to drive forward and he did, over the slight bump and up to the yellow line, faded over time, that said STOP HERE. Then he cut the engine. "Okay," he said. "I'm ready to be impressed."

I shot him a look. "You know," I said, "this is your first time, so for full effect, you really need to recline."

"Recline."

"It adds to the experience," I told him. "Trust me."

We both eased back our seats, settling in. His arm was resting against mine, and I thought of being at his house the other night, and how I'd come so close to kissing him, twice. As the machine began to whir behind us, I reached forward and turned on the CD again. "All right," I said as the jets came on overhead. "Here we go."

The water was pattering at first, then began to move down the glass in front of us in a wave. Owen shifted in his seat as a drop fell from over his head, landing on his shirt. "Oh, great," he said. "There *is* a hole in the roof."

He grew quiet, though, as the next cut on the CD began with a soft murmuring, followed by some plucking of strings. There was also a bit of buzzing, but with the water moving over us, the inside of the car seeming smaller, then smaller still, it seemed to dissipate, fading out behind us. I could hear the hum of the brushes as they moved in closer to the car, intermixed with the sad, sloping chords of a violin. Already I could feel it happening, that slowing of time, everything stopping for this one moment, here, now.

I turned my head to look over at Owen. He was lying there, watching as the brushes drew big, soapy circles across the windshield in front of us, his gaze intent. Listening. I closed my eyes, focusing on doing the same. But all I could think was that it felt like my whole life had changed—again—in just the few weeks I'd known Owen; and not for the first time, I wanted to tell him so. Find the right words, string them together in the ideal way, knowing that here they would have the best chance of sounding perfect.

I turned toward him again, thinking this, and opened my eyes. He was looking right at me.

"You were right," he told me, his voice low. "This is great. Seriously."

"Yeah," I said. "It is."

Then he shifted, moving closer to me, and I felt his arm press against mine, his skin warm. And then, finally, Owen kissed me—really kissed me—and I couldn't hear anything: not the water, the music, or even my own heart, which had to be pounding. Instead, it was just silence, the very best kind, stretching out forever, or only a moment, and then it was over.

Suddenly, the car wash was quiet, the music finished. Above me, I could see one big drop, dangling precariously over our heads. I kept my eyes on it until dropped, landing with a plunk on my arm just as a horn beeped behind us.

"Whoops," Owen said, and we both sat up. He cranked the engine as I glanced back at a guy in a Mustang who was waiting, windows already up, by the entrance. "Hold on."

When we pulled out of the bay, the sun was bright, catching the pools of water as they broke up, sliding off the hood. With the kiss, and the dark, I felt like I was still underwater, the brightness startling.

"Man," Owen said, blinking as he pulled over by the curb, "that was really something."

"Told you. Everything sounds better in the car wash."

"Everything, huh?"

He was looking at me as he said this, and I had a flash of his face just moments earlier, staring up at the windshield, listening so carefully. Maybe sometime, I would be able to say everything I'd thought at that moment. And even more.

"I wonder," he said now, running a hand through his hair, "if it works for techno."

"Nope," I said flatly.

"You're sure."

"Oh, yeah." I nodded. "Positive."

He raised an eyebrow at me. "Yeah, well," he said, pulling away from the curb and starting around the building again. "We'll see."

"Did you hear?"

It was six o'clock on the Saturday of the fashion show, and I was sitting in the makeshift dressing room at Kopf's, waiting. For the last few hours, while getting my hair and makeup done and my outfit fitted and tweaked, I'd managed to ignore the chatter around me. Instead, I focused on getting through this show so I could move on to the one I really cared about, at

Bendo, with Owen. It had been working just fine. Until now.

I looked to my left, where Hillary Prescott had just sat down beside a girl named Marnie. Like me, they were already done with hair and makeup, which left them with nothing to do but drink bottled water, examine their reflections, and gossip.

"Hear about what?" Marnie asked. She was a thin girl with a long face and high cheekbones. When I'd first seen her I thought she looked like Whitney, somewhat, although she was more pretty than beautiful.

Hillary glanced over one shoulder, then another, the classic double-check. "What went down last night at Becca Durham's party," she said.

"No," Marnie said, dabbing a finger over the gloss on her lips. "What happened?"

Hillary leaned in a little closer. "Well," she said, "from what I heard, there was total drama. Louise told me that about halfway through the party—"

She stopped talking, suddenly, staring at the mirror facing us just as Emily Shuster walked in. She had her arms crossed over her chest, her head ducked down slightly, and her mom was with her. I only got one quick glance, but that was all it took to see Emily looked terrible: Her face was puffy, her eyes red, rimmed with dark circles.

Hillary, Marnie, and I all watched as she and her mom passed, continuing toward Mrs. McMurty, who was on the other side of the room. Then Hillary said, "I can't *believe* she showed up here."

"Why?" Marnie asked. "What happened?"

Not my problem, I thought, turning my attention back to

the history notebook I'd brought with me to get some studying in during the downtime. As I did so, though, I felt a piece of hair stick to my cheek. I looked up at the mirror to brush it away just as Hillary leaned in a little closer.

"She hooked up with Will Cash last night," she said, her voice low, but not that low. "In his car. And Sophie caught them."

"No way," Marnie said, her eyes wide. "Are you *serious*?"

Because I was looking at my reflection, I was able to actually see myself react as I heard this. I watched myself blink, my mouth fall open just slightly before I shut it, quick, and looked away.

"Louise was inside," Hillary was saying now, "so she only heard about it. But apparently Will had driven Emily there, and someone saw them. When Sophie heard, she *freaked*."

Marnie glanced over at Emily, who was now standing with her back to us while her mom spoke to Mrs. McMurty. "Oh my God," she said. "What did Will do?"

"I don't know. But Louise said that Sophie had kind of suspected something lately. Like Emily had been flirting with him, always acting silly when he was around."

Silly, I thought. *Or just nervous*. I had a flash of Will's intense, flat stare, how slowly the time seemed to pass whenever we were alone in the car waiting for Sophie. Behind me, people were passing by, other models talking, the same noise and commotion. But all I could hear were these two voices, and my own heartbeat.

"God," Marnie said. "Poor Sophie."

"No kidding. They were supposed to be best friends." Hillary sighed. "I guess you can't trust anybody."

I turned my head. Sure enough, they were both looking at me. I stared back at them, and Marnie blushed, shifting her gaze elsewhere. But Hillary kept her eyes on me for a long moment before pushing back her chair and standing up, then shaking out her hair and walking away. After picking at her water bottle for an uncomfortable few moments, Marnie got up and followed her.

For a moment, I just sat there, trying to process what I'd heard. I looked at Emily, who was now sitting in a chair across the room. Her mom, standing beside her, was saying something, her face serious, and Mrs. McMurty, next to her, was nodding. Mrs. Shuster's hand was on Emily's shoulder, and every once in a while I saw her squeeze it, the fabric bunching, then unbunching.

I closed my eyes, swallowing over the lump that had risen in my throat. *She hooked up with Will Cash last night. Sophie freaked. They were supposed to be best friends. I guess you can't trust anybody.*

No, I thought, *you can't.* I had a flash of the last few months, my quiet summer, starting school alone, that awful day in the courtyard when I'd pushed Sophie away. Maybe I couldn't have changed any of that. But now, too late, I was realizing I might have been able to change something. Or one thing.

I tried to study, tried to think about Owen and what came next. But every time I managed to distract myself for even a moment, I'd find myself looking up and across the room, where Emily was sitting in front of a mirror. She'd been so late they were having to make her up quickly, a hairstylist and makeup person working in tandem, stepping around each other. In the room between us, people kept passing by, their voices high, movements busy, as the time to the show counted down, but Emily kept her gaze straight ahead, looking at herself and no one else.

When they called us out of the dressing room, she didn't walk out with the rest of us. Instead, she showed up after we were all in our places to take her spot second in line, three people ahead of me. There was a digital clock on a nearby mall directory—it was 6:55. Several states and miles away, Kirsten was getting ready to show her piece, and I had a flash of that green, green grass, suddenly not so perfect anymore.

Usually, this was the time I was the most nervous, these last few minutes before I had to walk. Ahead of me, Julia Reinhart was tugging on the hem of her shirt, and behind me I could hear one of the freshman models complaining that her shoes were too tight. Emily wasn't saying a word, her eyes on the slit in the curtain.

The music started—it was loud and poppy, total Z104 material—and Mrs. McMurty came around the corner, looking frazzled, her clipboard in hand. "One minute!" she said, and the girl at the front of the line, one of the seniors, tossed her hair, squaring her shoulders.

I stretched out my fingertips, taking a deep breath. Now, in the mall itself, everything felt brighter and more open. All I had to do was get through this, get out, and go find Owen, moving forward into what I wanted, not what I'd been.

The music stopped for a moment, then began again. We were starting. Mrs. McMurty made her way up the stairs to stand by the curtain, then pulled it aside and motioned for the first girl to step through. As she did, I caught a glimpse of the crowd—so many people in the chairs on either side, and more standing behind them.

When it was Emily's turn, she headed out with her head high, her spine ramrod straight, and as I watched her I wished I was like everyone else out there, who would see only a beautiful girl in beautiful clothes, nothing more or less. Another girl went out, then Julia, after which point Emily returned, walking off the other side of the stage to the dressing room. Then it was my turn.

When the curtain opened, all I could see at first was the runway stretched out in front of me, a blur of faces on either side. The music was pounding in my ears as I began to walk, trying to keep my eyes straight ahead, but still, I caught the occasional glimpse of the crowd. I saw my parents on the left, my mother beaming at me, my dad's arm around her. Mallory Armstrong was sitting with the red-haired twins from her party a few rows back on the other side. In the split second our eyes met, she waved excitedly, hopping up and down in her seat. I kept going, down the runway. When I got to the very end, I saw Whitney.

She was leaning against a planter in front of the vitamin store, a good fifty feet from the back of the fashion-show crowd. I hadn't even known she was coming. But what surprised me more than this was the look on her face, which was so sad that it almost knocked the wind out of me. When our eyes met, she stepped forward, sliding her hands in her pockets, and for a moment I just stared at her, feeling a tug in my chest. And then I had to turn back.

I could feel a lump rising in my throat as I willed myself forward, toward the curtain. I'd been through enough. I didn't want to think about anything that was happening or had happened, to Emily, or to me. I just wanted to be on the wall with Owen, talking music, and be the girl he saw, who was different, and in a good way. All the good ways.

I was at the midpoint of the runway by now, halfway there. Four more changes, four more trips, a grand finale, and this would be over. It wasn't my job to save anyone, anyway. Especially since I hadn't even been able to save myself.

"Annabel!" I heard a voice call out, and I glanced to my left to see Mallory, smiling widely as she lifted her camera to her face, her finger moving to the shutter. The redheads were waving, everyone was watching, but as the flash popped, all I could think of was that night in her room with Owen, looking at all those faces on the wall and not even recognizing my own.

I turned back to face forward, and then Emily stepped out from behind the curtain. As I saw her, I heard Kirsten's voice in my head, explaining why she was scared to show her film: *This is personal*, she'd said. *Real*. This moment was, too, even if you couldn't tell at first glance. It was fake on the outside, but so true within. You only had to look, really look, to tell.

The weird thing was that all fall, at school, rehearsals, anytime we passed, Emily wouldn't meet my eyes. It was like she didn't want to see me at all. But this time as we approached each other, I could feel her staring at me, willing me to turn my head, pulling my gaze in her direction. I fought it as hard as I could. But just as she passed me, I gave in.

She knew. I could tell with one glance, one look, one simple instant. It was her eyes. Despite the thick makeup, they were still dark-rimmed, haunted, and sad. Most of all, though, they were familiar. The fact that we were in front of hundreds of strangers changed nothing at all. I'd spent a summer with those same eyes—scared, lost, confused—staring back at me. I would have known them anywhere.

Chapter
THIRTEEN

"Sophie!"

It was the annual end-of-year party, the previous June, and I was late. Emily's voice, saying this, was the first thing I heard when I stepped in the door.

At the time I couldn't see her—the foyer was packed, the stairs crowded with people as well—but then, a moment later, she rounded the corner, a beer in each hand. When she saw me, she smiled. "There you are," she said. "What took you so long?"

I had a flash of my mother's face an hour earlier, how her eyes had widened when Whitney pushed back her chair, then slammed it against the table, making all our plates jump. This time, the issue had been chicken, specifically the half a breast my father had deposited on Whitney's plate. After cutting it up into quarters, then eighths, then impossibly small sixteenths, she'd pushed it all to the side before commencing to eat her salad, chewing each bite of lettuce for what seemed like ages. My parents and I acted like we weren't watching this, like we weren't even aware, keeping a conversation about the weather somehow aloft among the three of us. Still, a few minutes later, when Whitney dropped her napkin on her plate, I watched it drift down, draping the chicken like a magician's scarf as she willed it to disappear. No luck. My father told her to finish her food, and then she exploded.

By this point, we should have been used to her dinnertime histrionics—she'd been out of the hospital for several months, during which time they'd become routine— but there were still times when the volume and suddenness of her outbursts took us all by surprise. Especially my mom, who always seemed to take every raised syllable, every slam or crash, even the numerous sarcastic sighs like personal attacks. This was why I'd lingered after dinner, standing in the kitchen as my mother washed dishes. I could see her face reflected in the window over the sink, and I kept watching it closely, the way I always did when she got upset, worried I might see something besides her features that I recognized.

"I got held up at home," I told Emily now. "What'd I miss?"

"Not much," she said. "Have you seen Sophie?"

I looked around, past the clump of people beside us and into the living room, where I spotted her on a short couch by the window, a bored expression on her face.

"This way," I told Emily, taking one of the beers from her as I worked through the crowd over to the couch. "Hey," I called out to Sophie, over the din of a nearby TV. "What's going on?"

"Nothing," she replied, her voice flat. She nodded at the beer. "Is that for me?"

"Maybe," I said. She made a face at me, and I handed it over, then sat down as she took a sip, her lipstick staining the rim.

"God, I love your shirt, Annabel," Emily said. "Is it new?"

"Yeah. Pretty new." I reached up, running my hand over the pink suede top my mom and I had found at Tosca earlier the day before. It had been expensive, but we figured the whole summer's worth of wear I'd get out of it justified the price. "I just got it this week."

Sophie exhaled loudly, shaking her head. "This," she announced, "is officially the worst last-day-of-classes party ever."

"It's only eight thirty," I told her, looking around the room. There was a couple making out on a nearby armchair, and I could see a group of people sitting around the dining-room table playing cards. Music was coming from somewhere, probably out back, the bass thumping beneath our feet. "Things could improve."

She took another swig of her beer. "Doubtful. If this is any indication, this summer's going to be the worst yet."

"You think?" Emily said, sounding surprised. "There were some cute college guys outside."

"And you'd want to date a college guy who hangs out at a high-school party?" Sophie said.

"Well," Emily replied, "I don't know."

"Like I told you," Sophie said. "Lame."

There was a burst of noise to our left, and I turned to see a group of people pushing their way into the foyer. I saw a girl I recognized from my P.E. class, a couple of guys I didn't know, and, bringing up the rear, Will Cash.

"See? Things are looking up already," I said to Sophie. Instead of looking pleased, though, she narrowed her eyes.

They'd had some spat earlier in the week, but I'd thought it was resolved as much as anything ever was between them. Apparently not. Will only nodded at Sophie before following the people he'd come with down the hallway to the kitchen.

Once he was out of sight, she sat back, crossing her legs. "This sucks," she announced, and this time, I knew better than to disagree.

I stood up, holding my hand out to her. "Come on," I said. "Let's go circulate."

"No," she said flatly. Emily, who had started to get up, sat down again.

"Sophie."

She shook her head. "You two go. Have a fabulous time."

"So you just want to stay here and sulk?"

"I'm not sulking," she said, her voice cold. "I'm just sitting."

"Fine," I said. "I'm going to get another beer. You need anything?"

"No," she said, her eyes on the dining room, where Will was talking to the guy at the head of the table who was dealing out cards.

"You want to come with me?" I asked Emily. She nodded, putting her beer on the coffee table, and followed me down the hallway.

"Is she okay?" she asked me as soon as we were out of Sophie's earshot.

"She's fine," I told her.

"She seems upset," she said. "Before you got here, she was barely even speaking to me."

"She'll warm up," I told her. "You know how she is."

We walked through the kitchen and out onto the porch to the keg, which was surrounded by a few older guys. "Hey," one of them, who was tall and thin and smoking a cigarette, said to me. "Let me get you a beer."

"I'm okay," I said, giving him a mild smile as I picked up a cup and filled it myself.

"You two go to Jackson?" another asked Emily, who was standing off to the side, her arms crossed over her chest. She nodded, her eyes on me. "Man, these freshmen get hotter every year."

"We're not freshmen," I said as I turned away from the keg. A curly-headed guy was standing right in front of me now, blocking my path. I said, "Excuse me."

He looked at me for a second before moving aside. "Hard to get, huh?" he said as I stepped past him. "I like that."

I walked back into the kitchen, and Emily followed, shutting the door behind us.

"Those weren't the ones I was talking about earlier," she said quietly.

"I know," I said. "Those guys are at every party."

We started back to Sophie, but a bunch of people had just come in, and the hallway was packed with bodies and noise. I tried to push my way through, only to get stuck about halfway to the living room, with people crammed on all sides of me. I turned my head, looking for Emily, but she'd been waylaid by a loud girl named Helena we knew from the Models who, from the looks of it, was yelling in her ear.

"*Excuse* me," some girl I didn't recognize snapped as she

pushed past me, her elbow cracking against mine. I felt a splash, then looked down to see beer—hers or mine, it was hard to say—running down my leg. Suddenly the hallway seemed even smaller, not to mention hotter. So when a space opened up to my left, I took it, turning into a small alcove under the stairs where I could finally breathe.

I leaned back, pressing myself against the wall, and took a sip of my beer as people continued to push past. I was getting ready to go back into the throng when Will Cash walked by. He glanced over at me, then stopped.

"Hey," he said. Two guys passed him going the other way. One of them reached up, ruffling his hair, and Will made a face. "What are you doing?"

"Nothing," I said. "Just—"

He turned, then ducked under to where I was. There was barely enough room for both of us in the alcove—it was the kind of place for a small table, or maybe a piece of art—but I still tried to move to my left, putting some space between us.

"Hiding out, huh?" he asked. He wasn't smiling as he said this, even though I was pretty sure he meant it as a joke. That was the thing with Will. You just could never tell. Or I couldn't, anyway.

"It just . . . got a little crazy out there," I said. "Have you, um, caught up with Sophie yet?"

He was still looking at me, that flat gaze, and I felt myself flush again. "Not yet," he said. "How long you guys been here?"

"Oh, I didn't come with them," I replied as Hillary Prescott walked past. When she saw us, she slowed her pace, staring at us for a moment before moving on, disappearing around the corner. "I just got here . . . I got held up at home."

Will didn't say anything, just kept staring at me.

"You know how it is," I said, taking another gulp of my beer as a bunch of girls passed by, laughing loudly. "Family drama and all that."

I had no idea why I was telling him this, just as I had no idea why I did anything I did around Will Cash. Something about him unsettled me to a point where I felt so tentative that for some reason I compensated by being entirely too open.

"Really," he said now, his voice flat.

I felt my face flush again. "I should go catch up with Sophie," I said. "I'll, um, see you around, I guess."

He nodded. "Yeah," he said. "See you."

I didn't even wait for a break in the crowd, instead just pushing forward, bumping some football player who was passing and following him back toward the kitchen, where I found Emily leaning against the island, her cell phone pressed to her ear.

"Where'd you go?" she asked, flipping it closed and slipping it back into her pocket.

"Nowhere," I said. "Come on."

When we got back to the living room, Sophie was still on the couch, but now she wasn't alone. Will had joined her, and from the looks of it, they were having some sort of argument. Sophie was saying something, her face pinched, while Will seemed to be only half listening, glancing around the room as she talked.

"Better not bug them right now," I said to Emily. "We'll

come back. Anyway, I have got to pee. Any idea where the bathroom is?"

"I thought I saw one over there," she said, nodding toward a nearby hallway. "Come on."

There was a bathroom there, but also a line, so we decided to try our luck on the second floor. We were navigating a long hallway when I heard someone yell out my name.

I stopped, then doubled back to an open door we'd just passed to see Michael Kitchens and Nick Lester, two seniors I'd spent all semester suffering through art history with, playing pool.

"See?" Nick said. "I told you I saw Annabel!"

"What do you know," Michael, who was bent over the table about to take a shot, said. "And here I thought you were just hallucinating."

Nick turned around, then put a hand to his heart when he saw me. "No, it's Annabel," he said. "Annabel, Annabel, Annabel Greene."

"You promised when the year was over, you'd let that go," I told him. He'd done some senior project on Poe and had bugged me with this line endlessly. "Remember?"

"No," he said, grinning at me.

Michael took the shot, the balls splitting apart with a clank. "Nick's drunk," he informed us. "Consider yourself warned."

"I'm not drunk," Nick said. "I'm just cheerful."

"Is there a bathroom in here?" I asked. "We've been looking for one everywhere."

"Right over there," Michael told me, nodding across the room.

"Come on," I said to Emily, and she followed me inside. "This is Nick and Michael," I said, handing her my beer. "And this is Emily. I'll be back in a sec, okay?"

She nodded, looking a bit nervous. "Do you play?" Michael asked her, gesturing at the table.

"Kind of," she said.

He walked over to the wall, pulling off a stick for her. "Yeah, right," he said. "You say that, and then you'll beat me in ten seconds."

"She does have that pool-shark look to her," Nick said. Emily laughed, shaking her head. "It's always the quiet ones."

"Just go easy on me," Michael said to her. "That's all I ask."

By the time I came out of the bathroom two minutes later, Emily was holding her own. She was also in full-on flirt mode with Michael, who seemed more than happy to reciprocate. Which left me with Nick, who sat down beside me on the near-by couch and announced he had something to say.

"You know," he said as he took a sip of his beer, "since school is over now and all, I just think you should know that I'm aware of how you feel about me."

"How I feel about you," I repeated.

"Dude," Michael called out from the right corner pocket. "Stop before you say something you regret."

"Shhh," Nick told him, waving his arm. He turned back to me. "Annabel," he said, his voice serious, "it's okay that you have a crush on me."

"Oh, God," Michael groaned. "I'm so embarrassed for you right now."

"I mean, it makes sense," Nick said, slurring slightly as I

tried not to smile. "I'm a senior. An older man. It makes sense you'd look up to me. But . . ." Here he paused, taking another swig of his beer. "It's not going to work out."

"Oh," I said. "Well. It's better to know now, I guess."

Nick patted my hand, nodding. "I'm really flattered, but it doesn't matter how much you love me. I just don't feel that way about you."

"Like hell," Michael said, and Emily laughed.

"I understand," I told Nick.

"You do?"

"Totally."

He was still patting my hand, although, at this point, I was not sure he was aware of it. "Good. Because I'd really like, if you can get past your feelings, for us to remain friends."

"Me, too," I said.

Nick sat back, tipping his bottle to his mouth. Then he brought it back down, turning it up. One drop fell out. "Empty," he announced. "I need another."

"You really don't," Michael said, then winced as Emily shot the cue ball, knocking two of his stripes into a pocket.

"How about a water?" I asked Nick. "I was just about to get one for myself."

"A water," he repeated slowly, as if this was a foreign concept. "Okay. Lead the way."

"We'll be back," I said to Emily as I got to my feet, Nick then doing the same with considerably more trouble. "You need anything?"

She shook her head, bending down for another shot. "I'm good," she said.

"Too good," Michael said as two more of his balls disappeared. "'Kind of' play, my ass."

Nick and I only made it about halfway down the hallway before he announced he'd changed his mind. "Too tired," he said, plopping down next to a bedroom door. "Need to rest."

"Are you okay?" I asked him.

"Dandy," he replied. "You just go get that, that . . ."

"Water," I said.

"Water . . . and I'll meet you right here. 'Kay?" He sat back, his head bonking the wall. "Right here."

I nodded, then continued on to the stairs. On the way, I stopped to look down at the living room below, which was now considerably more crowded. Sophie was gone from the couch, as was Will, which I figured was either a good sign or a really bad one.

Downstairs, I located two bottled waters, then stopped to talk to a few people. When I got back to the hallway, Nick wasn't there. I figured he'd headed back to the game room. I was just about to do the same when I heard a voice.

"Annabel."

It was soft and faint. I turned. There was a bedroom to my right, the door slightly ajar. Handy if you were stumbling or, even worse, puking. *Poor Nick*, I thought. I stuck one water in my back pocket, opened the other one, then pushed the door open and stepped inside.

"Hey," I said. "Did you get lost?"

As I stepped over the threshold into the dark, I had my first prickling sense that something wasn't right. It was just how the room felt, like the entire space around me was unsettled. I stepped back, reaching for the knob, but I couldn't find it, my fingers only touching wall. "Nick?" I said.

Then, suddenly, I felt something bump up against my left side. Not furniture, or an object, but something alive. Someone. *It's Nick*, I told myself. *He's drunk*. But at the same time I started moving my hand behind me, faster now, searching for the light switch or doorknob. Finally, I felt the knob. Just as I was twisting it, though, I felt fingers closing over my wrist.

"Hey," I said, and even though I was trying to act casual, my voice sounded scared. "What's—?"

"Shhh, Annabel," a voice said, and then the fingers were moving up my arm, over my skin, and I felt another hand on my right shoulder. "It's just me."

It wasn't Nick. This voice was deeper, and not slurring at all, each syllable enunciated perfectly. As I realized this, I panicked, my hand gripping tighter around the water bottle in my hand. The top popped off, and suddenly I felt cold seeping into my shirt, onto my skin. "Don't," I said.

"Shhh," the voice said again, and then the hands were off me. A second later, they covered my eyes.

I jerked forward, trying to pull away. The water bottle, now half empty, fell from my hands, hitting the carpet with a dull thud, and his hands grabbed me by my shoulders, hard. I kept wriggling, trying to get loose and turn around, toward the door, but my hands were flailing in empty air. It was like the walls had slid back, out of reach; there was nothing to hold on to.

I could hear myself gasping, my breath beginning to sputter as he locked an elbow around my neck, pulling me up against him. My legs came up off the ground and I started kicking them, making contact with the door once—*bang!*—before he dragged me backwards a couple of steps. Then his other hand was moving around to my stomach, pushing aside my shirt, and thrusting down my jeans.

"Stop it," I said, but then his arm—warm, and smelling of sweat—was covering my mouth, blocking the sound. His fingers were sharp as he pushed aside my underwear, going deeper and deeper, his breath now hard little bursts in my ear. I was still trying to get away, squirming, even as his fingers probed farther, and then he was inside me.

I bit down on the skin of his arm, hard. He yelped, then yanked his arm off my mouth, pushing me forward. As I felt my feet under me, I reached for the wall, trying to get my bearings, my fingers only barely raking some solid surface before he grabbed the waistband of my jeans and turned me around to face him. Instinctively I put my hands out in front of me, shielding myself, but he pushed them aside, roughly, and then I was down.

In a second—it seemed impossible he could move so fast—he was on top of me, his fingers fumbling open the snap of my jeans. I could feel carpet beneath me, scratchy on my back, as I tried to push him away, the smell of wet suede filling my nostrils as he put one hand on my chest, his palm flat against my skin to hold me down, and began pulling down my jeans with the other. I was digging into the floor with my elbows, putting all I had into rising up, but I couldn't move.

I heard him unzip, and then he was back on top of me. I tried to push against his shoulders, throwing every bit of my weight against him, but he was so heavy, pressing into me, pushing one of my legs up—this was really happening—and then, just as I felt him on my leg and twisted myself one last, desperate time, I saw something: a tiny sliver of light, falling across us.

It was like a thread through the dark, and in it, I saw a bit of his back, freckled; the fine blond hair on the arm that was thrown across me; the tiniest bit of dark pink suede; and then, just before he pushed off me, his eyes, blue, the pupils widening, then narrowing, then widening again, as the light stretched wider. And then he was scrambling to his feet.

I sat up, my heart pounding, and pulled up my pants. Somehow, I was able to focus on zipping them, as if this, now, was the most important thing in the world. I had just gotten it when the light overhead clicked on, and there, standing in front of me, was Sophie.

She saw me first. Then she turned her head and looked at Will Cash, who was now sitting on the bed behind me. "Will?" she asked. Her voice was high, tight. "What's going on?"

Will, I thought. I had a flash of his arm covering my mouth, his hands over my eyes, then another of him earlier, standing so close to me in the alcove. *It's Will.*

"I don't know." He shrugged, then ran a hand through his hair. "She just . . ."

Sophie stared at him for a long moment. From the hallway behind her, I could hear laughter, and I had a flash of Emily and Michael still playing their game. Still waiting for me.

Sophie turned to me. "Annabel?" she said, then stepped forward, into the room, her hand still on the doorjamb. "What are you doing?"

I felt like I'd been shattered, everything that had just happened a fragment, no part of a real whole. I got to my feet, smoothing down my top over my stomach. "Nothing," I said, the word coming out in a gasp. I tried to swallow. "I was—"

Sophie cut her eyes back at Will, and even though she hadn't interrupted me, I stopped talking. He stared right back at her. Not a flinch. Not one. "Somebody," she said, "had better start explaining this. Right now."

But nobody said anything. Later, this would strike me as so surprising, that at that moment I was actually waiting for someone else to define this, as if I hadn't been there, had no words for it at all.

"Will?" Sophie said. "Say something."

"Look," he said, "I was waiting for you, and then she came up here . . ." He trailed off, shaking his head, but kept his eyes on her. "I don't know."

Sophie turned her attention back to me, and for a moment we just looked at each other. She had to see something was wrong, I thought. I shouldn't have to tell her. I wasn't some other girl, like the ones we'd driven around looking for all those nights. We were best friends. I honestly believed that. Then.

Her mouth pursed. I watched the lips come together. "You *slut*," she said.

It seemed so stupid, later. But I actually, honestly thought I'd heard her wrong. "What?" I said.

"You're a goddamn whore." Her voice was rising now, still shaky but gaining strength. "I can't believe you."

"Sophie," I said. "Wait. I didn't—"

"You didn't what?" she said. Behind her, I could see shadows, stretching forward across the opposite wall of the hallway. People were coming, I thought. People were hearing this. People would know. "You think you can just fuck my boyfriend at a party and I won't find out?"

I felt my mouth open, but no words came. I just stood there, staring at her, and then Emily appeared behind her in the doorway, her eyes wide. "Annabel?" she asked. "What's going on?"

"Your friend's a slut is what's going on," Sophie told her.

"No," I said. "It's not like that."

"I know what I saw!" she screamed. Emily, behind her, stepped backwards. Sophie leveled a finger at me. "You have always wanted what I have!" she said. "You've always been jealous of me!"

I felt myself flinch. Her voice was so loud it was like it was shaking my bones. I was so confused, and scared, and even though through everything else, I had not cried—how had I not cried?—now I felt a lump begin and then swell in my throat.

Sophie pushed through the door, taking two big strides until she was right in front of me, and the room seemed to shrink—Will, Emily, everyone else disappearing from my peripheral vision—until it was just her narrowed eyes, her finger still jabbing, so much anger and fury.

"You're so done," she said. Her voice was shaking. "It's over for you."

"Sophie." I shook my head. "Please. Just—"

"Get out of my face!" she said. "Get out!"

And then, as quickly as it had fallen away, my view came back and I saw everything. The crowd of faces that had somehow gathered in the hallway. Will Cash, in my side vision, still sitting on the bed. The sea-foam green of the carpet beneath my feet, the yellow glare of the light overhead. It was hard to believe that only moments earlier, all of these things had been cloaked in such a thick darkness, so hidden I wouldn't have been able to recognize a single one. But now, like me, they were exposed.

Sophie was still standing in front of me. It was quiet all around us. I knew I could have broken the silence, could have spoken up. It was only my word against his, and now hers. But I didn't.

Instead, I walked out of that room and everyone watched me. I could feel their eyes as I stepped around Sophie, then pushed out into the hallway and started for the stairs. Once in the foyer, I went to the door, pushing it open, then stepped out into the night, crossing the damp grass to my car. I did all of this very carefully and with purpose, as if having control over these actions would somehow balance out what had just happened.

The one thing I didn't do, though, all the way home, was look at myself. Not in the side mirror. Not in the rearview. At every stoplight, every time I downshifted, I picked a point up ahead—the bumper of the car in front of me, a distant building, even the broken yellow line of the road—to focus on. I did not want to see myself like this.

When I got home, my dad was waiting, like always, sitting up by himself. I could see the light from the TV, pale and flickering, the minute I stepped inside.

"Annabel?" he called out as the volume on the set began to

decrease, bit by bit, before falling silent entirely. "Is that you?"

I stood there for a second in the foyer, knowing that if I didn't show my face he'd suspect something. I reached up, brushing back my hair with my fingers, then took a breath and stepped into the living room. "Yeah," I said. "It's me."

He turned in his chair to look at me. "Good night?" he asked.

"It was okay," I said.

"There's a great show on," he said, nodding at the TV. "It's all about the New Deal. You interested?"

Any other night, I would have joined him. It was our tradition, even if I only sat down for a few minutes. But this time, I just couldn't.

"No, thanks," I said. "I'm kind of tired. I think I'll just go to bed."

"All right," he said, turning back to the TV. "Good night, Annabel."

"Good night."

He picked up the remote and I turned away, walking back into the foyer, where the moonlight was slanting in the window over the door and falling on the picture of me and my mother and sisters on the opposite wall. In that bright light, you could see every detail: the distant caps of the waves, the slight tinge of gray to the sky. I stood there for a moment, studying each of us, taking in Kirsten's smile, Whitney's haunted gaze, the way my mother cocked her head slightly to the side. When I got to my own face, I found myself staring at it, so bright, with dark all around it, like it was someone I didn't recognize. Like a word on a page that you've printed and read a million times, that suddenly looks strange or wrong, foreign, and you feel scared for a second, like you've lost something, even if you're not sure what it is.

The next day, I tried to call Sophie, but she wouldn't answer. I knew I should go over to her house, explain myself in person, but each time I began to I had a flash of being in that room, that hand over my mouth, the bang of my foot kicking the door, and I just couldn't do it. In fact, whenever I thought about what had happened, my stomach twisted and I felt bile rising in my throat. Like some part of me was trying to push it up and out, purging it from my body entirely in a way I could not seem to do on my own.

The alternative wasn't good either, of course. I'd already been labeled a slut, and who knew how the story had grown in the hours since. But what had really happened was worse than anything Sophie could make up and pass on.

Even so, deep down, I knew I hadn't done anything wrong. That this wasn't my fault, and in a perfect world, I could tell people what happened and somehow not be ashamed. In real life, though, this was harder. I was used to being looked at—it was part of who I was, who I'd been as long as I could remember. But once people knew about this, I was sure they'd see me in a different way. That with every glance, they'd no longer see me, but what had happened to me, so raw and shameful and private, turned outward and suddenly scrutinized. I wouldn't be the girl who had everything, but the girl who'd been attacked, assaulted, so helpless. It seemed safer to hold it in, where the only one who could judge was me.

Still, I had times when I wondered if this was the right decision. But as the days passed, and then weeks, it seemed like even if I could have told my story, now it was too late. Like the longer the distance from it, the less people would be willing to believe it.

So I did nothing. But a couple of weeks later, I was with my mother at the drugstore, picking up a few things, when she said, "Isn't that Sophie?"

It was. She was at the other end of the aisle, looking at magazines. I watched her turn a page, wrinkling her nose at something she saw there. "Yeah," I replied. "I think so."

"Then go say hello. I'll get this," she said, taking the list from me. "Just catch up with me up front, okay?" And then she was gone, shifting her basket farther up her arm and leaving us alone.

I should have just followed her. But for whatever reason, I found myself walking toward Sophie, coming up behind her just as she stuffed the magazine—which had a cover entirely devoted to the latest high-profile celebrity breakup—back onto the rack. "Hi," I said.

She jumped, startled, then turned around. When she saw me, she narrowed her eyes. "What do you want?"

I hadn't planned what I was going to say, but even if I had, this would have made it harder. "Look," I said, glancing over to the next aisle, where my mother was examining an aspirin display, "I just wanted to—"

"Don't talk to me," she said. Her voice was loud, much louder than mine. "I have nothing to say to you."

"Sophie," I said. I was almost whispering now. "It wasn't what you think."

"Oh, so you're psychic now, and not just a slut?"

I felt my face flush at this word, and instinctively looked over again at my mom, wondering if she'd heard it. She'd glanced up, and now smiled at us and moved on farther down to the next aisle.

"What, is there a problem, Annabel?" Sophie said. "Let me guess. Just the regular family drama?"

I just looked at her, confused. Then I remembered: This was what I'd said to Will in the alcove that night, for what reason I still didn't know. Of course he'd tell her, use this, the stupidest of confessions, against me. I could just imagine how he'd spun it, me confiding in him, then following him upstairs. *I don't know*, he'd said that night as I waited for him to explain himself. *She just . . .*

"If you know a guy has a girlfriend—especially if that girlfriend is me—there's absolutely no reason you should be doing anything with him that could be taken the wrong way," Sophie had said to me, all those months ago. "It's a choice, Annabel. And if you make the wrong one, you have only yourself to blame when there are consequences."

In her mind, it was that simple. I knew this wasn't true, but I felt a flicker of doubt and fear as the pieces came together, building against me, my worst fears realized. What if even if I had told, or did tell, nobody believed me? Or even worse, blamed me for it?

My stomach twisted, that familiar taste filling my mouth.

Sophie glanced over at my mom, watching her for a second, and I had a flash of her that night at dinner, wincing as Whitney slammed her chair into the table. I'd been so worried about her that night, so many nights, and I couldn't imagine what she'd make of this if it ever got back to her.

"Sophie," I said again. "Just—"

"Get away from me," she said. "I never want to see you again."

Then she pushed past me, shaking her head, and walked away. Somehow, I managed to turn around and make my way back down the aisle, the shelves blurring as I passed them. I saw a woman with a kid on her hip, an old man pushing a walker, some stock clerk examining a price gun, and then, finally, my mom, standing by a sunscreen display, looking for me.

"There you are," she said as I approached. "How's Sophie?"

I forced myself to take in a breath. "She's good," I said. "Fine."

It was the first lie I told my mother about Sophie, but by no means the last. Then, I'd still thought everything I felt about that night—the shame, the fear—would fade in time, healing like a onetime gash to a single, barely noticeable scar. But that hadn't happened. Instead, the things that I remembered, these little details, seemed to grow stronger, to the point where I could feel their weight in my chest. Nothing, however, stuck with me more than the memory of stepping into that dark room and what I found there, and how the light then took that nightmare and made it real.

That was the thing: Once, the difference between light and

dark had been basic. One was good, one bad. Suddenly, though, things weren't so clear. The dark was still a mystery, something hidden, something to be scared of, but I'd come to fear the light, too. It was where everything was revealed, or seemed to be. Eyes closed, I saw only the blackness, reminding me of this one thing, the most deep of my secrets; eyes open, there was only the world that didn't know it, bright, inescapable, and somehow, still there.

Chapter
FOURTEEN

"Hey," Owen said, smiling as he turned around to face me. "You made it."

And I had. I was there, at Bendo, standing in front of the stage. How, though, I wasn't exactly sure. In fact, everything since Emily and I had finally come face-to-face was a bit of a blur.

Somehow, I'd managed to finish the fashion show, modeling three other outfits and clapping as Mrs. McMurty pretended to be both totally embarrassed and completely surprised to be coaxed onstage for flowers, just like every other year. Afterwards, I'd gone backstage, where my parents were waiting.

When my mother saw me, she pulled me in for a hug, her hands smoothing over my back. "You were fantastic," she said. "Absolutely gorgeous."

"Although that dress is a little low-cut," my dad added, eyeing the white sheath I'd worn for the formal segment, the last one of the show. "Wouldn't you say?"

"No," my mom said, swatting him as she pulled away from me. "It's perfect. You were perfect."

I forced a smile, but my mind was still reeling. There were

so many people behind the stage, so much noise and commotion, but all I could think about was Emily. S*he knew*, I thought as my mom said something about finding Mrs. McMurty. *She knew.*

I reached up, tucking a piece of hair behind my ear. I felt nervous, jumpy, the noise of the crowd and the heat of all those bodies not helping, and now my mother was talking again.

". . . just wonderful, but we should get home. Whitney's fixing dinner, and I told her we'd be there ten minutes ago."

"Whitney?" I said as my dad nodded at a man in a suit as he passed, saying his name. "She's not here?"

My mom squeezed my shoulder. "Oh, sweetie, I'm sure she would have liked to come, but it's still hard for her, I think. . . . She wanted to stay home. But we loved it. We really did."

With everything that had happened with Emily, I felt crazy, but I knew one thing: That had been my sister, watching me from a distance as I reached the end of the runway. I would have bet my life on it.

I felt a hand on my arm, and turned to see Mrs. McMurty standing there, a tall, gray-haired man in a suit beside her. "Annabel," she said, smiling, "I want you to meet Mr. Driscoll. He's the head of marketing for Kopf's, and he wanted to say hello."

"Hi," I said. "It's nice to meet you."

"And you as well," he replied, reaching out his hand. His palm was dry and cool. "We're all big fans. We loved you in the back-to-school commercial."

"Thank you," I said.

"Great show." He smiled, nodding at my mom and dad, and

then he and Mrs. McMurty were moving on, through the crowd. My mother watched them go, her face flushed.

"Oh, Annabel," she said. She squeezed my arm again, not saying anything else, but I got the message. Loud and clear.

Just then, over my mom's head, I saw Mrs. Shuster, a coat folded over her arm, standing by the back edge of the stage. She looked at her watch, then glanced around, worried. A second later, her face relaxed, and I saw Emily walking toward her. Her hair was still up, her makeup on, but she'd changed back into regular clothes and wasn't talking to anyone as she made her way through the crowd.

"Um, I should go change," I said to my parents. "These shoes are killing me."

My mom nodded, then leaned in, giving me another kiss. "Of course," she said as Mr. Driscoll walked past again, this time without Mrs. McMurty. My mom watched him go, then said, "I'll put aside a plate for you, all right?"

"Actually," I said, "um, some of us were going to go out for pizza. You know, to celebrate the show being over, and all."

"Oh," my mom said. "Well, I know you must be exhausted, so don't stay out too long. Okay?"

I nodded as, behind her, I watched Mrs. Shuster reach out to Emily, handing her the coat and standing there, her face somber, as Emily shrugged it on. Then she slid her hand down her daughter's arm, rubbing it slightly, and they started toward the mall exit. I turned my attention back to my mother, quickly. "I won't be too late," I said.

"Eleven at the latest," my father said as he leaned down to give me a hug. "Right?"

"Right," I replied.

The entire time I was changing out of my outfit, then walking to my car and driving across town, I told myself I had to push what had happened with Emily out of my mind. I'd been looking forward to going to Bendo, and I was determined to enjoy it. Or try to.

Starting right now.

"So," I said as Owen turned back to the stage, "what'd I miss?"

"Not much," he replied as someone bumped me from behind. As I pitched forward he reached out, grabbing my arm. "Whoa," he said. "Watch the footing, this place is kind of a madhouse." There was a burst of feedback from the stage in front of us, and a group of people to our left let loose with a loud chorus of boos. Owen leaned his head down closer to my ear. "How was the fashion show?"

I didn't want to lie to him. At the same time, though, I knew I couldn't tell him what had really happened—not here, not tonight. Maybe not ever. "It's over," I replied, which was, technically, true.

"That good, huh?" he said as a tall girl in a sequined top, holding a drink, pushed past us, splattering as she went.

I smiled. "Pretty much."

"Well, never fear. When the band comes on, your night will improve."

"You think?"

"I know," he said just as he got bumped, hard this time, by a guy in a black coat who was passing by, a cell phone pressed to his ear. Owen glanced at him, and the guy shrugged, hardly bothered, and kept walking. "Okay. Time for a space break. Come on."

He turned and started back through the crowd, and I did my best to follow him as he led me to an open booth against the wall.

"Have a seat," he said, gesturing for me to slide in. "The view isn't as good, but at least no one's elbowing you in the spleen."

I could hear what sounded like someone tuning up, followed by a burst of feedback. "The opener," Owen said, nodding toward the stage. "They were supposed to go on a half hour ago, but—"

This thought was interrupted by Rolly, who suddenly slid in beside him, landing with a thump on the bench. "Oh," he said, breathless, "my God."

"Finally," Owen said, turning to look at him. "Where the hell have you been, man? I was beginning to think you'd been abducted or something."

"No," Rolly replied. "You are not going to *believe* what just happened."

"He went to get drinks about a half hour ago," Owen explained to me. "I mean, I know the crowd is big, but that's ridiculous. And where's my water?"

Rolly shook his head. "Dude. She's here."

"What?"

Rolly took in a breath, then held up his hands, palms facing out. *"She's here,"* he said again. Then he paused, letting this sink in before adding, "She's here, and she smiled at me."

"For thirty minutes?" Owen asked.

"No. Only for a moment."

"This is the girl that punched you?" I asked, clarifying.

"Yes."

"I can't believe you didn't get my water," Owen said.

"Would you just forget about that for a second?" Rolly pulled a hand through his hair. "I don't think you're getting the significance of this situation."

"So you talked to her," Owen said.

"No. Here's what happened." Rolly took a deep breath. "I was on my way to the bar and then, suddenly, there she was. Boom! Popped up right in front of me, like an apparition or something. But just as I'm about to speak to her, someone steps between us. And the next thing I know, she's gone, walking away, surrounded by people. Since then I've been hanging back, waiting for the perfect in to present itself. I mean, it has to be just right."

"Why don't you offer to go get her a water?" Owen suggested. "You can pick up one for me while you're at it."

Rolly just looked at him. "What is up with you and this water thing?"

"I'm thirsty," Owen told him. "And I was going to go, but you offered. *Insisted*, I might add."

"I will get you a water!" Rolly said. "But first, if you don't mind, I'd like to meet my destiny in the most ideal way possible."

There was another burst of feedback from the stage. Owen sighed. "Look," he said, "maybe you should just forget about the ideal moment."

Rolly just looked at him. "I'm not following," he said.

"It's taken a long time for you to see her again, right?"

Owen said. "And who knows how much longer until the perfect moment. Maybe you should just do it. That way—"

Rolly's eyes widened, suddenly. "Oh, shit," he said. "There she is."

Owen leaned out of the booth slightly. "Where?"

"Don't look!" Rolly said, yanking him back in. "God!"

Owen looked down at his sleeve, which Rolly was clutching. Rolly moved his hand.

"Okay," he said quietly. "She's standing by the door. In the red."

I watched as Owen leaned out of the booth again, took a quick glance behind me, then sat back straight again. "Yep, that's her," he reported. "Now what?"

"My point exactly," Rolly said. "I need an in."

By this point, I had to admit that the suspense was killing me. "I'm just going to do a quick over-the-shoulder survey of the room," I said to Rolly. "Okay?"

He nodded, and Owen shot him a look. "She's a girl," Rolly explained. "They can look without looking."

When I first turned around, all I could see was a heavyset guy in a Metallica shirt. But then he moved slightly, and I saw that there was a girl behind him. She had shiny black hair and was wearing little retro glasses, a red sweater and jeans, a beaded bag pulled across her. But I didn't need to see any of these things, really; I knew her with one glance.

"Wait," I said, turning back to Rolly. "The girl . . . it's Clarke?"

For a moment, Rolly just looked at me. Then he leaned across the table so quickly that I drew back, startled, bumping my head on the booth behind me. "Is that her name?" he asked. His face was now inches from mine. "Clarke?"

I nodded, carefully. "Um . . . yeah."

After staring at me for another second he moved back, slowly, until he was sitting upright. "She has a *name*. And it is Clarke. Clarke . . ." He trailed off, looking at me again.

"Reynolds," I said.

"Clarke Reynolds," he repeated. "Wow." He looked like he was in a trance. Then, suddenly, his eyes widened, and he snapped his fingers. "That's it! That's my in. You."

"Me?"

He nodded vigorously. "You know her."

"No," I said quickly. "I don't."

"You knew her name," he pointed out.

"We were friends once. It was—"

"You're *friends* with her?" he asked. "This is perfect!"

"It's really not," I said, shaking my head.

"You go up and talk to her, and then I'll walk by and you can introduce me. It's organic. It's ideal!"

"Rolly, seriously," I said. "I'm not the person to get you close to Clarke."

"Annabel." He leaned across the table again, sliding his hands out to mine. "Annabel, Annabel, Annabel Greene."

Shhh, Annabel. It's just me. I felt a chill run up my neck.

"Please," Rolly said. "Just hear me out."

I looked at Owen, who just shook his head. When I moved my right hand forward, Rolly instantly grabbed it.

"This girl," he said solemnly, his palm hot, "is my destiny."

"Okay," Owen said, "now you're officially freaking her out."

"Rolly," I said. "This thing is—"

"Please, Annabel," he said. He put his other hand on mine, so my fingers were completely enclosed. "Please just introduce me. That's all I'm asking. One shot. One chance. *Please*."

I knew I should tell him the real reason he did not want me to be his in, or any part of whatever happened, or didn't, between him and Clarke. Not just because he deserved to know it, but also because up until now I had been truthful with Owen—and all things having to do with Owen—and holding this back would mean that for the second time that night, I wasn't being the honest girl he thought I was. If I ever had been.

At the same time, looking at Rolly's hopeful face, I could feel myself wavering. On a night when what I'd done, or not done, was suddenly looming large, this seemed like a tiny way to somehow, in some distant way, make up for it. I couldn't fix the past, or change what had happened to Emily, but with this, maybe, I could help someone else's future.

"All right," I said. "But I'm just warning you: It might not work."

Rolly beamed, then hurriedly motioned for Owen to get out of the booth before sliding out himself. "I'll just go over by the bar," he said, "and wait until you've made contact. Then I'll casually happen by, and you can introduce us. Okay?"

I nodded. Already I was regretting agreeing to this, which Rolly most likely sensed, as he bolted out of there, fast, so I couldn't change my mind.

"You sure you want to do this?" Owen asked me as I got to my feet.

"No." I glanced over at Clarke, who was now sitting with a group of people at a table. "I'll be back in a second."

As I turned away, I felt his hand on my arm. "Hey," he said. "Are you okay?"

"What?" I asked. "Why?"

"I don't know." He dropped his hand, then looked at me. "You just seem . . . I don't know. Not yourself, or something. Everything all right?"

And here I'd thought I was hiding it. But like the difference between the picture on Mallory's wall and my face in the picture he took, this contrast—between who I'd been and who I felt myself becoming, again, with each step I took or was forced to take backwards—was obvious. To both of us. Which was why this time, I didn't hesitate and try to be honest, instead just going with what came naturally.

"I'm fine," I told him, but I could feel him watching me as I walked away.

Clarke was talking to a girl with blonde hair wearing heavy dark eyeliner, and didn't see me until I was right up on her. She glanced up, half smiling, reacting to something her friend had just said. When she saw me, she immediately affected her normal thin-lipped, stoic expression. It wasn't like I could turn back now, though. So I just dove in.

"Hi," I said.

At first, she didn't say anything, her silence stretching out long enough that I thought she might turn away, ignoring me completely. But just as the pause was getting excruciating, she said, "Hello."

Someone from down the table said something to the

blonde girl, and she turned away, leaving us alone. Clarke was still looking at me, a flat expression on her face. I had a flash of her at the pool, all those years ago, a hand of cards spread out between her thumb and forefinger.

"Look," I blurted out, "I know you hate me, okay? But the thing is—"

"Is that what you think?"

I stopped in mid-breath. "What?"

"You think I hate you?" she asked. Her voice, I noticed suddenly, was clear. Crystal. Not a sniffle to be heard. "Is that what you think the problem is here?"

"I don't know," I said. "I mean, I just thought—"

"You don't know," she repeated. Her voice was sharp. "Really."

Just then, I felt it: a hand clapping onto my shoulder with such force it almost sent me spilling forward onto the table. "Annabel! Hello!"

It was Rolly. When I turned, he was standing there with a wow-how-about-this expression, as if we were long-lost friends who hadn't seen each other in eons. At the same time, I could feel a dampness from his hand, already seeping through to my shoulder.

"Hi," I said, trying to sound casual.

"Hi!" he replied, doing no better than I had. "I'm going to go to the bar in a second to get some waters. You want one?"

Clarke was looking at us, her eyes narrowed. *Better get to it*, I thought.

"Sure," I said. "Thanks. Oh, um, Rolly, this is Clarke. Clarke, this is Rolly."

Rolly shot out his hand. "Hi," he said as Clarke, more slowly, offered up her own. "Really nice to meet you."

"You, too," Clarke said flatly. She turned back to me. "You were saying?"

"So you're here for Truth Squad, right?" Rolly said, looking from me to Clarke, then immediately back to Clarke again. "They're really good, have you heard them before?"

"Um," Clarke said, "no. I haven't."

"Oh, they're *great*," Rolly gushed. I took a step to the side, and he immediately moved into the space I'd been standing in, closer to her. "I've seen them tons."

"You know, I better see if Owen wants a drink," I said. Clarke shot me a look; now, she was definitely pissed. "I'll, um, be back in a minute. Or two."

And then I got out of there, quick. When I got back to Owen, he'd been joined by a guy with short dark hair and an intense look on his face.

"—a total shambles," the dark-haired guy was saying as I slid in. "It was better when we did the booking ourselves. At least then, we had some say in the dates, and the venues. Now we're just their pawns, in their sick little corporate game."

"That sucks," Owen said.

"It does." The guy shook his head. "At least the single's getting some airplay nationally. I mean, that's what they *say*. Who knows if it's true or not."

I glanced over at Clarke's table. Rolly was still standing up, talking animatedly, while Clarke seemed markedly less so as she listened to him.

"Annabel," Owen said, "this is Ted. Ted, Annabel."

"Hi," Ted replied, barely glancing at me.

"Hi."

From the stage, there was a thumping noise as someone tested the microphone. "Hey," a voice said. "This thing on?" Someone from the crowd booed in response.

Ted sighed, "See," he said, "this is what I'm talking about. These jokers were only supposed to do a mini set, and they haven't even started yet."

"Who are they?" Owen asked him.

"I don't even know," Ted said, clearly disgusted. "The original openers came down with some kind of intestinal flu, so they booked these guys to fill in."

"Should have just had you go on early," Owen said. "It *is* an all-ages show. Plus everyone's here to see you guys."

"My point exactly," Ted replied. "Plus, if we had longer sets, we could try out some of the new stuff I've been writing. It's, like, a total change for us."

"Really."

Ted nodded, suddenly looking much more animated. "I mean, it's not so far from our regular stuff. Just a little slower, with some more technical touches. Reverb, and all that."

"Technical?" Owen said. "Or techno?"

"It's hard to say," Ted replied. "It's kind of its own thing. Maybe we'll be able to get a couple in the second set. Tell me what you think, okay? It's, like, supposed to be out there but still accessible."

Owen glanced at me. "You know, if that's what you're after, you should ask Annabel what she thinks," he said. "She hates techno."

They were both looking at me now. "Well," I said. "Actually—"

"So if she likes it," Owen said, "it's not too far out there. If she hates it, though, it won't float with the masses."

"And she'd say if she hated it," Ted said.

"Yup." Owen nodded. "She's dead honest. Doesn't hold back."

As he said this, I felt some part of me just sink. Because I so wanted this to be true, enough that, once, I'd actually believed it was. But now, I just sat there, feeling them both looking at me, and felt like the biggest liar of all.

There was a burst of guitar music from the stage, followed by a few drumbeats. Finally, the opening band was starting. Ted made a face, then pushed himself out of the booth. "I can't tolerate listening to this crap; I'm going back. You want to come with?"

"Sure," Owen said. I heard someone yowl, and more feedback. To me he said, "Come on."

I followed him and Ted along the back of the crowd, passing Clarke's table on the way. Rolly was still there, talking excitedly, waving his hands as he did so. Clarke was listening to him, however, so that had to count for something.

Ted led us to a door by the bar, then down a hallway so dark I could barely make out the restrooms as we passed them. When he pushed open a door with a hand-lettered sign that said PRIVATE, the sudden bright light spilling out made me squint.

The first thing I saw inside was a guy with curly black hair crouching on the floor, reaching under a nearby couch. When he saw us, he got to his feet, breaking into a wide smile. "Owen! What's up, man?"

"Not much," Owen said as they shook hands. "What about you?"

"Same old, same old." The guy held up a cell phone and battery. "Just busted my phone. Again."

"This is Annabel," Owen said.

"Dexter," he said, offering his hand. To Ted he said, "What's the word?"

"The opener just went on," Ted replied as he walked over to a small fridge, pulling out a beer. "Are you guys pretty much ready?"

There were two guys at a nearby table, playing cards. One of them, a redhead, said, "Do we look ready?"

"No."

"Well, looks can be deceiving. Because we are."

The other guy at the table laughed, throwing down a card as Ted shot him a look, then plopped on the couch, propping his feet on the table in front of him.

"So," Dexter said, sitting down on the opposite end of the couch. He put the phone on his knee, then picked up the battery, examining it. "What's new on the local music scene?"

"Nothing worth talking about," Owen told him.

"No kidding," Ted said. "You should see the frat-rock cover band that's playing now. Total Spinnerbait wannabes."

"Spinnerbait?" I said.

"They're a band," Owen told me.

"Hate Spinnerbait!" the redhead said, throwing down a card with a smack.

"Now, now," Dexter said, placing the battery carefully back on his phone. When he removed his hand, though, it fell off again, hitting the floor with a clack. He bent down, picking it up. "That's the thing that's great about this town," he said, putting it on again. "There are so many bands to choose from."

"Doesn't mean any of them can play," Ted said.

"True. But variety is always a good thing," Dexter said as the battery fell off again. He turned the phone over, trying to fit it on that way: no go. "In some places," he said, "you really only have a few choices and that"—the battery fell off again—"sucks."

"Dexter." I turned around to see a blonde girl sitting in a chair in the corner of the room. She was holding a yellow highlighter, and a textbook was open in her lap. I hadn't even seen her. "Do you need help?" she asked him.

"Nope. I'm good. Thanks, though."

She got up, sticking the pen in the book and the book under her arm, then walked over to him. "Give it to me."

"No, I've got it," Dexter said, turning the phone over again. "I think it's busted for good this time, actually. Maybe something broke out of it."

She held out her hand. "Let me try."

He handed it over. Then, as we all watched, she looked at it for a second, stuck the battery in, and pushed down. There was a click, and then a trilling sound as the phone came on. She handed it back to him, then sat down on the couch.

"Oh," he said, turning the phone over and staring at it. "Thanks, honey."

"No problem." She opened her book—*Statistics for*

Business Applications, the spine said—then smiled at us. "I'm Remy," she said.

"Oh! Sorry!" Dexter said. He reached down, smoothing a hand over her hair. "This is Owen and Annabel. This is Remy."

"Hi," I said, and she nodded, pulling out the highlighter again.

"Remy's slumming, touring with us over her fall break," Dexter explained. "She goes to Stanford. She's *very* smart."

"Then why's she with you?" the redhead called out from the table.

"I have no idea," Dexter replied as Remy rolled her eyes, "but I think it's my mad make-out skills." He leaned over, planting a series of loud, sloppy kisses on her cheek. She winced, trying to push him away, but then he fell into her lap, his long legs splaying out across the couch.

"Stop," she said, laughing. "God."

From outside, we could suddenly hear more feedback, followed by booing. "Hopefully, they're cutting that set short," Ted said. "Would anyone else like to perhaps, I don't know, get ready for our show?"

"No," the redhead said.

"Absolutely not," the other guy added.

Ted glowered at them. Then he put down his beer on the table with a clank, walked to the door, and pulled it open. Once he was out in the hallway, he slammed it behind him. Hard.

The redhead threw down his cards. "Gin!" he said, lifting his hands over his head in a victory salute. "Finally!"

"Aw, man," the other guy said. "I was close, too."

"Off," Remy said, and Dexter disentangled himself from

her lap, getting to his feet. In the process, he dropped his phone again. This time, though, the battery stayed put.

"Ted's right," he said, although Ted was now gone. "We should get organized. Owen, you guys sticking around after?"

Owen glanced at me. "Sure," he said.

"Cool. We'll catch up with you then, all right?"

"Sounds good."

Then, everyone was suddenly in motion: Dexter sliding his phone into his pocket, the redhead pushing out his chair while the other guy gathered up the cards. Owen led me back into the hallway, where we passed Ted, who was leaning against the wall, still looking annoyed. Owen told him to have a good show as we passed, and he mumbled something in return, but I couldn't make it out.

On the way back to our booth, I glanced over at Clarke's table. She was still there, looking at the stage, but Rolly was gone. *Oh well*, I thought. *I tried.*

"All right," Owen said as we sat down. From the stage, I could hear the openers winding up their set. "Now comes the real music. You'll like this."

I nodded, leaning back against the wall and tucking a piece of hair behind my ear. When I glanced over at Owen, he was staring at me. "What?" I said.

"Okay," he said. "Something *is* up with you. What's going on?"

I froze. Here it was, the direct question. Maybe I could answer. Just say something, spit it out, finally. Maybe—

"I mean," he said, "when have you ever just assumed you'll

like what I like? This could be Ebb Tide Two about to come on here. You have a fever or something?"

He was smiling as he said this, and I tried to smile back. Deep down, though, I could suddenly feel the weight of all my withholding, so many lies and omissions.

"I'm fine," I said as someone played a few guitar chords. "Stop distracting me. I need to concentrate on the music."

The crowd was huge now, much bigger than for the previous band, and pretty soon all I could see was backs and shoulders. Owen got to his feet. "You should stand up," he said.

"I'm okay," I said.

"Part of seeing a band live is actually *seeing* them," he said. And then he held out his hand.

Ever since I'd left the mall I'd been trying to forget about what had happened between me and Emily on the runway. But looking up at Owen, it all came back. Not just the day that led up to this, but all the ones since he'd done this the first time, offering not only his hand but a friendship that had saved me. I'd been so alone and scared and, yes, angry, and somehow Owen had seen it, even when everyone else had chosen to look away and act like it wasn't happening. Just like I'd done, and was doing, to Emily tonight.

He was still holding out his hand. Waiting.

"I'm, um, going to go to the bathroom," I said, pushing off the wall and out of the booth. "I'll be back in a second."

"Wait," he said, dropping his hand. He glanced at the stage. "The band's coming on. . . ."

"I know. I'll be right back."

Then I started walking before he could say anything else. Mostly because I couldn't bear to lie again. But also there was that sourness in my mouth, something rising up. I had to get out of there.

The crowd was impossibly thick now, body after body in my way as I tried to get to the door. Meanwhile, Truth Squad started with a song that, judging by the amount of people who immediately began to sing along, a lot of the crowd knew; the lyrics had something to do with potatoes.

I kept pushing on, moving sideways through a crowd of people all facing forward, just one profile after another after another, some turning slightly, annoyed as I pushed past, others ignoring me entirely. Finally, the crowd began to thin. I was almost to the door when someone grabbed my arm.

"Annabel!" It was Rolly. He was smiling, his grin wide, and carrying an armful of bottled waters. "I'm in!"

I just looked at him as the crowd suddenly burst into cheers and applause. "What?"

"In," he said, holding up a water. "I went to get her a drink, even. It's working! Finally, it's really happening! Can you believe it?"

He was so happy, his face flushed. "That's great," I managed. "Actually, I was just—"

"Here," he said, cutting me off. He stuck one of the waters it in his shirt pocket, another under his arm, and then handed me the remaining two. "For you and Owen. Tell him I said he was right. About everything. Okay?"

I nodded, then he flashed me a thumbs-up and was gone. As I watched him disappear into the crowd, I wished I'd thought to give him a message for Owen, as well. I looked across the crowd, knowing he was somewhere on the other side, waiting for me. But now the distance seemed so vast and impossible, too much in between. So with my mouth sour and palms wet, I headed for the door.

Once outside, the cold air hit me like a smack, gravel crunching beneath my feet as I left the building behind me. It was all too familiar, this bubbling up inside me, my throat burning, never enough time to get away. I barely made it to my car before I was dropping to my knees, the waters spilling to the ground as I smoothed my hair back with my hand. This time, though, as I felt my stomach clench, my body retch, nothing came up. All I could hear was the raspy sound of my own breathing, my heart thumping in my ears, and in the distance, barely audible but still somehow playing, music.

Chapter
FIFTEEN

"Okay," my mother said, loosening a cart from the row in front of the automatic doors. She set her purse in the front, then pulled out her list, unfolding it. "Here we go."

It was the second week of December, and we were at Mayor's Market, where I'd been recruited to help with the grocery shopping for Kirsten's homecoming dinner. It was not something I was all that excited about, unlike my mother, who was in full-on holiday mode. But still, as she pushed the cart toward the doors, smiling at me, and they slid open, I tried my best to smile back. It was all about trying, these days.

The last month and a half had been a total blur. The only thing I was fully aware of was how completely things were back to how they had been when the school year began. It was like the time I'd spent with Owen hadn't happened at all. Yet again, I was alone at school, modeling even though I didn't want to, and somehow completely unable to do anything about either.

The Sunday after that night at Bendo, I woke up right at seven, just in time for Owen's show. It was only once I opened my eyes that I remembered this morning was different and turned away from the clock, trying to will myself back to sleep. But I could feel some part of myself stubbornly waking up, bit by bit, and then everything was flooding back.

He had to be furious with me. After all, I'd just bolted, no explanation, nothing. The worst part was I knew it was wrong, even as it was happening, and yet I still couldn't stop myself. The only way to fix it would be to explain openly and honestly why I'd left, and I just could not do that. Even for him.

As it turned out, though, whether we discussed that night or not wasn't entirely up to me. The next day, our first day back at school, Owen made the decision for us.

I was in my car, having just parked, when he suddenly appeared at my driver's-side window. He announced himself by knocking: three hard raps, *boom boom boom*. I jumped, then turned. Once he saw he had my attention, he dropped his hand and started around my front bumper to the passenger door. As he opened it I sucked in a breath, the way they say you should do if your car is ever immersed in water, one last gasp to hold you over. And then he was in.

"What *happened* to you?"

As I'd expected, there was no hello. No stony silence for me to fill. Just the one thing that had been on his mind for, oh, thirty-six hours or so. Even worse, he was looking at me so intently—angrily—that I couldn't keep my eyes on him for more than a moment. His mouth was a thin line, his face flushed, his unsettled presence filling the small space around us.

"I'm sorry," I said, and as the words came out I heard my voice break. "I just . . ."

This is the problem with dealing with someone who is

actually a good listener. They don't jump in on your sentences, saving you from actually finishing them. Or talk over you, allowing what you do manage to get out to be lost or altered in transit. Instead, they wait. So you have to keep going.

"I don't know what to say," I finally managed. "I just . . . don't."

He was quiet for what felt like a long time. *This is excruciating*, I thought. Then he said, "If you didn't want to be there on Saturday, you could have just told me."

I bit my lip, looking down at my hands as a couple of guys passed by my window, yelling something about football practice. "I wanted to be there," I said.

"Then what happened?" he said. "Why did you just bolt? I didn't know what was going on. I waited for you."

There was something in these last few words that made my heart just break. *I waited for you.* Of course he had. And of course he would tell me this, because unlike me, Owen didn't keep secrets. With him, what you saw was really what you got.

"I'm sorry," I said again, but even to me it sounded so lame and weak, meaningless. "I just . . . There was a lot going on."

"Like what?"

I shook my head. This was what I could not do, get into this place where I was backed up to a wall, no choice but to tell the truth. "It's just a lot of stuff," I said.

"Stuff," he repeated, and I thought in my head, *Placeholder*. But he didn't say this out loud.

Instead he exhaled, turning his head toward the window. Only then did I allow myself to really look at him, taking in all the familiar things: the strong line of his jaw; the rings on his fingers; his earphones, looped loosely around his neck. Distantly, through one of them, I could hear music, and I wondered out of habit what he was listening to.

"I just don't get it," he said. "I mean, there has to be a reason, and you just don't want to give it. And that's just . . ." He stopped, shaking his head. "It's not like you."

For a moment, everything was very quiet. No one was passing, no cars driving up the row behind us. So silent as I said, "It is, though."

Owen looked at me, shifting his bag to the other leg. "What?"

"It is like me," I said. My voice was low, even to my ears. "This is just like me."

"Annabel." He still sounded annoyed, like this could never be true. So wrong. "Come on."

I looked down at my hands again. "I wanted to be different," I said to him. "But this is how I really am."

I'd tried to tell him that first day. I'd said I didn't always tell the truth, that I didn't handle conflict well, that anger scared me, that I was used to people just disappearing when they were mad. Our mistake was that we'd both thought I was capable of changing. That I *had* changed. In the end, though, that was the biggest lie of all.

The first bell sounded then, long and loud. Owen shifted in his seat, then put his hand on the door handle.

"Whatever it is," he said, "you could have told me. You know that, right?"

I knew as Owen sat there, one hand on the door, he was waiting for me to be the bold girl he'd wanted to believe I was, to just tell him. He waited longer than I thought he would have before pushing the door open and getting out.

And then he was gone. Walking across the parking lot, his bag over one shoulder, already lifting his earphones to his ears. Almost a year ago I'd watched him this same way, just after he punched Ronnie Waterman out. Then, I'd been awed, and slightly scared, and I felt the same way now as I realized what my silence and fear had cost me, yet again.

I waited until second bell, when the courtyard was nearly empty, before I finally got out of my car and headed to class. I didn't want to see Owen; I didn't want to see anyone. All morning, I walked through the halls in a fog, deliberately blocking out the voices around me. At lunch, I went to the library and sat in a carrel by the American History section, books spread out in front of me, not reading one word.

As the period was winding down, I packed up my stuff and went to the bathroom. It was empty except for two girls I didn't know, standing by the sinks, who started talking as I went into a stall.

"All I'm saying," one said as a faucet was turned on and water began to splash, "is that I don't think she's lying."

"Oh, come on." The other girl's voice was high, and more nasal. "He could date any girl he wanted. It's not like he's desperate. So why would he do something like that?"

"Do you really think she'd go to the cops if he hadn't?"

"Maybe she just wants attention."

"No way." The faucet cut off, and I heard paper towels being yanked from the dispenser. "She and Sophie were best friends. And now everyone knows? Why go through all that for a lie?"

I froze. They were talking about Emily.

"What did he get booked for?" the first girl asked.

"Sexual assault. Or second-degree rape, I don't know which."

"I can't believe he actually got *arrested*," the other girl said.

"At the A-Frame!" her friend replied. "Meghan said when the cops pulled up, people were running in all directions. Everyone thought it was a beer bust."

"Not hardly." I heard a backpack pocket unzip. "Have you seen Sophie?"

"Nope. I don't think she came today," the other girl said. "Shit. Would you?"

They were leaving now, their heels clicking across the floor, so I didn't get to hear the response to this. Instead, I stood in the stall, one hand on the wall beside me, where someone had written I HATE THIS PLACE in blue ballpoint pen. I dropped my hand, then put down the toilet seat and sat, trying to piece together what I'd just heard.

Emily had gone to the cops. Emily had pressed charges. Emily had *told*.

This realization was so big I just sat there, hands locked in my lap, stunned. Will had been arrested. People knew about this. Ever since Saturday night, I'd assumed Emily, like me, had stayed silent and scared, sucked this story in and held it there. But she hadn't.

As the afternoon wore on and I actually started listening to the people around me, I got the rest of the story. I heard that Emily was supposed to get a ride from the A-Frame to the party with Sophie, but she'd gotten held up, so Will offered to drive her instead. That he'd parked on the street and then, depending on who you believed, either jumped on her or was surprised when she made a move on him. That a woman walking her dog past saw something happening and threatened to call the cops if they didn't move on. That this was how Emily had gotten out of the car and, after getting a ride home, told her mom everything. That she'd spent Saturday morning at the police station, filing charges. That when the cops came for Will on Saturday night, he cried when the cops cuffed him. That Will's dad bailed him out within hours, then hired him the best lawyer in town. That Sophie was telling everyone that Emily had always been hot for Will, and when he wasn't interested, she cried rape. And that while Sophie was not at school today, Emily was.

I didn't see her until just after final bell. I was pulling a notebook out of my locker when I felt a sudden, strange hush fall over the normal end-of-the-day commotion. It didn't get entirely quiet, just quieter. When I turned my head, I saw her coming down the hallway toward me. She wasn't cowering or alone. She had two girls with her, one on either side, both of them people she'd been friends with before Sophie. I'd just assumed that I had no one after what had happened, that everyone would just accept Sophie's side of the story. It hadn't even occurred to me that somebody would believe mine.

For the next few days, what happened between Emily and Will remained the hot topic, although I was doing my best not to pay attention to it. At times, though, this was impossible, like the day I was in my English class, doing some last-minute cramming before a midterm, and Jessica Norfolk and Tabitha

Johnson, who sat behind me, started talking about Will.

"What I heard," said Jessica, who was junior class treasurer and not, I thought, the gossip type, "is that he's done it before."

"Really?" Tabitha replied. She'd sat behind me all year and always clicked her pen, which drove me nuts. She was doing it now.

"Yeah. There were rumors when he was at Perkins Day, apparently. You know, girls who said similar stuff had happened to them."

"But nobody ever had him *arrested*."

"Well, no," Jessica said. "But it means that it could be, you know, a pattern."

Tabitha, still clicking her pen, sighed through her teeth. "God," she said. "Poor Sophie."

"I know. Can you imagine dating someone and then this?"

A lot of these conversations I'd overheard came back to Sophie, which wasn't surprising. She and Will were one of those couples people knew about, if only for their frequently public dramatics. So it was odd she wasn't at school that first day. If Emily surprised me, though, Sophie did, too. Not only by not showing up, but by how she acted when she finally did.

She didn't station herself in the courtyard to make it clear she was unaffected by what had happened. Or confront Emily in public, as she had me. In fact, the first time I saw her she was alone, walking down the hallway with her cell phone pressed to her ear. At lunch, when I glanced out the library window, she wasn't on her bench—which was populated instead by some sophomore girls I didn't even know—but sitting on the curb by the turnaround, waiting for a ride. As for

Emily, she was sitting at a picnic table, drinking a bottled water and eating some potato chips, surrounded by people.

So Sophie was alone. I was alone. And Owen was alone, or so I was assuming. Occasionally before or after school, I'd catch a glimpse of him, towering over everyone else as he cut across a pathway or disappeared around a corner. Sometimes when I saw him, all I wanted to do was tell him everything. The thought would crash over me like a wave, sudden and unexpected. In the next moment, though, I'd already be telling myself that he probably didn't even want to hear it, now. Watching him walking across the courtyard with no expression, earphones on, it was like he was receding, back, back, to the person he'd been to me before all this. Just a mystery, a boy I didn't know at all, one more face in the crowd.

If school was stressful, home was not much better. At least not for me. For everyone else in my family, however, things were just great. My mother, next to me, was at this moment pushing her cart through the bounty that was the Mayor's Market produce department, so happy the entire family was finally getting together. While Kirsten had talked about coming for Thanksgiving, she'd opted instead to stay in the city, ostensibly to work some extra shifts and catch up on schoolwork. Later, though, she'd mentioned eating a turkey dinner with Brian, her TA; however, in very non-Kirsten fashion, she hadn't offered more details. Now she was finally coming home early for Christmas, and my mom was going all out.

"We're doing two kinds of potatoes," Mom said to me, gesturing for me to pull a couple of plastic bags from the dispenser. "I'm doing my creamed casserole, and Whitney's doing some kind of roasted potatoes with olive oil."

"Really," I said, handing the bags over to her.

"It's some recipe Moira gave her," she said. "Isn't that *great*?"

It was. My own problems aside, I could not help but be impressed with Whitney's recent progress. A year ago everything had started; now, while she was still by no means cured, the changes in her were yet again evident, but they were all good ones.

First, she'd started cooking. Not a lot, and not constantly; it had started slowly, after the dinner she'd made for me. Apparently Moira Bell was big into natural foods and organic cooking, and when Whitney told her about making spaghetti, she'd lent her a couple of cookbooks. My mother's meals tended toward the creamy and hearty: lots of casseroles with cream of mushroom bases, heavy sauces, meats, and starches. Whitney's interest, not surprisingly, leaned in a different direction. She'd started by contributing salads to our dinners now and then, going to the farmer's market and loading up with vegetables, which she'd spend ages slicing and dicing. Her dressings were vinaigrettes, swirled with herbs; reach for the Thousand Island or ranch and she'd shoot you a look suggesting that you don't. Then, the weekend of the fashion show, she made grilled salmon with a lime sauce for my parents, followed by steamed green beans with fresh lemon to replace the gooey casserole with french-fried onion topping we normally had for Thanksgiving. My mother was a great cook, the kind who worked on instinct, with no real measurements, only pinches and dashes. When Whitney cooked, she was all about exactitude, and her natural bossiness—about the dressing, or how yes, we could live without butter on every side dish—was just part of the process. But even at its most annoying, it was still an improvement, and we were all eating better. Whether we liked it or not.

She was also writing. She'd finished her official history by the end of the October, but since then she'd kept at it, often sitting at the dining-room table scribbling on a notepad, or curling up by the fire chewing her pencil. So far she hadn't let me read anything she'd written, although it wasn't like I'd asked, either. Still, the couple of times I'd found her notebook on the stairs, or the kitchen table, I'd been tempted to open it, just to see what was within all those carefully written lines. But I didn't. After all, I could understand about keeping things to yourself.

The most amazing thing, though, was the herbs. After sitting in the window doing absolutely nothing for a couple of months, the rosemary had suddenly sprouted just before Halloween. It was just one tiny, green shoot, but in the next week the others followed suit. Whitney checked on them every single day, testing the dampness of the soil with her fingers, turning them slightly for the optimum amount of light. Where I'd once thought of my middle sister as a closed door, these days when I pictured her I saw another image: her hands, curved around a chopping knife, or a pen, the handle of a watering can, moving across the plants, helping them grow.

Kirsten, meanwhile, had not only survived the showing of her piece to her professors and classmates but emerged victorious, winning the first-place prize in the competition. I'd expected her to call and regale us with one of her typical monologues, full of stream-of-consciousness details, but instead she'd left a message—telling us about the win and that she was very pleased with it—that clocked in at under two minutes, which had to be a record for her. It was so strange we were all convinced something must be wrong, but when I called her back, she said it was just the opposite.

"Things are great," she told me. "Just great."

"Are you sure?" I asked. "Your message was awfully short."

"Was it?"

"I thought the machine had cut you off, at first," I said.

She sighed. "Well, that's not altogether surprising, I guess. I've really been doing a lot of work on how I convey myself these days."

"You are?" I asked.

"Well, sure." She sighed again, a happy sigh. "It's amazing what I've learned this semester. I mean, between the filmmaking and Brian's class, I'm learning a lot about the true meaning of communication. It's really opened my eyes."

I waited for her to go on, to explain. Especially about Brian. But she didn't. Instead, she told me she loved me and had to run, and that she'd see me soon. And then we hung up. In under four minutes.

Kirsten may have been mastering the art of true communication, but I was failing miserably. Not just with Owen, but with my mother as well, as I'd somehow, in the midst of everything else that was happening, agreed to do another Kopf's commercial.

It happened the same week I'd heard about Emily's pressing charges. When I got home from school that Friday, my mother was waiting for me at the door.

"Guess what!" she said, before I even stepped over the threshold. "I just got a call from Lindy. The Kopf's people contacted her yesterday morning. They want you for their new spring commercial."

"What?" I said.

"Apparently they were very pleased with how the fall campaign went. Although, I have to say, I think your meeting that man from marketing last weekend didn't hurt. They're shooting in January but they want to see you in December for a fitting. Isn't it great?"

Great, I thought. The truth was, a couple of months ago this would have been a much bigger deal. A couple of weeks ago, maybe I might have even been able to stop it. But now, I just stood there, and barely managed to nod.

"I told Lindy I'd call her as soon as I told you," she said, going into the kitchen and picking up the phone. As she dialed, she added, "From what Lindy said, the ad skewed really well with younger girls, and that's what really won the Kopf's people over. You're a role model, Annabel! Isn't that something?"

I thought of Mallory's room, the screen captures lined up on the wall. And then her face staring into the camera, the feathers from the boa floating up to the edges.

"I'm no role model," I said.

"Sure you are," she replied, so easily. She turned and looked at me, smiling again as she shifted the phone to her other ear. "You have so much to be proud of, honey. You really do. I mean—

Lindy? . . . Hi! It's Grace, I've been trying to get through . . . is your receptionist out? . . . Still? . . . That's horrible. . . . Yes, I've just talked to Annabel, and she's thrilled. . . ."

Thrilled, I thought. *Not quite.* And not a role model, either. Not that it mattered. As long as someone else thought I was those things, that was all that counted.

October had folded into November and then December somehow without my even noticing, the days getting shorter and colder, Christmas music suddenly on the radio. I went to school, I studied, I came home. Even when people did try to talk to me at school, I barely replied, so used to my isolation that now I preferred it. At first, on weekend nights, my mom and dad seemed curious as to why I didn't go out or have plans. But after a few times of telling them I was just so tired from the Models and school and trying to catch up on my schoolwork, they stopped asking.

Still, I was aware of what was happening around me. I knew from the rumor mill that Will's trial was coming up, and there was still talk that some girls from Perkins Day would come forward with stories similar to Emily's. As for Emily herself, she seemed to be doing well. She certainly wasn't hiding out. In fact, I saw her everywhere—in the halls, the courtyard, hanging out in the parking lot—always with a bunch of girls around her. A week or so earlier, in the hallway between classes, I'd caught a glimpse of her standing by her locker, laughing at something. Her cheeks had been flushed, her hand covering her mouth. It was just one moment, one thing, but for some reason it stuck with me, all that day and into the next. I could not get it out of my mind.

Sophie was not faring so well. Usually when I saw her, she was alone, and she now left for lunch almost every day, a black car sliding to a stop to pick her up. It wasn't Will, and I wondered if they were still together. Because I hadn't heard otherwise, I assumed they were.

It seemed like a million years ago now that school had begun, and I'd been so scared of her. Now when I saw Sophie, I just felt tired and sad for both of us. Only when I saw Owen did I feel a twinge of something like loneliness. But even though we weren't talking, I was still listening, in my own way.

Not to the radio show, although I still found myself waking like clockwork at seven A.M. on Sundays, a bad habit that proved impossible, for whatever reason, to break. Even harder to shake was the music itself. Not just his music, either, but all music.

I wasn't sure when it had started, exactly, but suddenly I was very aware of silence. Everywhere I went, I needed some kind of noise. When I was in the car, I instantly turned on my stereo; in my room, I hit the light switch first, my CD player ON button second. Even in class, or sitting at the table with my parents, I'd always have to have some song in my head, repeating itself again and again. I remembered Owen telling me how music had saved him in Phoenix, that it drowned everything out, and it was the same for me now. As long as I had something to listen to, I could blur the things I didn't want to think about, if not block them out completely.

It took a lot of music to do this, though, and after a few weeks, I'd burned through my entire collection multiple times. Which was why, on a recent Saturday night, I'd broken down and pulled out the stack Owen had burned me. *Desperate times*, I thought as I opened up the PROTEST SONGS one again and stuck it in.

I still didn't love it. Some of the songs were strange, and others I didn't understand. But while I'd expected it to be weird to listen to Owen's music, I found a surprising comfort instead. There was something nice about picturing him picking the songs for me, organizing them so carefully, hoping I'd be enlightened. If nothing else, they proved we had been friends, once.

For the past few weeks I'd been working my way through the discs, song by song, listening to every single track until I knew them all by heart. Each time I finished with one, I felt sad, knowing there were only that many more left before this, too, was over. Because of this, I was planning to save the one that said JUST LISTEN. Like Owen had been to me once, it was a total mystery, and sometimes one I thought maybe was best unsolved. Still, I pulled it out every once in a while, just turning it in my hands before sliding it back to the bottom of the stack and leaving it there.

When my mom and I finally headed out into the Mayor's Market parking lot, I was surprised to see it was snowing. The flakes were the big, fat kind, too pretty to stick or last, but we both stopped still for a moment, looking up at them as they fell. By the time we got in the car and pulled out of the lot, they were already slowing, some catching the wind, blowing in circles. My mom turned on the wipers as we sat at a stoplight, watching the flakes hit the windshield.

"It's beautiful, isn't it?" she said. "There's something about snow that just makes everything seem so fresh and new. Don't you think?"

I nodded. The light was a long one, and even though it was barely five P.M., it was already getting dark. My mom glanced over at me, smiling, then reached forward to the radio. As she twisted the volume, filling the car with classical music, I turned my head to the side. The window was cool against my cheek, those pretty flakes still falling, as I closed my eyes.

Chapter
SIXTEEN

The library carrel where I was spending my lunches was deep in the far right corner, out of sight and away from most foot traffic. I wasn't used to having company. Which was why when Emily came looking for me thirty minutes into the last lunch before Christmas break, I saw her first.

Initially, she was just a flash of red in the corner of my eye, blurring past once, then twice. I glanced up from my English notes, which I had spread out in front of me, doing some last-minute cramming, then looked around me: nothing. Same quiet shelves, same rows of books. A moment later, though, I heard footsteps. When I turned around, she was standing at the end of the stack just behind me.

"Oh," she said. Her voice was quiet but audible. "There you are."

Like I'd been lost. Misplaced, only now turning up, like a sock you find long after you've assumed it was eaten by the dryer. I didn't say anything, too distracted by a rising panic. I'd picked my spot because it was secluded, faced the wall, and was tucked away from everything, the same reasons it was the last place you wanted to find yourself trapped.

Emily started toward me, and without even realizing it I leaned back, bumping the carrel behind me. She stopped, crossing her arms over her chest.

"Look," she said. "I know things have been weird between us this year. But I . . . I need to talk to you."

Somewhere nearby, I could hear voices, one male, one female, chatting as they moved through the stacks. Emily heard it, too, turning her head at the sound, until it faded. Then she grabbed a nearby chair, dragging it closer to me, and sat down. Her voice was barely a hush as she said, "I know you've heard what happened. What Will did to me."

She was so close I could smell her perfume, something fruity and floral.

"Afterwards," she continued, keeping her green eyes level on me, "I started thinking about you. And that night at the party, back when school ended last year."

I could hear myself breathing, which meant she probably could, too. Behind her, the trees beyond the window shifted, and a shaft of sunlight spilled across the shelves of books, dust dancing within it.

"You don't have to talk to me about it," she said. "I mean, I know you hate me and all."

I thought of Clarke, looking up at me from that chair at Bendo. *Is that what you think?* she'd replied, when I'd said this same thing to her.

"But the thing is," Emily said, "if something did happen . . . something like what happened to me, it could help. Make it stop, I mean. Make him stop."

I still hadn't said a word. I couldn't. Instead, I just sat

there, immobile, as she reached into the pocket of her jeans, pulling out a small white card.

"This is the name of the woman who's been working on my case," she said, holding the card out to me. When I didn't reach for it immediately, she put it on the table, beside my elbow, faceup. The name was in black, a seal of some sort on the top left-hand corner. "The trial starts on Monday, but they're still wanting to talk to people. You could just call her and tell her . . . whatever you wanted. She's really nice."

The one thing that scared me more than anything, the reason I hadn't been honest with Owen about what was really bothering me that night at Bendo—she made it sound easy. If I couldn't tell him, the one person I actually thought could take it, how on earth could I be expected to confide in a stranger? There was no way. Even if I wanted to. Which I didn't.

"Just think about it," she told me. Then she took in a breath, like she might add something, but didn't, instead just pushing herself to her feet. "I'll see you around, okay?"

She pushed the chair back into place, then started down the nearest row of shelves. After taking a couple of steps, though, she turned back to face me. "And Annabel?" she said. "I'm sorry."

These two words just hung there for a moment in the air between us, and then she was walking away, disappearing around the empty carrel on the far end of the row. *I'm sorry.* It was the same thing that I wanted to say to her, that I'd wanted to say ever since that Saturday night at the fashion show. What did she have to apologize for?

But even as my mind grappled with this, trying to work the

logic, I could feel it, a visceral reaction to what had just happened, her coming closer than anyone to the truth. My truth. And just like that, I could feel something rising up inside me. I looked around, wondering where on earth I could get sick quietly and discreetly. But then something else happened: I started to cry.

Cry. Really cry, the way I hadn't in years, the kind of full-out sobbing that hits you like a wave, pulling you under. Suddenly the tears were just coming, sobs climbing up my throat, my shoulders shaking. I turned around clumsily, trying to hide myself, banging my elbow on the edge of the carrel, and the business card Emily had left fell to the floor, fluttering end over end before landing at my feet. I put my head in my hands, pressing my palms over my eyes to shut out everything, even as the tears continued. I cried and cried, there in the library, tucked away in the corner, until I felt raw inside.

I was so scared about being discovered, but nobody came. Nobody heard. In my own ears, though, my sobs sounded primal and scary, like something I would have turned off if I'd been able to. Instead all I could do was just ride it out, until it—and I—was done.

When that happened, I dropped my hands and looked around me. Nothing had changed. The books were still there, the dust dancing in the light, the card at my feet. I reached down for it, closing my fingers over one edge and lifting it up. I did not read it, or even glance at it. But I did slide it into the pocket of my bag, stuffing it down and away just as the bell rang and the period ended.

• • •

For the rest of the day, you could just feel the pre–holiday-break restlessness in the air, everyone counting down until vacation officially began.

After finishing my exam late, I headed to my locker, then to the bathroom, which was empty except for a girl who was leaning in close to the mirror, putting on liquid blue eyeliner. Soon after I went into the stall, I heard her leave, and I thought I was alone. When I came out, though, Clarke Reynolds, in jeans and a TRUTH SQUAD T-shirt, was leaning against the sink.

"Hi," she said.

My first instinct was to look behind me, which was crazy, as well as kind of stupid, as I could see in the mirror there was no one there.

"Hey," I said.

I stepped around her, to the next sink down, and turned on the water. I could feel her watching me as I rinsed my hands and pumped the soap dispenser, which was empty as always. "So," she said, as again I realized there was no stuffiness to her voice whatsoever, "are you okay?"

I turned off the water. "What?"

She reached up, adjusting her glasses. "It's not really just me asking," she said. "I mean, it is, obviously. But Owen's wondering, too."

Hearing her say Owen's name was so strange that it took me a moment to wrap my mind around it. "Owen," I repeated.

She nodded. "He's just . . ." She trailed off. "Concerned, I guess, is the word."

"About me," I said, clarifying.

"Yeah."

Something wasn't right here. "And he asked you to talk to me?"

"Oh, no." She shook her head. "He's just mentioned it to me a few times, so I got to wondering, and . . . then I saw you today. After lunch. You were leaving the library, and you just looked really upset."

Maybe it was because she'd brought up Owen. Or because at this point, I really didn't have that much to lose as far as she and I were concerned. Whatever the reason, I just decided to be honest. "I'm surprised," I said. "I didn't think you'd care if I was upset."

She bit her lip for just a second, something I suddenly remembered her doing a million times when we were younger. It meant I'd caught her off guard. "Is that what you really think?" she said. "That *I* don't like *you*?"

"You don't," I said. "You haven't, since that summer with Sophie."

"Annabel, come on. You were the one who blew me off, remember?"

"Yeah, but—"

"Yeah, but nothing. *You* don't like *me*, Annabel." Her voice was even, level. "That's the way it's been since that summer."

I just stared at her. "But you won't even look at me in the halls," I said. "You never have. And that first day, on the wall—"

"You hurt my feelings," she said. "God, Annabel. We were best friends and you totally dumped me. How did you expect me to feel?"

"I tried to talk to you!" I said. "That day at the pool."

"And that," she shot back, pointing at me, "was the *only* time. Yeah, I was mad. It had just happened! But then you never came around, you never called. You were just gone."

It was like Emily saying "I'm sorry" to me, a total reversal of how I saw things, which seemed crazy and impossible to process.

"So why now?" I said. "Why talk to me now?"

She sighed. "Well," she said slowly, "I have to be honest. Rolly's a big part of it."

Rolly, I thought. Then I remembered that night, him clutching those waters. *Tell Owen he was right about everything*, he'd said, so excited. "You and Rolly?" I said.

She bit her lip again, and I could have sworn she blushed, but only for a second. "We're talking," she said, reaching down to tug at the hem of her TRUTH SQUAD T-shirt, which, now that I noticed, looked awfully worn for someone who had only just seen the band for the first time a month and half earlier. "Anyway, that night at the club, when he got you to introduce him to me, you said that I hated you. It got me thinking about everything that had happened with us all those years ago. And with Owen talking about you . . . you've been on my mind. So when I saw you today, and you were—"

"Wait," I said. "Owen talks about me?"

"He hasn't said all that much," she told me. "Just that you guys were friends, and then something happened, and now you're not. Forgive me for saying so, but it sounded, I don't know, a little bit familiar to me. If you know what I mean."

I felt myself flush, imagining Clarke and Owen discussing

me and my avoidant behavior. How embarrassing.

"It's not like we discuss you," she added, as if I'd said this aloud. Which was another thing that I now remembered about Clarke: She could always kind of read my mind.

Clarke was worried about me. Emily was apologizing to me. This was a weird day.

"So are you?" Clarke asked now, as a group of girls came in, cigarettes already out, their faces falling when they saw us there. They grumbled, huddled, then walked back out, presumably to wait until we'd left. "Okay, I mean?"

I just stood there, wondering how to answer this. I realized that for the last few weeks I hadn't been missing just Owen, but also that part of me that had been able to be so honest with him. Maybe I couldn't do that here. But I didn't have to lie, either. So I went for the place I was working toward always: the middle.

"I don't know," I said.

Clarke looked at me for a moment. "Well," she said, "do you want to talk about it?"

I'd had so many chances. Her, Owen, Emily. For so long, I'd thought all I needed was someone to listen, but that wasn't really true at all. It was me that was the problem. I did this. And now, I did it again. "No," I said. "But thanks anyway."

She nodded, then pushed off the sink, and I followed her out of the bathroom. In the hallway, as we prepared to go our separate ways, she reached down to her bag, pulling out a pen and scrap of paper. "Here," she said as she scribbled on it, then handed it to me. "My cell number. Just in case you change your mind."

Her name was written beneath it, in the hand I still recognized—clean, block-print, the same little swoop on the final *E*. "Thanks," I said.

"No problem. Merry Christmas, Annabel."

"You, too."

As we walked away from each other, I knew I probably wouldn't call her. Still, I unzipped my bag, stuffing the paper in with the card Emily had given me. Even if I never used either, for whatever reason, it was nice to know they were there.

Another holiday, another trip to the airport. Just like I had about a year earlier, I sat in the backseat, behind my parents, as we headed down the highway, a plane rising from one corner of the windshield to the other as we took the exit. Whitney had stayed home, ostensibly to get dinner ready. So it was just the three of us waiting behind the barricade for Kirsten to emerge from the gate.

"There she is!" my mother said, waving as my sister appeared wearing a bright red coat, her hair pulled back in a ponytail. Kirsten smiled, waving back as she walked toward us, the wheels of her suitcase whizzing across the floor.

"Hello!" she said, immediately reaching up to hug my dad, then moving on to my mom, who was already teary-eyed, the way she always was at arrivals and departures. When it was my turn she hugged me tight, and I closed my eyes, breathing in her scent: soap, cold air, and the peppermint of her shampoo, all so familiar. "I am so happy to see you guys!"

"How was the trip?" my mom asked as my dad took the

handle of her suitcase and we started across the terminal. "Any trouble?"

"None," Kirsten said, linking her arm in my mine. "It was all good."

I waited for her to continue, but she didn't. Instead, she just smiled at me, then slid her hand down around mine, squeezing it as we stepped out into the cold.

On the ride home, my parents peppered Kirsten with questions about school, which she answered, and Brian, which she evaded cheerfully, blushing occasionally. The new Kirsten I'd noticed on the phone was clearly in evidence. Her responses, while not curt, were much briefer than any of us were used to, so much so that weird silences kept falling after she spoke, while the rest of us waited for her to start up again. But she didn't, just sighing instead, or looking out the window, or squeezing my hand, which she was still holding, which she held all the way home.

"I have to say," my mother said as my dad turned into our neighborhood, "there's something different about you, honey."

"Really?" Kirsten asked.

"I can't put my finger on exactly what it is . . ." my mother said, looking pensive. "But I think . . ."

"She's letting the world get a word in edgewise?" my dad finished for her, glancing at Kirsten in the rearview. He was smiling. And right.

"Oh, Daddy," Kirsten said. "I didn't used to talk *that* much, did I?"

"Of course not!" my mother told her. "We always loved to hear what you had to say."

Kirsten sighed. "I've just learned a lot about being more concise. As well as making an effort to hear what's being said to me. I mean, do you realize how few people actually *listen* these days?"

I did. In fact, I'd spent the time between school and leaving for the airport finishing up the last tracks of Owen's OLD SCHOOL PUNK/SKA CD, the final labeled one in the stack he'd given to me. After this, I only had JUST LISTEN left to go, which made me sad. I'd gotten used to spending some time each day or night hearing a few tracks here or there. The act was like ritual, a weird kind of steady comfort, even when the music wasn't.

While I listened, I usually just lay on my bed with eyes closed, trying to lose myself in what I was hearing. Today, though, as the CD began with the pumping beats of a reggae-style song, I'd pulled my backpack onto my bed, taken out the card Emily had given me and Clarke's number, then laid them in front of me on the bedspread. As the music played, I studied each one, as if it was important to commit them to memory: the slightly raised type of the D.A. assistant's name, ANDREA THOMLINSON, the lines across the middle sections of the two sevens in Clarke's number. I told myself I didn't have to do anything with either of them. They were just options. Like Owen's two rings, two messages. And it was always good to know your options.

When we got home, it was already dark, but the house was lit up, and I could see Whitney in the kitchen, stirring something on the stove. As we coasted down the driveway, Kirsten squeezed my hand again, and I wondered if she was nervous. But she didn't say anything.

Inside, the house was warm, and I realized I was starving. Kirsten took in a deep breath, closing her eyes. "God," she said as my dad led the way in, "something smells amazing."

"That's Whitney's stir-fry," my mother told her.

"Whitney cooks?" she asked.

I looked ahead to see Whitney standing in front of the island. She had a dishtowel in her hands. "Whitney cooks," she said. "It should be ready in about five minutes."

"You are in for a treat!" my mom said to Kirsten, her voice a little bit too loud. "Whitney is a natural in the kitchen."

"Wow," Kirsten said. Another silence fell. Then she said to Whitney, "You look great, by the way."

"Thanks," Whitney replied. "So do you."

So far, so good. Beside me, my mother smiled.

"I'll put your bag upstairs," my dad told Kirsten, who nodded.

"And I'll get the salad together," my mom said, "and then we can all sit down and catch up. In the meantime, you girls can go upstairs and freshen up. How's that sound?"

"Good," Kirsten said, looking at Whitney again. My father turned, heading for the stairs with the suitcase. "Sounds great."

Upstairs, I sat in my room, listening to the noises around me. Kirsten's room had been pretty much untouched since she'd left, so it was weird to hear activity—drawers being opened and closed, the bumping of furniture being moved around—from that side of the wall. On the other, there were the Whitney noises I was used to: the creak of her bed, the low hum of a radio. When my mom called up to us that everything was ready, we all came out into the hallway together.

Kirsten had changed her shirt and let her hair down. She

glanced back at me, then at Whitney, who was behind me, pulling a sweater over her head. "Ready?" she asked, as if we were going farther than just the table. I nodded, and she started down the stairs.

When we came into the dining room, the food was already out: the stir-fry heaped on a big platter, a bowl of brown rice, my mother's salad, with the dressing, of course, to Whitney's specifications. Everything smelled great, and my father was standing at the head of the table as we all took our places around him.

Once we sat, my mom poured Kirsten a glass of wine, and my dad, a true meat-and-potatoes person, asked Whitney to please explain, if she could, exactly what we were eating.

"Tempeh and vegetable stir-fry," she said, "in peanut hoisin sauce."

"Tempeh? What's that?"

"It's good, Daddy," Kirsten told him. "That's all you need to know."

"You don't have to eat it if you don't want to," Whitney said. "Although it is pretty much the best thing I've ever made."

"Just give him some," my mom said. "He'll like it."

My dad looked dubious, though, as Whitney picked up a spoon, putting some onto his plate. As she added the sides, I looked around the table at my family, so different now from a year ago. We would probably never be the way we had been again, but at least we were all together.

As I thought this, I caught a glimpse of lights. Sure enough, in the window behind the row of herbs, a car was passing. As it slowed, the driver looking in at us, I thought again how you could never really know what you were seeing with just a glance, in motion, passing by. Good or bad, right or wrong. There was always so much more.

The rule in our house was that if you didn't cook, you cleaned up, so after dinner Kirsten, my dad, and I ended up in the kitchen together on dish duty.

"That," Kirsten said, handing me a soapy pan to rinse, "was delicious. The sauce was to die for."

"Wasn't it?" my mother, who was sitting at the kitchen table drinking a cup of coffee—but still yawning—replied. "And your father had *thirds*. I hope Whitney noticed. That's the best compliment you can give a cook."

"I never cook," Kirsten said. "Unless ordering in counts."

"It does," my dad told her. He was supposed to be helping, although so far all he'd done was take out the garbage and take a long time to replace the bag. "Calling for delivery is my favorite recipe."

My mom made a face at him as Whitney, who had disappeared upstairs after dinner, walked in wearing her jacket, her keys in hand. "I'm going out for a little while," she said. "I won't be late."

Kirsten, her hands in the water, turned and looked at her. "Where are you going?"

"Just to this coffee shop to meet some people," Whitney told her.

"Oh," Kirsten said, nodding. Then she turned back to the sink.

"Do you . . ." Whitney paused. "Did you want to come?"

"I don't want to intrude," Kirsten told her. "That's okay."

"It's all right," I heard Whitney say. "I mean, if you don't mind hanging out there for a little while."

Again, I felt it: this tentative, careful peace between my sisters—not exactly flimsy, but not set in stone, either. My parents exchanged a look. "Annabel, you want to come?" Kirsten said. "I'll buy you a mocha."

I could feel Kirsten's eyes on me as she asked this, and I thought of her squeezing my hand earlier, and how she was maybe more nervous than she seemed. "Sure," I said. "Okay."

"Wonderful!" my mother said. "You all go and have fun. Your dad and I can finish cleaning up."

"Are you sure?" I asked. "We're only about halfway through—"

"It's fine." She stood up, then came over, gesturing me and Kirsten out of the way as she rolled up her sleeves. I looked over at Whitney, standing in the archway. How I'd gotten in the middle of this I wasn't sure. But here I was. "Just go."

"Hello, and welcome to open-mike night, here at Jump Java. I'm Esther, and I'll be your emcee tonight. If you've been here before, you know the rules: Sign up at the back, keep it down when someone's reading, and most importantly, tip your barista. Thank you!"

When we arrived, I'd figured this was just something that happened to be going on. But as Whitney's friends from her group waved us over, it was clear it was no coincidence.

"So are you ready?" a girl named Jane, who was tall and very thin, wearing a red sweater with a pack of cigarettes poking out of the front pocket, said to Whitney after we got our coffees and had introductions. "And, more importantly, are you nervous?"

"Whitney doesn't get nervous," Heather, the other girl, said. She looked to be about my age and had short black hair, cut spiky, and a variety of piercings in her nose and lip. "You know that."

Kirsten and I exchanged a look. "What would you be nervous about?" she asked Whitney, who was sitting beside me, rummaging through the purse in her lap.

"Reading," Jane told her, taking a sip from the mug in front of her. "She's signed up for tonight."

"She had to sign up," Heather added. "It was a Moira Must."

"Moira Must?" I said.

"It's something from our group," Whitney explained, pulling some folded papers from her purse and putting them on the table in front of her. "You know, like an assignment. Moira's one of my doctors."

"Oh," Kirsten said. "Right."

"So you're reading something you wrote," I said. "Like part of your history?"

Whitney nodded. "Kind of."

"All right, we're ready to get started," Esther said. "And first up, we have Jacob. Welcome, Jacob!"

Everyone applauded as a tall, skinny guy wearing a black knit cap wound his way through the tables to the microphone. He opened a small spiral notebook, then cleared his throat. "This is called 'Untitled,'" he said as the espresso machine hissed from behind us. "It's, um, about my ex-girlfriend."

The poem he began to read started with images about daylight and dreaming. Then it began to build quickly, his voice rising until it was just a staccato list of words that he spit out, one right after another. "Metal, Cold, Betrayal, Endless!" he was saying, as the occasional bit of spit arced over the mike. I glanced at Whitney, who was biting her lip, then at Kirsten, who looked completely entranced.

"What is this?" I whispered.

"Shhh," she said.

Jacob's poem went on for what seemed like a long time before ending, finally, with a series of long, breathless gasps. When he was done, we all sat there for a second before deciding it was okay to clap.

"Wow," I said to Heather. "That was really something."

"Oh, that's nothing," she said. "You should have been here last week. He did ten minutes on castration."

"It was disgusting," Jane added. "Compelling, but disgusting."

"Next up," Esther said, "we have a first-time reader. Everyone, please, give it up for Whitney."

Jane and Heather immediately burst into loud applause, and Kirsten and I followed suit. As Whitney walked up to the mike, I watched the crowd reacting to her, their heads turning, then double-taking, at her beauty.

"I'm going to read a short piece," she said, her voice kind of faint. She stepped closer to the microphone. "A short piece," she repeated, "about my sisters."

I felt myself blink, surprised, and looked at Kirsten. I

wanted to say something, but I kept quiet, not wanting to be shushed again.

Whitney swallowed, then looked down at her papers, the edge of which I could see fluttering, just barely. She looked scared, and it suddenly seemed too quiet. But then she began.

"I am the middle sister," she read. "The one in between. Not oldest, not youngest, not boldest, not nicest. I am the shade of gray, the glass half empty or full, depending on your view. In my life, there has been little that I have done first or better than the one preceding or following me. Of all of us, though, I am the only one who has been broken."

I heard the chime over the door sound, and turned in my seat to see an older woman with long curly hair come in and stand at the back. When she saw Whitney at the microphone she smiled, then began to unwind her scarf from around her neck.

"It happened on the day of my youngest sister's ninth birthday party," Whitney continued. "I'd been sulking around the house all day, feeling alternately ignored and entirely too hassled, which was pretty much my default setting, even at eleven."

Kirsten's eyes widened as, at the table next to us, a man laughed loudly, and I heard other chuckles as well. Whitney flushed, smiling. "My older sister, the social one, was going to ride her bike down to the neighborhood pool to meet some friends and asked me to come along. I didn't want to. I didn't want to be with anyone. If my older sister was friendly, and my younger sweet, I was the darkness. Nobody understood my pain. Not even me."

There was another laugh, this time from someone across the room, and she smiled. So Whitney could be funny. Who knew?

"My older sister got on her bike and headed for the pool, and I started to follow. I *always* followed, and once we were riding, I started to get angry about it. I was tired of being second."

I looked at Kirsten again; she was watching Whitney so intently, as if no one else was even there. "So I turned back. And suddenly, the road was empty ahead of me, this whole new view, all mine. I started to pedal as fast as I could."

I could hear Heather's spoon clinking as she added another packet of sugar to her coffee, as I sat silent, unmoving.

"It was great. Freedom, even the imagined kind, always is. But as I got farther away, and didn't recognize what was ahead of me, I started to realize the distance I was covering. I was still going full speed, away from home, when my front wheel suddenly sank, and I was flying."

Beside me, Kirsten shifted in her seat, and I moved my chair closer to her.

"It's a funny feeling, being suddenly airborne," Whitney said. "Just as you realize it, it's over, and you're sinking. When I hit the pavement, I heard the bone in my arm break. In the moments afterwards, I could hear the wheel of my bike, ticking as it spun. All I could think was what I always thought, even then: that this was just not fair. To get a taste of freedom, only to instantly be punished for it."

I looked back at the woman by the door. She was watching Whitney with full concentration.

"Everything hurt. I closed my eyes, pressing my cheek to the street, and waited. What for, I didn't know. To be rescued. Or found. But no one came. All I'd ever thought I wanted was to be left alone. Until I was."

I swallowed, hearing this, then looked down at my coffee mug, sliding my fingers around it.

"I don't know how long I lay there before my sister came back for me. I remember staring up at the sky, the clouds moving past, and then hearing her calling my name. When she skidded to a stop beside me, she was the last person I wanted to see. And yet, like so many times before and since, the only one I had."

Whitney paused, taking a breath.

"She lifted me up and settled me onto her handlebars. I knew I should be grateful to her. But as we pedaled toward home, I was angry. With myself, for falling, and with her for being there to see it. As we came up the driveway, my younger sister, the birthday girl, burst out of the house. When she saw me, my arm dangling useless, she ran back inside yelling for my mother. That was her role, always, as the youngest. She was the one who told."

I remembered that. My first thought had been that something had to be really wrong, because they were together, so close to each other. And that never happened.

"My father took me to the emergency room, where the bone was reset. When we got home, the party was almost over, presents unwrapped, the cake just being served. In the pictures taken that day, I am holding my arm over my cast, as if I don't trust it to keep me together. My older sister is on one side, the hero; my younger, the birthday girl, on the other."

I knew that picture. In it, I am wearing my bathing suit, a piece of cake in my hand; Kirsten is grinning, one hand on her hip, which is jutting out.

"For years, when I looked at the snapshot, all I could see was my broken arm. It was only later that I began to make out other things. Like how my sisters are both smiling and leaning in toward me, while I am, as always, between them."

She took a breath, looking down at her papers.

"It was not the last time I would run away from my sisters. Not the last time I thought being alone was preferable. I am still the center sister. But I see it differently now. There has to be a middle. Without it, nothing can ever truly be whole. Because it is not just the space between, but also what holds everything together. Thank you."

I just sat there, a lump rising in my throat, as applause began all around me, first here and there, and then everywhere, filling the room. Whitney flushed, pressing a hand to her chest, then smiled as she stepped out from behind the microphone. Beside me, Kirsten had tears in her eyes.

As Whitney made her way toward our table, people nodding at her as she passed, I was so proud of her, because I could only imagine how hard it must have been to read this piece aloud. Not just for strangers, but us, as well. But she'd done it. Sitting there, watching my sister, I wondered which was harder, in the end. The act of telling, or who you told it to. Or maybe if, when you finally got it out, the story was really all that mattered.

Chapter
SEVENTEEN

The clock beside my bed, glowing red, said 12:15. Which meant that, by my count, I'd been trying to fall asleep for three hours and eight minutes.

Ever since Whitney's reading the previous night, all the things I'd been trying to push away—my falling-out with Owen, Emily giving me the detective's card, Clarke talking to me again—were suddenly haunting me. The house felt full and busy, my parents were more relaxed than they'd been in months, and my sisters were not only talking to each other but actually getting along. This sudden harmony was so unexpected, it just made me seem that much more out of sorts.

The night before, on the way home from the coffee shop, Kirsten had told Whitney about her film, and how it was similar to the piece she'd read. Whitney wanted to see it, so tonight before dinner, Kirsten had set up her laptop on the coffee table and we all assembled to watch.

My parents sat on the couch with Whitney perched on the arm beside them. Kirsten took a seat at an angle, motioning for me to sit closer, but I'd just shook my head, hanging back. "I've already seen it," I told her. "You sit there."

"I've seen it a million times," she replied, but took the spot anyway.

"This is so exciting!" my mother said, looking around at all of us, and I didn't know if she meant that we were all there together, or the film itself.

Kirsten took in a breath, then reached forward to push a button. "Okay," she said. "Here it is."

As the first shot of that green, green grass, came up, I tried to keep my eyes on it. But slowly, I found myself looking instead at my family. My father's face was serious, studying the screen; my mom, beside him, had her hands curled in her lap. Whitney, on my dad's other side, had pulled a leg to her chest, and I watched the light flicker across her face as the piece continued.

"Why, Whitney," my mother said as the girls pedaled down the street, "this is kind of like that essay you let us read a while back, isn't it?"

"It is," Kirsten said softly. "Weird, right? We just figured it out last night."

Whitney didn't say anything, her eyes on the screen as, in the distance, the camera showed the smaller girl, now off her bike, the wheel spinning. Then there were the scarier images of the neighborhood: the lunging dog, the old man getting his paper. When it finally ended with that last flash of green, we were all quiet for a moment.

"Kirsten, my goodness," my mother finally said. "That was incredible."

"Hardly incredible," Kirsten replied, tucking a piece of hair behind her ear. But she did look pleased. "It's just a beginning."

"Who knew you had such an eye?" my father said, reaching across to squeeze her leg. "All that TV-watching finally paid off."

Kirsten smiled at him, but her real attention was on Whitney, who hadn't said anything yet. "So," she asked, "what did you think?"

"I liked it," Whitney told her. "Although I never thought you'd left me behind."

"And I never would have guessed you turned back," Kirsten replied. "It's so funny."

Whitney nodded, not saying anything. Then my mother sighed and said, "Well, I never realized that day was such a big deal for either of you!"

"What, you don't remember Whitney breaking her arm?" Kirsten asked.

"Your mother has a selective memory," my dad told her. "I, however, have distinct recollection of the collective trauma."

"Of course I *remember* it," my mom said. "I just . . . had no idea it had resonated with you both so much." She turned, glancing around behind her until her eyes found me. "What about you, Annabel? What do you remember about that day?"

"Turning nine," my father said. "Right?"

I nodded, because they were all watching me. In truth, though, I wasn't sure what I recalled most about that day, as so much of it had been retold now, through other eyes. It had been my birthday, I'd had a cake, I'd run to tell my mom Whitney was hurt. But the rest, I wasn't sure of.

All through dinner I watched my family: Kirsten telling stories about the intense people in her filmmaking class,

Whitney explaining the details of the sushi rolls she'd been working on all afternoon, my mother's cheeks, pink and flushed, as she laughed. Even my father was relaxed, clearly happy to have everyone together, under such better circumstances. It was a good thing, and yet I felt strangely disconnected. As if I were now a car on the street outside, slowing down to stare, with nothing in common at all but proximity, and barely that.

Now, I pushed back the covers, getting up, then went to my door, easing it open. The hallway was silent and dark, but as I suspected, there was a light visible from the stairs. My dad was still up.

As soon as he saw me crossing the living room, he muted the TV. "Hey there," he said. "Can't sleep?"

I shook my head. On the screen, I could see the grainy black-and-white images of an old news report, two men shaking hands over a table. Behind them, a crowd was clapping.

"Well," he said, "you are just in time to help me decide. It's either this fascinating show on the beginning of World War One, or something on A&E about the Dust Bowl. What do you think?"

I looked at the TV, which he'd flipped to the other channel. It showed a bleak landscape, a car moving slowly across it. "I don't know," I said. "They sound equally compelling."

"Hey," he said. "Don't knock history. This stuff is important."

I smiled, moving to the couch and sitting down. "I know," I said. "It's just hard to get excited about it. I mean, for me."

"How can you not get excited about this?" he asked. "It's

real. This isn't some silly story somebody made up. These are things that actually happened."

"A long time ago," I added.

"Exactly!" he said, nodding. "That's my point. That's why we *can't* forget it. No matter how much time has passed, these things still affect us and the world we live in. If you don't pay attention to the past, you'll never understand the future. It's all linked together. You see what I'm saying?"

At first, I didn't. But then, I looked back at the screen, those images moving across it, and realized he was right. The past did affect the present and the future, in the ways you could see and a million ones you couldn't. Time wasn't a thing you could divide easily; there was no defined middle or beginning or end. I could pretend to leave the past behind, but it would not leave me.

Sitting there, I could suddenly feel myself getting more anxious, even as I tried to focus on the images on the screen. My mind was racing, too fast to even think, and after a few minutes I went back to bed.

This is crazy, I thought as I found myself again staring at the ceiling, my sisters quiet in their rooms on either side. I closed my eyes, the events of the last few days blurring across my vision in bits and pieces. My heart was pounding. Something was happening I didn't, or couldn't, understand. I sat up, kicking off the covers; I needed something to calm me down, or just even take away these thoughts, if only for a little while. Reaching over to my bedside drawer, I grabbed my headphones and plugged them into my CD player, then went to my desk. In the bottom drawer, after digging through all the CDs Owen had made me, I finally found it: the yellow disc that said JUST LISTEN.

You might totally hate it, Owen had told me. *Or not. It might be just what you need. That's the beauty of it. You know?*

When I hit the PLAY button, all I could hear was static, and I settled in, closing my eyes, and waited for the first song to begin. It didn't. Not in the next few minutes, not ever. Then I realized: the CD was blank.

Maybe it was supposed to be a joke. Or something profound. But as I lay there, it only seemed like silence filling my ears. And the thing was, it was so freaking loud.

It was the weirdest thing, so different from music. The sound was nothing, empty, but at the same time, it pushed everything else out, quieting me enough that I began to be able to make out something distant, hard to hear. But it *was* there, albeit softly, coming to me from some dark place I'd never seen but still knew well.

Shhh, Annabel. It's just me.

But these words were only the middle of the story. There was a beginning here, too. And I knew suddenly that if I stayed where I was, in all that quiet, and didn't run from it, I would hear it. I'd have to go back, all the way to that night at the party when I'd first heard Emily call out Sophie's name, but that was okay. It was the only way, finally, to get to the end.

All I'd ever wanted was to forget. But even when I thought I had, pieces had kept emerging, like bits of wood floating up to the surface that only hint at the shipwreck below. A pink shirt, a rhyme with my name, the feeling of hands on my neck. Because that is what happens when you try to run from the past. It doesn't just catch up: it overtakes, blotting out the future, the landscape, the very sky, until there is no path left except that which leads through it, the only one that can ever get you home.

I understood now. This voice, the one that had been trying to get my attention all this time, calling out to me, begging me to hear it—it wasn't Will's. It was mine.

Chapter
EIGHTEEN

"This is WRUS, your community radio station. It's seven fifty-eight, and this is Anger Management. Here's one final song."

There was a twang, followed by a burst of feedback. Something experimental, different, and not altogether listenable. Just another Sunday on Owen's show.

It was not, however, just another Sunday for me. Somewhere between sliding on my headphones the night before and now, something had changed. After lying there for a long time, letting myself retrace the steps of that night at the party, I'd drifted off into that silence, the voice inside my head finally talked out. When I'd woken up at seven, my headphones were still on, and I could hear my heart in my ears. I sat up, sliding them off, and the quiet around me did not, for once, seem empty and vast. Instead, for the first time in a while, it felt like it already was full.

When I'd first turned on the radio, the show had just started with a blast of old-school metal, someone wailing over some heavy-duty guitars. After following up with what sounded like a Russian pop song, Owen finally came on.

"That was Leningrad," he said, "and this is Anger

Management. I'm Owen. It's seven oh-six, thanks for hanging out with us. Got a request? A suggestion? Issues? Call us at 555–WRUS. Here's Dominic Waverly."

The song that followed was a techno one, beginning with several bouncy beats, seemingly out of sync, which eventually blended together. All those other Sundays I'd listened so intently, wanting to like or at least understand what I was hearing. When I hadn't, I'd never hesitated to tell Owen. If only I'd been able to just tell him everything else, as well. But you can't always get the perfect moment. Sometimes, you just have to do the best you can, under the circumstances.

Which was why I was now in my car, pulling out of my neighborhood, heading toward WRUS. It was 8:02 when I turned into the lot. The Herbal Prescription, the syndicated show that followed his, was just starting. I parked between Owen's and Rolly's cars, then reached over to the passenger seat for the CD there and went inside.

The station was quiet, a voice murmuring about ginkgo biloba as I made my way across the lobby. To my right, at the end of a hallway, I could see the booth, enclosed in glass. As I approached, the first thing I saw was Rolly at the controls in the little room adjacent to it; he had on a bright green T-shirt and a baseball hat turned backwards, his headphones over it. Clarke was beside him, drinking from a to-go coffee cup, the Sunday paper crossword puzzle in front of her. They were talking, and neither of them noticed my arrival. When I turned to the main booth, though, Owen was looking right at me.

He was sitting at the microphone, a stack of CDs spread out in front of him. Judging by the look on his face, he was not happy to see me. It was worse than the day in the parking lot. Which made it that much more important that I push the door open and go inside. So I did.

"Hi," I said.

He just looked at me for a second. "Hey," he said finally, his voice flat.

There was a buzz, and then Rolly's voice came from over my head. "Annabel!" he said, his sunny tone a distinct contrast to Owen's barely tolerant one. "Hey! What's going on?"

I looked over him, lifting a hand to wave. He waved back, as did Clarke. He was leaning in to say something else to me when he glanced at Owen—who was glaring at him—and slowly drew back, deciding against it. There was a click, and the microphone went off again.

"What are you doing here?" Owen asked me.

Of course he would come right out with it. "I need to talk to you," I said.

Out of the corner of my eye, I was aware of some sudden movement in the other room. I looked over to see Clarke hurriedly stuffing her newspaper into a bag, while Rolly took off his headphones, standing up. *Who's conflict-adverse now*, I thought as they exited the room at a breakneck pace, Rolly slapping the light off as he went.

"We're, um, going to go ahead to the bacon," he said to Owen as they passed behind me. "See you there?"

Owen nodded, and Rolly smiled at me again before turning away. Clarke lingered for a moment, her hand on the open door. "You okay?" she asked.

"Yeah," I said. "I'm fine."

She pulled her bag over her shoulder, giving Owen a look I couldn't make out. Then she was running to catch up with Rolly, linking her hand with his, and they disappeared around the corner into the lobby.

When I looked back at Owen, he was packing up as well, coiling the cord around his headphones. "I don't have much time," he said, not looking at me. "So if you've got something to say, go ahead and say it."

"Okay," I said. "It's—" My heart was beating fast, and I felt sick. Normally this was where I stopped, chickened out, and turned back. "It's about this," I said, holding up the CD in my hand. My voice sounded shaky, so I cleared my throat. "It was supposed to blow my mind? Remember?"

He glanced at it again, his expression wary. "Vaguely," he said.

"I listened to it last night," I said. "But I wanted to be, um, sure that I got it. Your intention, I mean."

"My intention," he repeated.

"Well, you know," I said, "there's a lot left up to interpretation." My voice sounded more solid now, finally. The power of music, indeed. "So I just wanted to make sure I really, you know, got it."

We just stared at each other, and it was all I could do not to look away. But I managed. And then, after a moment, he stuck out his hand for the CD.

He looked at the case, then turned it over. "There's no track listing on here," he said.

"Don't you remember what you put on it?"

"It was a long time ago." He shot me a look. "And I made you a lot of CDs."

"Ten," I told him. "I listened to them all."

"Really."

I nodded. "Yeah. You told me you wanted me to before I put that one on."

"Ah," he said. "So now you care about what I want."

Outside, I could see Rolly and Clarke in his car, backing out of their parking space. He was saying something, and she was laughing, shaking her head.

"I always cared about that," I said to Owen.

"Really? It's been kind of hard to tell, by the way you've been avoiding me for the last two months." He reached out to the console in front of him, hitting a button. The drawer slid open, and he put the disc in.

"I figured that *was* what you wanted," I said.

"Why?" he said. He reached down, nudging up a knob beneath the player.

I swallowed, hard. "You were the one who got out of the car in the parking lot that day and walked away," I told him. "You'd had it with me."

"You ditched me at a club and wouldn't even tell me why," he shot back, his voice rising. He turned the knob a bit more. "I was pissed, Annabel."

"Exactly," I said, and now I could hear static over our heads. "You were pissed. I'd let you down. I was not what you wanted me to be—"

"—and so you just bolted," he finished, hitting the knob

again. The static grew louder. "Disappeared. One argument, and you're out of there."

"What did you want me to do?" I said.

"Tell me what was going on, for one," he said. "God, tell me *something*. It's like I said, I could have handled it."

"Like you were handling my not saying anything? You were furious with me."

"So what? I was entitled," he said. He glanced at the console again. "People get mad, Annabel. It's not the end of the world."

"So I was supposed to just explain myself, and let you be mad at me, and then maybe you might have gotten over it—"

"I would have gotten over it."

"—or not," I said, glaring at him. "Maybe it would have changed everything."

"That happened anyway!" he said. "I mean, look at us now. At least if you'd told me what was going on, we could have dealt with it. As it was, you just left everything hanging, no resolution, nothing. Is that what you wanted? That I be gone for good, rather than just mad for a little while?"

I just stood there as he said this, the words sinking in. "I didn't," I said. "I didn't realize that was an option."

"Of course it was," he said, looking up at the speaker overhead; the static was even louder now. "Whatever it was, it couldn't have been that bad. All you had to do was be honest. Tell me what really happened."

"It's not that easy."

"Is this? Ignoring and avoiding each other, acting like we

were never friends? Maybe for you. It's sucked for me. I don't like playing games."

As he said this, I felt something in my stomach. It wasn't the clenching sickness I was used to, though. More of a slow simmer. "I don't like that, either," I said. "But—"

"If it's so big that it's worth all this," he said, waving his hand to include the studio, the static, and us in the midst of it all, "all this crap and weirdness that's happened since then, it's too big to keep inside. You know that."

"No," I said, "*you* know that, Owen. Because you don't have problems with anger—yours or anyone else's. You just use all your little phrases, and everything you've learned, and you're always honest and you never regret a thing you say or how you act—"

"Yes, I do."

"—and I'm not like that," I finished. "I'm just not."

"Then what *are* you like, Annabel?" he shot back. "A liar, like you told me that first day? Come on. That was the biggest lie of all."

I just looked at him. My hands were shaking.

"If you were a liar, you would have just lied to me," he said, glancing at the monitor again as the static grew louder. "You would have just acted like everything was fine. But you didn't."

"No," I said, shaking my head.

"And don't tell me this is easy for me, because it's not. These last couple of months have sucked, not knowing what's going on with you. What is it, Annabel? What's so bad you can't even tell me?"

I could feel my heart beating, my blood pulsing. Owen turned back to the console, raising the volume of the CD even higher, and as the sound filled my ears it hit me, all at once, what this feeling was. I was angry.

Really angry. At him, for attacking me. At myself, for waiting until now to fight back. At every other chance I hadn't taken. All these months, I'd been having this same reaction, but I'd blamed it on nerves, or fear. It wasn't.

"You don't understand," I said to him now.

"Then tell me, and maybe I will," he shot back, pushing the empty chair in front of him toward me. "And what," he said, his voice loud, "is going *on* with this CD? Where's the music? Why can't we hear anything?"

"What?" I said.

He pushed a few buttons, swearing under his breath. "There's nothing on this," he said. "It's blank."

"Isn't that the point?"

"What?" he said. "What point?"

Oh my God, I thought. I reached forward for the chair he'd pushed toward me, then eased myself down into it. Here I'd thought this gesture was so deep, so profound, and it was just . . . a mistake. A malfunction. I was wrong, all wrong.

Or not.

It was all so loud, suddenly. His voice, my heart, the static, filling the room. I closed my eyes, willing myself back to the night before, when I'd been able to hear the things I'd kept silent for so long.

Shhh, Annabel, I heard a voice say, but it sounded different this time. Familiar. *It's just me.*

Owen began to turn down the volume, and the static above us receded bit by bit. There comes a time in every life when the world gets quiet and the only thing left is your own heart. So you'd better learn to know the sound of it. Otherwise you'll never understand what it's saying.

"Annabel?" Owen said. His voice was lower now. Closer. He sounded worried. "What is it?"

He had already given me so much, but now I leaned toward him, asking him for one last thing. Something I knew he did better than anyone. "Don't think or judge," I said. "Just listen."

"Annabel? We're just about to start the movie. . . ." My mother's voice was soft; she thought I'd been sleeping. "You about ready?"

"Almost," I said.

"Okay," she said. "We'll be downstairs."

The day before, I hadn't just told Owen about what happened to me at the party. I told him everything. The stuff with Sophie at school, Whitney's recovery, Kirsten's movie. Agreeing to do another commercial, talking with my dad about history, and listening to his blank CD the night before. He just sat there, listening to every single word. And when I was finally done, he said the two words that usually don't mean anything, but this time, said it all.

"I'm sorry, Annabel," he told me. "I'm so sorry that happened to you."

Maybe this was what I'd wanted, all along. Not an apology—and certainly not one from Owen—but an acknowledgment. What mattered most, though, was that I'd gotten through it, finally—beginning, middle, and end. Which did not, of course, mean it was over.

"So what are you going to do?" he asked me later, when we were standing by the Land Cruiser, having had to leave the booth to make room for the next show, which was hosted by two cheery local realtors. "Are you going to call that woman? About the trial?"

"I don't know," I said.

I knew that in any other circumstance he'd be telling me exactly how he felt about this, but this time he held back. For about a minute.

"The thing is," he said, "there aren't a whole lot of opportunities in life to really make a difference. This is one of them."

"Easy for you to say," I said. "You always do the right thing."

"No, I don't," he replied, shaking his head. "I just do the best I can—"

"—under the circumstances, I know," I finished for him. "But I'm scared. I don't know if I can do it."

"Of course you can," he said.

"How can you be so sure?"

"Because you just did," he said. "Coming here, and telling me that? That's huge. Most people couldn't do it. But you did."

"I had to," I said. "I wanted to explain."

"And you can do it again," he replied. "Just call that woman and tell her what you told me."

I reached up, running a hand through my hair. "There's more to it than that," I said. "What if she wants me to come testify or something? I'd have to tell my parents, my mom. . . . I don't know if she can take it."

"She can."

"You don't even know her," I said.

"I don't have to," he replied. "Look, this is important. You know that. So do what you have to do, and then go from there. Your mom just might surprise you."

I felt a lump rise in my throat. I wanted to believe this was true, and maybe it was.

Owen dropped his bag to the ground, then crouched down beside it, rummaging around. I had a flash of him that day behind the school, doing this same thing, and how I'd had no idea in the world what he would come up with, what on earth Owen Armstrong had to offer me. After a moment, he pulled out a picture.

"Here," he said, handing it to me. "For inspiration."

It was the one he'd taken of me the night of Mallory's photo shoot. I was standing in the powder-room doorway, no make-up, my face relaxed, the yellow glow of the light behind me. *See*, he'd said then, *that's what you look like*, and as I stared down at it, it seemed like proof, finally, that I was not the girl from Mallory's wall or the Kopf's commercial or even the party that night in May. That something in me had changed that fall, because of Owen, even if I only now could really see it.

"Mallory told me to give it to you," he said. "But . . ."

"But?" I said.

". . . I didn't," he finished.

I knew maybe I shouldn't ask. But I did anyway. "Why not?"

"I liked it," he said with a shrug. "I wanted to hang on to it."

It was the picture I was holding that afternoon when I finally got up the nerve to call Andrea Thomlinson, the woman whose card Emily had given me. I left a message on her voice mail, and she called back within ten minutes. Emily was right: She was nice. We talked for forty-five minutes. And when she asked if I'd come to the courthouse the next day, in case they needed me, even though I knew what it meant to do so, I agreed. As soon as we hung up, I called Owen.

"Good for you," he said when I told him what I'd done. His voice was warm, pleased, and I pressed the receiver closer, letting it fill my ear. "You did the right thing."

"Yeah," I said. "I know. But now I have to get up in front of people. . . ."

"You can do it," he said, and when I sighed, not at all sure of this, he said, "You can. Look, if you're nervous about tomorrow—"

"If?" I said.

"—then I'll go with you. If you want."

"You'd do that," I said.

"Sure," he replied. So easily, no question. "Just tell me where and when."

We arranged to meet at the fountain in front of the courthouse, just before nine. I knew that even without him, I still wouldn't be alone. But it was nice to have options.

Now, I took one last look at the picture, then slid it into my bedside-table drawer.

On my way to the living room, where my family was gathered, I stopped to look at the photo in the foyer. As always, my eyes were drawn to my own face first, then those of my sisters, and finally my mother, looking so small between us. But I saw it differently now.

When that picture was taken, we were all gathered around my mother, sheltering her. But that was just one day, one shot. In the time since, we had arranged and rearranged ourselves so many times. We'd all gathered around Whitney, even when she didn't want us to, and Kirsten and I had gotten closer when she pushed us both away. We were still in flux, as had been clear at the table that night as I watched my mother and sisters come together again. Then, I'd been convinced I was on the outside, but really, I'd always been within arm's reach. All I had to do was ask, and I, too, would be easily brought back, surrounded and immersed, finding myself safe, somewhere in between.

I walked across the living room to where my family was gathered around the TV. No one saw me at first, and I just stood there for a second, looking at them all together. Finally, my mom turned her head, and I took in a breath, knowing that whatever I saw in her face, I could do this. I had to.

"Annabel," she said. Then she smiled before moving over to make a place for me beside her. "Come join us."

For a moment I hesitated, but then I looked at Whitney. She was watching me, her expression serious, and I thought of that night a year ago, when I'd pushed open a door and flipped a switch, exposing her to the light. What had happened to her had scared me to death, but she'd survived it. So I kept my eyes on her as I crossed the space between and took my seat.

My mother smiled at me again, and I felt a wave of sadness and fear come over me, knowing what I was about to do. *You about ready?* she'd asked me earlier, and then, I hadn't been. Maybe I never would be. But there was no way around it now. So as I got ready to tell my story again, I did what Owen had done for me so many times: I reached out a hand, to my mother and my family. And this time, I pulled them through with me.

Chapter
NINETEEN

When I first got into the courtroom, I could only see Will Cash in glimpses. The back of his head here, the arm of his suit there, a profile, fleeting. At first this was frustrating and made me even more nervous, but as the time grew closer to when I'd be called, I began to think this was a good thing. Pieces and parts were always easier to process. The full picture, the entire story, was another thing entirely. But you just never knew. Sometimes, people could surprise you.

Telling my family had been harder, in the end, than telling Owen. But I did it. Even through the hard parts, even when I heard my mother catch her breath, could feel my father's eyes narrowing, felt Kirsten shaking beside me, I kept on. And when I felt myself really wavering, I looked at Whitney, who never flinched. She was strongest of us all, and I kept my eyes on her, all the way to the end.

My mother had surprised me most. She had not fallen apart, or crumpled, although I knew hearing what had happened to me was not easy for her. Instead, while Kirsten cried, and Whitney helped my dad find Andrea Thomlinson's card in my room so he could call her for more details, my mother sat beside me, her arm around my shoulder, just smoothing her hand over my head, again and again.

That morning, on the way to the courthouse, I'd sat in the backseat between my sisters, watching my parents. Every once in a while my mother's shoulder would move, and I knew she was reaching over to pat my father's hand, as he had done to her on another drive, on another day when secrets had begun to come out, not so long ago.

All my life, I realized, I'd only seen my parents one way, as if it was the only way they could be. One weak, one strong. One scared, one bold. I was beginning to understand, though, that there were no such things as absolutes, not in life or in people. Like Owen said, it was day by day, if not moment by moment. All you could do was take on as much weight as you can bear. And if you're lucky, there's someone close enough by to shoulder the rest.

When we walked up to the courthouse it was just before eight forty-five, and I scanned the crowd in the square around the fountain, looking for Owen. He wasn't there. Not then, and not after my mother and I met with Andrea Thomlinson in a nearby office to go over my story again. Not even when the courtroom opened and we filed inside, taking our seats just down the row from Emily and her mom. I kept looking for him, thinking he would slide in at the last minute, just in time, but he didn't. It was so not like him, and it worried me.

An hour and a half later, the prosecutor called my name. I stood up, my palm slick on the bench in front of me as I slid my hand along its back, walking past my sisters to the end of the row. Then I stepped out into the aisle and was on my own.

As I crossed the floor I finally had a clear view of every-thing—the crowd, the judge, the prosecutors and defense attorneys—and I made a point of focusing only on the bailiff, who was waiting for me by the witness stand. I took my seat, feeling my heart pounding as I answered his questions and the judge turned, nodding at me. It was only after the prosecutor stood and started toward me that I finally let myself look at Will Cash.

It wasn't his fancy suit I noticed first. Or his new haircut, short and schoolboyish, which was probably intended to make him look young and innocent. The look on his face—narrowed eyes, pursed lips—didn't really register, either. The only thing I could see, actually, was the black circle around his left eye, the redness of the cheek beneath. Someone had tried to cover it up with makeup, but it was still there. Clear as day.

"State your name for the record," the prosecutor asked me.

"Annabel Greene," I said. My voice was shaking.

"Are you acquainted with William Cash, Annabel?"

"Yes."

"Could you point him out to me, please?"

After being silent for so long, I felt like I had talked so much in the last twenty-four hours. But with any luck, this would be the last time for a while. Which was maybe why it wasn't so hard to quiet myself, to take in that first breath, to begin.

"There," I said, raising my finger and pointing at him. "He's right there."

• • •

When it was finally over, we walked through the dark of the courthouse lobby into a noontime sun so bright it took my eyes a moment to adjust. When they did, Owen was the first thing I saw.

He was sitting on the edge of the fountain, wearing jeans and a white T-shirt, a blue jacket over it, his earphones hanging around his neck. It was lunchtime, and the square was packed with people crossing back and forth: businessmen with briefcases, students from the university, a bunch of preschoolers walking in a line, all holding hands. When Owen saw me, he stood up.

"I think," my mother was saying, running a hand down my arm, "that we should all go get something to eat. What do you think, Annabel? Are you hungry?"

I looked at Owen, who was watching me, his hands now in his pockets. "Yeah," I told her. "Just give me one second."

As I started down the steps, I could hear my father asking where I was going, and my mother responding she had no idea. I was sure they were all watching me, but I didn't look back as I crossed the square, walking up to Owen, who had the strangest look on his face, one I'd never seen before. He was shifting in place, clearly uncomfortable.

"Hey," he said quickly, as soon as I was in earshot.

"Hi."

He took in a breath, about to speak, then stopped, running a hand over his face. "Look," he said. "I know you're pissed off at me."

The weird thing was that I wasn't. While initially, I'd been surprised, then worried when he hadn't shown up, the entire experience had been so overwhelming—although cathartic— that I'd kind of forgotten about it once I got up on the stand. I opened my mouth to tell him this, but he was already talking again.

"The basic fact is that I should have been here. I have no excuse. There is no excuse." He looked down at the ground, scuffing his foot across the pavement. "I mean, there is a reason. But it's not an excuse."

"Owen," I said. "It's—"

"Something happened." He sighed, shaking his head. His face was flushed, and he was still fidgeting. "Something stupid. I made a mistake, and—"

Then, and only then, did I put it altogether. His absence. This shuffling embarrassment. And Will Cash's black eye. *Oh my God*, I thought.

"Owen," I said, my voice low. "No way."

"It was an error in judgment," he said quickly. "And something I regret."

"Something," I repeated.

"Yes."

A businessman talking loudly on a cell phone passed us, talking about mergers. "Placeholder," I told him.

He winced. "I thought you might say that."

"Come on," I said. "You *knew* I would say that."

"Fine, fine." He pulled a hand through his hair. "I was having an in-depth discussion with my mother. One that I could not easily extract myself from."

"A discussion," I repeated. "About what?"

Again, he flinched. This was killing him. And yet I could not help myself. After being on the other side of the truth for so long, I realized I kind of liked asking the questions.

"Well," he said, then coughed. "Basically, I'm supposed to be under punishment right now. For the foreseeable future, in fact. So I had to negotiate a furlough. It took longer than I expected."

"You're grounded," I said, clarifying.

"Yes."

"For what?"

He winced, then shook his head, looking over at the fountain. Who knew the truth could be so hard for Owen Armstrong, the most honest boy in the world. But if I asked, he would tell. That I knew for sure.

"Owen," I said as he squirmed, noticeably, his shoulder wriggling, "what did you do?"

He just looked at me for a minute. Then he sighed. "I punched Will Cash in the face."

"What were you *thinking*?"

"Well, clearly I wasn't." He flushed a deeper red. "I didn't intend to do it."

"You punched him by accident."

"No." He shot me a look. "Okay, you really want to know?"

"Am I not asking?"

"Look," Owen said, "the truth is, after you left yesterday, I was really pissed off. I mean, I'm human, right?"

"You are," I agreed.

"I really only wanted to get a good look at him. That was all. And I knew he sometimes plays with that shitty Perkins

Day band that was in a showcase last night at Bendo, so I figured he might be there. And he was. Which, really, when you think about it, is despicable. What kind of a person goes to a club—to see a shitty band, no less—the night before he's due in court? It's—"

"Owen," I said.

"I'm serious! Do you know how much they *suck*? Seriously, even for a cover band they're pathetic. I mean, if you're going to just come out and admit you can't write your own songs, at least be able to play other people's well. . . ."

I just looked at him.

"Right," he said. He ran a hand through his hair again. "So anyway, he was there, I got a look at him, end of story."

"Clearly," I said sternly, "that is *not* the end of the story."

Owen continued, reluctantly. "I watched their set. Which, as I said, sucked. I went out for some air, and he was outside smoking a cigarette. And he starts talking to me. Like we know each other. Like he's not the freaking scum of the earth, a total fucking asshole."

"Owen," I said softly.

"I could feel myself getting more and more pissed off." He winced. "I knew I should breathe, and walk away, and everything else, but I didn't. And then, when he finished his cigarette, he clapped me on the shoulder and turned to go back inside. And I just—"

I took a step closer to him.

"—snapped," he finished. "I lost it."

"It's okay," I said.

"I knew even when I was doing it I'd regret it," he said.

"That it wasn't worth it. But by then it was already happening. I'm really pissed off at myself, if you want to know the truth."

"I know."

"It was just one punch," he grumbled, then added quickly, "which doesn't make it okay. And I'm so freaking lucky the bouncer just broke us up and told us both to get out of there, and didn't call the cops. If he had . . ." He trailed off. "It's just so stupid."

"But you told your mom anyway," I said.

"When I got home, she could tell I was pissed. So she asked me what happened, and I had to tell her—"

"Because you're honest," I said, taking another step.

"Well, yeah," he said, looking down at me. "She was livid, to say the least. Laid down this hardcore punishment, totally deserved, but then today, when I tried to leave to come here, things got kind of sticky."

"It's okay," I said again.

"It's not, though." Behind him, the fountain was splashing, sunlight glinting off the water. "Because I'm not like that. Anymore. I just . . . freaked out."

I reached up, brushing his hair out of his face. "Huh," I said. "Really."

"What?"

"I don't know." I shrugged. "It's just to me, that's not freak-ing out."

"It's not," he said. Then he just looked at me for a second. "Oh," he said finally. "Right."

"I mean, to me," I said, moving closer, "freaking out is dif-ferent. More of a running away, not telling anyone what's wrong, slowly simmering until you burst kind of thing."

"Ah," he said. "Well, I guess it's just a matter of semantics."

"I guess so."

People were still moving all around us, on their way here and there, filling up their lunch hour however they could before the rest of the day began. I knew that somewhere behind me, my family was waiting, but still I reached my hand down to brush his.

"You know," Owen said, as his fingers found mine, "it sure seems like you have all the answers."

"Nah," I told him. "I'm just doing the best I can, under the circumstances."

"How's that going?" he asked.

There was no short answer to this; like so much else, it was a long story. But what really makes any story real is knowing someone will hear it. And understand.

"Well, you know," I said to Owen now. "It's day by day."

He smiled at me, and I smiled back, then stepped closer, turning my face up to meet his. As he leaned down to kiss me, I closed my eyes and saw not the flat black of the dark but something else. Something brighter, closer to light, shining small but ever steady. More than enough to go on as a part of me pushed up and out, finally, to meet it there.

Chapter
TWENTY

I slipped on my headphones, then looked over at Rolly. When he flashed me a thumbs-up, I leaned into the microphone.

"It's seven fifty, and you're listening to your community radio station, WRUS. If you're looking for Anger Management, it will return in"—I glanced at my notepad, where, above my neatly written playlist, there was a big number two, followed by an exclamation point—"two weeks. In the meantime, I'm Annabel, and this is Story of My Life. Here's The Clash."

I kept my headphones on, watching Rolly until the first notes of "Rebel Waltz" were audible. Then I finally let out the breath I felt like I'd been holding forever, just as the speaker over my head popped and Clarke came on.

"Nice," she said. "You barely sounded nervous."

"That's still nervous," I told her.

"You're doing great," Rolly said. "And I don't know why you get so worried anyway. It's not like you're walking in front of people in a bathing suit." Clarke turned, shooting him a look. "What?" he said. "It's true!"

"This is harder," I said, sliding off my headphones. "Much harder."

"Why?" he asked.

I shrugged. "I don't know," I said. "It's more real. Personal."

And it was. In fact, I'd been terrified when Owen had first asked me to fill in when his mom decided that taking away the radio show was the only sufficient punishment for what he'd done to Will Cash. But once he'd convinced me that Rolly (and Clarke) would be there to help with the technical stuff and make sure I stayed on time every week, I'd agreed to try it at least once. That had been four weeks ago, and while I was still nervous, I was also having fun. So much that Rolly was already bugging me to take the community radio prep course and apply for my own time slot, but I wasn't quite ready for that yet. But never say never.

Of course, Owen was still involved with the show. When I'd first started subbing for him, he'd insisted that I stick to his playlist, even when it meant forcing music I hated on the masses. After the first week, though (and once he realized that he really couldn't stop me), he'd relented, and I'd started putting my own songs in here and there. There was something really great about being able to put something out into the world—a song, an introduction, even my voice—and let people make of it what they wanted. I didn't have to worry about how I looked, or if the image of me people had fit who I really was. The music spoke for itself and for me, and after so long being watched and studied, I was finding I liked that. A lot.

Rolly knocked on the glass between us, then signaled to me to get the next song ready to go. It was a Jenny Reef single, for Mallory—my first true fan—who made a point of setting her alarm each week so she could call in a request. I cued it up, then waited until The Clash began to fade out before hitting the button to begin its bouncy beats (a segue that I knew would annoy Owen, who for various reasons insisted on listening to the broadcast of the show in the car, alone). Once it had fully started, I shifted in my chair, glancing over at the row of pictures I had lined up next to my monitor. When I'd first started, I'd been so nervous I figured I could use all the inspiration I could get. So I'd brought in the shot of Mallory with the feather boa circling her face, to remind me at least one person was listening. The one of me Owen had taken, so I'd keep in mind that it didn't matter if she was the only one. And then one more.

It was shot of me and my mother and sisters, taken at New Year's. Unlike the one in the foyer, it was hardly professional, with no dramatic vista behind us. Instead, we were all standing at the kitchen island. We'd just been talking, about what I couldn't even remember, and then Kirsten's boyfriend Brian— with the class over, they were now free and clear to make their relationship public—was telling us to look here, and the shutter snapped. It was not a great picture in the technical sense. You can see the flash in the window behind us, my mother has her mouth open, and Whitney is laughing. But I loved it, because it was what we looked like. And best of all, this time no one was in the middle.

Every time I looked at it, I was reminded how much I liked this new life, without a secret hanging over me. It was a fresh start, and now I didn't have to be the girl who had everything, or nothing, but another girl altogether. Maybe even the one who told.

"Two minutes until next break," Rolly said now, and I nodded, sliding my headphones back on. As he leaned back from the microphone, Clarke reached over, ruffling his hair. He smiled at her, making a face as she went back to the Sunday crossword, which she made a point of trying to complete every week during the hour the show was on. Clarke was competitive, even with herself. It was one of many things I'd forgotten about her, but was now remembering—like how she always sang along with the radio, refused to watch scary movies, and could make me giggle uncontrollably over the stupidest things—as we cautiously worked our way back into a friendship. It wasn't like it had been, but then neither of us would have wanted that anyway. As it was, we were just happy to be hanging out. Everything else, we took day by day.

This was how I was dealing with everyone and everything lately, taking the good when it came, and the bad the same way, knowing each would pass in its own time. My sisters were still speaking, as well as occasionally still arguing. Kirsten was in her second filmmaking class, working away on a piece about, strangely enough, modeling, which she promised would "rock our world" (whatever that meant). In January, Whitney had enrolled in classes at the local university, where, along with a few requirements, she was taking two writing classes, one on memoir, the other fiction. In the spring, with her doctor's blessing, she was moving into her own apartment, a place she'd made sure had enough light for some plants. In the meantime, her herbs were still in the windowsill, where I made a point to pass them whenever I could, reaching down to smooth their pungent leaves between my fingers, releasing their scent to linger to the open air behind me.

As for my mother, she had accepted all these changes with a few tears—of course—as well as a strength that continually surprised me. I'd told her, finally, that I was done with modeling, for good, and while it was hard for her to let go of that part of my life, and her own, she'd compensated by taking a part-time job with Lindy, who was still desperately in need of a receptionist. It was a good fit. Now she sent other girls out to calls and dealt with clients, keeping one foot in the world where she, out of all of us, always felt the most comfortable.

Still, I knew it would probably be hard for her when the new Kopf's commercial began running in a few weeks. From what I heard, they'd stuck to the same idea as the one I'd done, focusing on the Ideal Girl as she moved through spring sports and prom. It probably would have bothered me, for all the reasons the other one had, if not for the girl they'd picked to replace me: Emily. After all, if anyone could be a role model, it was her.

As far as Emily and I went, we weren't exactly friends. But we both knew what we'd been through would link us forever, whether we liked it or not. Whenever we passed each other in the hallway now, we made a point of saying hello, even if that was all we said. This was more than I could say for Sophie, who studiously ignored both of us. After Will's conviction and sentencing for second-degree rape—six years, although he'd probably be out earlier—she'd laid low for a while, clearly uncomfortable with being the subject of so much discussion. There were times when I saw her alone in the halls, or at lunch, and thought that ideally, I'd be able to go up to her, heal this rift, do for her what she'd never done for me.

Or not.

Thinking this, I looked down at my thumb, slipping off the thick silver ring there to read these same words. It was too big for any of my fingers, and I'd had to wrap some tape on it so it would fit, but it was just fine for now while I was still figuring out what I wanted on the one Rolly had promised me. Until then, Owen had said I could hold on to his, if only to remind me that it's always good to know your options.

"Thirty seconds," Rolly said in my headphones.

I nodded, moving my chair closer to the microphone. As the seconds counted down, I looked out the window to my left and saw a blue Land Cruiser turning into the lot. Right on time.

"And . . ." Rolly said, "you're on."

"That was Jenny Reef, with 'Whatever,'" I began, "and this has been Story of My Life, here on WRUS. I'm Annabel. The Herbal Prescription is next. Thanks for listening. Here's one last song."

The opening notes of Led Zeppelin's "Thank You" came on, and I pushed back my chair. Then I closed my eyes to listen, as I did every time I heard this song, my own little ritual. Just as the chorus began, I heard the door open and, a moment later, felt a hand on my shoulder.

"Please tell me," Owen said, flopping down dramatically in the chair beside me, "that I did not just hear Jenny Reef on my show."

"It was a request," I said. "And besides, you said I could play what I wanted as long as we called the show something else."

"Within *reason*," he said. "I mean, you just have to keep in mind that my listeners are going to be confused. They're still tuning in, and they expect quality. If possible, enlightenment. Not commercial, mass-produced crap sung by a teenager completely controlled by corporate marketing."

"Owen."

"I mean, there's room for some irony, but it's a delicate balance. Too much either way and you lose all credibility. Which means that—"

"Are you even listening to what I'm playing now?" I asked.

He stopped in mid-rant, then looked up at the speaker overhead, listening for a second. "Oh," he said. "Well, this is what I mean. This is my—"

"Favorite Led Zeppelin song," I finished for him. "I know."

In the booth, Clarke rolled her eyes.

"Okay, fine," Owen said, moving his chair closer to mine. "So you played some Jenny Reef. I thought the rest of the show was pretty good. Although I'm not sure about the juxtaposition you did in the second pairing—"

"Owen."

"—following up that Alamance track with the Etta James. It was a bit much. And—"

"Owen."

"What?"

I leaned closer to him, pressing my lips to his ear. "Shhh," I said.

He started to say something else—of course—but stopped as I slid my hand over to his, locking his fingers in mine. It wasn't over. Eventually, he'd make his point, or at least argue

it into submission. But for now, the chords were building overhead, the chorus starting up again. So I moved closer to Owen,
leaning my head on his shoulder to listen, as we settled into the
sunlight coming through the window beside us. It was bright
and warm, catching the ring on my thumb as Owen reached for
it, spinning it slowly, slowly, as the song played on.

ACKNOWLEDGMENTS

It takes a village to see a book from beginning to end, and I am lucky to have good neighbors. Thanks to Leigh Feldman, the most honest person I know, and the fabulous Regina Hayes, who always takes my best and makes it so much better. Joy Peskin gave her perspective and experience when I needed it most. I am also indebted to Marianne Gingher and Bland Simpson at UNC–Chapel Hill, who gave me the second best job I've ever had and, more importantly, continue to understand why writing is the first. I'm grateful to Ann Parrent at WCOM 103.5 Community Radio, and Jeff Welty, dashing vegan criminal defense attorney, for facts and information, and to my parents for yet again talking me down off the ledge. But in the end, this book, like all the others, is really for Jay, who gave me Bob Dylan, Tom Waits, Social Distortion, and a million other songs still playing. Thanks for listening.